"How do you feel, Seven?" the Doctor inquired.

"Fine," Seven assured him. "Is that all?"

"For the time being," he replied. "I suspect we'll be rejoining the fleet soon, and if possible, I will keep you apprised of any new developments in the interim."

"Thank you, Doctor." She nodded. "Safe travels."

"And to you." He smiled.

She spent the few moments it took for her to walk from sickbay to the transporter room trying to dispel the anxiety that had welled up within her. As she stepped onto the platform, it occurred to her that unless she could pinpoint its source, it would be difficult to quell.

Then, it hit her, as she felt the transport beam begin to take hold. The tune the Doctor had hummed during the procedure had taken her back to a time when he had been forced to try and extract information from her mind without the benefit of his ethical subroutines. It had been years earlier, when *Voyager* had encountered the *Equinox,* another Starfleet vessel lost in the Delta Quadrant, and the Doctor's program had been intentionally sabotaged.

PROTECTORS

KIRSTEN BEYER

Based on *Star Trek*®
created by Gene Roddenberry
and
Star Trek: Voyager
created by Rick Berman & Michael Piller
& Jeri Taylor

POCKET BOOKS
New York London Toronto Sydney New Delhi

Pocket Books
A Division of Simon & Schuster, Inc.
1230 Avenue of the Americas
New York, NY 10020

This book is published by Pocket Books, a division of Simon & Schuster, Inc., under exclusive license from CBS Studios Inc.

First Pocket Books paperback edition February 2014

POCKET and colophon are registered trademarks of Simon & Schuster, Inc.

For information about special discounts for bulk purchases, please contact Simon & Schuster Special Sales at 1-866-506-1949 or business@simonandschuster.com.

The Simon & Schuster Speakers Bureau can bring authors to your live event. For more information or to book an event, contact the Simon & Schuster Speakers Bureau at 1-866-248-3049 or visit our website at www.simonspeakers.com.

Cover art and design by Alan Dingman

Manufactured in the United States of America

10 9 8 7 6 5 4 3 2 1

ISBN 978-1-4767-3854-3
ISBN 978-1-4767-3855-0 (ebook)

For my Maggie

and her amazingly bright future

HISTORIAN'S NOTE

As the Federation struggles to recover from the Borg Invasion (*Star Trek: Destiny)*, a Starfleet that has already taken heavy losses is challenged by the emerging power of the Typhon Pact (*Star Trek: Typhon Pact: Rough Beasts of Empire*).

The Full Circle fleet has been devastated by the force of the Omega Continuum. The narrative begins just after the return of Vice Admiral Kathryn Janeway (*Star Trek: Voyager: The Eternal Tide)* and unfolds from September 2381 through January 2382.

"The truth is this: The march of Providence is so slow and our desires so impatient; the work of progress is so immense and our means of aiding it so feeble; the life of humanity is so long, that of the individual so brief, that we often see only the ebb of the advancing wave and are thus discouraged. It is history that teaches us to hope."

—ROBERT E. LEE

Prologue

STARBASE 185, BETA QUADRANT

"Welcome to the graveyard, Verdell."

Ensign Lawrence Verdell, who had graduated from Starfleet Academy "without distinction," as his father liked to say, or "in the bottom third of his class," as his mother preferred, had not come to the nether regions of the Beta Quadrant with high expectations. He knew full well that gamma shift on a remote Starbase was the place Starfleet careers went to die, so his commanding officer, Lieutenant Hars Kaydn's ominous greeting did not trouble him in the least.

Many other cadets like Verdell whose formal notices of separation from the Academy indicated that they'd merely "met all standard requirements" had managed to secure posts on one of Starfleet's many exploratory vessels. Hundreds of ships and tens of thousands of officers had been lost in the Borg attack seven months ago leaving a vast number of positions to be filled as ships were constructed. Most of those in Verdell's class who were "exceeding all standard requirements" had graduated early and spent half of what should have been their final year of study on active duty. But Verdell had never dreamed of such things, and though he knew it was probably wrong to feel relief when he was passed over for similar honors, he couldn't help himself. He would do his job as well as he could and sleep the untroubled sleep of the angels knowing that he was about as far from the white-hot center of the galaxy and its seemingly ever-present conflict and imminent destruction as it was possible to be and still call oneself a Starfleet officer.

"Thank you, sir. Honored to be here," Verdell replied cheerily to Lieutenant Kaydn as he took his post and made the controls of the ops station his own for the first of what he assumed would be many quiet and mind-numbingly boring shifts. He suspected Kaydn's ominous "welcome" when he had entered the command center was meant to unnerve him a bit. A fair amount of hazing for the newbie was to be expected. He thought it best to play along patiently until it subsided. It was likely that nobody else in the room was a future admiral either or they wouldn't be here.

"See anything interesting out there?" a gruff voice asked over his shoulder.

Verdell turned to nod at Lieutenant Terral, who was manning the security station for the evening's festivities. Lawrence's bunkmate, a garrulous Bolian named Lud, had already warned him that Terral was a hard-nosed stickler, and Verdell wanted badly to find his way into what few good graces the man possessed.

"No, sir," Verdell replied as he double-checked his console's readings for good measure.

"Just the way we like it, eh, Terral?" Kadyn observed.

An impatient "Harrumph" was Terral's terse response.

"You any relation to Admiral Verdell?" Kaydn asked, though Lawrence was certain the Lieutenant knew the answer.

"His third-born son," Verdell said without looking up.

He wasn't a telepath, but he could still hear the unspoken thoughts of Kaydn, Terral, and Stacker, gamma shift's science officer. *Son of an admiral and the best he could do is this lousy post?*

Acutely conscious of three sets of eyes boring their way into his back, Verdell was grateful for the sudden appearance of a crimson-hued blip on his console. Though it was likely nothing, it pushed the unwanted attention of his comrades to the back of his mind as he automatically realigned the station's sensors for a better look.

"What the . . . ?" he murmured a few seconds later as a series of improbable readings appeared before him and simultaneously the station's alert klaxons, which he had not activated, began to wail all around him.

"We have incoming," Terral confirmed as Kaydn rose from his chair and stepped closer to the main viewscreen.

Verdell did his best to quiet the panic welling inside as he tried to make sense of the data before him.

"From where?" Kaydn asked.

Ensign Stacker obliged him by responding. "It emerged from some sort of subspace aperture, sir, less than four hundred thousand kilometers to port."

"Can you identify it, Ensign Verdell?" Kaydn barked.

Finally, Lawrence could, at which point his shaking ceased, and he manually deactivated the deafening alarm.

"Okay, you got me," he said with a self-deprecating shrug. "Good one, guys."

He lifted his face to Kaydn's, expecting to see a wide smile as communal chuckling erupted around him. Their lame attempt at a practical joke might have been more effective if they'd given him a little time to settle into his shift or had chosen a more realistic "emergency." But there was no way he was falling for this one. "The automated red alert was a nice touch," Verdell began, but he stopped short when he saw Kaydn's wide-eyed glare.

"Report, Ensign," Kaydn ordered.

"It's . . . it's," Verdell stammered, suddenly wondering if he might have been wrong.

"It's what?" Kaydn demanded.

"It's impossible, sir," Verdell replied.

"Ensign Verdell!" Kaydn bellowed.

"The approaching vessel does not match anything in our databases, sir," Verdell said, "but several unique attributes register as . . ." Verdell swallowed hard before he added, ". . . Caeliar."

"Caeliar?" Kaydn said. "Look again."

"Aye, sir." Verdell nodded and did so. After a moment he was forced to accept the best information at his disposal. "Confirmed, sir. Caeliar vessel approaching."

"Life signs?" Kaydn asked.

"Yes, sir," Verdell went on, locking his knees to keep his legs from shaking. "One . . . very faint."

"We don't actually have a good baseline for Caeliar life signs, sir," Ensign Stacker advised from her science station.

"Hail them," Kaydn ordered.

It took a fraction of a second longer than it should have for Verdell to remember that this was his job. He was too busy trying to wrap his brain around the fact that an individual from one of the most advanced and mysterious races Starfleet had ever encountered, the race that had single-handedly transformed the Borg and then, according to all reports, departed the galaxy for parts unknown, had apparently decided to pay a visit on the most remote starbases in Federation space.

Finally, Lawrence's shaking fingers found the appropriate controls as he sent a standard greeting to the incoming vessel and requested that it identify itself.

"No response, sir," he said a few moments later.

"The vessel is on a collision course," Terral noted, as if Verdell needed any more pressure.

"Open a channel," Kaydn ordered.

"Channel open, sir," Verdell reported.

"Incoming vessel, this is Lieutenant Hars Kaydn of Federation Starbase 185. Alter course immediately to avoid collision, and please advise if you require assistance."

Kaydn's words were answered by several moments of miserable silence.

Releasing a quick breath of frustration, Kaydn turned to Terral. "Can we nudge it off course without destroying it?"

"I wouldn't advise attempting that, Lieutenant," Stacker jumped in. "What little intelligence we have on the Caeliar indicates that their vessels, their entire civilization, is powered by Omega particle generators."

"Would you advise allowing even a small vessel powered by Omega to run into the station, Ensign?" Kaydn asked pointedly.

Verdell was grateful to be able to relieve a little of the suffocating tension now enveloping the command center. "Energy readings are not Omega, sir," he said with more confidence than he felt. "I can't tell you what is powering that vessel, but it's not . . . you know . . . *that*."

"Either way, I don't know if we want to open fire on a species that could probably destroy us in one shot if it wanted to," Terral added.

Kaydn nodded, clearly considering his options.

"Time to impact?"

"He's coming in pretty fast," Terral noted.

"Three minutes, fifty-one seconds," Verdell clarified.

"Kaydn to transporter control."

"Go ahead, sir."

"Can you get a lock on the pilot of the incoming vessel?"

During the thirty seconds that it took the transporter room to reply, Verdell busied himself wondering why he hadn't told his parents to go to hell when they demanded he follow his brothers into Starfleet and instead opened the small Mediterranean restaurant he'd always dreamed about.

"No, sir," the transport officer finally replied.

"Damn it," Kaydn hissed.

"Warning, intruder alert," the maddeningly calm voice of the station's computer advised, bringing Verdell fully back to the present moment.

"Where?" Kaydn asked, but before the computer could reply, the air between the command chair and the viewscreen began to ripple. Kadyn stepped back automatically and almost tripped into his chair as the distortion resolved itself into a shimmering reflective surface. It appeared to Verdell as if someone had just hung an oval, full-length mirror in front of the viewscreen. Moments later, a figure broke through the surface and tumbled headfirst onto the deck as the mirror vanished behind him.

Everyone else reached for his own phaser. Verdell brought both of his hands to his mouth to keep the contents of his stomach from adding to the grisly sight now before him.

A man, or what had perhaps once been a man, his body a mangled mass of flesh and dried blood mingled with fresher putrid ooze, was curled in a fetal position on the deck. His bald scalp revealed numerous deep gashes, and a hole where his ear should have been was the only visible orifice. The rest of him looked like it had been haphazardly reconstructed by a surgeon who had no idea what the original shape of the man's body might be. There was no clothing, no scraps or tattered rags to cover even an inch of the horrifying spectacle.

"Kaydn to sickbay," the Lieutenant shouted.

"Sickbay here," a light, feminine voice said.

"Janis, we're initiating a site-to-site transport of an injured man who has just appeared in the command center. When he arrives, put him behind a level-ten force field before you do whatever you can for him. He's in pretty bad shape. And you'd better wake up Doctor Mai."

Turning to Verdell, Kaydn barked, "Why is he still here, Ensign?"

Right. Site-to-site transport; that's my job, too, Verdell realized and searched his panel for the controls. Even once he'd found them and the figure mercifully vanished in the transporter's standard luminescent display, the stench the man had brought with him lingered.

"Time to impact?" Kaydn demanded of Terral.

"Two minutes, nineteen seconds," Terral replied.

"Verdell, Stacker, lock every sensor we have on that ship

for the next seventy-nine seconds. I want as much data as we can get. At one minute out, destroy it, Terral."

"Aye, sir," all three responded in unison.

Verdell immediately retuned his station's sensors to the most detailed analysis of which they were capable. He didn't know how much information Starfleet had about the Caeliar. If his father's comments in the heady days after the cessation of hostilities with the Borg were to be believed, the answer was "not nearly enough." Verdell briefly glimpsed life as someone who could actually add something meaningful to the organization he had reluctantly chosen to serve, and applied himself diligently to coaxing as much usable information as he could from this brief encounter.

A bright flash of light followed by a shockwave that shook the station forcefully as it dissipated, ended the information-gathering process too soon, but Verdell had already seen enough to know that his end-of-duty report this night was going to take days to compile. Surprised, Lawrence found himself looking forward to it.

It was disappointing when seconds after the ship had vanished in a blaze of particles, his console went suddenly haywire before sputtering into darkness.

Kaydn was headed for the door to the turbolift as he said, "Kaydn to Captain Dreshing."

A groggy voice replied, *"Dreshing here. Go ahead, Lieutenant."*

"Please join me in sickbay immediately, sir. We have an unexpected guest."

"On my way. Dreshing out."

As Kaydn headed for the turbolift he tossed back over his shoulder, "Good work, everybody. Well, almost everybody," he added with a sharp glance in Verdell's direction. "I know it's your first day out of the Academy, Verdell, but gods almighty damn, you just about screwed up one of the most important contacts Starfleet has ever made because you decided it was a joke."

"I'm sorry, sir," Verdell said.

"I want your initial analysis in my hands in an hour, Ensign."

"I'd like to comply, sir," Verdell said, shaking his head as his stomach heaved.

"Is there a 'but' coming, Ensign?"

"I'm sorry, sir, but my station has been rendered inoperable."

"What?" Kaydn demanded, halting his steps.

"It's not just Verdell, sir," Stacker added. "My station is out, too. I think that ship transmitted a virus over the open channel just before we destroyed it."

Kaydn shook his head, disgusted.

"Do what you can to recover any data possible, Ensigns."

"Aye, sir," Verdell and Stacker said.

Lawrence immediately set to work, certain that if he was unable to retrieve or reconstruct the data requested, his service to Starfleet would end an hour after it had begun. And while "shortest career in history" was still an accomplishment, Verdell had no doubt where his father would put him when he learned of the dubious achievement.

Welcome to the graveyard, Verdell.

Chapter One

VOYAGER

"This is absurd," Vice Admiral Kathryn Janeway said, crossing her arms and fixing her gaze on the streaks of starlight visible from the long bay window in Counselor Hugh Cambridge's office.

The counselor did not reply immediately, a tactic Janeway had become all too familiar with in the last few days of regular morning sessions with *Voyager*'s resident therapist. She didn't need to turn back to know that despite her outburst, she would find him as she'd last seen him, resting comfortably in the deep black chair he favored, his long legs crossed at the knee, and his hands resting in his lap. His features would be placid, though occasional hints of ironic mischief would flash from his eyes.

"Can they actually do this?" she demanded of the heavens.

"Starfleet Command?" Cambridge replied drolly enough for Janeway to infer his meaning: *How well do you know the lunatics currently running our high-tech asylum?*

Finally facing him with the full sum of her fury, Janeway said, "They already offered me the damned job."

A faint smile flickered too quickly across Cambridge's lips for her to demote him for it on the spot.

"They did," Cambridge agreed.

"So what's the problem?"

"You didn't accept," Cambridge replied.

"I didn't accept *immediately*," Janeway corrected him. "The issue was first raised twenty-four hours after I had witnessed the deaths of Captain Eden and my godson while doing all I could to prevent the end of the entire multiverse. Hell, I'd only been alive again at that point for three days. And those three days were a little fraught, even by the Delta Quadrant's standards."

"Mmm-hmm," Cambridge murmured.

"They *ordered me* to think it over," Janeway said.

"And you excel at following orders?" Cambridge asked.

"I do," Janeway said, genuinely surprised at the implied criticism.

Cambridge said nothing, obviously wondering if she was going to dig this hole any deeper before tossing her a rope.

Janeway's shoulders fell as she released her arms to her sides, finally saying, "I excel at following the important ones."

A chuckle finally escaped the counselor's lips. "Congratulations, Admiral. We've been at this for days, and that might be the closest you've come to dispassionate self-reflection."

"What do they want from me?" Janeway asked.

"How should I know?" Cambridge countered, matching her bewildered tone.

"You've served under Admiral Montgomery for almost four years now," Janeway shot back.

"And you served right next to him for almost three," Cambridge said. "I'd hazard a guess that you know him better than I ever wish to."

Janeway paused for a moment to consider Admiral Kenneth Montgomery, who now held the future of the *Starship Voyager,* along with *Galen* and *Demeter,* in his hands. There was no denying that Montgomery and Janeway had begun their acquaintance at odds. But once the unpleasantness of Starfleet Intelligence Director Covington's bizarre and reckless attempt to turn herself into a Borg Queen had been put behind them, they had certainly become allies if not friends. While he didn't tend to reflect as deeply as she would have liked before taking action, Montgomery was hardly unreasonable and could be downright pleasant when the mood struck him. He had certainly seemed patient and understanding enough during their lengthy conversations of the past few days.

"Maybe he changed his mind," Janeway ventured.

"That would require him to acknowledge that his initial assessment was flawed," Cambridge said. "A useful ability, but not one I've seen Montgomery display, oh let me think . . . ever."

Janeway felt her face falling into hard lines. "Montgomery and his superiors sent nine ships to the Delta Quadrant five months ago. Although they were equipped with slipstream drives and staffed by Starfleet's finest, this fleet has suffered unimaginable losses in that short time, including the destruction of five ships, the deaths of more than eight hundred officers and crewmen, and the loss of two fleet commanders. He asked me if I would be willing to assume command of what's left to us: an *Intrepid*-class ship never truly designed for deep space exploration, an experimental medical vessel staffed largely by untested holograms, and a third, small ship that as best I can tell is little more than a roving airponics bay. With these resources, I am tasked with continuing exploration of one of the most dangerous areas of space Starfleet has ever entered in search for the remnants of the Borg, who were responsible for sixty-three billion deaths a few months ago, and the Caeliar, a species advanced enough to destroy the greatest threat the Federation has ever faced through the use of technology that our best scientists still classify essentially as magic."

"A tall order, I'll grant you," Cambridge allowed.

"So when Montgomery said I should take as much time as I needed to *think about it,* it never occurred to me that actually doing so might be construed as a character flaw."

"You think *that's* why the offer was rescinded?" Cambridge asked.

"You just said . . ." Janeway began.

"Admiral, please," Cambridge cut her off. "You are many things, but you are not stupid. I realize the new orders you received only moments before stepping into this office are troubling, but gather yourself and think for a moment."

Janeway did so, forcing herself to take the frustration now engulfing her and set it aside. Her breath settled into a deep slow rhythm, and moments later, a new thought jumped to the forefront of her mind.

"Montgomery didn't make the call."

Cambridge smiled. "See, that wasn't so hard, was it?"

The admiral then took a few moments to visualize the current chain of command above Montgomery, and her heart stilled as she realized that the new order in question could only have realistically come from one place.

"Admiral Akaar?" she asked.

"He is Starfleet's current commander in chief," Cambridge noted.

"But why would he trouble himself . . . ?"

"Because he doesn't have a dog in this hunt," Cambridge replied. "His perspective is going to be a little different than Montgomery's."

"Akaar is the top of the food chain, Counselor. All the dogs are his."

Nodding, Cambridge continued, "Yes, well, *whoever* made the choice you are now fretting didn't do so after hours of discussion with you. They had a series of cold hard facts as their only guide."

"And those facts led Admiral Akaar to conclude that I am not capable of leading this fleet?" Janeway asked.

"Put yourself in his shoes," Cambridge suggested.

"I realize I have made my fair share . . . all right, perhaps more than my fair share of questionable calls over the years," Janeway allowed.

"I don't think this about the distant past, Admiral," Cambridge said. "I'd guess ninety-five percent of those calls led to your promotion when *Voyager* first returned home from the Delta Quadrant."

"Yes, but that calculus might have changed a bit in light of some of the more far-reaching consequences of those choices," Janeway added.

"You think Akaar holds you personally responsible for the Borg Invasion?"

"It's not a huge leap."

"No, it's an impossible one," Cambridge insisted.

Janeway shook her head. They'd already spent several hours discussing what Cambridge felt was her misplaced need to assume responsibility for the recent actions of the Borg that resulted in the deaths of sixty-three billion and the loss of hundreds of ships and several planets. There was no arguing that her choice four years earlier to destroy a transwarp hub in the Delta Quadrant seemed to have led the Borg to reconsider their tactics against the Federation and to target them for annihilation. But Cambridge had rightly pointed out that without a crystal ball, there was no way Janeway could have predicted that her choice would have such cataclysmic results. Based on the intelligence she had at the time, it would have been dereliction of duty for her to have refused to attempt to cripple the Borg, regardless of the eventual consequences. Intellectually, she could see his point. Her heart, however, remained unconvinced.

"Then why?" Janeway asked.

Cambridge sat up abruptly. "For pity's sake, Kathryn, you've only been *alive* again for a week and a half. You were presumed dead for the last fourteen months, but that time never happened for you. Two weeks ago, by your internal reckoning, you were on a routine mission to investigate what you believed to be a dead Borg cube. You arrived, were eaten by a wall, and transformed into a Borg Queen who then rained fiery death down upon your former comrades at arms. Violence on that level, violations of that nature, are incomprehensible to most of us. That assault left you with a wounded, terrified shred of yourself that was somehow saved by the Q and that tender shred was then asked to rationally decide whether or not to release itself into oblivion or return to the life you once knew in order to prevent the multiverse from combusting trillions of years ahead of schedule. Within hours of returning to this existence, you were faced with the death of the man you love, the man on whom you had pinned many of your hopes and expectations of the future. And despite the fact that he ultimately survived, the only solution to the Gordian knot you were trying to unravel did include the deaths of a fellow captain you respected and a godson you would gladly have sacrificed yourself to save."

Janeway felt heat rising to her cheeks but remained silent.

"The wonder here is not that calmer heads have prevailed upon Montgomery and ordered you back to the Alpha Quadrant to undergo a course of evaluations and recuperation before making final determination regarding your future career. What you should be questioning is why Montgomery would have ever offered you the job in the first place. What demons must be driving the man who would so callously set you up to fail?"

"You don't think I'm ready to lead this fleet?" the admiral asked.

"You are, inarguably, one of the finest officers who has ever worn the uniform. You eat the impossible for breakfast. You seek out challenges most would never contemplate, holding yourself to ridiculously idealistic standards, and you do it with a ready smile, keen wit, formidable intelligence, and a compassionate heart. You are a bloody beacon in the darkness, an inspiration to anyone dedicating their lives to Starfleet. To a man, those who have served with you in the past would walk naked through fire for you, but right now, I wouldn't follow you to the mess hall."

"I see," Janeway said, placing her hands on the back of the chair opposite the counselor.

Cambridge searched her face warily.

"And did you, by any chance, share these thoughts with Admiral Montgomery or Admiral Akaar?" Janeway asked.

Cambridge shook his head, clearly exasperated. "They didn't *ask,* Kathryn," he replied.

Her heart began to pound slowly but with considerable force. "They didn't?"

Again, Cambridge shook his head. "I kept waiting, assuming they would. But no one has yet."

"That's . . ." she trailed off, unable to find the right word.

". . . troubling," he finished for her. Rising, he moved to her side, and she turned to face him.

"Someone up there has made a decision they believe to be final and are not the least bit interested in anyone else's opinion on the matter. How they reached that decision is irrelevant. Be prepared to listen very hard, to what they say and don't say. The truth will slip through the cracks somewhere.

"But make no mistake. That can't be your primary focus right now. Even after you left command of *Voyager* to Chakotay, you maintained what some might call an unhealthy attachment to your former command. You crossed lines few in your position would have risked for those you once led. You did it because you are constitutionally incapable of doing otherwise. But if you truly hope to lead them again, if you actually want this job, which I can't imagine you could reasonably decide right now, you need to shift your priorities.

"You need to spend as much time as it takes to grieve your former life, to process this extraordinary transformation, and to decide who you are now. The Kathryn Janeway who stepped onto that Borg cube wouldn't have blinked when command of this fleet was offered to her."

"But *I* did," Janeway said softly.

"Precisely. And well done, I might add. That alone tells me your deeper wisdom is already serving you well."

"Wonderful." Janeway sighed.

"You will never again be the woman you once were. You

have glimpsed yourself on a subatomic level. You have been altered forever by events both within and beyond your control. The mysteries of the universe, of existence, are no longer abstractions you can idly consider over drinks on a late night. They are staring you coldly in the face. They will not be ignored or postponed. There isn't a clinical diagnosis that can contain the many levels of psychic stress you have endured or the emotional toll they have taken, never mind a treatment plan. You are now, much as you were when *Voyager* was first lost in the Delta Quadrant, countless light-years from your home.

"But this journey, you must walk alone. You must somehow integrate all of the violence, pain, and loss as well as the love and light that are yours into a new functioning whole. And it's going to take a little longer than you're ready to admit right now. It's not a task I envy you, though I do regret not being able to be the one to walk beside you as you take your first steps."

"I appreciate that, Counselor," Janeway said. "And on one level, I know you're probably right."

"But?"

"I think I'd feel better about this if the decision had been mine. You make it sound as if I have no choice in the matter."

"Of course you do. You could march straight into Montgomery's office the day you arrive and demand he reconsider. You could bully your way past the counselors assigned to evaluate you. You could make Akaar's life personally and professionally miserable by reminding him and anyone else who will listen that you just saved this ship and the entire multiverse and that alone should earn you the right to do as you damn well please.

"You could try to avoid this work for the rest of your life, Kathryn. But do that and I promise, eventually, it will bring you to your knees."

The admiral smiled mirthlessly. "Maybe. But not for long."

"I'm rooting for you, Kathryn. You can do this. You *will*

if I know you at all. But even I wouldn't dare guess at this point what your final choice will be once you've found the path. And neither should you. What I do know is that *if* you return, it needs to be for the right reasons. And *if* that day comes, I'll likely follow you anywhere."

Lieutenant Commander Thomas Eugene Paris entered Captain Chakotay's ready room at precisely 0700 hours, as ordered. And that was no mean feat, given that his morning had started three hours earlier and consisted almost entirely of nursing his wife through her worst bout of morning sickness to date. Had Paris not seen it, he would never have believed it was possible for any individual to eliminate that much of anything from her body continuously and over so many hours. He had wondered, but not found the courage to ask B'Elanna, if one of the redundant Klingon organs was the stomach. If this morning was any indication, she must have six of them.

Paris had finally prevailed upon her to go to sickbay, over her strenuous objections. He had then activated Miral's holographic nanny to watch over her, hurriedly replicated a fresh uniform, and rushed to the ready room for his morning meeting with the captain. Thankfully, the thought of breakfast hadn't even been tempting or he would have been late.

He found Chakotay seated at his desk and staring out through the windows of the ready room, several padds stacked untouched before him.

"Good morning, sir," Paris greeted Chakotay briskly.

As his captain turned to meet his eyes, Paris registered deep consternation tinged with a smidge of anger.

"Chakotay?" Paris asked, dropping the official pleasantries at once.

"We have a problem, Tom," Chakotay began.

When isn't that the case? Paris thought, but was wise enough to keep to himself. Instead, the first officer did a quick mental inventory of the ship's status, ongoing personnel issues, pending duties, last-known orders, and came up with absolutely nothing to account for Chakotay's mood. True, in a few hours, *Voyager* would arrive at New Talax to regroup with its last remaining fleet vessels, the *Galen* and *Demeter,* and a few hours after that, a lengthy memorial service no one could be looking forward to would begin.

But Chakotay had spent the last few months in *Voyager's* center seat turning calmness in the face of chaos into an art form. And less than two weeks ago, he had unexpectedly been reunited with Admiral Janeway, the only woman Paris believed Chakotay had ever truly loved, and whom all of them had thought dead for the last year or so. If anything, this unlikely turn of events had seemed to deepen Chakotay's reserves of strength while bringing a new and healthy light back into his eyes.

"What happened?" Paris asked, when his best efforts came up empty.

Chakotay clasped his hands before him and began to knead them, as if he could force some insight from them.

"We have new orders from Starfleet Command," Chakotay replied.

"Okay," Paris said, wondering how bad this could possibly be.

Chakotay rose from his desk and moved to place his back against the railing that separated his work space from a small raised lounge—the room's most comfortable and inviting feature. "Once the memorial ends, Admiral Janeway will board the *Galen* and return to the Alpha Quadrant for an extended period of recuperation."

Paris's stomach turned so hard he was grateful it was empty.

"I thought they had offered her command of the fleet," he said.

"They did." Chakotay nodded. "And I was certain that the only way they were going to allow us to stay out here in the Delta Quadrant was if she accepted."

"So . . . she passed on their offer?" Paris ventured hesitantly.

"No." Chakotay shook his head. "It took some convincing, but she decided to accept it. And when she advised them this morning of her intentions, the offer was rescinded."

"Then this isn't Admiral Janeway taking some much-needed and well-earned rest," Paris realized.

"No."

"This is going to be weeks or more of intensive psychiatric evaluations, and wait a minute." Paris paused as too many thoughts rushed through his sleep-deprived brain at once. "Are we going home?"

Chakotay's eyes met Paris's, searching them with the precision of a laser scalpel.

"No," he said softly.

"Then I don't understand," Paris admitted.

Chakotay sighed. "I don't either. *That's* the problem."

The first officer made his way up the low step into the seating area where he had an unobstructed view of streaking starlight.

"So we're supposed to continue to do the work that was once assigned to nine ships all by ourselves?"

"*Demeter* is staying as well."

"What about *Achilles*?"

"She is still officially connected to the fleet, but there's been no word of her returning to the Delta Quadrant any time soon."

Paris turned back to face Chakotay. "You think they've written us off?"

"Resources are pretty scarce these days in the Alpha Quadrant, and Admiral Janeway has mentioned some new political developments that are troubling. But clearly they don't trust us to assist with any of that."

"Have we been assigned a new mission?"

"Captain's discretion," Chakotay replied.

"Huh."

"I know."

Paris placed his hands on the rail as Chakotay turned to face him. "I think it's fair to say that from command's point of view, the last few months haven't gone as well as they probably hoped for our fleet."

"Maybe. But I look at the last five months and see amazing, if qualified successes," Chakotay insisted. "I know the costs have been great, but I also know that they should have been greater, and would have been if not for the dedication and resourcefulness we've all displayed. But I don't see how we can possibly fulfill our mission, a thorough investigation of this quadrant, with our two small ships. And for now, they're not offering any reinforcements."

"You think they want us to fail?"

"I wouldn't go that far. I think they don't know which end is up right now. I think the sheer volume of catastrophic change they've had to absorb in the last year probably has everyone still connected to their behinds looking for a way to cover them. Putting Admiral Janeway immediately back in command was a tidy solution on paper, but obviously they must question her fitness right now. It took a lot less than being assimilated, killed, and resurrected for them to question mine."

Not that much less, Paris thought, but held his peace.

"They have to know that one *Intrepid*-class vessel and a special-mission ship can't make a dent in unraveling this quadrant's mysteries, but bringing us home now is tantamount to admitting that sending us out in the first place was a mistake. And I don't think anyone is eager to add that to their resume right now."

"Do you think it was a mistake, Chakotay?"

"No," he replied as if offended by the thought.

"You want to stay?"

"I know this is where we can do the most good right now, even if they don't."

"So how do we show them that?"

"We do what we've always done . . . we prove them wrong . . . *again.*"

"Yes, but *again* I ask, how?"

The captain stepped back from the railing and began to pace the small area before his desk. "We need to avoid any appearance of impropriety or renegade impulses. We need to demonstrate to Starfleet that we take our responsibilities seriously and that we can play by the rules. But we also need to show Command that continuing to explore this quadrant is a worthy investment of time and resources.

"I want you to compile a list of possible targets for exploration. When we first left the Delta Quadrant behind, we'd barely scratched the surface of its depth and breadth. We need to find a mission that could yield significant results, not just for us, but for the Federation."

"So no baby stars, uninhabited systems, or interesting nebulas?" Paris quipped.

"First contact would be nice," Chakotay mused.

"Agreed, but those can be a little unpredictable. I know things ended well with the Children of the Storm and Riley's people, but we ticked off the Indign and the Tarkons pretty well, and there's still that little matter of our lost hologram to consider."

"Unless Reg has found any promising leads in our absence, I'm not sure where to begin looking for Meegan."

"We can't just let her go."

"Call it instinct, but my sense is if she plans to move against us in any way, she'll find us when she's good and ready."

Paris shrugged. "If in the meantime you're suggesting we revisit any of the territories we already know a little about, we do have something of a reputation preceding us to deal with."

"Not everybody called us the 'ship of death.'" Chakotay smirked.

"No, just the ones who survived our first visits." Paris chuckled.

"You know what I mean," Chakotay insisted.

"I do." Paris nodded. "And with your permission, I'm going to ask Seven and Harry to help me create this list."

"Absolutely. Be prepared to present it first thing tomorrow morning."

"I was planning to spend most of the day finalizing preparations for the memorial service, and then, attending it."

"And?"

"Sleep is for sissies."

"Don't you just love being first officer?" Chakotay teased.

"Yes, sir."

After a moment, Paris added, "Are you going to be okay?"

Chakotay had moved to take his seat, but paused. "How do you mean?"

Paris considered testing the waters but honestly no longer had the patience for anything less than a reckless dive. "Without the admiral," he replied.

"Yes." Chakotay smiled, and Paris sensed he meant it. "She'll be back. And when she returns, we're going to have done ourselves proud in the interim."

Paris wanted to take this at face value, but he knew he needed to push a little further. "You lost her once and it didn't go all that well. You're not afraid of losing her again?"

Chakotay might have punched anyone else for insubordination at this, but coming from Paris, who had come painfully close to losing his wife and daughter, it was a fair question.

"I'm not going to lie. The thought is too awful to contemplate. But I'm not going to live every day of the rest of my life in fear. And neither is she. Tomorrow is promised to no one. We can't waste today. A few thousand light-years between us changes nothing. She will come back."

"And if she doesn't?"

"You think they'll decide she's not up to the job?"

"I think on her worst day, she's overqualified," Paris replied sincerely. "But I don't like the idea of her facing all of this alone. I wonder if she needs us right now even more than we need her."

"She has us," Chakotay insisted. "That's never going to change."

"No, it isn't," Paris agreed.

As Paris crossed to the door to begin what was going to be a much busier day than he hoped for when he arrived, Chakotay called after him.

"Conlon submitted her morning engineering report and indicated B'Elanna wasn't present. Is she okay?"

"She's fine," Paris said. "Just a little under the weather this morning. I'm sure Doctor Sharak will have her back on her feet in no time."

"Good. As you were." Chakotay dismissed him.

Paris continued out the door, slightly chagrined at withholding his and B'Elanna's happy news. Paris had only known for a few days that his family was about to get a little bigger, and B'Elanna had forbidden him to tell any of their friends for a few more weeks. It was an understandable request, but Paris couldn't help but think that especially today, Chakotay could have used a little good news.

Still, he was determined to provide the captain with some by the next morning, come what may.

"The proper term is hyperemesis gravidarum, Commander," Doctor Sharak said in his most soothing voice.

Lieutenant Commander B'Elanna Torres responded by heaving once again and depositing the results in a small basin Sharak had offered her the moment she had entered sickbay.

"Don't . . . care . . . what you call it . . ." B'Elanna finally said through ragged breaths. The last several hours had sapped every ounce of strength she possessed. "Just . . . make it . . . stop," she finished, and punctuated the thought by retching again.

"I can't," Sharak said.

Exhausted and dispirited, B'Elanna lay her head against

the inclined biobed. "Do your people have a position on euthanasia?" she asked.

Sharak seemed to seriously consider the question. "We do," he finally replied, "though it is a personal choice rather than one imposed by society as a whole."

B'Elanna turned her head to make sure Doctor Sharak knew that last question had been her extreme distress talking and not a serious request. Although he was the first Tamarian she had ever met and the nuances of the expressions of his wide, dark-brown mottled face were often difficult to decipher, an assured smile and twinkle in his eyes put her fears to rest.

"But do not despair, Commander. This condition has arisen much later in your pregnancy than is normally encountered and will likely subside shortly as the hormones currently aiding the fetus's early growth diminish to the more normal levels you will maintain for the next several months. In the meantime, I will monitor and supplement your fluid intake and electrolyte levels. I will also provide daily injections of vitamin supplements to replace those you will likely be unable to keep down until your appetite returns."

"You mean to tell me we can communicate via subspace, create warp fields, dematerialize and rematerialize complex matter at will, and manufacture weapons that operate in multiple phase states but Federation medical science still hasn't cracked the code on morning sickness?" B'Elanna demanded.

"Oh, we have," Sharak replied. "We now understand the precise hormonal and chemical interactions that produce your symptoms and have learned through years of experimentation that the wisest course of action as long as your health is not seriously jeopardized is to allow nature to act as it must."

"*This* is natural?"

"Yes," Sharak replied, "and in your particular case, its intensity is likely related to the genetic issues present in your son's mixed heritage."

"Tom and I already have one child, and my first pregnancy was nothing like this."

"Every union of genetic material is unique, Commander," Sharak assured her, "as is every ensuing gestation."

B'Elanna paused as Sharak's words finally registered.

"My *son's* heritage?" she asked.

"Yes, Commander."

"It's a boy?" B'Elanna asked as wonder momentarily replaced her general misery.

Sharak's face fell. "I am sorry, Commander. Did you not wish to know the gender of your child prior to its birth?"

The fleet engineer's stomach heaved again, and she immediately rolled to her side and grabbed the basin. When the sensation had subsided, she sat back and replied, "It's okay." Placing her hands protectively over her belly that had yet to show even a hint of rounding, she imagined the look in Tom's eyes when she told him they were about to have a son.

It more than made the last several hours worth it.

Like most expectant mothers, B'Elanna had been hoping for ten little fingers and ten little toes. The rest, including the child's gender, was gravy. But something in the knowledge that this was her son, *Tom's son,* filled her with awe.

It's going to be okay, my little man. Your mom is a Klingon warrior. I've been through worse.

Lieutenant Harry Kim, *Voyager*'s security chief and tactics officer, was pleased with his handiwork. He stood beside the chief engineer, Lieutenant Nancy Conlon, and Seven of Nine in what had once been cargo bays two and three. For the time being, they had been merged into one vast compartment, empty but for a newly erected command console and the presence of dozens of specially designed holographic generators.

"Let me see it one more time?" Kim asked.

Conlon and Seven exchanged a knowing, weary glance, but the lieutenant complied without comment. At her command, the bleak gray bulkheads were replaced by a large reception hall decorated in somber earth tones. A small raised area at one end had been designated for representatives from each fleet vessels, save *Plank*'s, whose loss had already been memorialized. The rest of the space was filled with rows of long, low, cushioned benches running the length of the room, on which the surviving crews from the vessels *Voyager, Quirinal, Esquiline, Hawking, Curie, Achilles, Galen,* and *Demeter* would sit during the formal part of the ceremony.

"And the park?" Kim requested.

In a flash, the interior location shifted, and the same dais and benches sat in an open-air recreation of Federation Park in San Francisco at night. This would be used for a brief time at the end of the service. Once it was done, the space would be reset to an interior but populated by casually arranged tables and chairs to allow the various crews to interact more personally.

Kim and Conlon, with Seven and Paris's help, had spent the last several days considering the most appropriate and personal forum in which those who had served together but a few short months and had recently been separated by tragedy could come together as a fleet to commemorate the lives of those lost. It had been Conlon's suggestion to make contact with the survivors who had hastily returned to the Alpha Quadrant less than a week ago and hold the service together in real time using the communications buoys the fleet had launched when they first arrived in the Delta Quadrant. Kim had initially envisioned mounting ceiling-to-floor viewscreens to create the illusion that those assembled were sharing one space. It had been Seven's suggestion to simply create a holodeck large enough to house *Voyager, Galen,* and *Demeter*'s two hundred plus crew while simultaneously allowing them to actually interact directly with the more than seven hundred who would be gathering in the Alpha Quadrant.

This minor miracle could never have been accomplished

without the assistance of the officers at Project Pathfinder who had worked years earlier to reconnect *Voyager* with the Alpha Quadrant when they had been lost in the wilds of the Delta Quadrant. Although Pathfinder's work had been refocused when *Voyager* first returned home, many on staff there now still felt a certain kinship with *Voyager*'s crew, and a small contingent had been assigned to monitor the fleet's relays and enable continuous communications capabilities when the new fleet had launched. Seven had made direct contact with an old acquaintance, Commander Varia, and he had dropped everything to assist her in making the necessary preparations from his end.

Real-time holographic communications of this size had been reserved for only high-level meetings of Federation and Starfleet authorities. When Kim and Seven had briefed Varia on their intentions for the service, he'd agreed it was possible, and in this case, absolutely appropriate.

"Do you think we should . . . ?" Kim began.

"I'm not contacting Varia again, Harry," Conlon cut him off. "The relays are stable. We've already tested the matrix fifty times, and everybody who will be running the technical side of this thing knows their job. We're ready," she assured him.

"Seven?" Kim asked, hoping she might countermand Conlon's completely accurate assessment.

"While I am a little concerned at fluctuations in relays nineteen and twenty-six's power levels, we can bypass them if necessary," Seven replied.

"Are they still acting up?" Conlon asked, double-checking her own console.

"We are ready, Lieutenant Kim," Seven said.

Kim nodded. While he took a moment's pleasure in the results of their labors, certain that in a few hours hundreds of men and women now separated by more than twenty-thousand light-years would, for a short time, believe that they were standing right beside one another, that happiness was too quickly replaced by the unavoidable heaviness of the circumstances that necessitated their gathering.

"Okay," Kim agreed. Now, he only looked forward to the evening's end, when he could tear the thing down and begin the much more difficult process of putting the devastation of the last few weeks behind him.

Chapter Two

VOYAGER, NEW TALAX

Once Captain Chakotay had grown accustomed to her holographic presence, as vivid as everyone else on the dais, he had been unable to suppress the amusement that had risen unexpectedly throughout Captain Regina Farkas's remarks.

If anything, Farkas was shorter than he remembered; a trim woman in her seventies with white hair and a fading scar running down the right side of her face. She had served Starfleet for almost fifty years, and the wisdom she had accumulated in that time was not lost on him. Her voice was warm, her tone quaint and conversational. Everything about Farkas made him wish that her ship, the *Quirinal,* had not been one of those recently lost and that during the few months they'd served the same fleet, he'd actually found some time to get to know her a bit.

"*. . . at which point Parimon turned to his mother, tossed the sheet tied around his neck jauntily over his shoulder, and shouted defiantly, 'Parimon to the rescue!'*" Farkas paused here as light laughter rippled through the assembly. "*He then proceeded, wearing only his underpants and that magical cape, to assault that tree with all the might of his five years, and damned if that keekit wasn't back on the ground a few minutes later.*" Farkas paused again as the luster the memory had brought to her eyes seemed to dim. "*I know some of you might think that little recollection inappropriate for a gathering such as this.*

But I've known his parents, Lukas and Selena Dasht, for forty years, and while duty made it impossible for me to witness most of his life, I'll never forget that first meeting or the certainty it left me with that young Parimon Dasht had great things in his future.

"That's the problem with moments like this. We want to think about the good times, our best memories of those we have lost. But now that we know how their lives ended, those memories are tainted by all of the untapped potential; the sense that it shouldn't be this way.

"I've read the final reports Captain Eden filed before her death, and included in them were notes of things she witnessed in the Omega Continuum while many of you sitting here before me were marshaling every resource at your disposal to save my ship, Parimon's, Itak's, and Chan's. I don't know what to make of her reports. But I am disinclined to doubt the word of a fellow Starfleet officer, so the impressions she recounted have now been added to my understanding of events as I prepare to move into the future.

"According to Captain Eden, there were four officers present, sharing some sort of meeting, just prior to the destruction of Quirinal, Esquiline, Hawking, *and* Curie. *They included Captains Itak and Chan, as well as Lieutenant Waverly of the* Esquiline *and Ensign Sadie Johns, a member of my crew I did not have the pleasure of knowing well. What strikes me as odd is that Parimon wasn't there. He should have been. There is nothing in Captain Eden's report to explain this, so I have come to my own conclusion. Parimon wasn't there because he had another battle to fight. Somewhere among the seven hundred and eighty-five of our fellows who were lost in Omega, someone needed him. So he delegated whatever task the others were performing to a trusted subordinate, and at that critical moment, was somewhere else, rushing to the rescue."*

Chakotay had spoken briefly with Eden after she had experienced this vision and had committed the logs Farkas referenced to memory. He knew that Eden believed that hundreds of minds had been unable to function in the terror that was the Omega Continuum before they had died, and likely Parimon's was among them. That was the only reason Chakotay could imagine for a Starfleet captain to forego a gathering where the result had been the intentional destruction of his vessel. But Chakotay couldn't fault Farkas for choosing to come to her own conclusions about Captain Dasht. History was written by those who survived it, and her explanation was certainly easier to live with than the likely truth.

Although the captain's subsequent comments about Captains Itak and Chan and several of her own officers were of necessity less personal, they were no less poignant. But her final words were the ones Chakotay found hardest to forget.

"Memorials are nice. They are necessary. They begin to bring acceptance to those who participate. And acceptance is perhaps the most critical of the stages of grief. Without it, it is impossible for us to continue to navigate our own lives in any semblance of wholeness. Because I honor the lives every single man and woman aboard those ships lived and the nobility of the choice they made to serve among the stars, I will accept that they were taken from us too soon by a force beyond my comprehension. I will do so because the only tribute I can offer that is worthy of their sacrifice is my continuing devotion to the duty that defines us all. But I will never forget the debt I owe them that can never be repaid or the lessons writ large by their choice to die so that we could go on living. It is not enough to make peace with this. We must consider our choices as well.

"The Klingons begin each day with a saying: 'Today is a good day to die.' I've certainly found myself meditating on those words in some of my darkest moments. But what occurs to me now is that they are not meant to teach us to covet death or to glorify it. The truth they reveal is that every day must be lived to its absolute fullest. We must move through every moment of every day certain that the choices we are making are those we would want others to remember us by. The Klingons are not calling to the warriors within us to seek out death. They are calling us to

live every moment of every day as our best selves, so that should death arrive unbidden, we may face it without regret.

"I do not know what regrets our fellows may have nurtured in their last moments, but I hope they were few. We demonstrate our love and respect for them by dedicating ourselves here and now to doing what we must to ensure that when death inevitably comes for us, we will meet it untroubled by thoughts of what we should have done differently."

At this, the entire assembly rose to its feet and remained there until Captain Farkas had taken her seat beside Admiral Janeway. Chakotay caught the admiration in Kathryn's eyes as she regarded the captain. Farkas kept her eyes forward, glued to the men and women who seemed determined to answer her call.

Chakotay's turn had finally come. Brief comments by Lieutenant Vorik, the senior officer to have survived *Hawking*'s destruction, and Lieutenant Downs, one of *Curie*'s few remaining crew, had preceded those of Captain Farkas.

"Please be seated," Chakotay said softly as he took the podium. Once the assembly was settled, he began. "My fellow officers have already paid tribute to those who served with them. It falls to me to speak briefly of the loss I am uniquely capable of addressing.

"Project Full Circle was Captain Afsarah Eden's vision. She spent the years between *Voyager*'s return to the Alpha Quadrant and this fleet's launch going over every aspect of our journey; cataloging, summarizing, and distilling what we learned, giving meaning to all we endured by ensuring that our unique experience was not lost to future generations. Through that work, she became convinced that continued exploration of this area of space was vital to Starfleet's ongoing mission.

"When I stood on *Voyager*'s bridge the day we began our journey home and imagined the seventy thousand light-years we would have to travel, it seemed an impossible distance. It was so big, I found it difficult to visualize. I did the only thing

I could. I focused on the small steps. The goal was always in sight, but the quality of the journey became my priority.

"Afsarah Eden never tore her eyes away from the big picture. As soon as our technology caught up with her relentless passion for exploration, Captain Eden made sure that technology was put to its best possible use.

"I know many of you might still harbor questions about her role in the recent tragedy. Among the more disappointing rumors I've heard is one that she only supported this mission and chose to lead it for selfish reasons. Nothing could be farther from the truth. As Commander Drafar of the *Achilles* has reported and I can attest, her primary concern, once the threat of Omega had been revealed, was to ensure the safety of as many of the people under her command as possible. *Achilles* was ordered to return to the Alpha Quadrant to preserve the lives of those we managed to rescue.

"This might have been the only selfish choice she ever made.

"Afsarah Eden gave her life for every single creature now in existence and for countless more to come. 'Humanity is a stubborn thing,' she said. 'It hopes, even when all hope is gone.' It is only because of her choice to hope that we are all standing here right now.

"Every single one of you knows intimately the power this existence has to humble us. It bestows benign and beautiful gifts with one hand, wonder, awe, inspiration, and love, while wrenching those same things from us with the other. Violence, destruction, senseless conflict, and paralyzing loss are always ready to tip the scales toward despair. They teach us to fear the unknown, to risk only small things, and to temper our dreams with realistic expectations.

"But we are the ones who grant them that power.

"Even as she drew her last breath, Afsarah Eden refused to despair. She reached for the best in herself and in all of us, determined to vanquish the darkness. She taught me many things, but her greatest lesson, the one I will hold close when that darkness creeps near, is to put my faith in our greatest weapon and the very definition of our humanity: our capacity to hope."

Admiral Janeway had requested the honor of reading the names of those lost aloud, and Chakotay had agreed. As he stepped aside to grant her the podium, his heart swelled at the sight of her face. He knew she felt the lion's share of responsibility for what the fleet had lost. But in this moment, she had clearly set that aside to serve as a focal point for the grief of all those present.

"Thank you, Captain." Janeway nodded toward Chakotay as she took her place. "For those of you I have not yet had the honor to meet, I am Vice Admiral Kathryn Janeway. I know that some of you attended my memorial service a little over a year ago, and having done so, my presence here now might be disconcerting. To be honest, it surprises me as well."

This elicited soft laughter as she continued. "I am here because those we honor now thought more of us, more of those they had sworn to protect when they began their service than they did of themselves. Each and every one of them reminds us that the work we undertake on a daily basis is perilous. But it is purposeful. It falls to us now to take our memories of each of them and sear those memories into our hearts and minds. We will never forget who they were or what they have given us. And neither will Starfleet, or the Federation."

After a brief pause, Janeway nodded toward the back of the room, and a few seconds later, what had been a tranquil interior room was replaced by a grassy plain beneath a star-filled sky. Murmurs of confusion diminished as the admiral continued.

"As we speak, night has fallen on Federation Park on Earth where the sacrifice of those we honor will be forever memorialized. Even the miracles of our technology do not permit us to share the field tonight with those who have assembled there for their own ceremony. We join them in spirit for the official dedication of the monument to those lost as we recall our fellow crew, family, and dear friends."

Janeway's voice remained steady as she began to speak the names aloud. "Captain Afsarah Eden. Captain Parimon Dasht. Commander Sebastian Dagny . . ." She was perhaps twenty names into the long list to come when Chakotay noticed several of the officers before him pointing up at the sky. The admiral continued, untroubled, and soon enough, Chakotay understood. Finally, the tears he had held at bay throughout the formal remarks began to fall freely in the sanctified darkness.

As each name was read, one of the stars above the assembly disappeared.

Chakotay watched the faces of those before him turn to solemn reflection, and he nodded faintly. Tom, Harry, Nancy, and Seven had accepted the difficult task of preparing this event. The captain was proud and grateful that they had found a way to ritualize this ceremony that was both powerful and appropriate.

By the time the list of names neared its end, everyone in the room's eyes were lifted to the imaginary heavens above. Most were tear streaked, but all seemed determined to witness the dying of the light to the last.

When the admiral had read the final name and the room was shrouded in darkness, she paused. A moment later, a white-hot sphere burst into light above them, giving off waves of incandescence almost too brilliant to behold. Many looked away as it descended and came to rest atop a low stone basin that had appeared just before the dais through the magic of holographic technology.

Finally, Janeway continued. "As many of you will not be at liberty for some time to see the memorial Starfleet has erected to honor the crew of the *Esquiline, Quirinal, Hawking,* and *Curie,* we felt it appropriate that each of you see it re-created here tonight. Once the service has concluded, feel free to approach it, if only to reflect on the words chosen to honor our fallen comrades. They were written by an English poet, Sarah Williams, more than four hundred years ago, and are as follows:

"'Though my soul may set in darkness, it will rise in perfect light; I have loved the stars too fondly to be fearful of the night.'"

With that, Admiral Janeway stepped aside as the entire room erupted in spontaneous, deafening applause.

As Janeway descended the dais and moved into the crew that was beginning to intermingle, she caught sight of B'Elanna Torres moving quickly to meet Lieutenant Vorik as he stepped down for a closer look at the monument. Ignoring his Vulcan restraint, she grabbed him fiercely in a hug the moment their eyes met. Janeway continued to observe long enough to see Vorik finally return some of the firmness of her embrace. Having served with Vorik for many years, Janeway, like B'Elanna, had been relieved when she learned that he had been among the survivors.

Chakotay remained near the podium, his head bent low as he spoke with Captain Farkas. A tall human woman in dress uniform who was likely in her eighties stood at Farkas's other side, waiting patiently for the captain's attention.

Although many were casting hesitant glances toward Janeway, she was soon face-to-face with Seven of Nine.

"How long should I wait before resetting the program to the reception hall?" she asked.

"I'd give it a little more time," Janeway suggested. "And Seven?"

"Yes, Admiral."

"Well done."

Seven smiled faintly, but could not help adding, "The shift to the park setting was, as I told you, Lieutenant Kim's suggestion. I merely facilitated it."

"I know you didn't sleep last night with the extra programming required to re-create Federation Park," Janeway admonished her. "But the effect was lovely, and I believe it meant a great deal to everyone present."

"Then the extra effort required was not wasted," Seven said.

Janeway turned as the sounds of a scuffle registered to her right. Weaving his way toward her and moving aside none too gently any unfortunate enough to block his path, was Neelix.

She closed the distance between them and soon was enveloped in an embrace so intense, it left her momentarily breathless. When he finally pulled away, Neelix's eyes were awash in tears of joy.

"Mister Ambassador," she greeted him warmly.

"I just can't . . ." he began. "How . . . I mean, Seven tried to explain but . . . oh, never mind, I don't care how," he decided, pulling her close again.

After several minutes spent ensuring her old friend who had attended the ceremony among the representatives of New Talax of her health and well-being, a furtive tug of her sleeve ended this pleasant reunion all too quickly. Promising to find Neelix again before the evening had ended, she turned her attention to Chakotay.

"I know we've got some time left, but I think Captain Farkas might be signing off a little early, and she wants to speak with you."

"Of course." Janeway nodded and followed him through the crowd to a secluded area where Farkas stood alone.

"I need to find Icheb," Chakotay said softly as he left her side. Nodding in understanding, Janeway turned to face *Quirinal*'s former captain.

Farkas's face was set in harder lines than Janeway had seen throughout the evening, and she was clearly not in a mood to mince words.

"How do they do that, exactly?" Farkas asked.

Unsure, Janeway replied, "The holo-presence technology?"

"No, the creation of the memorial," Farkas clarified.

Janeway shook her head. "I don't know. I think there's a dedicated office at Command."

"We do this so often as an organization, we've actually carved out a space in our headquarters for the planning of our memorials," Farkas said bitterly.

"Captain?" Janeway asked gently.

Farkas's eyes met hers, filled with cold resolve.

"Permission to speak freely, Admiral?"

Though Janeway had never known these words to be followed by any she enjoyed hearing, she stiffened her spine and nodded. "Of course."

"I've spent the last week camped out in Admiral Montgomery's office. I know he offered you command of the fleet, and I know that the offer has been temporarily placed on hold."

"That's right."

"I'd like you to do me a favor."

"If I can."

"I'd like you to help me understand, now that all of the consequences of your past choices have been laid bare, how you'd even entertain the notion that a command such as this, a trust such as this, should rest in your hands."

Janeway's cheeks stung as surely as if she'd been slapped.

"Which choices are you referring to?" she asked.

"The only one that matters," Farkas replied. *"The one that as best I can tell set this entire chain of events in motion. Some future version of you decided that the life she had was so unbearable, the only appropriate course was to alter the time line so she could bring her crew home early and spare them some painful losses? When you look around this room, when you feel the suffering of those assembled here, do you weigh their misery any less than yours? Because you did this, Admiral."*

Janeway had leveled similar charges against herself constantly over the last several days, but hearing them read to her now by a fellow officer who had already earned her regard was nearly unbearable.

"It's a fair question," Janeway acknowledged. "The problem is I can't answer it."

"What with my ship being destroyed and all, I've got a little time on my hands, Admiral, and I'm here to tell you, unless you try, I'm going to spend that time making sure you never see a starship from the inside again," Farkas said.

Janeway didn't doubt this.

"When I was with the Q, I was given an unusual gift. Apart from the obvious one," she added quickly. "I experienced the lives and deaths of many versions of myself in countless time lines. Still, I can't tell you what specifically drove *that* Admiral Janeway to take such reckless actions. I can tell you that my initial response to her suggestion was to avoid any further alterations of the time line. It went against everything I'd learned, everything I believed. But I also knew, or *thought I knew,* the future. The consequences of inaction weighed heavy. And the fact that we might, through our choices, cripple the Borg, was a major consideration."

"We all know now how well that turned out," Farkas said, not giving an inch.

"We do," Janeway agreed. "I can offer no defense now, nor would I, given the magnitude of my apparent miscalculation." Janeway paused before meeting Farkas's eyes again, this time with her own healthy resolve. "What I *can* tell you is that the woman who made that choice no longer exists. As best I can tell, she never will now. And if you think for one instant that I don't spend every waking moment wondering how I could ever have come to such a place, how I could conscience such purely selfish instincts, you don't know me at all."

Farkas started to speak again, but Janeway raised a hand to silence her.

"We all have regrets, Captain," Janeway insisted. "You cannot imagine mine, and I would never wish them on you. But you're the one who said we need to make every day left us a promise to do better. Those are words I planned to live by, even before you spoke them. I could never be that woman now, knowing all I know. It's not possible. I can't make those mistakes again. I can certainly make new ones, but I won't live in fear of them.

"You will, of course, proceed as you see fit. I will do the same," she added. "And perhaps when the grief has dissipated a bit, you might take some time to walk a few miles in my boots. You saw the devastation wrought by the Borg firsthand and just survived the destruction of your vessel. I suspect we have a great deal in common, more than you'd like to admit. Perhaps one day we will meet under circumstances that will grant you the opportunity to see this. I hope so."

"Admiral," Farkas replied.

Janeway nodded sharply and turned away, certain that Farkas had ended that thought internally by adding, *"Don't hold your breath."*

Cadet Icheb had come home. *Voyager* was the only place he'd ever occupied for any length of time that seemed worthy of the designation. Starfleet Academy had become familiar, comfortable. But it was transitory. His few memories of Brunali were unpleasant. And he had never known individuality among the Borg. He'd only been back onboard *Voyager* a few days, but he slept better in his temporary quarters than any dorm room, and the renewed companionship of old friends like Seven, the Doctor, and the Paris family had put him entirely at ease.

Once he had arrived and ascertained the status of *Voyager,* Icheb had put in a formal request to Starfleet Academy that they allow him to finish his final year of studies with the fleet. He couldn't imagine that any curriculum devised on Earth could rival the experiences he would accrue in the Delta Quadrant. He had not, however, received a response to his request.

As he stood among the throngs of those present at the service, now clustered in small groups, Icheb wondered if he should seek out Seven to see if she required any assistance, until he saw Captain Chakotay making his way through the crowd in his direction.

"Cadet," Chakotay greeted him warmly.

"Captain," Icheb replied. "This has been a most unusual experience."

"How do you mean?"

"I have attended several memorial services in my years on Earth, but none of them felt like this one."

"Were you personally acquainted with those whose services you attended?" Chakotay asked.

"Yes."

"And did you know anyone among the fleet who was lost?"

"No. That is what is odd about it," Icheb added. "In the past I felt almost nothing, even at Admiral Janeway's memorial. I remember being so cold, so confused. But standing here tonight, I was deeply moved."

Chakotay's face clouded over. "Why do you think that was?"

"Perhaps because of my connection to you and the rest of *Voyager*'s crew," Icheb suggested. "I was saddened for all of you, all that you've lost. And I couldn't help thinking about Q."

"You don't have that same sense of belonging among your friends at the Academy?"

Icheb shook his head. "It's different. It's all so competitive. You wish to trust, but it is hard to know where to place that trust. Here there is no question."

Chakotay swallowed hard. "I knew this wasn't going to be easy, but now it's even more difficult."

"To what are you referring, sir?"

"I received word from the Academy this afternoon," Chakotay replied. "They have denied your request to remain with the fleet. You will return to Earth tomorrow aboard the *Galen*."

Icheb's cheeks burned and his eyes stung. "Did they say why?"

Chakotay paused to consider his response. Finally he said, "When *Voyager* was too far from the Alpha Quadrant for you to go there and begin your work at the Academy, it made sense for you to do so here. But that is no longer the case. Because it is possible for you to return, they feel you must. Yes, things get interesting out here, and there is much you will learn when you are once again on a starship, but you have almost a full year left in your course requirements. And I think they want to make sure that you are being evaluated as objectively as possible."

"I studied at the Academy under both Commander Tuvok and Seven of Nine. I assure you that neither of them allowed our personal relationships to affect their evaluations of my performance," Icheb insisted.

"Knowing both of them, that's not surprising." Chakotay smiled. "But it's more than that. Part of being at the Academy is living outside your comfort zone. They're preparing you to function at your best in the most inhospitable of circumstances. Returning is the harder road, Icheb."

Icheb sighed, unable to contain his disappointment.

"Should I request that they reconsider?"

Chakotay shrugged. "I don't think it would make any difference. But we're scheduled to be out here another two and half years, and you can bet I'll be requesting that you join us as soon as you graduate."

This lifted Icheb's spirits a bit. "Thank you, Captain."

Chakotay placed an arm over Icheb's shoulder. "Hard as it might be to imagine right now, Icheb, I'm certain there are lessons for you back there still to be learned. I wonder if you realize how much the connection you feel to this crew resulted from your own choices as much as ours. We accepted you with open arms, but you returned our affections. You earned our trust. Maybe it's time to open yourself to the possibility that you could have friendships just as meaningful among your peers at the Academy."

Icheb nodded. "I will try, Captain."

"But we can't do that!" Lieutenant Reginald Barclay insisted vehemently.

His superior officer, the captain of the *Galen,* Commander Clarissa Glenn, seemed to take his outburst in stride. She was a lithe woman with delicate features and long reddish-blond hair that hung loosely tonight over her dress uniform. She was also as serene as any Starfleet officer Barclay had ever known.

"We serve at their pleasure, Lieutenant," she reminded him. "They can and will order us to go where they please."

Barclay tried to collect himself. "Have you read my latest reports, Commander? Our survey of the asteroid field surrounding New Talax is not yet complete, but I'm certain that with more time, or by adding *Voyager*'s astrometrics sensors to our work, we will find the asteroid where Meegan buried those other canisters."

Glenn placed a gentle hand on his arm. "I know how you feel about this. I know you feel guilty about Meegan's fate, and that guilt has been driving you to work this problem to the exclusion of your other duties. For the last few months, that wasn't a problem. And I will advise Captain Chakotay of your work and suggest strongly that he complete the survey before he departs on his next mission. But we are setting our course for the Alpha Quadrant in the morning, and you will be with us when we do."

"You don't understand, Commander!"

"Lieutenant," Glenn said softly but forcefully.

Knowing he had stepped right up to, if not over, the line, Barclay took a deep breath as he searched for another argument.

"Meegan is incredibly dangerous. She is the most advanced hologram ever created, and she is under the control of an entity its own people condemned to permanent incarceration. It was trapped in a disembodied state for thousands of years. And now she's out there, with seven more just like her. She must be found and stopped."

"I agree, but we aren't the only people out here capable of doing that," Glenn reminded him.

"Then let me stay," he pleaded. "You're going straight home and will return shortly, I presume. What use am I to you on a quick run like that? Transfer me to *Voyager* in the interim."

Glenn's eyes widened. "The *Galen* is a ship staffed almost entirely by holograms you helped create. You are my senior holographic specialist on board. You don't think your presence is vital? What if something goes wrong on our 'quick run'?"

"It won't," Barclay hoped, but also knew when he was beat.

As his shoulders fell, he caught sight of Admiral Janeway moving through the crowd, head bent low. Immediately, he moved to block her path.

"Admiral Janeway," he greeted her enthusiastically.

She looked up and it was obvious even to Barclay that she was struggling. Her cheeks were ruddy and her eyes glistened.

"Can it wait, Reg?" she asked.

"I . . ." Barclay began, until her distress moved him beyond his own cares. "Of course, Admiral," he replied and moved to allow her to pass.

After a moment, Glenn said softly, "I may not know her as well as you do, but I don't honestly think she would have countermanded my orders on this one. *Galen* is taking her home tomorrow."

This was almost as troubling to Barclay as his visceral need to find Meegan, but he sighed in acceptance.

"Understood, Commander."

Chapter Three

GALEN

"You wished to see me, Doctor?" Seven asked as she entered the holographic doctor's private office just off the main sickbay of the *Galen.*

He looked up from the padd he was studying with his most gracious smile and replied, "I did. And thank you for obliging me at this early hour. We're scheduled to depart shortly, but I have a request to make, which I hope you will consider."

"Of course," Seven replied. Although there was nothing in his manner to suggest anything less than cordial camaraderie, she was a bit surprised to see it so flagrantly focused in her direction. Only a few days earlier, the Doctor had become aware that she had entered into an intimate relationship with *Voyager*'s counselor, Lieutenant Hugh Cambridge. She had already witnessed in the Doctor a certain amount of distress at this development and believed that the next time they had an opportunity to speak privately, the subject would take priority. She did not believe the Doctor was jealous of the counselor. They had enjoyed a purely platonic relationship for years now. His misgivings more likely arose from his general dislike of Cambridge, and on that count, she could not necessarily fault him. Hugh could be maddening. It had taken her some time to warm to him and see past his carefully constructed, rather acerbic façade.

She was both relieved and troubled as he moved past her into the main bay and gestured for her to stand beside him at a data console. His attention was clearly elsewhere. Seven chided herself for imaging that her private life should be a source of concern to the Doctor. He'd had several days now to process the development and obviously decided to offer her what support he could, if only by his silence.

As she turned her attention to the data now displayed before her, Seven wished that she actually believed this assessment. Unfortunately, her years of proximity to the Doctor belied it.

"I wasn't sure until last night that what I am about to propose would even be possible," he began. "I've spent the last several months studying the catoms the Caeliar left in you in place of your Borg implants, and as you know, that work has been largely hypothetical in nature. I understand what this programmable matter is and does, but it had been interwoven so seamlessly into your organic tissue that differentiation has been all but impossible."

"Are you saying you have isolated the catoms, Doctor?" Seven asked, surprised. She had come to believe that such a feat could take years.

The Doctor smiled in feigned humility. "You doubted me, Seven?" he teased.

"Of course not," she replied quickly. "But even at their subatomic level, they mimic the organic tissue that surrounds them."

"They do," the Doctor agreed, pointing to a display of two neural cells that seemed to be identical. "Here we have isolated two cells from the area of your brain that once housed your cortical node. It's worth noting that my previous familiarity with your Borg implants was instrumental in this work. I may not have known what I was looking at, but at least I knew *where* to look."

"I see no obvious differences between these two cells, Doctor," Seven said.

"At this level of magnification, you wouldn't. But let's look closer, shall we?" he suggested. He then increased the display's reference beyond the cellular level, to the molecular.

Seven studied the display, but again, saw nothing to explain the Doctor's enthusiasm. As the molecules in question seemed to float freely before her eyes, she searched the display hungrily for evidence of the Doctor's breakthrough.

"There," he said, freezing the display and pointing to a particular structure.

Seven looked, and for a brief moment wondered if the Doctor had brought her here as a pretense. Then, without his permission, she again increased the magnification, and her breath caught in her chest.

"What is that?" she asked softly.

"It is a synthetic marker, coded into the molecular structure of this catom that identifies it as unique to you and designates its current purpose," the Doctor replied.

Seven turned to the Doctor and smiled. "That's amazing," she said sincerely.

He shrugged as if it were nothing.

As Seven considered the possibilities this discovery now made real, she asked, "What is your next intended course of action?"

"With your permission, I would like to extract a few of these molecules. I can now state to a certainty which ones are catomic in nature, and it is essential that I study them in their pure form."

Seven did not wish to dampen his enthusiasm, but something in her revolted at the thought. "Are you certain that's wise?"

"It's the next logical step," the Doctor argued.

"Are you certain I can survive without them?" she clarified.

The Doctor appeared stricken. "I wouldn't suggest it otherwise," he insisted. "I actually believe now that your catoms are self-replicating."

This was news to Seven and left her thunderstruck. "Upon what do you base that hypothesis?"

"When you were contacted by Doctor Frazier, you experienced a blackout, did you not?"

"I did."

"Your scans following that incident, like those I took after your lengthy telepathic conversations with the Indign, indicated slight damage to the areas of your brain surrounding your catoms. But now that I know what I'm looking at, I can also confirm that the damage done was repaired by an infusion of more catoms. You should study the data yourself if you don't believe me," the Doctor suggested.

"You're saying my damaged neural tissue was replaced by new catoms?" Seven asked.

"Yes." He nodded. "You have only to compare your initial scans from when you arrived on *Voyager* to your most recent ones."

"Does that suggest that my catoms will continue to replicate indefinitely should I experience a more serious neural injury?" Seven asked.

"I don't think so," the Doctor replied. "We've already established that these catoms are 'powered,' so to speak, by your body's internal system. I don't know if they could keep you alive or continue to regenerate in the presence of massive trauma. But they are hearty little fellows, nonetheless. And who knows? What I can isolate and study, I might at some point be able to replicate."

The thought was intriguing, and if the Doctor was right, the risks of removal of a tiny population of catoms did not seem to outweigh the potential of one day perhaps duplicating this technology—for Seven, and others. It would, by any estimation, be a great leap forward for medical science.

"Very well." Seven nodded. "How do you wish to proceed?"

The Doctor smiled again, clearly reassured by her confidence in him. "If you'll lie down here, I'll begin the extraction," he said, gesturing to the nearest biobed. "It shouldn't take long."

Seven did as she was bidden, and the Doctor set to work double-checking his instruments and displays. As she tried to relax, a question formed in her mind.

"You said you made this breakthrough last night?" she asked.

"I did," he replied.

"Didn't you attend the memorial?"

"I did," he said. "I left a little early."

"How early?" she asked.

At this, the Doctor turned on her, clearly vexed. "Just after Admiral Janeway began the recitation of names, if you must know."

Seven rose up on her elbows. "I am not criticizing you, Doctor. I am merely surprised."

"As soon as the final complement of the fleet was established, complete medical records of every officer and crewman present were added to my memory buffers. I received the casualty list several days ago and have already marked those files as deceased. You'll forgive me if my zeal to continue working on a project that might ultimately result in saving lives, including your own, overcame my desire to waste time listening to data that has already been integrated into my stored memory files."

Taken aback, Seven resumed her supine position. But her mind whirred as she considered this revelation, as well as the heat with which it had been delivered.

She could not remember the Doctor speaking so callously of himself in a long time. Yes, he was a complicated holographic program, but he also was sentient and usually took great care to think of himself as much more than a collection of matrices, processors, and files. He tended to dismiss others who thought of him only as a creation or a tool. The Doctor had, long ago, surpassed his programming, and to Seven, this felt like a regression. She was certain that had anyone else described him this way, the Doctor would have been highly insulted.

"I apologize," she began.

"There is no need," he said, returning to a more casual tone. "Shall we begin?"

Seven paused but decided she did not care to risk upsetting him further.

"Of course."

"And if you don't mind, I need to concentrate. I'll let you know as soon as I'm finished."

Seven nodded, though she was stung by his clinical manner. He had been trying to help her, and she had offended him. It wasn't the first time, but she had thought herself long past such lapses, particularly where one so dear to her was concerned.

She did not expect to feel anything as the procedure began, and she didn't. She was conscious, however, of a slight increase in her respiration as well as an uncomfortable twinge in her stomach as the Doctor began to hum absentmindedly and so slightly off-key that only her enhanced auditory senses would have registered it.

Soon enough, he was finished, and Seven had never been so grateful to reach the end of a procedure. She moved to sit up the moment he indicated she was free to do so.

"How do you feel, Seven?" he inquired.

"Fine," Seven assured him. "Is that all?"

"For the time being," he replied. "I suspect we'll be rejoining the fleet soon, and if possible, I will keep you apprised of any new developments in the interim."

"Thank you, Doctor," she said. "Safe travels."

"And to you." He smiled.

She spent the few moments it took for her to walk from sickbay to the transporter room trying to dispel the anxiety that had welled up within her. As she stepped onto the platform, it occurred to her that unless she could pinpoint its source, it would be difficult to quell.

Then, it hit her, as she felt the transport beam begin to take hold. The tune the Doctor had hummed during the procedure had taken her back to a time when he had been forced to try and extract information from her mind without the benefit of his ethical subroutines. It had been years earlier, when *Voyager* had encountered the *Equinox*, another Starfleet vessel lost in the Delta Quadrant, and the Doctor's program had been intentionally sabotaged.

They had actually sung the song together in perfect harmony after those troubling events. It had been part of the healing process for both. Seven could not recall the Doctor humming or singing "My Darling Clementine," slightly off-key in her presence since then.

"What do you think?" Kathryn asked as Chakotay stepped into the quarters that would serve as her home for the next few days.

"I know it's a small ship," Chakotay replied, surveying the close, efficient space that would barely have accommodated his ready room on *Voyager*, "but is this really the best they could do?"

The admiral shrugged. "Commander Glenn offered me her quarters for the duration, but I refused. It's got a workstation, a replicator, and a bunk. I won't need anything else."

"Low maintenance." Chakotay grinned. "I like it." His instinct was to move toward her, but her stance, hands on hips and chin tilted upward, demanded a little distance. He settled for, "I was a little surprised when I woke up alone in my bed this morning."

Kathryn turned away and busied herself organizing a few padds on her tiny desk. "I spent most of the evening, once the service had concluded, with Neelix and Dexa. He's sending me home with about a hundred letters for Naomi Wildman. After that, Tom Paris found me and asked if I would pay a visit to his mother when I reach Earth, circumstances permitting. I would have done so anyway, but now it seems

I'm obligated. At any rate, I wouldn't have been able to join you until breakfast."

Chakotay nodded. "I assumed as much." It was the first night they'd spent apart since Kathryn returned and the last night they could have shared for several weeks to come. "I lost track of you at the service."

At this, Kathryn turned again to face him and crossed her arms, resting against the workstation. "Did you know what Captain Farkas wanted to speak to me about?"

"No," he replied. "She only asked that I facilitate the introduction."

"I see."

"What did she want to speak to you about?" Chakotay asked.

"She's furious with me," Kathryn replied simply. "In fact, now I'm wondering how much influence she might have with Ken Montgomery or the rest of Starfleet Command."

"There's no way she could have influenced Montgomery's decision," Chakotay insisted.

"Maybe. Maybe not." Kathryn shrugged. "But damn, she speaks her mind. I've got to give her that. There's something refreshing in it. Not that she's got anything on Hugh Cambridge."

"What exactly did she say?"

Kathryn waved the question off. "Nothing I haven't already accused myself of, or that future Admiral Janeway."

Chakotay nodded. He knew too well the demons she was wrestling and was more than willing to give her the space she needed to battle them. But he was a little surprised to hear of this coming from Captain Farkas, who, as best he could tell, was one of the more seasoned and even-tempered officers in Starfleet.

"I can't help but feel how much has changed in the last fourteen months," Kathryn finally admitted.

"A lot of us who lived through them are still raw. It can be hard to hold your tongue," Chakotay offered.

"It's more than that," she continued. "Maybe I spent too much time among the brass. I certainly grew accustomed to a fair amount of deference from those I outranked, and the political maneuvering among my peers was done in subtext. It appears that's not how we do things anymore."

Chakotay considered her words. "Everything feels almost too close to the bone right now. I don't know many who have the patience for lying. I think because none of us are sure anymore that there will be time in the future to speak the truth."

Kathryn nodded. "Good to know."

"Commander Glenn to Admiral Janeway," the captain's voice bleated over the comm.

Tapping her combadge, Kathryn replied, "Go ahead."

"We're ready to depart when you are, Admiral."

"Understood. Captain Chakotay will be on his way to the transporter room momentarily."

"Thank you, Admiral."

Stepping closer to Chakotay, Kathryn remarked, "Not this one, though," clearly referring to Commander Glenn. "She does everything by the book."

"She's young." Chakotay smiled. "Give her time."

Wordlessly, Chakotay finally took Kathryn in his arms and held her close for the few moments left to them. When she pulled away, her eyes met his and he saw defiance there.

"There's no reason to say good-bye," she said. "I'll see you in a few weeks."

Chakotay wanted this to be true, and for her sake, refused to allow any other option to enter his mind. "You will be missed," he said. "And I assume it goes without saying that if there is anything at all you need from us while you are away, you have but to ask."

Kathryn smiled faintly.

Chakotay bent his head low to kiss her lightly. She lingered there a bit longer than he'd anticipated, ending the moment on her terms.

"A few weeks," she said again, willing it to be true.

Taking her face in his hands, he replied, "And then, no matter what happens . . ."

Kathryn nodded in understanding as she took his hands in hers, kissed each of them tenderly, and released them.

The morning briefing had already gone on almost an hour, and as best Lieutenant Kim could tell, Captain Chakotay had yet to be impressed. The suggestions he, Tom, and Seven had spent several hours preparing had clearly failed to pique his interest for their next mission. Commander Liam O'Donnell, *Demeter*'s captain, had remained silent, as if he had mentally checked out. His fellow senior officers—Lieutenant Commander Atlee Fife and Lieutenant Url, Kim's counterpart aboard *Demeter*—had asked the occasional pertinent question. Fleet Chief B'Elanna Torres and the rest of *Voyager*'s senior staff—Lieutenant Conlon, Counselor Cambridge, science officer Lieutenant Devi Patel, operations officer Lieutenant Kenth Lasren, and the CMO, Doctor Sharak—seemed to hope that Chakotay would just settle on *something* so they could get on with their duties.

In a way, Kim shared their desire. The fleet's original mission profile had consisted largely of continued sweeps of former Borg territory. Much had been explored by *Quirinal, Hawking, Esquiline,* and *Curie* before their encounter with the Omega Continuum, but they had only scratched the surface of the space that was once held by the Collective. Apart from *Voyager*'s last mission to learn the fate of a small group of Borg severed from the Collective prior to the Caeliar transformation, none of the efforts of the Full Circle fleet had produced any evidence of any interesting activity, Borg or otherwise, except for a few cranky Malon. Continuing along the same path seemed likely to produce more tedium.

After the fleet's encounter with Omega, however, Kim wondered if this was a bad idea. From the moment *Voyager* had arrived, they had stumbled into one catastrophe after another. The Delta Quadrant had rarely been boring in Kim's experience, but giving everybody time to regroup and get their feet under them sounded like just what the crew needed as a morale booster.

The captain was convinced, however, at least to hear Tom tell it, that for the fleet's mission of exploration of the Delta Quadrant to continue after all they'd lost, they were going to have to demonstrate beyond a shadow of a doubt that their work was vital to the Federation.

Kim had found some of Tom and Seven's proposals interesting. Seven was keen to attempt to make contact with several races known to have partially escaped assimilation, including Arturis's people. Given how angry Arturis had been with Captain Janeway and the lengths he had gone to exact revenge, Kim wasn't sure that would end well. Tom had proposed, among other things, that they attempt to find Kurros and his Think Tank. They, too, had proved themselves untrustworthy during *Voyager*'s initial encounter. It was likely, however, given their interests and expertise, that the Think Tank might have learned more than most about local changes of significance since the Borg's presumed disappearance.

It wasn't so much the potential hazards of these and similar missions that Chakotay found objectionable. It was that they were treading over old ground. The captain wanted at least the potential for significant new information to be added to their databases, and thus far, nothing suggested seemed to fill that bill.

"Is there anything else?" Chakotay asked, clearly disappointed but trying to remain encouraging. "The floor is open."

Paris's shoulders slumped visibly, and Seven sat back, resting against her chair, clearly nonplussed. Kim was inspired by the general level of discontent to take a risk.

"There might be," he said and was suddenly conscious of eleven pairs of eyes shooting toward him. O'Donnell alone remained lost in his own thoughts.

"Go ahead, Lieutenant." Chakotay nodded.

"It was a while ago," Kim began, sitting forward and interlacing his hands before him on the table. "Just after we started our journey home," he went on. "We were celebrating Kes's second birthday on the holodeck, and we encountered a spatial distortion ring that pretty much twisted the ship into a pretzel as we moved through it."

The first officer's eyes widened, as if he could not believe Harry would bring up the encounter. Kim remembered well how difficult it had been for all of them to accept the fact that there was nothing they could do to combat the distortion and the few minutes they had spent awaiting what they believed would be their destruction surrounded by some of Tom's more annoying holographic creations had been a low point in those early years.

"I remember," Chakotay said.

"As do I," Torres said, her displeasure evident.

"We didn't learn much initially about the phenomenon," Kim allowed.

"We didn't learn anything," Paris corrected him. "It dumped a ton of information into our databases and uploaded ours, but the data was too corrupted to be of any use."

"We purged it all a few months later, didn't we?" Torres asked of Seven, who shrugged. "Sorry," she quickly realized, "that was before you joined us."

"Did I miss much?" Seven quipped, bringing a slight smile to Cambridge's lips.

"We did purge the data," Kim said. "But I kept a copy in my personal files."

"Why?" Paris demanded.

"Because it always bothered me," Kim replied. "It was a powerful device of some sort, and it obviously had a purpose. It seemed like such a waste that it would have tried to provide us with all of that data we could never use."

"You felt bad for the poor distortion ring?" Paris asked, incredulous.

"He was looking for a shortcut home," Torres suggested more gently. "You thought there might be one buried in all that information, didn't you, Harry?"

Kim sighed. "At first, yes. I knew it was a long shot, which is why I never mentioned it. It became a pet project of mine. Whenever I had time on my hands, and there were some stretches over the years, I went back to it, tried a few new algorithms. It was a puzzle, but almost too complex to ever solve."

"Did you solve it?" Chakotay asked.

"Some of it," Kim replied. "Most of the data was beyond retrieval. A lot of what I did recover was star charts of areas we had already scanned. But there were also bits and pieces that seemed to be expressions of *want* or *need* on the part of the phenomenon. I'm not saying it was a life-form—I believe it was constructed by someone or something. I got the sense that it had surpassed its original parameters. I also know, for a fact, that it came from a considerable distance from where we encountered it. I found the distortion ring's initial coordinates. It had traveled more than twenty thousand light-years in the course of at least two hundred years before we encountered it. We thought it had just passed by to say 'hello,' but I think it was asking for help."

"You found a distress call?" Chakotay asked.

"It sounded like one to me." Kim nodded.

"Why didn't you say something back then?" Paris asked.

"It took me six years to decipher what I did," Kim countered. "By that time, answering the call would have taken us forty thousand light-years or so in the wrong direction."

"It would not have been practical to suggest," Seven concurred.

Kim shook his head. "And it's not something I was supposed to be working on. But we could investigate now. I know it's been more than nine years, but in the life of that phenomenon, it was the blink of an eye."

"Perhaps two blinks and a nod," Cambridge suggested.

"Are you certain it was technological and not a life-form of some sort?" Patel interjected, clearly intrigued.

Kim shrugged. "None of the readings we were able to take during our first encounter showed anything other than high EM discharges. But it altered space and subspace as we moved through it. And it did manage to make what might have been a telepathic connection with Admiral Janeway. It was an incredibly complex and powerful entity."

"One I'd like to avoid encountering again," Paris mumbled.

As silence fell around the table, all eyes turned back to Chakotay.

Before he could speak, Commander O'Donnell asked, "What did it say, exactly?"

"It was twenty million gigaquads of data," Kim replied.

"You said it asked for help," O'Donnell clarified.

You were listening? Kim thought. "The exact phrasing was something like '. . . require aid . . . unable to sustain as ordered . . .'"

"Unable to sustain what?" O'Donnell asked.

"The next retrievable data was a set of coordinates."

"What were those coordinates?" Chakotay asked.

"A moment, please." Kim rose to cross to the room's main data interface panel. He quickly tapped into his personal archive and a brief search yielded the required results. He then activated them for display. "This is much farther out than our previous mission was intended to take us. We have no idea what's out there."

At this, Seven leaned in to take a closer look. After a moment she said, "This region is more than ten thousand light-years from any area of space ever held by the Borg."

"Well, that settles it then, doesn't it?" O'Donnell said.

"Sir?" Paris asked, clearly not having reached the same conclusion.

"This has to take priority over any other mission. We're

still in the business of answering distress calls, aren't we?" O'Donnell asked.

Paris looked to Chakotay. Kim saw a familiar glint lighting his captain's eyes.

"We are," he agreed. "Excellent work, Harry."

"Thank you, sir," Kim said, relieved.

Chakotay turned to Paris and said, "Tom, have Gwyn plot a course. Nancy, bring the slipstream drive online and coordinate our flight plan with *Demeter*. Devi, I'd like you and Seven to work with Doctor Sharak. Review all of the information from our first encounter with the distortion ring and everything Harry was able to coax from the data it provided. I'd like to know before we arrive at those coordinates if we're dealing with a life-form."

"It took two hundred years to find us some forty thousand years from this location," Paris interjected. "You don't think it was headed home or made it there in the last nine, do you?"

"No," Chakotay replied. "But there's a chance it wasn't one of a kind, either, isn't there? Dismissed," Chakotay ordered, then rose and crossed to Kim.

Paris warned him softly, "So help me, Harry, if another one of those things is out there and comes at us again with the bending, twisting maneuver, I'm throwing you out of an airlock to meet it."

"Hey, you wanted exciting." Kim shrugged.

Paris was prevented from further comment by Chakotay's presence behind him. "You have your orders, Commander," he said pointedly.

"Do you want me to cancel or postpone our final high-resolution sensor sweep of the asteroid belt for Lieutenant Barclay?" Paris asked, rising.

"Train sensors aft, get what data you can," Chakotay ordered.

Paris moved on, joining the others returning to their posts as Chakotay paused before Kim.

"A pet project?" he asked.

"I almost abandoned it until we entered that void, about five years in, remember?"

"I do." Chakotay nodded.

"I hadn't made any headway. But I could only stand losing to Tuvok at *kal-toh* so many times. I found another brick wall to bang my head against." Kim shrugged. "There were actually a number of Borg-inspired algorithms that came in handy, along with some of the enhanced linguistic tools we picked up from Arturis before he tried to send us back to Borg space."

"Obviously we're going to need countermeasures in the event there are more distortion rings out there, but I'm entering a commendation in your file now for sheer tenacity."

"Thank you, sir," Kim said.

"I want you to take point with our research groups. You've earned it, Lieutenant," Chakotay added.

"Happy to."

"Let's get to work."

As Kim turned to follow the captain out, his step was a little lighter. He had always suspected that his transfer from operations to tactical and security was as much a promotion as an effort by his superiors to give him the widest possible range of experiences before moving to the command track. Kim certainly hoped that one day, he would have a ship of his own to lead. If he was right, and if this mission did turn up anything interesting, he might be closer to that now than he'd ever been at any time in his career.

And that felt awfully good.

Chapter Four

GALEN

Kathryn Janeway had actually put this moment off longer than she should have. Her obligations to Starfleet and those who had survived the recent tragedy had taken priority, along with her early work with Cambridge to try and regain her equilibrium.

Still, she wasn't certain her mother was going to understand.

She felt light-headed, and her pulse began to race while she waited for the ship's operations officer to establish the necessary connection. Her anxiety intensified as the Federation insignia on the small screen before her stretched and clouded with static. Several unbearable moments later, however, the screen was filled with the careworn yet still undeniably beautiful face of Gretchen Janeway.

At first, Kathryn could find no words. She simply stared at her mother and watched Gretchen squint a little as if she couldn't clearly see the image she was receiving.

At last, the worry lines creasing Gretchen's face opened into a soft smile. *"Kathryn,"* she said softly.

"Yes, mother." Kathryn nodded. "It's me."

Gretchen brought her hands to her mouth, an obvious effort to contain the emotion ready to overspill them. Her eyes glistened as they remained glued to those of her daughter.

Kathryn felt her own smile blooming as she reached for the sides of the screen in an unconscious desire to pull her mother closer to her.

"Are you all right?" Kathryn asked.

"You're alive," Gretchen managed, as if that were answer enough.

It almost was.

"I'll be back on Earth in two days. I have to get settled in San Francisco first, but as soon as I'm able, by dinner at the latest, I'll transport home."

"Give me a little warning?" Gretchen asked. *"I can't wait, but don't just pop into the living room. I don't know if my heart could take it."*

Kathryn chuckled. "I won't. I promise."

After a moment, Gretchen's face fell into softer lines. She was the source of Kathryn's emotional balance. No matter how extreme the circumstances she faced, Kathryn had rarely witnessed any that could conquer her mother's resolve. *"Admiral Montgomery notified me a week ago that I should expect your call. He did his best to explain the circumstances, but Kathryn, I still don't understand. Were they wrong when they declared you dead?"*

Kathryn sighed. Her mother possessed a sharp intellect and had spent more than thirty years married to a Starfleet officer. But she had always been a civilian and was never inclined to dig too deeply into the scientific wonders that had claimed the hearts of her husband and oldest daughter. "They weren't, as far as it was possible for them to know," Kathryn replied. "They didn't lie to you, or put you through this intentionally. The rest, I want to explain to you in person. Some of it, I'm still not sure I understand."

"It's okay, my darling," Gretchen assured her. *"We'll figure it out together. Whatever you need from me is yours."*

"I know that, Mother. And I love you so much. I'm so sorry you had to . . ." But sadness too deep for expression stilled her words.

"Don't be," Gretchen chided her. *"You came back. That's all I care about now."*

Kathryn nodded.

Wiping away her own tears with her palms, Gretchen said, *"Phoebe is on her way home now. She'll be in tomorrow night. Should I contact anyone else to be here when . . . ?"*

"No," Kathryn replied quickly. "Not at first, please. I just want to see you, both of you," she corrected herself quickly. "The rest can wait until I'm a little more settled."

"Of course." Gretchen nodded.

They spent the next few minutes chatting about more mundane matters, glorying in the simplicity of familiar concerns and events. Too soon, Kathryn realized that their communications window was about to close.

"I need to go," Kathryn said. "We're still a ways out and can't maintain a longer connection en route."

Gretchen nodded. *"That's fine. Please be safe for the next few days."*

"You have my word," Kathryn assured her.

"I think I'm going to do a stew. That'll keep in case you run late," Gretchen decided, *"and obviously, my caramel brownies."*

"As long as Phoebe makes the coffee," Kathryn teased lightly.

"Kathryn, you aren't still drinking more than a few cups a day are you?" Gretchen suddenly demanded. *"You promised you were going to cut back."*

Almost fifty years later, some things between mothers and daughters just never changed.

"I am," Kathryn replied. "But I really don't think this is the time for me to make any other really big life changes, okay, Mom?"

Gretchen's disappointment was evident, but she held her peace.

"I'll see you soon," Kathryn assured her.

Gretchen nodded as she quickly, almost involuntarily, reached for the screen. Kathryn did the same, their fingertips touching though thousands of light-years remained between them.

"Don't worry," Kathryn insisted as the image distorted and was quickly replaced by the standard insignia.

Alone again, she took a few moments to bask in the comfort of their brief connection. So much of her life had been lived beyond her mother's arms. Weeks, months, and, unintentionally, years had passed between conversations in the past. But it didn't matter. When she was younger, Kathryn had believed that who she was had been shaped by her father. She had followed in Edward Janeway's footsteps. She was with him on a shuttle test mission when he was killed. He had been the taskmaster little Kathryn Janeway had always striven to please. Only now did she begin to see how much of her intestinal fortitude had come from her mother. Challenging as it was to live among the stars, the greater challenge by far must be borne by those left behind, who waited.

She could almost feel her mother's arms around her again. There, she knew she was loved without condition or reservation. And whatever parts of herself Kathryn might have lost along the way, Gretchen would have kept safe in her heart.

Two days, she reminded herself, knowing now that they would creep by.

Forcing these thoughts aside, Kathryn turned her attention to unfinished personal business. She had already prepared a private message for her childhood friend and former fiancé, Mark Johnson. She didn't want to see Mark via subspace. Too many of their conversations had happened that way. This one needed to happen in person.

The other person she was most anxious to speak with was Tuvok. They had served together for more than twenty years. Duty had separated them for much of the last few. It was impossible to contact Tuvok directly now as he was on a deep-space assignment in the Beta Quadrant aboard the *Titan.*

But she did not want more time to pass without Tuvok

receiving word from her, and Kathryn did not doubt that as soon as he was able he would arrange for them to speak. She looked forward to it, just as she had her initial reunions with her former crew aboard *Voyager*.

Having ordered the ship's computer to transmit these messages as soon as *Galen* was in range of the next communications buoy, she left her desk and sat on her rack. Part of her wanted to rise and spend a little time touring the ship. She knew the Doctor was eager to acquaint her with the most minute details of the amazing creation he had helped design.

But something stayed her. Kathryn was about to spend the next several weeks being dissected by counselors and her superiors; likely as not, her mother, sister, and old friends as well. She imagined the long hours she would spend talking and chose for now to seek refuge in a few hours of silence.

The Doctor was annoyed, a state of being he had grown quite accustomed to in the last several days. For the first time, since he had learned of the existence of the Caeliar catoms and the crucial function they played in keeping Seven of Nine alive and healthy, he was actually able to see one. Understanding how they operated, assessing their limitations, hopefully learning how to re-create them would take months, perhaps years, but he was finally well on his way.

Neither Icheb nor Reg seemed to appreciate the gravity of the moment or the magnitude of his work. Normally this wouldn't have troubled the Doctor. He had been underappreciated for most of his existence. But the pair had chosen to come to his sickbay to commiserate, thus making it all but impossible for the Doctor to focus his concentration and best efforts on unraveling the technological marvel now before him.

In Barclay's case, this was nothing new. The man was brilliant. However, from the first days of their friendship, the Doctor had realized that too many years spent in his technological comfort zone at the expense of a normal, healthy attention to his emotional and social skills had left Reg stunted. His was a staggering intellect, paired with the emotional intelligence of an adolescent male.

Icheb could be forgiven as he was just beyond his own adolescence. That he possessed any social graces at all was admirable, when one considered that more than half of his life and his most crucial formative years had been spent in a Borg maturation chamber. Icheb was growing into a disciplined and sensitive young man, and normally the Doctor found his company quite pleasant.

Today was proving an exception.

"This is a waste of time," Barclay opined. "Sometimes I find it impossible to understand Command's priorities."

"As do I, Lieutenant," Icheb added.

"Do they not understand the threat posed by Meegan?"

"If you have provided them with the same data you showed me, they would not have underestimated Meegan," Icheb said sincerely. "But it is also possible that they are unconvinced that your investigation is likely to reveal further relevant information."

"There is no other reason for her to have abandoned the Starfleet shuttle she stole in favor of a mining vessel," Barclay insisted. "No." Shaking his head vigorously, he went on. "She took the mining vessel because it served a purpose. Meegan clearly intended to bury the other canisters she stole somewhere in that asteroid field to hide them while she plotted her next move."

"It is possible," Icheb agreed. "But it is also just as likely that she simply wanted to make it more difficult for you to track her. Despite the damage she did to the shuttle, she had to know it would be easier for you to find than the mining vessel. The transfer might have been intended to buy her time."

"Don't try to reason with him, Icheb," the Doctor pleaded. "Reg remains wedded to his current course because it is the only one likely to produce meaningful information. If you are right, and odds are you are, we are no closer to determining her present whereabouts."

At this, both Barclay and Icheb turned to face him, mirroring each other's puzzled expressions.

Summoning the subroutine that contained appropriate chagrin when one has trespassed socially, the Doctor added gently, "Both of you might put this time to more productive ends by assisting me."

Icheb's face lit up, while Barclay only crossed his arms and muttered something under his breath.

"I would be happy to, Doctor," Icheb enthused as he moved to stand behind the Doctor and immediately began studying his display.

Though this increased the Doctor's discomfort somewhat, it was preferable to disengaging his audio-processing subroutines to enable him to ignore their conversation.

"That is a catom?" Icheb asked softly.

"Yes."

"What aspect of it are you currently analyzing?" Icheb asked.

"When this catom was part of Seven's anatomy, it mimicked the organization of a molecule in a neural cell. Shortly after it was removed, its configuration altered completely."

"In what way?"

The Doctor quickly altered the display view to show the catom's molecular structure both before and after extraction side by side.

"If I had to theorize, which is all I can do at this point," the Doctor replied, "I would say that it became less specialized."

"That is not entirely unexpected, is it?" Icheb asked as he peered at the screen intently.

"It was to me," the Doctor replied.

"This is programmable matter," Icheb clarified. "It is possible that it takes its essential coding from the matter that surrounds it, in this case, Seven's neural tissues. In the absence of any input, it might revert to a neutral state in preparation for receiving new input and reorganizing itself appropriately."

"That would suggest a degree of mutability I had not anticipated," the Doctor noted.

"Why not?" Icheb asked sincerely.

The Doctor shrugged. "I supposed I assumed that once programmed to replace Seven's cortical array, these catoms would not be capable of performing any other function."

"As long as they remained within her body, they might not be," Icheb suggested. "But as with Borg nanoprobes, these catoms must be capable of performing a wide variety of functions. Rather than create them specifically for each function, on their most basic level, the catoms could have been designed to assimilate data from their immediate environment and adapt accordingly."

The Doctor looked up at the young man, suddenly glad he had asked for Icheb's input. As a former drone, Icheb had intuitively seen a connection between the Borg and Caeliar that the Doctor had not yet considered. Given what he understood of the Borg's origins, the Doctor believed Icheb might be right. Clearly nanoprobes and catoms were unique technologies, the Caeliar's much more powerful and elegant. But as the Borg had been spawned by the Caeliar, the nanoprobe might be the crudest possible descendent of the catom.

This explosive train of thought was diverted by the voice of Captain Glenn as she entered the sickbay. "Oh, good," were the words that drew the Doctor reluctantly back to the present.

"Good morning, Captain," Barclay greeted her immediately. "I was just . . ." But here, he was suddenly at a loss.

"Both Reg and Icheb have been assisting me this morning, Captain," the Doctor interjected quickly. Annoyed as he was with Reg at the moment, his instinct to protect him was greater than his ire. In Icheb's case, the statement was actual fact.

"A happy coincidence for me," Glenn replied, "as I can now advise you simultaneously of our new orders."

"New orders?" Barclay asked, clearly distressed at the

thought that this development might further delay his return to the Delta Quadrant.

Glenn nodded briskly. "As soon as we reach Earth and offload our passengers, we will depart immediately for Starbase 185." Approaching the Doctor, she continued, "Within the next few hours, you will receive several files from the base's sickbay on a patient they are currently attempting to treat. They have requested you specifically, Doctor."

The Doctor felt himself beaming at the compliment.

"Do you know anything more?" he asked.

"You are the only medical officer in Starfleet with firsthand knowledge of Caeliar catoms," Glenn went on. "While the specifics of your work with Seven of Nine have remained segregated in your personal files, Starfleet is aware of the basics of her transformation. Until now, they have furthered their own studies based upon the sensor readings gained during the *Enterprise, Titan,* and *Aventine*'s brief exposure to the Caeliar, as well as the physical evaluations of Seven just after her implants disappeared. That will no longer suffice."

"Why not?" the Doctor asked, suddenly alarmed. From the day she had joined the fleet, Seven had specifically requested that the Doctor classify his work on her catoms. Necessity had required that Doctor Sharak be granted access to those files. Counselor Cambridge understood their nature in the broadest possible strokes, but the Doctor understood Seven's fear that wider dissemination would make her an object of inquiry.

"Because it appears the patient they are attempting to save is Caeliar," Glenn replied. "Until we reach the Starbase, you are ordered to suspend all other projects and devote yourself entirely to studying the data they will transmit. I will provide you any assistance I can. I'm sure that once we arrive, they're expecting a miracle."

"The Doctor will not disappoint them," Icheb said.

For his part, the Doctor hoped the cadet was right.

Chapter Five

VOYAGER

Tom Paris was catapulted into alertness from a deep sleep. Somewhere nearby, a steady, persistent beeping had begun. The adrenaline rush was likely a result of the combined loud whoosh he associated with fire-suppression systems and the acrid fumes now assaulting his nostrils.

He was on his feet and at the door separating the family's sleeping quarters from the main living space in an instant. The deep pounding of his heart ricocheted throughout his entire body.

Their quarters were filled with smoke, and he could faintly make out the figure of his wife in the middle wielding a handheld flame suppressant. Surprisingly, Miral slept soundly.

Lunging into the fray, Tom stumbled toward B'Elanna, who was ordering the ship's fire-response system offline for their quarters. "Stay back!" she ordered Tom, focusing the canister in her hands on what Tom believed was their replicator.

Tom began to cough violently. B'Elanna ordered the room's environmental controls to maximize the venting systems to clear the smoke. His wife then turned to him, frustration rolling off her, while he waited for his heart to steady itself. It left him quivering from head to toe: an unpleasant sensation.

When the room's air was again clean, Tom asked, "What happened?"

B'Elanna tossed the empty canister to the deck and moved

back to the replicator. "Nothing," she replied, disgusted. "Go back to bed."

"I'm not even sure I'll be able to sleep tomorrow," Tom said, joining her before the mess she had just created. Just beneath the viscous fluid now covering the replicator's surface, he thought he saw exposed control panels. "And the rest of the night is out of the question," he added. "So what gives?"

B'Elanna was clearly attempting to figure out the quickest way to clean up the mini-disaster, and she was in no mood to answer questions. "I was hungry," she replied roughly.

On the one hand, this was good news. Tom hadn't heard his wife utter these words in a week. Perhaps the acute morning sickness was beginning to subside.

On the other hand . . .

"Did the replicator malfunction?" he asked as gently as possible. *Or attack you?*

B'Elanna turned back to him, mortification overtaking indignation. "No," she admitted.

Seeing her like this, Tom wanted only to make whatever was wrong better. He tenderly reached out for her, ignoring the acrid fumes and sticky spots, and pulled her close. "Want me to head down to the mess hall and get you something?"

B'Elanna shook her head against his chest. Finally a muffled explanation met his ears. He had to pull back a little and ask, "You wanted what?"

"A *ghabjebaQ joqngogh,*" she repeated.

"Gesundheit." Tom smiled.

"And I don't want it," B'Elanna added, miserably. "I *need* it."

"Just point me in the right direction, and I promise I'll go kill one for you and bring it right here," Tom assured her. "What is it?"

"It's kind of a vegetable and fried meat sandwich," B'Elanna replied, attempting to conjure one from thin air with her hands. "But it is made with this grilled flat bread done over a fire. It's amazing," she went on. "My mom used to make them for me when I was really little."

"I take it the replicator can't do it justice," Tom deduced. When it came to really specific tastes and textures, this magnificent technology often fell short.

B'Elanna shook her head. "I tried ten different versions before I came up with a better idea."

"Better?

"I needed an open flame, so I decided to rig a quick burner." B'Elanna shrugged, as if it should have been obvious.

Tom couldn't find it in himself to be angry with her right now. But double-checking her sanity didn't seem out of the question.

"You remember we're on a starship right now, don't you, honey?"

B'Elanna stepped back, now clearly ready to punch him.

"I was the one who installed Neelix's burners in the galley our first time out here," she reminded him. "It can be done."

Tom considered his options. Only one seemed likely to end in both of them living through the night.

"Back to bed," he ordered her.

"I have to . . ." she began.

"Get some sleep," he finished for her. "I'll get a couple of Nancy's gamma shift folks in here to clean up and repair the replicator. And then I'll head to the mess hall and find something resembling your *ghabjeba* . . . whatever," he finished.

"I can't ask someone else to . . ." B'Elanna argued.

"But I can," Tom reminded her. "There are lots of young officers aboard right now eager to earn points with their XO. And they will be sworn to secrecy."

B'Elanna sighed, considering this. She blinked her eyes a few times, then lowered them to half-mast. "Come to think of it, I'm not that hungry," she replied. Her shoulders slumping, she trudged back toward the bedroom.

"Honey?" he called after her.

"I know," she replied. "Sonic shower first."

"Set and match to Lieutenant Kim," the computer reported.

"Yes!" Kim said jubilantly.

Nancy Conlon, who had executed a perfect dive toward the ball as it shot back into her quadrant—perfect except for the part where her swing missed—rolled over onto her back and stared up at the overhead holodeck grid. She was drenched in her own sweat and breathing in quick gasps but only really conscious of her extreme frustration with herself.

"Good game," Kim offered from above, reaching out a hand to help her up.

"Best three out of four?" Conlon asked, using his weight to pull her to her feet.

Kim smiled with sincere regret. "Can't. I want to get to the bridge early. We're set to arrive at our destination in a little over an hour, and I don't want to miss a minute of it."

The chief engineer moved to the low bench resting along the wall that faced the velocity court and retrieved a small towel and a jug of water. Her wind was coming back and a few swigs of the cool beverage were restorative, but her competitive spirit remained unsatisfied.

"Just one more set then?" she asked. "Winner take all?"

Kim shook his head as he took a few gulps of his own water. "You played a great match," he assured her, wiping his mouth with the back of his hand. "You'll get me next time."

He might be right. They'd begun to exercise together regularly in the early mornings even before *Voyager* had returned to New Talax and had quickly moved from parallel workouts, weights, runs, and hikes, to oppositional ones. Most games found them well matched, but twice now she'd come up short in velocity, and it had begun to irritate her. It was ridiculous. There was no reason she needed to be better than Harry at anything, let alone everything. But she despised losing.

"You afraid?" she asked.

The smile fled from Kim's face.

"One set," he said softly.

Finding her own smile, Conlon ordered the computer to begin the game.

She took the first two points easily. Though Kim was as intent on winning as ever, his concentration was divided between rising to her challenge and getting to the bridge as soon as possible. This gave Conlon an advantage, one she could easily exploit. As she added the next two points to her score, she realized there wasn't as much fun in beating someone incapable of performing at his best.

Frustration seemed to give Kim focus and he took the next three volleys, albeit with some difficulty. He was moving swiftly to meet her next service when she actually saw him hesitate just long enough to miss the ball.

It could have been another concentration lapse, but Conlon didn't think so.

"Computer, pause program," she ordered.

"What's wrong?" Kim demanded through labored breaths.

"You let that go," she accused him.

"No, I didn't."

"Harry?"

"I didn't."

She stared at him, wondering if her imagination was getting the better of her.

"I might have," he finally admitted, dropping his head.

Conlon tossed her racquet to the bench and took a seat. Kim moved to his own bench but seemed to think better of it and crossed instead to sit beside her.

"It's just a game," he said.

"Don't ever do that," she replied seriously.

"What?"

"Less than your best," she said. "Don't let me win."

"It was one point," he pleaded.

"Doesn't matter," she insisted. "I don't want a victory I haven't earned."

Kim nodded, conscious of the insult he had just inflicted on her.

"Okay," he agreed. "Let's finish this, then."

Conlon shook her head. "No. You need to get to the bridge. I shouldn't have pushed it."

"I've got a few minutes."

Conlon smiled and placed her hand over his where it rested on his thigh. "That's sweet of you, but I want to beat you when you can give it your all. Not when your mind is already at your station."

"Is it really the end of the world if you don't?" Kim asked, genuinely curious. "I mean, there's going to be stuff you do better than me, and I'm going to have to learn to live with it, right?"

"Oh, yes," she assured him. "But don't think you know what I need better than I do. If there's a question in your mind, ask."

Kim squeezed her hand gently and brought his face close to hers. "I have a question."

She replied by touching her lips to his.

"And now you have your answer." She smiled, pulling away.

Nodding, Kim rose to collect his things. He turned back to see her standing, hands on hips, shaking her head slowly.

"What now?" he asked.

"When we get to the middle of nowhere we're going to find something really fascinating, and we're going to learn a ton, and Chakotay is going to add a commendation to your file, and you're going to be the one who handed him exactly what he wanted."

Kim considered her words. "And . . ."

"You're so excited just by the possibility that you can't keep your head in the game. When all that happens, there's going to be no living with you at all," she teased.

"You won't be happy for me?"

"I'll be thrilled for you," Conlon said honestly. "You

deserve it, Harry. We're both serving with some of the brightest lights in Starfleet. It's easy to get lost in the shadows of their brilliance."

"Not everything is a competition," Kim said.

"No, it isn't," she agreed. "But ever since you set foot on this ship, I'd bet you've been dying to distinguish yourself. You're going to have to if you ever want to serve anywhere else."

Kim shrugged. "The same is true of every officer on this ship."

"No, it really isn't," she replied. "Plenty just want to keep their heads down and do their duty and stay alive. You want more."

"Maybe," Kim agreed. "But I learned a long time ago that when you are surrounded by the best and the brightest, more can be a long time coming. Thing is, you have to keep your sights set on your goal."

"A ship of your own?"

"Yes."

"Go get it," Conlon encouraged him.

"Of course, every starship needs a great chief engineer." Kim smiled.

"Go," she ordered, stepping aside and pointing toward the door.

"Talk to you soon," he said, jogging lightly past her.

Once he had gone, Conlon sighed. Her initial attraction to Harry had been simple. He was a good guy; smart, funny, and cute as hell. The honesty and insight he had offered her lately—even when she tried her best to push him away—had come as a surprise, but they had cemented her impressions that this relationship was worth pursuing.

Lieutenant Harry Kim was, without doubt, the most optimistic individual she had ever known. No matter how close the darkness came, his determination to overcome it and certainty that goodness would prevail was refreshing.

Conlon remained unsure about the universe's tendency

toward beneficence. She could only function in the here and now, moving through one moment at a time. She might hope and work like hell for the good, but she didn't think she could ever believe in it as completely as Harry did.

DEMETER

Commander Liam O'Donnell had arrived on his bridge less than five minutes earlier. He had spent the majority of the last few days with Brill and DeFrehn tweaking several of the hybrids they had just developed for New Talax. Colonizing asteroids was a risky business. It was a challenge to create a wide enough range of edible substances from soil that tended to be homogenous and lacked the renewal the life-forms and water sources a more diverse ecosystem provided. To their credit, the scientists of New Talax were aware that their people were already showing signs of nutrient deficiencies. Synthetic supplements could only go so far to replace these. They needed greater variety in their diet. Figuring out which fruits, vegetables, and grains would solve this was easy. Coaxing them from the available soil was another matter.

Demeter's crew had made great strides in the past weeks, infusing the soil with several natural compounds and overhauling the waste-processing facilities to maximize the amounts of usable fertilizer produced. They had also managed to create from scratch more than two dozen new seed varieties, several hearty bacteria, and a bunch of annelids, most of which were flourishing by the time they departed.

But O'Donnell wanted more.

Right now, every bit of usable space on the main colony was spoken for. As the population continued to grow, they were going to have to find significantly more generous trading partners or begin maximizing the resources available to them. Getting to the other asteroids wasn't a problem. Creating livable and workable environments within them was a challenge, and one for which the colonists did not have sufficient resources. O'Donnell's chief engineer, Lieutenant Elkins, had suggested creating small, heavily shielded areas on the outside of the local rocks that could be filled with appropriate atmosphere and turned into productive fields. The next time they visited New Talax, O'Donnell was bound and determined to make sure that he had fifty or more species of seeds that would thrive in such an environment.

The optimal soil properties for three versions of tomatoes were foremost in the commander's mind when his first officer, Lieutenant Commander Atlee Fife, announced that the slipstream field was dispersing. O'Donnell had settled on two of the three tomatoes when Fife ordered Ensign Thomas Vincent at ops to begin long-range scans of the uncharted area of space while cautioning Lieutenant Url at tactical to keep a sharp eye for anything that might be coming their way.

Five minutes later, O'Donnell had narrowed the field to a single variety of tomato, settled on the precise soil configuration and its complementary atmospheric profile, and digested his crew's initial scans.

For good measure, he double-checked the main viewscreen, then rose from his seat.

"Captain?" Fife asked cordially.

"If you find anything interesting you'll let me know," O'Donnell said.

"Aye, sir." Fife nodded and moved to take the seat the commander had just left.

O'Donnell smiled internally as he exited the small bridge. A few months ago, Fife would have taken his choice to leave the bridge as evidence that he was unsuited for Starfleet service, let alone command. One near mutiny and many long conversations later, Fife had come to accept their unique command structure. O'Donnell was the captain, but his skills were best utilized working the problems the *Demeter* had been charged with when the ship joined the fleet. As one of the Federation's preeminent botanical geneticists, O'Donnell felt those problems did not include the various and sundry tactical and operational concerns or the scientific mysteries present in vast areas of space most Starfleet captains considered their purview. Those O'Donnell was content to leave to Fife.

The commander smiled because finally, Fife was done questioning this and seemed content to simply live it.

VOYAGER

Harry Kim didn't know what to think. When not answering inquiries from the rest of the senior staff about the sensor logs and data he had recovered from the distortion ring, he had spent most of the last few days theorizing about what they might find when *Voyager* and *Demeter* reached their intended coordinates. He thought it was too much to hope to find a planet or space station busily manufacturing the distortion ring technology. He considered it possible one or more of the phenomena might be detectable nearby. At the very least he expected to find a part of interstellar space with visible stars and planetary systems within scanning range.

He did not expect to find nothing. Unfortunately, that seemed to be exactly what they'd found.

Everyone else on the bridge was busy. Short- and long-range scans were being continuously run, and there were a few very distant stars visible from the occasional angle of inquiry.

Otherwise, *Voyager* and *Demeter,* at Kim's suggestion, had just arrived at the edge of a massive void.

To Paris's credit, he waited a few minutes before saying, "Is it me or does the Delta Quadrant seem to have more than its fair share of these?"

The tactical officer caught Chakotay's stern glare in Tom's direction, but with every scanning frequency Kim tested, his heart sank further, and he waited for the captain's disappointment to focus in his direction.

"What do we have, Lieutenant Lasren?" Chakotay asked.

"Nothing, sir," the ops officer replied. "No contacts in any visible spectrum for several million kilometers. If we set course bearing one two six mark three, long-range sensors are picking up a few star systems several days' journey from here at maximum warp. Less, if you wish to engage the slipstream."

"Any EM discharges matching those of the distortion ring?" Chakotay asked patiently.

"No, sir," Lasren replied.

"Do we have any idea how far this void extends?" Chakotay asked.

"Long-range sensors are at maximum, sir," Patel advised from the science station. "Apart from the sector Lieutenant Lasren noted, there are no visible stars or systems discernible for at least a parsec. Beyond that, we won't know for sure unless we set a course into the void."

Kim had already tuned his tactical sensors to search all EM frequencies for discharges comparable to those first detected with the distortion ring. *Nothing.* And while he fervently hoped there was more to this than met the eye, that wasn't going to be enough for him to persuade his captain to waste their time exploring all that nothing. Past experience suggested there could be some interesting phenomena undetected in the darkness. But it hardly seemed likely. If he'd had more to go on from the ring's original data, he might have been able to make a few intelligent suggestions, but it seemed they had just invested several days and their precious benamite reserves to travel to one of the Delta Quadrant's least-interesting swaths of space.

Chakotay resettled himself in his seat and ordered, "Continue long-range scans for the next hour. If nothing comes up, we'll set course for the nearest visible system, maximum warp, and take a closer look."

Kim resisted the urge to apologize for this fiasco, but he was pretty sure he'd be doing so privately to his captain in about fifty-nine minutes.

Chakotay began studying the sensor data routed to the small screen embedded in the arm of his chair. Paris ambled toward Kim's station and leaning in said softly, "That's not just nothing, Harry. That's a whole lot of nothing."

"You think I don't already feel bad enough about this?" Kim replied for Tom's ears only.

At that moment, a faint wave registered on tactical. It disappeared so quickly, Kim wasn't sure he'd even seen it, but he quickly narrowed the frequency.

"Do you see that, Lasren?" Kim asked, transmitting the data to the ops station.

Lasren studied it quietly for a moment. The young Bajoran was thorough and maddeningly slow to commit to an analysis where the available information was this sketchy.

"Looks like a sensor echo, sir," Lasren finally replied.

Kim had already decided this was a definite possibility. The EM frequency was so low it could have been any number of things, none of them terribly promising. But still, it was *something*.

In the interest of thoroughness, Kim decided to expand the search grid of the low frequency. To his surprise, this resulted in the immediate detection of several more "sensor echoes." It wasn't inconceivable that this would occur naturally. They knew next to nothing about this area of space, and any number of natural phenomena could account for it. But so could a handful of unnatural ones.

Tapping his combadge, he said, "Kim to engineering."

"Go ahead," Conlon replied.

"Please prepare to target the coordinates I am sending you now with a low-level tachyon pulse."

"Why?" Paris asked.

"I want to make sure the scattered low-level EM radiation surges I'm reading aren't indicative of stealth technology," Kim replied.

At this, Paris ordered, "Helm, adjust our orientation for optimum deflector alignment."

"Aye, sir," Aytar Gwyn replied.

A few moments later, the tachyon pulse was emitted from

the main deflector dish, and in an instant, Kim's tactical display lit up with a multitude of varied contacts, this time unmistakable in their purpose.

"Wow," he said softly.

Noting the readings on Kim's panel, Paris immediately ordered, "Raise shield. Yellow alert."

"Report, Lieutenant," Chakotay said.

Kim gave Paris a knowing nod before saying, "That's not a void, sir. That's cloaked space."

Chakotay smiled. "Good work, Harry."

Given Kim's assessment, Chakotay seriously considered taking the ship to red alert, but decided raising the threat level could wait. In his experience, cloaking technology was used for a relatively small number of things: people and ships. Rarely, planets or planet-sized technology could be cloaked. But the power required to sustain such things was massive.

"Do we have any idea what is generating the cloak?" Chakotay asked.

"Not yet, sir," Lieutenant Kim replied. "I've asked Seven to begin astrometrics analysis."

"Good." Chakotay nodded.

His thoughts suddenly turned to *Demeter*. No doubt, their science and tactical staff had reached the same conclusion as his people. But the small special mission ship was not really suited or intended for combat. If the fleet still had a *Vesta*-class ship with them, Chakotay's misgivings would have been mitigated. As it was, *Voyager* was the only thing standing between the *Demeter*'s capture or destruction, if hostilities broke out.

The captain knew he might be getting ahead of himself, but there was no denying that anyone or anything with the capacity to generate a cloaking field this size could pose a threat.

He didn't wish to deny *Demeter*'s crew the opportunity to contribute to the fleet's work, but he also didn't want to jeopardize them needlessly. Though the fleet did not have a commander at the moment, Chakotay had seniority, giving him the authority to order *Demeter* to fall back. It seemed to Chakotay that the time had come to broach the topic.

Rising from his chair he said, "Paris, you have the bridge. Continue scans and advise me immediately if anything changes out there."

"Aye, sir," Paris replied, stepping back to the command well as Chakotay crossed to his ready room.

Once at his desk, he opened a channel to the *Demeter*, where he was surprised to see the ship's first officer, Lieutenant Commander Atlee Fife. He was a young, lean man with eyes that seemed to take up altogether too much of his face.

"Commander Fife," Chakotay began, "have you detected the cloaking field?"

"Yes, sir," Fife replied officiously. *"We were picking up some strange EM readings when Voyager fired the tachyon pulse. We were about to request you do that, but clearly we're all on the same page."*

"Where is Commander O'Donnell?"

"His quarters, sir."

Chakotay hesitated, perturbed by the commander's lack of interest in the proceedings. "Is he aware of this discovery?"

"I have forwarded all pertinent data to his personal terminal. If he has any questions or recommendations, I'm sure he will apprise me of them in due time."

"Thank you, Commander. Patch me down there," Chakotay ordered.

When O'Donnell appeared, Chakotay got the distinct impression that the man was annoyed by the interruption. A balding human in his fifties, O'Donnell had already demonstrated his brilliance with the Children of the Storm contact. However, the two men had exchanged few words, and Chakotay still didn't quite know what to make of him.

"Is there a problem, Captain?" O'Donnell asked, cutting right to the chase.

"I was wondering, Commander, if you were concerned that the cloaking field we just discovered might pose a threat to your ship, given its limited maneuverability and armaments," Chakotay replied.

O'Donnell's brow furrowed. *"For the moment, it's Fife's call. Is he causing trouble up there?"*

Chakotay had been briefed on *Demeter*'s odd command structure. O'Donnell was the senior officer and titular captain. But when Command staffed the fleet they had specifically assigned O'Donnell a first officer with command level and tactical experience to compensate for O'Donnell's deficiencies. Fife reported to O'Donnell, but when it came to daily operations and hostile encounters, for the most part, O'Donnell deferred to Fife. For every other aspect of *Demeter*'s mission profile, a science vessel equipped to grow and house a wide variety of botanical life and to study unusual discoveries of the same, O'Donnell was in charge.

Still, Chakotay found it hard to understand how any ship's captain wouldn't be on the bridge at this moment.

"Commander Fife is acquitting himself admirably," Chakotay replied. "But my concern is for your ship's safety. You should consider falling back a bit until we have thoroughly evaluated the area."

"Fall back how far?" O'Donnell asked. *"The Alpha Quadrant?"*

Chakotay was sorely tempted to end this exchange by pulling rank, but he knew he had to find a way to make this unusual situation work.

Finally, he replied, "For now, we'll both continue our explorations. Advise Commander Fife that at the first sign of trouble, *Demeter* should move immediately out of the area and let *Voyager* take the lead. In addition, he should keep an open channel with *Voyager* and coordinate with us before testing the field in any way or maneuvering too close to it."

"Anything else we can get you?" O'Donnell asked. *"You guys hungry?"*

"If you disagree with my assessment, Commander . . ." Chakotay began, emphasizing his rank.

"I didn't say that, sir," O'Donnell replied. *"I realize* Voyager *has had a rough few weeks, and I appreciate that your ship took the brunt of Fife's reckless actions with the Children of the Storm. But, as best I can tell, my people have a firm a grasp on this discovery, and assuming you're willing to allow it, they might even surprise you by contributing to the work ahead. Fife knows our limits. And he's not going to put us, and by extension, you in any unnecessary danger. If things go south, he'll do what's right."*

"You're comfortable letting him take the lead on this?" Chakotay asked sincerely.

"I know what he knows so far. Somebody out there who apparently went looking for help a long time ago thought it necessary to hide at least a parsec's worth of space. I'm sure everybody else working the problem will figure out how they did it soon enough. In the meantime, I'm sitting here wondering why."

"If you asked that question of your bridge officers, they might have some valuable input to offer," Chakotay suggested.

O'Donnell shrugged. *"I think better when I'm alone. But when I come up with something, you'll be the first to know."*

"Just so we're clear," Chakotay began.

"Yes, yes, yes, yours is the last word out here, Captain. I know that. Fife does too. But, as long as we're out here together, just the two of us, why don't you let me handle my ship and you handle yours, unless we prove ourselves unworthy of that modicum of respect."

Chakotay nodded, stung, but not entirely surprised. Eden had briefed him on O'Donnell's personal quirks. Despite them, she considered him a valuable resource, and Chakotay knew it would be unwise to dismiss her judgment. But it had taken minutes for Chakotay's vague misgivings to ratchet up to concern.

"Both you and Lieutenant Commander Fife have my respect, Commander," Chakotay replied. "You also have been advised of my concerns. Keep the lines of communication open as things develop."

"Will do." O'Donnell nodded.

Chakotay signed off, frustrated. He had more than enough on his plate without navigating *Demeter*'s unique command structure. Fife had lost Chakotay's trust the moment he'd turned against his captain when they faced the Children of the Storm. Despite O'Donnell's apparent confidence, from Chakotay's point of view, Fife had a ways to go before he earned it back. O'Donnell might be a genius, but that didn't make him a leader. *What was Command thinking?* Chakotay wondered for the hundredth time since he'd returned to *Voyager*'s center seat.

Setting his grim thoughts aside, Chakotay returned to his bridge.

Chapter Six

STARFLEET HEADQUARTERS, SAN FRANCISCO

By the time the *Galen* arrived at McKinley Station, Kathryn Janeway was more than ready to meet with Admiral Montgomery. Although she expected most of her time to be spoken for over the next few weeks, as she bid farewell to Icheb, Janeway promised to check in with him and encouraged Icheb to apply himself diligently to his studies. She had spoken briefly to the Doctor and Reg and asked that they keep her apprised of their work on Starbase 185. Given the uncertainty of her position, she could not make this an order. Their friendship made it unnecessary. They had offered her any support they could provide, and she accepted it with gratitude.

Admiral Kenneth Montgomery's aide admitted her to his office without hesitation. Clearly she had been expected. As Montgomery rose from his desk to offer his hand, Janeway was struck by how much he seemed to have aged in the last year. He had maintained a lean, toned build well past the time many admirals had let their bodies go to seed. His deeply tanned skin lent an air of health, in spite of ragged lines, but his gray eyes, while alert as ever, were now rimmed with dark circles. His fair, sandy hair was more generously flecked with silver. But most telling was his movement. Where once she would have described him as spry, he now carried himself like a man who had recently taken several body blows and was still tender.

His relief at seeing her seemed genuine enough, though

his smile might have been a bit forced as he said, “Kathryn, so good to see you again.”

“And you, Ken,” she replied, taking his hand and shaking it firmly.

“Your journey was uneventful?” he asked.

Janeway had never possessed much patience for small talk. This morning, her reserves were thoroughly depleted.

“Why am I here, Ken?” she asked simply. “On your orders, I have just left the vast majority of the people most dear to me in the universe tens of thousands of light-years from my aid or Starfleet’s. They’ve been through hell for the last five months, and while they remain ever ready to do their duty, they are no longer properly equipped to do so. I realize there are those among Command inclined to question my ability to lead, given the unusual circumstances of my return, as well as the actions I have taken in the past. But I didn’t get the impression that you were one of them.”

Montgomery shook his head as he moved to lean his back against his desk and cross his arms.

“You haven’t changed a bit, have you?” he observed lightly.

Having successfully released a little steam, Janeway relaxed a smidge. “Of course I have,” she replied honestly. “You don’t visit the Q Continuum and experience your life and death in countless alternate universes without gaining a little perspective and humility. Choices I made with the best of intentions unraveled into the most horrific ends. I know a little time spent taking stock is warranted. But before I begin, I need to know something.”

“What’s that?”

“Is the choice you gave me two weeks ago still mine to make?”

Montgomery’s eyes met hers briefly.

“Maybe,” he replied honestly.

“Maybe?”

“As you have no doubt surmised, it is no longer my call.”

Janeway assumed a more defensive posture, crossing her arms and stepping toward him. "What changed?"

"When I first extended the offer for you to assume command of what is left of the Full Circle fleet, I based that decision on the reports filed by Captains Eden and Chakotay and our initial conversations. Since then, my office has been flooded with inquiries from superior officers, raising concerns about that decision."

"Is the pressure coming from above or below?" Janeway asked.

"Both," Montgomery replied.

"What do I have to do to ease your mind?"

"Were you any other ranking officer who had just undergone trauma on the field of battle, I would tell you to answer all the inquiries of your evaluators honestly and succinctly and to analyze, as dispassionately as possible, your ability to cope with the stresses resuming command will bring."

"I'm no longer just any ranking officer?" Janeway asked.

"You died, Kathryn; or came close to it. Yes, other officers have died and been resurrected in various ways, but none of them immediately resumed duties on par with command of the Full Circle fleet. It is difficult for us to evaluate your experiences because they fall too far outside the bounds of our understanding.

"And your 'near death,' shall we say, came as a result of a particularly brutal form of assimilation."

"I'm not the only officer serving Starfleet who survived assimilation."

"No," Montgomery agreed. "But it's more than that. The bond you share with those who served with you in the Delta Quadrant is unique. It was forged under extreme circumstances, and in many ways, can be considered an asset. But it is possible that you lost sight of the fact that those you led served something bigger than themselves or you. You have made choices in the past that arguably blur the line between the obligations of command and the needs of those you think of as family.

"Leadership requires, above all, perspective. I'm not sure that when it comes to 'your people,' you have sufficient perspective to make giving you command of them appropriate."

"You think I put their needs ahead of what's best for Starfleet or the Federation?"

"I don't know. Can you stand here and honestly tell me without a doubt that you trust yourself to let them risk what they must to do what duty requires? Has coming so close to your own demise, and theirs, at the hands of Omega *not* affected your ability to make instantaneous judgments unclouded by personal considerations? They're not your family, Admiral. They don't need a mother, a lover, or a friend. They need a commanding officer. Can you ever be just that to them?"

Had the question not been at the forefront of her mind for weeks, Janeway might have been able to summon an immediate affirmative response. Further, Montgomery's use of the word "lover" suggested to her that someone had been telling tales out of school. There were only a handful of people who knew that her relationship with Chakotay was more than professional.

"That's why you're here," Montgomery finished.

Janeway nodded. "I understand," she replied. "But I do have one more question."

"Please," Montgomery offered.

"If *I* decide it is no longer in my best interest, or theirs, to resume command, who will take my place?"

"That should not figure into your calculations, Admiral," Montgomery replied.

Janeway nodded again. It was a strange sensation to feel so powerless after so many years of wielding considerable authority.

"Admiral Montgomery?" The voice of his aide interrupted them.

"Yes?" he barked.

"Admiral Akaar and Vice Admiral Verdell have arrived."

"Show them in at once," Montgomery replied.

The doors to his office slid open, and the frame was filled by Starfleet's commander in chief, Admiral Leonard James Akaar, a Capellan mountain of a man who carried himself like a well-fortified building. Janeway had met Akaar before he had risen to his present post, but she still found his physical presence awe-inspiring. His personal history and sterling record were the only things more impressive than the man.

Behind him, a portly officer—who barely reached Akaar's elbows—with serious eyes and a pronounced cranial ridge entered. He appeared to be perhaps a decade older than Janeway. She assumed this was Verdell.

With two full strides, Akaar was beside her and immediately extended his hand to Janeway. "I apologize for my tardiness, Admiral. I meant to be here when you arrived."

"Thank you, Admiral, but it is entirely unnecessary," she replied with sincere appreciation.

"On the contrary, Admiral Janeway, on behalf of all of Starfleet, I wish to welcome you home. I've been briefed on your encounter with the Omega Continuum. I am pleased that you and the fleet's crew were able to end the threat it posed. I would also like to offer my personal condolences on the losses you suffered."

Janeway nodded, swallowing hard. "Thank you, sir."

"Allow me to introduce you to Vice Admiral Verdell," Akaar continued, gesturing to his right. Verdell shook Janeway's hand with a solid grip, his face betraying little beyond polite acknowledgment.

"A pleasure, Admiral," he said, his cadence rather clipped.

"Admiral," Janeway replied.

"Verdell has been brought up to speed on the progress of the Full Circle fleet and will have many questions for you in the coming weeks. I know your time for the foreseeable future will be at a premium," Akaar continued. "I am certain there are many people here on Earth you are eager to see. While I do not wish to overburden you, I would appreciate it if you would make a priority of familiarizing yourself with the many changes to our political, tactical, and strategic landscape."

"Of course," Janeway said.

"It has been a year of unexpected developments, Admiral. But I do not doubt that your expertise and knowledge will aid Starfleet tremendously going forward."

"Thank you, sir."

"I assume she has an office?" Akaar inquired of Montgomery.

"And an aide," Montgomery replied. "No one expects you to assume normal duties immediately," he quickly added.

"As soon as you are ready." Akaar nodded. "Take all the time you need."

Janeway paused, considering the wisdom of making a personal plea to Akaar while he was obviously in such a gracious mood. But it seemed clear to her that he had already settled matters in his mind as to her ultimate dispensation. Akaar did not intend to waste the years of experience she had accumulated. But he was the unmovable mass she would have to force into a new orientation should she wish to return to the fleet. And unless she was much mistaken, Vice Admiral Verdell was his hand-picked replacement for her. At least it was good to know that for now, Akaar did not seem inclined to recall the fleet and redistribute its resources. That would ease Chakotay's mind, but she could not apprise him of this development.

"Carry on then," Akaar said and left the office briskly, Verdell trailing at his heels.

When they were alone again, Janeway turned back to Montgomery. His doubts were real and justified. Clearly they had been planted by others, but they'd quickly found fertile ground and already formed vigorous roots.

Acceptance seemed the easiest course. She could make

Montgomery's life, Akaar's life, and for all she knew now, her own life, a lot easier by simply bending to the political realities before her. She would be kept busy and find new ways to contribute to Starfleet. Chakotay would continue to protect those they both loved, guiding them through the next few years. No matter how long they were apart, one day, they would find each another again.

Let go, a strangely familiar voice echoed in her mind.

Like hell, another quickly replied.

"My office?" Janeway asked of Montgomery.

"This way," he replied, gesturing for Janeway to precede him out.

A few minutes later, Janeway was deposited in a completely sanitized and anonymous space in the farthest corner of the floor occupied by Montgomery and dozens of other admirals. A single padd lay on her desk containing a schedule of appointments beginning that afternoon with a counselor named Pyotr Jens. If history was any guide, within days the surface of her desk would be buried beneath several more padds. The aide she had been promised had not yet materialized in her office's reception area.

A single flashing light on her computer terminal indicated a priority message awaiting her attention. It took a few minutes for Janeway to authenticate her identity at the terminal and acquire her new command codes, but shortly thereafter, she retrieved the message.

Its sender was a surprise, but not unexpected. Its urgent tone was disconcerting. With the next few hours clear and a promise to fulfill, Janeway left word for her aide to expect her after lunch and headed for the facility's transporter room.

MONTECITO, CA

Julia Paris, wife of the late Admiral Owen Paris, mother of Lieutenant Commander Tom Paris and Kathleen and Moira, mother-in-law of B'Elanna Torres, and grandmother of

Miral Paris sat alone at her kitchen table. A Starfleet wife and mother knew better than to expect constant or even regular communication from those in her family in Starfleet. She honored their choices by accepting their absence unconditionally. Her daughters, a university professor and a doctor, had careers that kept them occupied, but their regular visits and calls filled some of the empty spaces.

It had not yet been a year since Owen's death aboard a distant starbase at the height of the Borg Invasion. Less than five months earlier, Julia had begun to grieve the loss of her daughter-in-law and beloved granddaughter, coping as well as could have been expected. Others had lost more. She kept herself busy reviewing the latest scholarly articles from her long-ago abandoned field of study, paleontology, and toyed with the idea of joining a research group. She had insisted that her daughters stop checking in so often. She refused to burden them with her grief.

The losses she had suffered, great as they were, had not broken her. It had taken a letter, written by her son, dispatched from the Delta Quadrant to do that.

A chiming from the front door jolted her, but Julia composed herself as she went to answer it. She knew that Admiral Kathryn Janeway stood outside. She had attended the admiral's funeral and did not understand how she had been recovered and restored to life. Among the many surprising revelations contained in Tom's letter was news of Janeway's return, and it was the only information therein that filled her with unreserved relief.

The rest . . . well, perhaps Kathryn, a dear family friend who had been one of Owen's protégés since she was a cadet, would help her understand.

"Hello, Julia," Janeway's warm, rich voice greeted her, and Julia's fears were quieted. There was no mistaking the reality of her solid comforting presence, and Julia immediately opened her arms to Janeway.

"It's so good to see you again," Janeway said as Julia held

her close. Both women were petite, but Janeway felt strong as ever, while Julia sensed herself disappearing slowly, reduced to little more than bones covered by a thin veneer of flesh.

"Thank you for coming so quickly," Julia said, struggling to hold her warring emotions at bay.

"I promised Tom I would, and when I saw your message, I didn't think it should wait," Janeway said.

"Coffee?" Julia asked, her hosting skills kicking in with a vengeance.

"Please." Janeway smiled, and Julia led her into the kitchen, warming her own cup after pouring a large mug for her guest.

"I only learned of Owen's passing a few weeks ago," Janeway began. "I'm so sorry."

"Thank you," Julia said as she settled herself in a chair beside the admiral. "I had actually convinced myself that he was invincible," she added ruefully. "He survived so many missions he shouldn't have. Obviously, I was wrong."

Janeway shook her head and placed a warm hand over Julia's. "It's never wrong to live in hope."

Julia's faint smile vanished. "I take it Tom was the one who told you about Owen?"

"Yes." Janeway nodded. "I know he's still struggling with it, but you'd be so proud of him, Julia . . . the man he has become."

"Then you don't know . . ." Julia began.

"Know what?" Janeway asked, her face clouding over with concern.

"What he did?"

Janeway searched her memories for a moment, but she shook her head at a loss.

Julia's lips began to quiver, not with sadness, but with rage. "He lied to me. *Again.* He promised after that business at the Academy that he was done with deception, that he had learned the error of his ways. And even when he betrayed Starfleet, he did it honestly and for a cause he could justify.

But he let me believe, he let me live for months thinking that my only granddaughter was dead. His father died thinking Tom's marriage had ended. Owen sat here with me at this very table, agonizing over Tom's pain, trying to figure out how he had failed as a father."

Julia paused to collect herself. "I don't know who my son is now or how you could possibly think I'd be proud of him."

The confusion writ plainly on Janeway's face only fortified Julia's certainty that her son had completely disgraced himself.

"Of course he wouldn't tell you," she realized. "Your good opinion still matters to him."

Janeway shook her head slowly, interlacing her fingers and resting her hands on the table before her. "This must be a mistake . . . some misunderstanding," she insisted.

"It's all here," Julia said, her voice rising as she moved to the counter to grab the padd containing Tom's letter. Passing it to Janeway, Julia sat again and gave her a few moments. As she read, Janeway's confusion vanished, replaced by what looked suspiciously like understanding.

"I see," she finally said and sighed.

"You can't possibly condone what he did?" Julia asked.

"'Condone' is probably too strong a word," Janeway agreed, "but, 'understand,' yes."

"Subterfuge in the name of protecting the interest of Starfleet or the Federation is one thing," Julia granted her. "The wife of a Starfleet admiral learns to live with many a half-truth. But this was a family matter. You don't tell lies like this to your family. I remember the day he told me that B'Elanna and Miral's names were on the casualty list. He let me comfort him. He let me go on and on about how it could be a mistake. He wouldn't arrange a formal service for them. He made *me* do that. I'm actually glad his father never lived to see this, because he would never have forgiven him. I can't either."

"Oh, Julia, no," Janeway said softly. "His choices might not have been mine. But I stood beside him when the Warriors of Gre'thor took Miral from him. The threat they posed was real. His fear that they would eventually find and murder Miral was not imagined or overstated. I had no idea he and B'Elanna had concocted this ruse to throw them off. But it might very well have been the best way to keep Miral safe."

"Fine," Julia conceded. "Lie to our enemies all day long. But lie to your mother?" she demanded.

"To keep you safe as well," Kathryn insisted.

"Me?"

"There was nothing to prevent the Warriors of Gre'thor coming after you, forcing you to provide them with Tom, B'Elanna, or Miral's whereabouts. It was possible. Had they done so, you could only have told them honestly what you knew . . . that Miral was dead."

"Nothing could have forced me to betray Miral to anyone."

Vivid pain streaked across Janeway's face. Her tone chilled as she said, "You wouldn't have *wanted to,* Julia. But there are many ways they could have forced you, most of which you would not have survived."

Julia knew that many years ago, Janeway had been captured along with Owen by Cardassians. Owen had been tortured, and while he hadn't spoken of it, Julia knew that the scars had been permanent. She had never known what Janeway suffered during that mission, but she sensed now that it had been something akin to what Owen had endured.

Shaking her head, grasping for the fury now sustaining her, Julia replied, "Now I almost wished they had."

"You don't mean that."

"I do. You didn't know Tom when he was a cadet. I know you've read his permanent file so you know about the accident that claimed the lives of three of his best friends and how he lied about it at the initial inquiries to spare himself harsher punishment. I was the one who stood up for him, even after the truth came to light. I was the one who insisted he could survive it. My love was unconditional.

"Owen spoke often in the last few years about his doubts, wondering what Starfleet had become in the face of so much aggression. The Parasites, the Dominion, the Borg, so many species determined to exterminate our way of life. Every time we faced them, we seemed to lose a little more of ourselves. He worried that we could no longer produce young men and women with the drive to explore the universe's mysteries with open minds and hearts.

"If Tom is an example of Starfleet's finest . . . I don't know what the hell we think we're doing anymore."

"You need to give it some time, Julia. Tom, B'Elanna, and Miral are all healthy and so happy to be together as a family again. Miral is a beautiful, curious, bright young girl. Tom only learned a few days ago that the Warriors of Gre'thor were killed by the Borg. And the minute he was free to do so, he told you the truth. You need to talk to your son. Let him explain to you what was in his heart when he did this."

"*My son*? He's not my son," Julia replied bitterly. "When will the fleet return to the Alpha Quadrant?"

"I don't know," Janeway replied, shocked by the abrupt question.

"Most of it was destroyed, wasn't it?" Julia demanded. "Surely Command isn't going to leave them out there now? I assumed the fact that you are here means they can't be far behind."

"We'll know more in the next few weeks," Janeway replied cagily, "but they are still slated to continue the mission for another two and a half years."

Julia rose from her seat and began to pace the cavernous kitchen. It had been designed as the heart of a house meant to be filled with multiple generations of Parises. Finally she stopped. "I don't think so," she said.

Janeway stood and approached her warily. "This is a matter for Starfleet Command, Julia. It's beyond your purview."

"Owen was beloved by the organization he served. I don't think my request will fall on deaf ears."

"What request do you intend to make?" Janeway asked.

"If Starfleet still considers my son fit to serve, that's their problem. But there is no question in my mind that he is not fit to parent my granddaughter. She's a civilian, and I can petition the Federation courts for custody."

The color fled from Janeway's face. "Julia, no," she pleaded.

"Watch me," Julia replied coldly.

Chapter Seven

VOYAGER

Twenty-seven hours after *Voyager* had arrived at the edge of the cloaking matrix, Seven had devised a means to pinpoint its field generators and to render a navigational chart that would allow the ship to enter the area without impacting any of the objects currently cloaked to the ship's sensors.

Lieutenant Kim and Captain Chakotay stood beside her at the astrometrics lab's main control station, studying the grainy image displayed on the room's massive viewscreen.

"The field generators are in subspace?" Chakotay asked, clearly seeking to solidify his understanding of the technology Seven had spent the last several minutes laying out in painstaking detail.

"Within a triaxilating subspace fold, yes," Seven replied. "They are tetryon based and similar in structure to the first distortion ring we encountered. They are less complex but appear to produce a harmonic resonance that sustains the cloak."

"I still don't understand why we aren't reading even minimal tachyons," Kim noted.

"The rotating modulations of the fold are neutralizing the tachyons, burying them in deeper subspace layers," Seven replied. "The modulations are essential to masking the generators."

"How many generators have you detected thus far?" Chakotay asked.

"Fourteen thousand six hundred and nineteen," Seven replied. "As we move deeper into the field, I expect we shall find more," she added. "It is impossible to theorize how far the matrix might extend beyond our sensor's limits."

"This is the best image you can compile of what is hidden by that field?" Chakotay continued.

Seven chaffed at the implied criticism. The fact that she had been able to compile the image they were now viewing was an extraordinary accomplishment. "It is sufficient for navigational purposes," Seven replied, "but if you find it aesthetically lacking, I could create a program that would extrapolate the images in more realistic detail, though it would take several more hours."

Chakotay bowed his head and smiled faintly. Placing a hand on Seven's shoulder he replied, "I'm sorry, Seven. That won't be necessary. This is more than sufficient, and you are to be commended for a job extremely well done."

"Thank you," she said.

"I don't get it," Kim finally said.

"The matrix, like most cloaking technology, is effectively bending the light and energized particles around the objects contained within it, thus rendering them invisible to our standard sensors. But minute traces of the objects are retrievable at the intersection point where the light and particles are refracted. Once you locate the precise frequency of the cloaking matrix, that point becomes visible. I cannot tell you to a certainty *what* the objects are, but their mass and locations have been mapped . . ."

"I'm sorry, Seven," Kim interjected. "I understand the math. What I meant to say is that what we have here is what appears to be a lot of empty space until we reach this sector," he continued, indicating a point on the display, "which looks like part of an asteroid field."

"Why would anyone trouble themselves to hide this?" Chakotay asked.

"Exactly." Kim nodded.

"There is one star system, almost two light-years from our present position, containing several masses of planetary configuration and size," Seven offered.

"Obviously we won't know until we get closer if there's anything worth seeing in that star system," Chakotay noted.

"Unless we can disable the cloaking matrix, we won't even know then, sir," Kim corrected him.

"Any thoughts on how to do that?" Chakotay asked.

"Are we sure we want to?" Kim asked.

Chakotay appeared taken aback. "You getting cold feet, Harry?"

"No," Kim replied. "Exploring is one thing. But this field was put in place by someone or something a long time ago. For all we know it's their sovereign space and this is how they encourage travelers to stay out of it. I'm not sure we have any right to try and disable their means of protection."

"That's a fair point," Chakotay replied. "Just because we're curious doesn't mean we are entitled to have our curiosity satisfied. But," he added, "that distortion ring directed us here and if you're right, it required assistance. I'd like to provide that if we can."

"Perhaps venturing into the cloaked area, now that we can safely do so, will encourage anyone out there who might need help to show themselves," Kim posited.

"I'm not yet thoroughly satisfied that we can enter it safely," Chakotay corrected him.

"Sir?" Seven asked.

"Prepare a class-1 probe," Chakotay ordered. "Plot a direct course toward that star system. Equip it to send out standard greetings on all frequencies. Let's see if that gets anyone's attention."

"Aye, sir." Kim nodded.

"Do you require assistance, Lieutenant Kim?" Seven asked.

"Yours? Always," Kim replied with a wide smile.

Lieutenant Commander Atlee Fife ordered his flight controller, Ensign Sten Falto, to put a greater distance between *Voyager* and *Demeter*. *Voyager* had discovered the power sources of the matrix well before Lieutenant Url had cracked that mystery. Fife concurred wholeheartedly with Captain Chakotay's intention to launch a probe into the cloaked area before allowing either vessel to enter it. From their present position, they would be able to access all data retrieved by the probe and be able to escape should anything untoward occur. Url had maintained contact with *Voyager,* and now, all both ships could do was wait.

Fife rested on the edge of his chair, his spine perfectly aligned maximizing both comfort and potential freedom of motion. He had activated a link between the main viewscreen and Captain O'Donnell's quarters should he have any interest in the proceedings. As the probe launched, Fife honestly wondered what he hoped would result from the effort. Not too long ago, his focus would have been on the tactical dangers posed. He would have expected a hostile response and been mentally running scenarios to combat it. Now, he was satisfied to remain curious. Having barely survived a first-contact situation with the Children of the Storm, he was committed to at least considering the possibility that less-invasive, more diplomatic efforts could yield better results. A product of his training, Fife had begun his service as hostilities with the Dominion were escalating. But he was beginning to see how those early experiences had restricted his thinking. How many other possible responses were there in a situation such as this?

He actually wished that Captain O'Donnell had come to the bridge for the launch. No doubt, if Fife were to pose the question, the captain would have several alternatives, and he wanted to hear them right now. He made a mental note to discuss the question with the captain at the next opportunity.

"Commander," Url called from tactical, "we are detecting a response to the probe's entry into the cloaked field."

"Onscreen," Fife ordered, his pulse quickening.

He found the spectacle that played out before him disappointing on several levels.

"Report," Chakotay demanded.

The first response to the probe's contact had come only a few minutes after it passed into the cloaked area. EM readings had spiked, followed by detection of low-level tetryons.

"Something is emerging from subspace, sir," Kim replied.

"Specify."

Kim paused, studying the readings and immediately ordering the computer to run a comparison with the distortion ring. As he waited for the computer's response, Kim settled for a visual analysis. Swirling greenish gas burst forth several thousand kilometers from the probe's position. A dark point at its center began to expand, edged by sharp spikes Kim couldn't help but think of as "teeth." The ovoid darkness expanded as it moved to intercept the probe.

"Lieutenant Lasren, let's see what the probe is seeing," Chakotay ordered.

The image on the main viewscreen was split between *Voyager*'s sensor's display of the probe's course and an image taken directly from the probe's visual sensors. Kim decided that from the probe's point of view, the encounter was significantly more terrifying. As the swirling mass approached, a gaping maw opened, filled with jagged energy discharges. Were the probe capable of thought, it might have realized it was about to become dinner.

"Lieutenant Kim?" Chakotay asked again.

"It's a wave form, sir," Kim replied. "The EM readings are consistent with the distortion ring, but there are numerous other energy signatures previously unseen."

"I don't think its intention is terribly mysterious," Paris added.

"How long until it reaches the probe?" Chakotay asked.

"Thirty seconds," Kim replied. "Should I attempt to adjust the probe's course?"

"No," Chakotay said.

Thirty seconds later, the wave form reached its target. Its "mouth" had opened to a diameter of ten meters, wide enough to completely surround the probe. The moment it was engulfed by the wave form, the probe ceased transmission. Lasren reset the viewscreen to display sensor readings. An oval shape clamped down, and the gaseous mass around it was lit by streaks of orange and white light, evidence of the probe's destruction. Seconds later, the gas began to disperse, and all evidence of the wave form vanished from the viewscreen.

Paris turned to Chakotay. "The probe was programmed to transmit our standard friendship greetings as well as an offer to assist anything that needed our help," he said. "I think we have our answer, sir."

Chakotay brought his hand to his chin, leaned forward, and nodded somberly.

As the computer finally began to relay its comparative analysis at Kim's station, sensors registered two new EM spikes: one within ten thousand kilometers of *Voyager,* and the other an equivalent distance from *Demeter.*

"Two new wave forms are emerging from subspace, sir," Kim reported at once.

"Red alert," Chakotay ordered. "Helm, evasive maneuvers."

"*Demeter* is altering course as well, sir," Lasren advised.

"Is the comm link stable?" Chakotay asked.

"Aye, sir," Lasren replied.

"*Demeter,* status?" Chakotay said.

"We've detected the wave form, sir," Fife replied, unruffled. *"We can evade at impulse speeds for now, but if necessary, we can go to warp. The drive is online."*

"Belay that!" a new voice ordered gruffly.

"Commander O'Donnell?" Chakotay asked.

"The EM frequency of this wave form is slightly different from the one that just destroyed the probe. We need to see what it wants, Captain," O'Donnell replied.

"Even if that's true," Chakotay countered, "contact cannot be permitted at this time. The first one of these things we encountered halted us in our tracks and altered the physical configuration of our ship as it moved through us."

"Is it saying anything, Lieutenant Vincent?" O'Donnell asked of his operations officer.

"No communications are incoming on any subspace bands, sir," Vincent replied.

Chakotay looked to Lieutenant Lasren, who echoed Vincent's response with a sharp shake of his head.

"Commander O'Donnell, I am ordering you to move your ship clear of harm's way," Chakotay said, rising from his chair.

"That's a mistake, Captain," O'Donnell said.

"No, that's an order," Chakotay said more forcefully.

After too long a pause, O'Donnell finally replied, *"Understood."*

Kim watched as *Demeter* began to put significant distance between itself and the approaching wave form.

"Can we stop this one, Lieutenant Kim?" Chakotay asked.

"Yes, sir," Kim replied. He'd spent six years studying the distortion ring and creating several tactical responses.

"Its speed is increasing, Captain," Gwyn advised from the helm.

"Full impulse," Chakotay ordered.

"Aye, sir."

"Time to impact?"

"Three minutes at present speed," Gwyn replied.

"Harry?" Chakotay demanded.

"Permission to attempt communication?" Kim requested.

"How?" Chakotay asked.

"I'm encrypting our standard greetings using the same

code the first wave form used," Kim replied. "If we can show it that we understood its message, maybe it will answer us."

"Go ahead." Chakotay nodded.

"Lasren?" Kim asked.

"Transmitting now," Lasren replied.

Kim waited breathlessly for the wave form now approaching *Voyager* to halt its progress, transmit a reply, or give any sign that it had received the message. When a minute had gone by and none of these things had come to pass, Lasren said with obvious regret, "No response, sir."

"One minute to contact," Gwyn added.

"Neutralize the wave form, Lieutenant Kim," Chakotay ordered.

"Aye, sir. Venting tetryon plasma," Kim replied.

The tactical officer watched as the plasma dispersed from the ship's nacelles into the path of the wave form. As expected, the concentrated gamma radiation disrupted the portion of the form that was still in subspace and the ever-widening dark center distorted visibly before collapsing altogether.

"The wave form has been forced back into subspace, sir," Kim reported.

"Good work, Lieutenant Kim. Any additional contacts?"

"No, sir."

"What is *Demeter*'s status?"

"The wave from approaching *Demeter* is accelerating," Kim reported.

"Why haven't they gone to warp?" Chakotay asked.

"I'm not sure they can now," Paris suggested.

"They waited too long," Chakotay murmured, clearly frustrated. "Ensign Gwyn, put us between *Demeter* and the wave form. Kim, prepare to vent plasma," Chakotay ordered.

"Aye, sir," Gwyn replied. Inertial dampers struggled to compensate as *Voyager* made a sharp turn to port.

Even moving at full impulse, the distance was too great. "We're not going to make it," Gwyn reported.

Kim watched as *Demeter* attempted to go to warp. The proximity of the wave form was disrupting subspace sufficiently to make formation of the warp bubble impossible.

"Options?" Chakotay asked.

"I'm realigning the deflector dish," Kim replied. "Emitting a tetryon pulse."

Kim wasn't sure the pulse would have the same effect as the plasma, but it was *Demeter*'s only chance.

Bright flares shot forth from the deflector and flew into the heart of the wave form. For a few breathless seconds, they appeared to have no effect. Then, the wave form collapsed, less than a thousand meters from its target.

"Helm, set course six one nine mark three and engage at warp six," Chakotay ordered. "Lasren, relay that course to *Demeter*."

"Aye, sir," Gwyn replied.

"Course transmitted," Lasren reported. "*Demeter* has achieved warp speed and is following."

Chakotay released a deep sigh and finally said, "Stand down red alert."

Kim's relief was palpable, but so was his curiosity. Was it possible he had misinterpreted the data? Did the wave forms no longer require help? They seemed eminently capable of defending their territory. But the request he had decoded had such a plaintive tone to it. And despite the many inconveniences of the first encounter, the distortion ring had done no real damage to *Voyager*. It seemed intent only on communicating with them.

What had Commander O'Donnell seen that he had missed?

"Captain?" Kim asked. "As soon as we have reached a safe distance, I would like to request permission to confer with Commander O'Donnell."

"Noted," Chakotay replied.

From his tone, Harry sensed that Chakotay probably intended to do a fair amount of "conferring" with O'Donnell as well.

Chapter Eight

STARFLEET MEDICAL, SAN FRANCISCO

Had her morning been even slightly less fraught, Admiral Janeway might have been able to cobble together some patience for Counselor Pyotr Jens. He had to be in his forties, but his boyish face belied any experience he might have gained in those years. A quick glance at his service record indicated that he had spent most of his career at Starfleet Medical. She didn't want to judge him too harshly. Maintaining a positive attitude was essential, especially in trying times. But his earnestness read as condescension, his enthusiasm, forced.

Adding to a long list of worries was what Julia Paris was about to do to Tom, B'Elanna, and Miral. Unless Janeway managed to convince the very green Mister Jens to provide her with a sterling evaluation, she would quickly find herself without the authority to aid them in any way.

The problem was she had no idea who she was dealing with and therefore no way to formulate responses sure to satisfy him. For all his too-obvious sincerity, he remained aloof. She actually missed Hugh Cambridge. At least with him, she'd never had cause to doubt her footing or the savage truth of his assessments.

Just be honest, she reminded herself as each new question made her want to grab Jens and shake him. Instead, she kept her hands folded in her lap and did her best to keep her face neutral.

They had briefly discussed major events following *Voyager*'s return to the Alpha Quadrant. Jens then indicated that he wished to use most of this day's session to cover her presumed death and experiences with the Q. "How much do you remember of the assimilation process?" he asked.

Enough.

"Not much," she replied. "I had experienced a version of assimilation before."

"Yes." Jens nodded, clearly pleased with himself to already know this. "Stardate 54014, you, Commander Tuvok, and Lieutenant B'Elanna Torres allowed yourselves to be assimilated in order to gain access to the central plexus of a Borg vessel."

"Yes." Janeway nodded stoically, though Jens's mispronunciation of B'Elanna—*Buh Alana*—almost sent her over the edge. "But we had been injected with neural inhibitors prior, which allowed us to retain our individuality during and after the assimilation process."

"One wonders why such a miraculous innovation was not more widespread among the fleet during last year's Borg attack. At the very least, it should have become a standard safeguard for anyone facing the Borg," Jens mused. "It might have come in handy when you led the *Einstein*'s away team aboard the cube that assimilated you."

No, one doesn't.

"In the first place, it wasn't entirely successful," Janeway said curtly. "Lieutenant Tuvok was almost lost to the Borg. Second, almost every weapon and tactic successfully used against the Borg worked once, twice if we were lucky. Their ability to adapt was one of their greatest strengths. Our ability to innovate was the only thing that leveled the playing field. Finally, when the Borg came last year, they didn't come to assimilate. They came to annihilate."

"Yes, of course." Jens seemed to realize on the spot. He should have been mortified to display such limited understanding of the subject, but he wasn't.

"The two assimilations were nothing alike," Janeway finally went on. "The first I seemed to watch, as if it were happening to someone else. The second was like drowning. It felt like a very long time before I realized that I still existed in some fashion, apart from the Queen they made from me. Where once I'd had full run of the house that I think of as myself, it seemed I was now locked in a very small closet and only granted access to what was being done with my body in brief, horrifying glimpses."

"Do you now find yourself fearful of small places?" Jens asked.

"Not especially," Janeway replied wearily.

It didn't matter. Nothing she could say here was going to help her. The work she needed to do to come to terms with her recent past required the aid of an intellect and the wisdom of years this energetic young man simply did not possess. Janeway had no doubt that Montgomery had known this when he assigned Jens as her counselor. This exercise was meant to occupy her time, nothing more. Montgomery was going to cave to Akaar's pressure, and Admiral Verdell was probably already working on salvaging whatever the admirals thought they could of the fleet's mission.

Before she set foot on Earth, Janeway had readied herself to consider as honestly and deeply as possible the pros and cons of fighting for command of the fleet. She wanted to find the right answer to this question, both for herself and for those she loved. Farkas's anger had shaken her, and Montgomery's words about her ability to maintain perspective had struck at the heart of her misgivings. Janeway needed to satisfy herself that she *could* and *would* do what she must, and in the absence of that certainty, she would accept Command's choice with grace.

The resistance to that acceptance now grew stronger with every word that fell from the counselor's lips. It flowed from an irrational determination to refuse to bow to the political winds, not from an inner certainty that she *should* return to the fleet. It was empowering and felt all too familiar. Beating impossible odds was her comfort zone. But she could not say for sure that this was the battle she was supposed to be fighting.

For all his well-intended efforts, Counselor Jens wasn't even capable of seeing the field, let alone joining her on it.

"Do you believe now, knowing all you know, that were you again faced with the choice to board that cube, you would still do so?" Jens asked, his batting average in obliviousness nearing one thousand.

"No," Janeway replied. *But who among us ever gets that chance?* she shouted internally.

You did, a soft voice reminded her. *You chose to rewrite history once when you didn't like the outcome.*

"That wasn't me," Janeway murmured.

"Admiral?" Jens asked.

"I'm sorry, Counselor," she said quickly. "What was your question?"

Jens did not immediately reply, instead busying himself making a notation on his padd.

This can't last forever, she reminded herself.

But she had no doubt that the outcome of these sessions would haunt her nearly that long.

STARBASE 185

The Doctor's first thought entering Starbase 185's sickbay was that it was badly in need of retrofitting. Data terminals, biobeds, even the tricorders were several years out of date.

He had downloaded the files of the patient designated as "C-1" into his memory buffers and spent the past two days analyzing the contents. The Starbase's CMO, Doctor Sakrys Mai, was obviously at a loss and had made a number of errors in her initial evaluation. A treatment plan would have to wait until the Doctor could examine the patient personally.

Commander Clarissa Glenn accompanied the Doctor to

the sickbay, where Doctor Mai, a short, plump woman from Cestus III, stood within the visible level-10 force field erected to protect the rest of the base from the patient. As the Doctor and Glenn entered, a nurse at a control panel lowered the field, allowing Doctor Mai to exit. The field was quickly restored as Mai crossed to offer the EMH her hand.

"It's a pleasure to meet you, Doctor," she said sincerely. Her voice had a lilting, almost musical quality that the Doctor found appealing. "And you, Commander Glenn," Mai added.

"Has there been any change in his condition since your last report, Doctor Mai?" the Doctor asked as he stepped toward the force field.

"No," Doctor Mai replied. "Patient C-1 showed minimal life signs when he arrived. After tending to the areas of infection, I induced coma to maximize his body's ability to heal. There has been little progress over the last five days. I suspect I've done little more than postpone the inevitable."

"I don't believe that's the case," the Doctor said. "May I?" he asked, gesturing toward the curtain of energy that separated him from his patient.

"Of course," Mai replied and nodded toward the nurse who obliged her by lowering the field again.

The Doctor moved to the biobed where the man rested beneath a medical arch, covered with a thin sheet. He performed a complete visual examination of the man's body. The multiple obvious injuries the patient had sustained were more troubling than the reports suggested. The arch readings showed there were numerous internal and external wounds, most of which were several months old. That the patient had not already died of them was amazing, but no real mystery to the Doctor. A quick scan with his tricorder revealed the unmistakable presence of catoms. Unlike Seven's, however, they did not appear to be repairing the damaged tissues around them. At first blush, the Doctor believed they might be dormant.

After a few moments spent confirming his suspicions as well as his dismay at the sickbay's status, the Doctor turned to Mai and Commander Glenn and said, "We need to transport him to the *Galen* immediately."

"Why?" Glenn asked.

"Absolutely not," Mai added over her.

"I see," the Doctor said. "Please lower the force field."

The nurse complied as Mai stared openmouthed while the Doctor moved to leave the sickbay.

"Doctor?" she demanded.

"Yes?" he replied pleasantly.

"Patient C-1 poses a serious security risk," Mai began.

"Not while comatose," the Doctor said. "And with all due respect, Doctor, *Galen*'s security capabilities dwarf yours. Further, I cannot help him without access to several systems and programs unique to my sickbay."

"You've been ordered to help him," Commander Glenn reminded the Doctor.

"Fine." The Doctor nodded. "Computer, begin Mark One level nineteen cellular composite neural scan."

A sharp bleat was followed by the computer's response. *"Unable to comply."*

The Doctor nodded, then turned to Glenn. "The catoms currently sustaining his neural functions will not be visible on any other scan. I need to know how many catoms are in there and how well they are functioning before I can begin to figure out how best to help them do their work."

Mai nodded subtly. "Then he is Caeliar."

"No, he isn't," the Doctor said.

"How can you be sure?" Mai demanded.

"You have access to the same classified reports I do, Doctor Mai," the Doctor chided her. "While his injuries make it difficult to precisely visualize his 'normal' anatomy and physiology, he bears absolutely no resemblance to any of the life-forms described by *Titan*'s crew."

Mai's lips tightened into a thin line. "Those reports were

only made available to me a few days ago. It's an incredible amount of data. I'll admit my review was probably not as thorough as it should be. But Captain Erika Hernandez, who was Caeliar by the time our officers encountered her, was described as a female human apparently in her twenties."

"I would suggest that you consider Captain Hernandez a special case," the Doctor said. "I doubt seriously we will ever see her like again."

"Starfleet Medical reports on Seven of Nine indicate she also retained her human appearance even after the Borg implants disappeared."

"A less-special case, but more instructive in this instance," the Doctor allowed.

"His genetic profile shows mixed humanoid characteristics of no known species. But he arrived on a Caeliar vessel," Mai argued.

"So that's it?" the Doctor asked sharply.

"Doctor," Glenn warned softly.

"There was nothing in my files about Caeliar *vessels,*" the Doctor went on. "Do they even have them? They traveled in city ships. However, there were many images of transformed Borg vessels. I believe that's what we have here. The Caeliar, as best we understand them, are comprised completely of programmable matter, or catoms. This man possesses a limited quantity of catoms. Most of his tissues are humanoid, and the only reason we can't identify them is because we've never encountered his species before."

"Where does a humanoid containing Caeliar catoms come from?" Mai asked.

"The Borg," Glenn replied.

"Yes." The Doctor nodded. "This man was clearly once a drone. Before the Caeliar transformation happened, he'd either had some of his Borg implants removed or more likely, tried to forcibly remove them himself. Obviously, he made an absolute mess of it. I would hazard a guess that he was suffering intense psychological trauma at the time and was likely already severed from the Collective when he performed the excisions."

"Wasn't all Borg technology, including all drones, transformed by the Caeliar?" Mai asked.

"Recent discoveries by the Full Circle fleet have confirmed that most, but certainly not *all,* former drones were taken into the Caeliar gestalt."

"You are referring to Seven of Nine?" Doctor Mai asked pointedly.

"Among others," the Doctor replied. "What we do know now is that all drones were offered membership in the gestalt. None were forced to accept it. In every case of those who did not join the Caeliar, any remaining Borg technology was replaced by catoms coded to perform very specific and limited functions. Our patient's catoms are the only thing keeping him alive. If you want to know the rest of his story, I'm going to have to help them restore his body completely. But as I said, I can't do that here."

"Very well," Mai replied. "I will process the orders for his transfer immediately. I will join you aboard *Galen*."

"That won't be necessary," the Doctor said. "I will keep you apprised of his progress."

"You're a consulting physician here, Doctor," Mai reminded him. "Patient C-1 is and will remain under my direct supervision."

Off a sharp glance from Glenn, the Doctor nodded with feigned amiability even as he moved the files containing all of his new research on Seven into a discreet protected buffer. Those present in *Galen*'s computer were already segregated and would not be accessible to Doctor Mai or anyone else unless he authorized it.

"Thank you, Doctor Mai," Commander Glenn added cordially, obviously troubled by the friction between the two physicians.

"I'll await both of you aboard the *Galen,*" the Doctor retorted and left the sickbay without a backward glance.

INDIANA

Kathryn Janeway had been as good as her word. A little after six in the evening, local time, she had transmitted a message indicating she had reached the nearest transporter station and would arrive at her family home within minutes.

Unable to contain herself any longer, Gretchen had rushed out the front door and onto the large wooden porch. Even in the fading light, Kathryn's form and gait were unmistakable as she made her way up the long path that led from the residence to the main road. It did not surprise Gretchen that Kathryn would take a few minutes to gently reacquaint herself with her home. Vast fragrant fields and ancient trees surrounded the property and had always been a refuge for her family. Gretchen knew Kathryn had missed them as much as the home's occupant.

As soon as Kathryn caught sight of her, her pace quickened, and Gretchen's feet found unusual speed for her eight decades. Within moments, they were in each other's arms, and as soon as they were, the world was a perfect place.

Soon enough, Gretchen stood back, examining her daughter at arm's length while still keeping firm grasp of her triceps.

"What's wrong?" Gretchen asked immediately.

"Nothing that a night at home won't cure," Kathryn offered, smiling with her lips but not her eyes.

As they approached the porch, her younger daughter, Phoebe, stepped into the threshold. Until the day she had heard the miraculous news of Kathryn's recovery, Phoebe had held on to her anger, both at Kathryn and Starfleet. Kathryn stepped onto the deck, saying her sister's name softly and opening her arms to embrace her. Phoebe's face was a mask of shock. She looked almost like a startled deer, ready to flee. Trusting her instincts, Kathryn slowed her steps, giving Phoebe the time she needed. The moment their hands touched, Phoebe dissolved into violent tears, made all the more intense because they had been restrained for so long.

Kathryn took her sister in her arms and comforted her with soft words. Gretchen moved past them to the kitchen, content to give her daughters time alone.

After several minutes, they walked arm in arm into the kitchen where the table had already been set for three. Kathryn finally looked relaxed, and though Phoebe's fair skin was blotched with severe red patches and her eyes still glistened, she smiled at her sister in unreserved adoration.

"Mmm," Kathryn said, inhaling deeply. "Is that venison?" Detaching herself from Phoebe, she moved to the stove and removed the lid from the largest pot.

"No fingers," Gretchen ordered, offering Kathryn a large wooden spoon she then used to retrieve a sample. There was nothing feigned or forced in the pleasure that lit her face as she swallowed her first bite.

"Oh, Mom," she said. "That's heaven."

"Sit," Gretchen ordered, and Kathryn pecked her on the cheek as she passed her and crossed to the table.

No culinary effort had been spared on this night. Freshly baked wheat bread, newly churned butter, and homemade preserves were already on the table, along with a tall pitcher of iced tea. The stew was filled with vegetables from Gretchen's garden. When they were younger, the girls had chided their mother relentlessly for her "traditionalist" ways. Modern technology had made such efforts a waste of time. Finally both had come to appreciate that there were some things no technology could replicate, and whole natural foods were one of them. There were certainly no complaints as they settled themselves and began to eat.

Dinner conversation was light and peppered with outbursts of laughter. Fond memories were recalled, gentle teases exchanged. For Gretchen, who had never thought to sit again in Kathryn's company, it was a stolen hour of absolute joy.

Finally, Phoebe's coffee and Gretchen's caramel brownies were served. Kathryn had eaten heartily enough, but she was content to pick at dessert as her thoughts drifted back to whatever had been bothering her when she first arrived.

It was Phoebe, of course, who turned the conversation to more troubling subjects. Though she loved her sister dearly, their adult relationship had been filled with challenges, most stemming from Phoebe's insistence that Kathryn share more than she was inclined, or allowed to do.

"Mom said Command is forcing you to undergo some sort of test," Phoebe began as she reached for her second brownie.

Kathryn nodded. "It's typical under the circumstances."

"Typical?" Phoebe chuckled. "How many officers have returned from the dead?"

"A few." Kathryn smiled.

"So how long until you're free?" Phoebe asked.

Kathryn's brow furrowed. "Free?"

"Won't they retire you once their curiosity is satisfied?"

Kathryn stole a glance toward her mother. Gretchen shook her head. She had not wanted anything to taint Kathryn's homecoming and had not shared her suspicions that Kathryn would return to active duty once her evaluations were complete.

"My next assignment has not been decided," Kathryn began. "But whether I remain here on Earth, or return to the fleet, I won't be retiring, Phoebe."

Phoebe glanced between her mother and sister, the lightness that had graced her features settling into brittle lines. "They haven't taken enough from you yet?" she demanded.

Both of her girls were tough. Kathryn favored her father, particularly his temperament—her cool reserve and stubborn willfulness masked deep wells of intense passion and almost infinite capacity for delight and wonder. Phoebe was Gretchen's doppelganger, with curly brown hair and icy blue eyes that stormed gray when she was angry. Her passion was no less than her sister's, but she expressed it without hesitation or thought. Kathryn had followed Edward into Starfleet's service, but Phoebe had never entertained the notion. She'd spent most of her life exploring a variety of creative endeavors before settling into a career of painting and collage construction.

Clearly determined not to completely spoil the evening, Kathryn replied gently, "*They* have taken nothing from me, Phoebe. *They* have given me the unique opportunity to explore the mysteries of our universe; to be of service to all people of the Federation."

"They're not sending you back out there?" Phoebe demanded, horrified at the thought.

"I don't know yet," Kathryn said.

Phoebe sat back in her chair, her face again erupting in streaks of red. "But you want to go?"

"I don't know."

Phoebe shook her head in disbelief. "Why would you?"

"It's what I'm best at," Kathryn replied, with honesty that seemed to take her by surprise.

"You've never raised a hand to anything you did not ultimately master," Phoebe argued.

"There was ballet," Gretchen interjected, hoping to bring a little levity back to the table. Off Kathryn's surprised look she added, "You were, of course, gorgeous, my angel, but a prima ballerina . . . never."

"Yes, well," Kathryn grudgingly agreed.

"This isn't funny, Mom," Phoebe admonished her.

"I'm sorry, Phoebe," Kathryn said.

"No, you're not," her sister retorted. "You have no idea what your death did to the people who love you. You weren't here. You're *never* here. Starfleet told us to give you up for dead when you were lost in the Delta Quadrant. *We* didn't. But when the Borg turned you into a monster and then the ship you were on was destroyed, we *had* to."

"Phoebe," Gretchen said sharply.

"Daddy's death, Justin's death, I know what they did to

you, Kathryn. I was there. Believe it or not, *your* death was harder to take. It wasn't an accident. You chose to go out there, chose to risk everything for what? Curiosity? And now you're ready to do it again? When is enough, enough, Kathryn? When will you accept the reality that not every problem out there is yours to solve? Does it matter to you at all that you aren't the only one who pays for your choices?

"You know what?" Phoebe said, rising from her chair. "I won't do it again. I won't grieve your inevitable loss one more time. I can't."

Phoebe turned and stormed out, slamming the front door behind her. Likely as not, she was headed out to the old willow tree. In days past, Kathryn would have risen to follow her. This time, she remained in her chair, her face swirling with a tempest of emotions.

Gretchen placed a comforting hand over Kathryn's. Her daughter's flesh was so cold. "She just needs time, darling. It's a lot to take in."

Kathryn's eyes met hers, filled with doubt. "It's odd," she finally said. "I've spent my entire life determined to do what is right. Looking back now, I can only see all the ways I went wrong."

"Welcome to middle age." Gretchen smiled. "Just remember, regrets are powerful, but they are also lousy companions. That's a truth waiting for you on the other side of middle age."

Kathryn rose to refresh her coffee.

"I've done up your room for you upstairs," Gretchen reminded her. "You're probably exhausted."

Kathryn nodded. "I'll just spend a few minutes in dad's office. I want to check in before I go to bed."

"Of course," Gretchen said. It had been more than two decades since her husband's death. Fewer since her daughters had moved out. And while their childhood rooms had eventually been redecorated and transformed for more utilitarian purposes, Edward's office was still as he had left it: a permanent memorial.

Gretchen busied herself with the dishes. She was just pouring the remains of the stew into a container when Kathryn returned to the kitchen, more calm, but seemingly energized.

Gretchen knew that look all too well.

"You have to return tonight?"

Kathryn nodded.

"You're not letting your sister run you off, right?"

Kathryn smiled, shaking her head, and moved again to embrace her mother. "I'll check in tomorrow. And I'll be back here as often as I can over the next several weeks. This isn't good-bye, Mom."

Gretchen hugged her firmly. "It never is, my angel."

SAN FRANCISCO

Less than ten minutes after leaving her mother's home, Janeway was again at her desk at Starfleet headquarters. Although many offices were empty, there was still a fair amount of activity, even this late in the evening. Janeway could easily have read the letter she had just received, the one that had driven her from Indiana, at her main computer terminal. But her office felt far too confining. She needed air.

Transferring the letter onto a padd, Janeway left her office. There was moderate foot traffic in the wide plaza that fronted the building. Heedless of her direction, Janeway turned and began walking. The simple exercise was intoxicating.

Her mother could never suffocate her. She had mastered the art of letting go, first learned at the hands of her husband. Janeway knew she would return for several more lengthy visits with her mother, and she looked forward to them.

Her sister was another matter. Phoebe's will was a force to match Janeway's, and when it was directed toward her with such ferocious pain, it was excruciating. Janeway had known that many people had suffered when she'd been declared dead. But until now, none of them had shared that suffering with her so viscerally. Part of her wanted to ease Phoebe's pain. But she also knew that her sister was holding on to that pain for her own reasons and trying to use them as a cudgel to force Janeway to do her bidding. The admiral did not believe she had ever attempted to manipulate another's emotions so callously. But she understood the desire. Where love was given, power was granted. Janeway could never take back the elemental love that was the bond between her and her sister, but she would hold her own power close, until Phoebe realized that she was guilty of the same trespass she'd leveled against her sister. Janeway's problems were not hers to solve, no matter how well-intentioned Phoebe's desire to see her sister live a long life. Phoebe was accustomed to living life on her own terms, but when she disagreed with another's choices, she was usually unwilling to grant them the same consideration. Phoebe thought she knew what was best, and damn anyone who disagreed with her.

Janeway knew she shared this trait, but she had been struck this night by Phoebe's audacity. Still, she knew that she could not avoid the mirror forever. What gave her the right to decide who should live or die? The pips on her collar? They were mere symbols, meant to demonstrate the experience she had gained and the trust her superiors placed in her. They conveyed power to those who wore them, but not necessarily character. Janeway had never doubted her ability to trust herself. Now it seemed everywhere she turned, she was surrounded by people who did not trust her, and it was becoming more and more difficult not to allow their misgivings to be added to her own.

The admiral paused as she walked into a large pool of light cast from a lamp above. To her right was a small bench. The brisk walk had warmed her, and the paths around her were all but deserted. Settling herself, she took the padd and placed it on her lap to read. It was a transmission from *Titan.* She anxiously opened the letter.

Admiral Janeway:

I am writing to you on behalf of my husband, Tuvok. I know he has not yet responded to your message, and while I understand his reticence, I also believe you should not be forced to interpret his silence in the absence of data.

My husband and I are now living aboard the Federation Starship Titan. *Tuvok continues to perform his duties conscientiously and to the best of his abilities. We were on* Titan *when we learned of your death. It was a particularly difficult loss for Tuvok to endure, but his deep and abiding respect for you was a source of strength.*

Our son, Elieth, and his wife, Ione Kitain, were both killed when Deneva was destroyed by the Borg. Tuvok had not been able to see Elieth or meet his wife prior to their deaths. Their loss, coupled with the intense stresses shared by all who witnessed the assault of the Borg, has left my husband struggling to assert the imperatives of logic over his emotional responses. His discipline is formidable, and I do not doubt that in time, he will again master them. Indeed, he works tirelessly toward this end.

My husband believes it would be unwise to speak with you at this time. I will not question the wisdom of his choice. I can only assume that to do so might make his efforts more difficult. I am certain eventually he will wish to express appropriate sentiments regarding your return. It is to Starfleet's benefit that your death was presumed in error. Until he is able to do so, on behalf of us both, I wish you peace and long life.

T'Pel

After reading it twice, Janeway set the padd beside her and inhaled deeply. She was more worried than wounded. What she read between the lines was T'Pel's concern for Tuvok's emotional well-being. For Tuvok's pain and ongoing struggle to warrant his wife's response on his behalf, Janeway could only assume that whatever pleasure Tuvok might have experienced in learning of her return had been mitigated by much darker unresolved issues regarding his son and daughter-in-law's deaths.

Janeway did not see Tuvok's actions as a sign of diminished affection on his part. Had he cared less, it would have been no trouble for him to respond cordially and positively to her message. But he could not reach beyond his pain at this time to offer Janeway any relief of her own. That Tuvok had apparently lost this much of himself was terrifying to contemplate.

She could hear the accusations now. *Why had she been spared? Billions had died, but she alone merited some special consideration on the part of the universe?* Her death would have been difficult to accept, but death was part of the natural order of things. Her return defied logic.

Shaking these haunting thoughts aside, she rose. A chill had entered her bones as she sat, and she looked around for a source of warmth. Turning, Janeway found herself at the gates of a large park. Passing through the stone archway, she realized at once where she was and wondered if subconsciously she had intended to come here all along.

Federation Park was a vast plain of manicured grass sloping down toward the San Francisco Bay. Spaced throughout were monuments of assorted shapes and sizes, tributes to Starfleet personnel lost in the line of duty. To her right, in the distance, a white sphere blazed. It was the memorial that had been raised to the fallen of the Full Circle fleet.

Unconsciously, Janeway turned to her left and began to walk among the stones, putting as much distance as possible between herself and the blazing reminder of the cost of her choices.

She wandered aimlessly for a time, content to allow the peace of the park to seep into her bones. She stopped short when she saw, several meters ahead, a large pillar topped by an eternal flame. Their second night together, in some detail, Chakotay had described her memorial service and the monument erected in her honor. He had spoken of a long night spent there and the choice he had made to leave Starfleet.

It was impossible for her to avoid the structure's magnetic properties. Her feet moved toward it as Janeway wondered idly why it had not been removed. She didn't know the protocol, but she was determined to rectify the situation as soon as possible.

Up close, the masonry was imposing. She passed over the plaque embedded near the base. It was odd to see her name there, and it sent spiders of ice running up and down her spine.

Here, not that long ago, her lover, partner, and dearest friend had found solace and direction. He had moved beyond personal concerns and emotional demands and chosen a new path. That choice had ultimately led Chakotay back to his place in command of the crew she would always think of as *theirs*. Janeway wondered if the tall, cold stone would have similar inspiration to offer her.

Curious, she bent low and began to poke at the ground at the pillar's base. It took a little doing, but soon enough, her fingers touched cold metal. Moments later, she unearthed the combadge and pips Chakotay told her he had buried there.

Janeway was not in uniform. She had changed into a casual shirt and pants for dinner at home. Even if she were, she knew at this moment, she would *not* have placed her own symbols of command beside Chakotay's. Her desire to be of service to Starfleet had not diminished. All she had suffered, lost, and endured over what felt like only a month had left her disconnected, a stranger to herself in many ways. But that one definition remained basic and true.

Less clear was *how* she could be of service. And try as they might, none of those around her now could help her see that path clearly. Her blood relations were on Earth, but as she gently rubbed the dirt from Chakotay's badge and pips, she knew that *her family* was thousands of light-years away.

Heavens knew that none of her fellow officers at Command, or the well-meaning Counselor Jens, could offer helpful advice. They could imagine her challenges, but they could never truly understand them.

Suddenly Janeway knew what she needed. So alarming was the insight, she laughed involuntarily.

She needed to speak to someone who had walked the same path. Thankfully, his current mission was relatively close to Earth.

The matter settled, Admiral Janeway hurried from the park. First thing in the morning, she would sign out a shuttle and set course to *Enterprise.*

Chapter Nine

VOYAGER

"There, there, and there," Commander O'Donnell said, pointing out the visible discrepancies between the wave form that had destroyed *Voyager*'s probe and the two that had emerged later. The shift in frequency was subtle and within the sensor's miniscule error margin, but Chakotay had to admit that they were present. Believing that O'Donnell had not personally followed the interaction, Chakotay had been surprised by the thoroughness of his understanding of the wave forms and the intuitive leaps he had made regarding them.

Liam O'Donnell was not to be underestimated.

Chakotay looked to Kim and Seven expecting to see skepticism. Instead, both appeared intrigued. To his left, Lieutenant Patel and Doctor Sharak conferred quietly as they studied the image Commander O'Donnell had brought up on the conference room's three-dimensional display.

"Computer, display image O'Donnell six alpha," the commander ordered, and the frequency display was replaced by a magnified projection of the center mass of the two wave forms. Here, the differences were more striking. The wave form that had crushed the probe emitted powerful visible fields, streaks of energy radiating from its outer edge toward its center. The second wave forms did not.

"Despite its appearance, Commander," Seven said, "the second wave forms were capable of emitting high frequency

EM discharges. The fact that they had not yet done so when these images were captured does not necessarily indicate passive intentions on its part."

"But now, we'll never know, will we?" O'Donnell asked.

After a moment Kim shook his head. "Even without the energy discharges, this wave form was more than capable of surrounding our ship, penetrating our shields, disabling many systems, and making it impossible for us to create a warp field."

"Yes, but *Voyager* survived that once, didn't she?" O'Donnell asked. When Kim nodded, he went on. "I realize the hours you spent in the company of that distortion ring were unpleasant, but isn't it worth it for the possibility of making contact with this thing. What if it's a life-form?"

"It isn't," Patel said.

O'Donnell favored her with a withering gaze.

Doctor Sharak jumped in. "Commander, nothing in *Voyager*'s first encounter suggested life was present. Motion, intention, limited communication capabilities, yes, but not metabolism."

"It's a piece of technology, Commander," Patel finished for him. "Very powerful technology."

"And technology has never yet surpassed its creator's designs and achieved sentience, has it?" O'Donnell asked rhetorically. "Oh, wait . . ." he added, tapping his palm to his forehead a little too theatrically.

"I'm less interested in its potential for sentience than its intentions toward us," Chakotay said. "We believe the first wave form we encountered wanted help. Thus far, nothing confirms that these are the same or that they require assistance."

"A moment, Captain," Patel said. Turning toward O'Donnell, she asked, "Would you mind restoring the image of the frequencies?" The *Demeter*'s commander complied, and Patel added a third image to the display. "This is a complementary image of the distortion ring *Voyager* first encountered. When considered in its wave state, it is nearly identical to the two forms that approached the ship. Its particle form, however, is a little more interesting."

"How so?" Chakotay asked.

The science officer entered commands into the data panel, the image shifted immediately to display the atomic structure of all three. Significant gaps were present in the distortion ring, but otherwise, the image was identical to that of the wave forms. "One thing we never considered about the first distortion ring was that it might have been damaged during the two hundred years it spent wandering open space. This image suggests that it was. That might also explain why its transmission was so difficult to decode. It is highly likely that the wave forms that approached our ships a few hours ago were an undamaged version of the same technology."

"Is it likely that this is a means of communication? A transfer of data that was triggered from the first wave form once its scans of us were complete?" Chakotay asked.

"There's no way to tell at this point," Patel replied.

"There might be," Kim countered.

"How?" Chakotay asked.

"When I tried to make contact with the wave form, I encrypted our hails to match the coding we received from the distortion ring," Kim said.

"That wouldn't have worked," O'Donnell said.

"It didn't." Kim nodded. "And now I know why."

"Enlighten us, Harry?" Chakotay asked.

"The original data we received was so corrupted that no reverse encryption I could create would have been recognized. It had already been run through several complex linguistic algorithms, and many of them would have created transcription errors when run in reverse."

"We need to transmit the original data we received," Chakotay said.

Kim and O'Donnell nodded simultaneously.

"We also need designations for the two distinct types of

wave forms we have now discovered." O'Donnell added, "Just to minimize any confusion going forward."

"Let me be clear," Chakotay said. "I will not allow *Voyager* or *Demeter* to be surrounded again by one of these wave forms, even if that is the only way to communicate with it. *Voyager*'s previous encounter did not result in lasting damage. But I am not convinced that would be the case now. Both of these wave forms are more powerful than the first."

"Sentries and proctors," Kim offered.

"One is designed to protect this region and the other to gather information," O'Donnell interpreted.

"Scanners would be more precise than proctors," Seven suggested.

"No," Kim argued. "The distortion ring *Voyager* first encountered could have transmitted its data to us at any time while it was in contact with us. It only did so *after* its scans were complete."

"It was testing you," O'Donnell said. "The first time, you passed."

Kim shrugged. "This time we failed."

"Well, why don't we see if we can improve our grade?" Chakotay asked.

Voyager had returned to its previous position bordering the cloaked area. O'Donnell kept *Demeter* within the proximity of the ship's long-range sensors. If all went well, they could join *Voyager* within a few hours.

Lieutenant Kim had retrieved the original transmission and provided it to Lieutenant Lasren. As soon as the ship was in range, the ops officer sent out the transmission on all subspace bands.

"Transmission complete," Lasren reported.

The bridge crew waited, tense for some sort of reply.

"Helm, prepare to go to warp if . . ." But Chakotay did not have time to finish the statement. Seconds later, the ship rocked beneath him, and multiple alarms began to sound.

"Warning, shields have been breached," the computer advised.

"Report!" Chakotay shouted.

"It's a proctor," Kim advised. "It emerged from subspace directly beneath the ship and has surrounded us."

"Lasren, give me ship-wide," Paris requested. Off Lasren's nod, he ordered, "This is Commander Paris to all hands. Remain exactly where you are until further advised."

"Navigation?" Chakotay asked.

"Helm not responding," Gwyn reported.

Silence descended around them. A faint tingling began in Chakotay's extremities, followed by a dull roar in his head. The sensation ended so abruptly, he wondered if he had imagined it.

Seconds later, the alarms ceased.

Kim was the first to speak. "It's gone, sir."

"That was it?" Paris asked, both surprised and relieved.

"Our database has been uploaded," Lasren advised.

"Did it leave any messages for us?" Chakotay asked.

"No, sir," Lasren replied.

"I'm not so sure," Kim interjected. "Captain?"

Chakotay's eyes turned to the main viewscreen where it seemed as if a veil had been lifted. Suddenly, it was no longer black. The darkness had been replaced by hundreds of pinpoints of light.

"Several sections of the cloaking matrix have been disabled, Captain," Kim reported.

"Sections?" Chakotay asked.

"I'd like to confirm with Seven and compare this to her initial navigation chart," Gwyn said from the helm. "It looks like they've cleared a path for us through the field."

Chakotay smiled. "Advise *Demeter* to join us, and to prepare to be scanned," he ordered Paris. "Ask Counselor Cambridge to report to astrometrics. Lieutenant Kim, you're with me. Mister Paris, you have the bridge."

Counselor Hugh Cambridge hadn't had many opportunities over the years he had served on *Voyager* to utilize his skills as a first-contact specialist. When Chakotay ordered him to astrometrics, he knew he'd be dusting them off, and he looked forward to it. Cambridge was relieved that contact with the new wave form had not produced the same effects as the ship's first encounter, though the thought of a few hours trapped in Seven's company had its charms. She had been intently focused on her work over the past few days, and he had not pushed her to make time for more personal liaisons. They had all the time in the universe to explore one another, but to push her was to court resistance.

"Seven, Counselor," Chakotay greeted them energetically as he entered the lab. "What do we have?"

Nodding to the large screen before them, Seven began. "Approximately thirty-point-four percent of the field has been disabled."

"Where's the star system you detected?" Kim asked, studying the screen.

"It does not fall within the visible area," Seven replied. "There is, however, a vast asteroid field ahead, a section of which is now visible that we will have to navigate if we intend to follow the course provided to us."

"You said they did not transmit any data to us?" Cambridge asked, puzzled.

"I believe their intention is clear, nonetheless," Seven replied. "A section of space has been revealed, and it seems likely that if we follow it, we will reach the far end of this protected space."

"Does this look like an invitation to you, Hugh?" Chakotay asked.

"That's one possibility," Cambridge allowed.

"There are others?" Kim asked.

"Assuming this is an answer to the transmission we sent,

they know why we came here. Their scan of our vessel must have apprised them of our capabilities, as best they can understand them. They might be saying, 'Welcome. Keep to the path and proceed.' But showing us this intensely uninteresting area of their space could also be interpreted as, 'Nothing to see here . . . move along.'"

"They didn't have to show us anything," Chakotay said.

"I think our first foray into their territory clearly demonstrated that we knew them. They don't want anyone in there. Otherwise, they wouldn't go to so much trouble to hide this much space. Most would conclude that what they've shown us is not worth investigating further."

"Might they be directing us to an area of their space not yet in sensor range?" Kim asked.

"Perhaps an area with a denser population of sentries capable of destroying our ship," Seven suggested.

"An unpleasant, but not improbable, hypothesis," Cambridge agreed.

"Bridge to Captain Chakotay," Commander Paris's voice called.

"Go ahead," Chakotay said.

"Demeter *has arrived."*

Chakotay appeared dumbstruck. "They were hours away at maximum warp."

"They did a quick slipstream jump, sir," Paris said. *"And they have just been scanned by a proctor."*

"Any damage?" Chakotay asked.

"None, sir," Paris reported.

"Advise Commander O'Donnell to hold position until I contact him personally."

"Aye, sir."

Cambridge chuckled internally. Watching Chakotay work with O'Donnell amused him considerably. Chakotay was determined to demonstrate the fleet's ability to work cohesively, while following Starfleet guidelines to the letter. Sadly, these priorities had no appeal to O'Donnell.

His attention was diverted by a shocked intake of breath from Seven. Cambridge turned to her and found her staring openmouthed at the lab's viewscreen. He followed her gaze.

"What just happened?" Kim asked.

"The entire cloaking matrix has just been disabled," Seven replied, clearly awed by the development.

"Anything significant?" Chakotay asked.

"The star system is now visible," Seven said. "It contains one Class-M planet with billions of life-forms."

Chakotay considered this for a few moments, then turned again to Cambridge. "What do you think now, Counselor?"

"I think they liked something they saw in *Demeter* more than us, sir," Cambridge replied. "If they were, in fact, testing us, *Voyager* passed, but *Demeter* aced it."

A flurry of complicated emotions passed over the captain's face.

"Are we going to investigate, Captain?" Kim asked.

"Yes," Chakotay replied. "But, we're going to let *Demeter* take the lead."

Chapter Ten

GALEN

The Doctor watched intently as patient C-1's vital signs crept erratically upward. Several days of study had allowed the Doctor to pinpoint all of the catoms present in his body. There were significant clusters in his neural tissue, surrounding his heart, stomach, and intestines. The Doctor knew from his initial extractions of Seven's Borg technology when she was severed from the Collective that these areas would have contained various nodes enabling the drone's link to the Borg Collective and fortifying its vulnerable yet essential internal organs. Many normal bodily processes were circumnavigated by these nodes, allowing a drone to ingest the energy it required to function through regeneration, rather than the messier and more time-consuming processes of eating and eliminating waste.

The catoms present in these areas were plentiful and most likely all that had allowed the man to survive. However, they were noticeably absent at some of the areas of greatest physical trauma, including his left auditory canal and left arm. Numerous superficial wounds covering his torso and legs complicated matters as they had become infected and were only now responding to antibiotic therapies.

It seemed clear to the Doctor that patient C-1 had forcibly removed a specialized auditory receptor, or at least the part that had once replaced his left ear, much of the Borg armor that covered his body, and whatever grotesque appendage had been grafted to the remains of his left hand. C-1 still possessed a left thumb, but most of that hand and the other fingers had been severed, presumably at assimilation. While those areas were not critical to his survival, they had also become infected before the introduction of the Caeliar catoms. He could have suffered for weeks, working haphazardly on the extractions, and growing ever weaker before the Caeliar transformation saved his life.

Superficial damage was now almost fully healed. The catoms the Doctor had initially believed were dormant were also showing increasing signs of activity. Given this, he had decided it was safe to risk reviving the patient. Naturally, the Doctor would not induce consciousness until he was certain C-1's body was stabilized, but his vitals had begun to fluctuate the moment the trinephedrine had been administered.

"His pressure is elevated, Doctor," Commander Glenn noted.

"As is his heart rate," the Doctor added. "Injecting twenty milliliters of lectrazine."

"It's still climbing, Doctor," Glenn advised.

"Five cc's quadroline," the Doctor ordered, and Glenn immediately injected it into the patient's neck.

"No change," Glenn said.

"Reducing flow of trinephedrine."

Glenn looked up. "You're not going to . . ." she began.

"I can't stabilize him like this. We bring him any further out, he'll go into shock."

Glenn nodded as all of the patient's vitals began to fall, returning to the levels at which they had been sustained for almost a week.

The Doctor turned away to study the neural monitor. He nodded to himself, satisfied that the attempt had not done any further damage to C-1's central nervous system.

Once it was clear that the patient was out of danger, Glenn moved to stand by his side. "What now?" she asked.

The Doctor shook his head, frustrated. "I don't know. I've

seen Seven's catoms do such miraculous things. I just don't understand why those present in his body aren't being more assertive. I know they can repair the rest of the damage and restore him to full health. But they aren't."

"What if he doesn't want them to?" Glenn asked.

"Commander?"

"This man, whoever he was, somehow managed to escape the Collective *before* the Caeliar transformation. At some point after that escape, he began to forcibly remove all of the Borg technology he could access with his bare hands, and he wasn't exactly careful about it. He did not join the gestalt, which means the Caeliar must have been honoring a choice they felt him capable of making. But maybe he didn't want to join them because he didn't want to live. Powerful as these catoms are, do we know if they have any effect on psychological damage? We may be looking at an intentional suicide."

"Are you saying we shouldn't try to save him?" asked Doctor Mai, who had observed the proceedings.

"I'm saying I don't know if we can," Glenn clarified.

The Doctor moved to the bay's central data panel and brought up his most recent scan of C-1's catoms. He was unwilling to display Seven's catoms beside them but was running his own internal comparative scan when a new piece of data came to his attention. "What is this?" he asked of Glenn.

The commander moved to his side and replied, "I completed the coding analysis you requested. It took some time as we only have one sample to use for comparison."

"Seven's," the Doctor said.

"Yes. According to his catoms, the Borg identified this man as Five of Twelve, Secondary Adjunct of Trimatrix Nine Four Two."

That piece of data was immediately flagged by the Doctor's long-term memory buffers and routed to his segregated files. When the data match was confirmed, the Doctor walked briskly back to the patient's side and studied his face.

"Doctor?" Glenn asked.

"I . . ." the Doctor hesitated.

"Doctor?" Mai repeated, clearly hoping to draw him out.

"I . . . that is to say, Seven knew this man."

"Seven of Nine provided you with a comprehensive listing of every drone present in the Collective while she was a part of it?" Mai asked dubiously.

The Doctor shook his head. He knew his face was registering shock, but the realities and possibilities of this new information were overloading his analytic subroutines.

"Who is he?" Glenn asked.

"His name, before he was assimilated, and when Seven knew him in Unimatrix Zero, was Axum," the Doctor replied.

"So?" Mai demanded.

"We're going to try one more thing," the Doctor replied.

STARBASE 185

Once the Doctor had briefed her on his plan to attempt to fortify "Axum's" catoms, Doctor Mai excused herself from his sickbay and transported back to her office aboard the starbase.

She hadn't had much to report to her superiors in the last few days, but the revelation of the patient's identity and his connection to Seven of Nine required action on her part; action she could not take while aboard *Galen* as she could not risk Commander Glenn or her crew discovering it.

Mai quickly composed a message and encrypted it, forwarding it to Starfleet Medical. From there, she knew it would be routed to the Federation Institute of Health.

The doctor had no idea what the result of this transmission would be, only that she was under orders to relay any significant developments with patient C-1 immediately.

She then considered stopping in the mess hall for a quick bite, but troubled by the certainty that the Doctor had been less than forthcoming in his plans for C-1, Mai opted to return to the *Galen.* Hunger she could manage. Failing to do her duty was out of the question.

ENTERPRISE

The first face Admiral Janeway saw when she stepped out of her shuttle onto the deck of the *Enterprise* was that of its commanding officer, Captain Jean-Luc Picard. He looked weary but well, and his lips formed a mischievous smile as their eyes met.

"It seems the rumors of your death were premature," he said warmly as he stepped forward to take her hand.

Grinning sincerely, she replied, "I've heard another rumor, Captain; one I found almost impossible to believe."

"What was that, Admiral?"

"You are a father?" Janeway teased.

"Guilty as charged." Picard sighed. "I can produce the evidence, should my assurances fail to convince you."

Janeway laughed lightly. "It's the middle of the night. Let him sleep."

"Sleep?" Picard chuckled. "I've never in my life wished so dearly to know the identity of the man who coined the phrase 'sleeping like a baby.' Either he was badly translated or is long overdue for a flogging."

"Congratulations, Jean-Luc," Janeway replied through her mirth, "to you and Doctor Crusher."

"Thank you. I left her pacing our quarters, René in her arms, and I will place no wagers as to who will collapse first."

"My money is on René," Janeway replied.

"A safe but not certain bet," Picard assured her.

By the time they reached the captain's ready room, Janeway had dissolved more than once into fits of unseemly laughter as he regaled her with the details of the last few weeks of his life since his son's birth. If fatherhood did nothing else for Picard, it had certainly enhanced his sense of humor.

"What is his full name?" Janeway asked as she settled

herself on the sofa and gratefully accepted black coffee delivered in a lovely porcelain cup.

Picard smirked as he took a sip of his tea and replied, "It was more challenging than I expected to settle on a name for him."

"I was thinking of having a blanket monogrammed," Janeway encouraged him.

"Very well," Picard replied. "He is René Jacques Robert François Picard."

Janeway brought a hand to her lips to hold back her amusement. Forcing her face into more serious lines she asked, "Because being the son of the captain of the Federation flagship and the former head of Starfleet Medical wasn't enough to live up to?"

Picard dropped his chin, laughter shaking his belly. "I must say, though, he already wears it well, all three-point-six kilograms of him."

"I have no doubt," Janeway said.

Their eyes met and the levity they had used to dispel the tension between them evaporated.

"But you didn't come all this way to tease me mercilessly about my son, did you?"

"I haven't laughed this hard, or this much, since I can't remember when," Janeway replied seriously. "Already I know the journey was not wasted."

"It never is, Admiral," Picard said.

Janeway was suddenly taken aback. A most unwelcome wall of rank was rising between them.

"For now, I would prefer Kathryn, if you don't object."

"How can I help you, Kathryn?" he asked, settling himself beside her.

Now that the moment had come, she found herself at a loss. They had shared so many common experiences, but they really did not know each other well. Janeway felt that she was trespassing on his kindness. The least she could grant him was the courtesy of not wasting his time.

"I don't know how much you know of the circumstances of my reported death and return," she began.

"The formal communiqué was less than generous with details," he said.

Janeway nodded. "You know I was assimilated by that cube."

"I was there," he noted somberly, "and I do not bear you the slightest ill will or hold you in any way responsible for the actions of the Borg."

"Thank you," she said, wondering how many times he had told himself this before he had been able to accept it.

"Some part of me remained trapped but present after I was assimilated," Janeway said, noticing the confusion furrowing his brow as he nodded for her to continue. "It was that part of me that Seven of Nine reached and which enabled her to deliver the virus that destroyed the cube."

"The Federation is in her debt and yours."

"I don't care about the credit, Jean Luc."

"No," he agreed, "I don't imagine you would."

"It was that part of me that was taken into the Q Continuum once my body was destroyed."

"Q?" Picard asked, clearly taken by surprise.

"My godson, Q's son, convinced me that he was confronting a problem he could not solve without me. He taught me how to restore my body so that I could live again."

At this, Picard's eyes widened. "'Of all the wonders that I yet have heard . . .'"

"Indeed." Janeway smiled faintly. "The problem was the incursion of a continuum into our space/time as powerful as the Q's but its polar opposite in purpose. It was the Omega Continuum. To seal it once and for all and to end the premature destruction of the entire multiverse required the sacrifice of Q's son and the Full Circle fleet's former commanding officer, Captain Afsarah Eden."

Picard bowed his head, fully absorbing the enormity of

the situation. "There's always a price, isn't there?" he asked softly.

"Q said as much, repeatedly as we were working to solve the problem, and is furious with me now," Janeway said flatly. "He said I had made an enemy of him."

"Why?" Picard asked in utter disbelief.

Holding up a hand, Janeway continued. "A few years ago, an Admiral Kathryn Janeway, whose life took a very different path from mine, tried to convince me to use a transwarp hub we discovered to bring *Voyager* home. I opted to destroy it, hoping to cripple the Borg. That action made it possible for *Voyager* to return home sixteen years before it had in her time line. But it also erased an encounter *Voyager* should have had with Omega that would have made my godson and Captain Eden's sacrifice unnecessary."

"Is there anything else Q deigned to lie at your feet?" Picard asked, now obviously angered. "The Borg Invasion, perhaps?"

"It's hard to argue that had I not destroyed that hub . . ." Janeway began.

"Q!" Picard shouted to the heavens.

Janeway's breath caught in her chest as she considered the possibility that Q would answer Picard's summons. When a full minute had passed in silence, Picard went on, "No, he wouldn't admit to such frailty, would he?"

It seemed most unwise to Janeway to tempt fate or Q. But she also found Picard's anger on her behalf comforting.

"Frailty?" she finally asked.

"It's not his irrational anger that surprises me," Picard replied. "Indeed, I refuse to imagine how I would feel should anything like that befall my son. But coming from Q? How often has he reminded us how far beyond our comprehension he is? How often has Q justified his arrogance by asserting his omnipotence? Q was better than us. Until now. Brought low by events beyond his control, he lashes out at you. But even a cursory glance at this time line's history reveals the lie. You faced the Borg many times in the Delta Quadrant, didn't you?"

"Yes."

"Had you known nothing about them, what do you think would have happened to *Voyager* the first time you crossed their path?"

"We would have been destroyed fighting them," she replied.

"You would have been assimilated to the last man," Picard assured her.

"Probably," Janeway admitted.

"You would never have survived to return to the Alpha Quadrant in seven or seventy years, let alone deal with this Omega Continuum."

She nodded.

"But you were prepared to face them because *we* had already encountered them. And who made that possible?" Picard asked.

Janeway's head was suddenly light. She had committed Picard's reports about the Borg to memory without ever making this simple connection.

"Q."

"Q. He first threw us into the path of the Borg. Guinan told me that event had happened several years before it should have. I don't pretend to understand how Guinan knew such a thing, but she's never lied to me. Had Q been so wise, or so committed to safeguarding his eventual offspring, he would *never* have erred so casually. Q said he meant to frighten us, to put us in our place.

"His anger is not with you, Kathryn. Q knows his blame in this. His anger was misplaced because, however briefly, he could not bear to level it against himself, where it belongs."

"You don't think he'll come after me?"

"For all we know, he has. Q could have ended your life countless times, but none would have brought him comfort.

I dare say he regrets his folly now because it has revealed a weakness he would die rather than admit."

"He's more like us than he would ever wish to be," Janeway realized.

Picard nodded. "I wouldn't spend another moment worrying about his retribution, Kathryn."

"Believe it or not, I haven't been."

"Then, what?"

"The Full Circle fleet has suffered catastrophic losses in the last few months. Four ships out of nine remain, and right now only two are still in the Delta Quadrant. Admiral Montgomery asked me to assume command of the fleet, but then rescinded the offer. I've been brought home to undergo a series of evaluations, I believe at Admiral Akaar's insistence."

"Annoying, I'll grant you," Picard said, "but not entirely unexpected."

"I've only met with one of my counselors so far," she went on, "but I don't think he was chosen for this assignment to aid me in any way. If he was, he is incredibly ill-equipped to do so."

"I've been through more than one of those sessions myself, Kathryn. Keep your head down, answer them honestly, and you'll do fine."

"I don't know, Jean-Luc," Janeway admitted. "I don't think they want me out there."

"Will they recall the fleet?"

"It doesn't look like it, but they can't have high hopes for their success if they leave them out there under strength."

Picard turned to look her directly in her eyes and asked, "Do you want the post?"

The question tormented her. When the command was hers, she had accepted it almost grudgingly and certainly with doubts. Chakotay's assurances had quieted them, but they had soon come roaring back with a vengeance. The moment it was taken from her, her determination to reclaim it had become so all-consuming it was difficult to trust.

"Would you?" Janeway asked. "Tens of thousands of light-years beyond Starfleet's aid in the wilds of unexplored space, with so many lives to protect?"

Quietly, Picard replied. "We've been tasked with putting the best possible face on the Federation's rebuilding efforts. What you describe sounds like pure heaven to me right now."

"I don't know if I am the best person for the job or if all I've experienced has broken me in some elemental way. I don't know if the errors of my past are so egregious they make me unfit for command. I don't know if the deep and abiding love and respect I have for those who have served with me for so many years has left me unable to lead them."

"The ability to admit that you do not know is the surest indication of your enduring strength, Kathryn," he insisted. "Absolute certainty might seem comforting, but is actually proof that you've given up. You will learn no more once you have decided you know. Yes, it's harder to live with the certainty that you don't know, that you will surely fail again. But it is essential if you intend to take command of that fleet."

Janeway smiled. "I've been told I have work to do before I even contemplate my future; that if I do not take time to process all I've experienced, it will hinder my ability to be an effective leader."

Picard came just shy of rolling his eyes. "And did those who offered this advice give you any indication of how long that might take? Life doesn't stop at our convenience. And perhaps this 'processing' is best done in the company of those you trust the most."

The *Enterprise*'s captain leaned forward. "Do you know when to ask for help?"

"I'm here, aren't I?" she asked.

"Does your heart still skip a beat when the simplest or greatest wonder appears before your eyes?"

"It does," she said.

"And when the tide finally turns again in your favor, are you humbled with gratitude?"

"Absolutely." She nodded.

"Then you are alive and functioning as well as the rest of us. I know it isn't that simple, Kathryn, but it has become so for me. I was terrified before my son was born that I had finally gone too far, dared to grasp for too much happiness. Now that he is here, those fears are confirmed, but completely powerless. I've made mistakes, been broken by evil, and wished fervently for my life to be taken from me. The past will never change. But my imperfect past brought me here, and it's a remarkable place to be. All I've suffered, all you have suffered, Kathryn, has not made us weak. It has made us wise."

"I belong there," she said softly.

"You do," he said with a gentle smile.

"But they may not allow me to return," Janeway said, giving voice to her darkest fear.

"*They*?" Picard asked. "Do what I do."

"Ask for forgiveness rather than permission?" she asked.

"Exactly," he replied. "Proceed as if all you want has already been granted to you. Become the solution they require. Don't worry about doing what you're told. Do what you must."

"Thank you, Jean-Luc," Janeway said.

"I haven't told you anything you don't already know," he insisted.

"But there are times it is good to be reminded nonetheless," she said. Placing her cup on the table before her, she rose. "I have taken too much of your time."

"Not at all," he assured her, standing and extending his hand.

As she took it she said, "It occurs to me that you might harbor some ulterior motives here."

"How so?"

"If I return to the Delta Quadrant for the next few years, I will be unavailable to question your every move."

"The thought had crossed my mind, Admiral," he teased gently.

"I hope you know . . ." Janeway began as her thoughts

turned back to the last time they had spoken and the way he had flouted her direct orders.

"You weren't entirely wrong," Picard admitted. "My efforts to stop that cube were a dismal failure, mitigated only by the brilliance of my crew."

"Do us all a favor and keep failing," Janeway said seriously.

SAN FRANCISCO

Admiral Leonard James Akaar was relieved when he received word of Admiral Janeway's incoming transmission. He'd heard enough of Ambassador Florian's dismay with the accommodations for his delegation aboard the *Aventine* as they were ferried to Betazed. Apologizing curtly, he accepted Janeway's call. His personal aide, Lieutenant Clarington, stood ready to take any appropriate notes.

"Admiral Janeway," he greeted her briskly.

"I have a question for you, Admiral." Janeway began.

"Go ahead."

"Right now, almost a thousand former crew members of the Full Circle fleet are awaiting reassignment. I have a post for many of them, if you approve."

Intrigued, he said, "What?"

"A slipstream-enabled vessel is lying in pieces at Utopia Planitia."

"If you are referring to the ship I think you are, you should know it took a hell of a beating during its test runs and was dismantled. She'll never be space-worthy again."

"Two months ago the Quirinal *crash landed on a planet. More than sixty percent of its systems were catastrophically damaged and sixteen decks were ripped open. The crew of* Achilles *had her flying again inside of six weeks. Don't underestimate my people, Admiral,"* Janeway said.

Akaar hesitated, but only momentarily. He had given considerable thought in the last few weeks to the ultimate disposition of *Achilles* and the remaining crews of *Quirinal, Esquiline, Hawking,* and *Curie.* He had also harbored grave doubts about leaving *Voyager* in the Delta Quadrant with only *Demeter* and *Galen*. Starfleet's resources were stretched to the point of breaking at the moment, but that didn't change the Full Circle fleet's needs. It had taken Kathryn Janeway all of two days to solve these problems.

Akaar liked that in those he commanded.

"Have you run this proposal by Admiral Montgomery?" Akaar asked, wondering if Ken had suggested that she should still consider the fleet's personnel *hers*.

"The last time we spoke, Ken said that no resources could be spared. I just wanted to make sure he was right," Janeway replied, not giving an inch.

"I'll advise him immediately that I have approved your request, Admiral," Akaar stated. She wasn't observing the chain of command. But he had yet to meet a Starfleet officer of any worth who did when they knew they were right and time was of the essence. Akaar suspected Janeway was aware that *he* was the one now preventing her reinstatement.

"Thank you, Admiral," Janeway said. *"I'll issue new orders at once for Captain Drafar, Captain Farkas, and Lieutenant Vorik."*

"Carry on," Akaar said, signing off.

When the channel had closed, Lieutenant Carrington, clearly worried that she had missed something, asked, "Has Admiral Janeway been reinstated as commander of the Full Circle fleet?"

"No," Akaar replied evenly.

Carrington didn't need to voice her obvious confusion.

"Admiral Janeway has just proven that she's going to do all she can to keep them safe," Akaar clarified for her.

"Are you reconsidering your reservations about her fitness, Admiral?"

"Not at all, Lieutenant," Akaar replied, then ordered, "get me Admiral Montgomery."

Chapter Eleven

VOYAGER

A week of analysis by both *Voyager* and *Demeter* had begun to yield interesting results. Chakotay's morning had begun with a call from Lieutenant Kim asking that he join him in *Voyager*'s main shuttle bay. When he started to leave the bridge, Lieutenant Lasren was just beginning his duty shift and was eager to provide a report to Chakotay. The captain ordered Waters to remain at ops for a few minutes and asked Lasren to accompany him to the shuttlebay.

"Lieutenant Vincent and I have now confirmed that this asteroid field is actually one of several within range of our scanners," Lasren began.

"Vincent, the ops officer on *Demeter*?"

"Yes, sir," Lasren confirmed.

"The *Demeter* was focusing her efforts on the planet," Chakotay said.

"Vincent has been working with me in his off hours, and Seven's most recent sensor enhancements came online in the middle of gamma shift," Lasren replied.

"Remind me to order Seven to get some sleep," Chakotay said semi-seriously. Lasren was still young enough to wonder if his captain meant it and discreet enough not to use his empathic abilities to check for himself.

"Shall I . . . ?" he began.

"It was a joke, Lieutenant," Chakotay assured him.

"Vincent hypothesized, given the mass visible to our

sensors, its relative motion, and its proximity to other planetary bodies, that this is not a typical asteroid field," Lasren went on. "Normally, fields like this are the work of millions if not billions of years of accretion and collisions. What happened here happened in the last five hundred years, or less. There is also a discernible lack of metallic asteroids, but a higher than normal concentration of S-type bodies."

Chakotay halted in the middle of the corridor, taking this in. "What could do this in five hundred years?" he asked.

"The destruction of dozens of planetary bodies by some very powerful energy weapons," Lasren replied.

"Dozens?"

"Maybe more," Lasren confirmed. "Long-range sensors now confirm the planetary debris extends throughout the mass once hidden by the cloaking matrix."

Chakotay nodded somberly., "Half a millennium ago, someone or something moved through this area, essentially strip-mining every terrestrial planet it came across down to their cores."

"They were efficient," Lasren noted. "They took almost every resource available, reducing several star systems to dust and debris. A handful of larger gas giants remain around some of the primary stars, but they were otherwise quite thorough."

"If Seven wasn't certain that the Borg never made it out this far, I would say this sounds like something they might have done," Chakotay mused.

"What is more troubling, however, is where it all went," Lasren added.

Chakotay asked, "If they were harvesting resources for their own use, where are the ships or starbases or worlds where those resources were allocated?"

"It is not outside the realm of possibility that some sort of space-born life-form might have ingested them," Lasren offered.

"Let's hope not. But good work; keep it up," Chakotay allowed as they reached the shuttlebay.

"Thank you, sir. I'll see you on the bridge," Lasren replied.

"Thank you, Lieutenant," Chakotay said, dismissing him.

As he entered the shuttlebay, Chakotay immediately noticed a large metal fragment. Most of the shuttles usually housed here were currently on recon, or there would not have been room for it.

Harry Kim was speaking with a small group of officers, including Lieutenant Url from *Demeter.* Chakotay started to wonder if Captain O'Donnell actually needed any of his senior officers for anything. *Let him run his ship.* In the last week no further contacts had been made by the proctors or sentries, so O'Donnell could reasonably spare his tactical officer.

Kim's face lit up as Chakotay approached. The metal fragment was scarred and pitted and had obviously once been part of a large vessel. It was heavily coated with interstellar dust and streaked with what appeared to be residue from high-energy weapon discharge. A small area near the aft end had obviously been recently scrubbed clean to reveal distinct alien markings.

"Report," Chakotay said as he approached.

"We've found part of a hull of an alien vessel, sir," Kim replied, confirming the captain's initial assessment.

"Has the computer been able to translate these?" Chakotay asked, indicating the markings.

"It is incomplete: 'the Worlds of the First Quadrant,'" Kim replied.

"The First Quadrant?" Chakotay asked.

Kim shrugged. "Maybe they never got the memo about the Alpha Quadrant, sir," he joked. "This fragment predates the founding of the Federation."

"How old is it?" Chakotay asked.

"Metallurgic analysis places it between three hundred and three hundred fifty years old," Kim said.

"Any signs of these 'Worlds' yet?"

"No, sir," Kim said. "Lieutenant Lasren's current analysis

suggests they aren't within our sensor range. They could begin where this cloaking matrix ends."

"You've already read Lasren's report?" Chakotay asked.

"I helped Seven compile the data last night," Kim replied.

"Your devotion to duty is admirable, Lieutenant," Chakotay said, "but this isn't a crisis situation. We've got time to spend out here. Normal duty shifts should be observed. I don't want you or anyone else burning themselves out on this."

Kim's jaw tightened as he asked, "Then you haven't spoken to Captain O'Donnell yet this morning?"

"No," Chakotay replied.

"He's heading over now," Kim advised. "According to Url, he's pretty concerned about conditions on the planet and has a proposal for you."

"I look forward to hearing it." Chakotay nodded. "Keep me advised, and good work, Harry."

"Thank you, sir." Kim smiled, then added, "Lieutenant Patel and Doctor Sharak are also preparing a briefing on the origination of the wave forms."

"Sounds like it's going to be a busy morning," Chakotay said.

As Chakotay turned back toward the shuttlebay entrance, two thoughts troubled him. The first was the identity and location of these "Worlds of the First Quadrant." The second was if anyone on either ship was getting any sleep.

When Tom Paris emerged from his bedroom, in uniform and ready to finish whatever Miral had left on her breakfast plate, he tripped on a stack of small padds, scattering them over the deck.

What the . . . ? he thought, taking in the scene before him.

Miral was seated at the breakfast table, which had been pushed against the room's far wall beneath the hastily repaired replicator. She was watching her mother with wide, curious eyes. An end table and coffee table that had once occupied their small seating area, along with his prized replicated antique television set, were piled haphazardly near the room's door, and the short sofa had been pushed into a corner. Most of the deck was littered with padds, puzzles, toys, and small magnetic construction tiles along with several spherical objects that were covered with bright flashing lights and a few of which seemed to be playing various musical compositions. A small bassinet had also appeared and been placed where the unfortunate end table had once resided, next to the couch.

"Oh, good. You're up," B'Elanna said and offered him a quick peck on the cheek before moving past him into the doorway he had just vacated. Once there, she retrieved a small seat meant to be suspended by two elastic bands from the doorframe. As she began to install it, Tom crossed to Miral and kissed her good morning before settling himself in the seat opposite her.

"You've been up for a while then?" he asked.

"Couldn't sleep," B'Elanna replied. Her face glowed and her skin glistened with a thin layer of perspiration. Whatever she was doing, she was working hard at it and clearly enjoying herself.

Once she had installed the swing, she turned to him and said, "What do you think?"

"I love it," Tom replied automatically. "But assuming it's for the new baby, it doesn't have to start living there just yet, right?"

"Of course not," B'Elanna replied, but she made no move to take it down. Instead, she crouched down and began rifling through the padds he had knocked over.

"Um," Tom hesitated, his eyes now mirroring his daughter's in width, "what else do you have there?"

"I've replicated a new curriculum for Miral," she said without looking up.

"Preschool?" Tom asked.

"Yes."

"And where were you thinking we might store these new materials?" he asked.

"I'm working on it," B'Elanna replied, finally looking up and meeting his eyes with a gaze that dared him to find fault with her.

"Great." Tom smiled, hoping his terror wasn't too obvious.

"We're going to need all of this and more when the baby comes," B'Elanna said, rising and placing her hands on her hips, studying her handiwork.

"Right, but that's not going to be for several more months, and in the meantime, couldn't we just replicate these things as we need them and then recycle them?"

"It's a waste of time and energy," she said, shaking her head. "I'm planning some storage units for this area," she went on, indicating the space just below the room's long window.

Tom had harbored no illusions that once the new baby came, their living space was going to be very tight, but he wouldn't have considered seriously tackling the problem for months. B'Elanna, obviously, had other ideas.

"Have you checked in with Nancy this morning?" he asked as casually as possible. "She might . . ."

"She's fine." B'Elanna cut him off. "This is essentially downtime for the engineering staff. They're running standard diagnostics and tweaking the warp and slipstream drives for efficiency. They don't need me," she assured him.

Tom rose and moved to her, stopping short of an embrace. "I know we have to figure this out, and I'm more than happy to leave it in your beautiful and capable hands, but don't be afraid to take your time, honey. You need your rest."

Their eyes met again and he saw fear radiating from hers.

"I don't know how we're going to make this work," she admitted softly.

Finally, he wrapped his arms around her. "I'll talk to Chakotay," he said.

"Not yet," she reminded him, pulling back.

"Soon," he insisted. "I know there isn't a square inch of this ship that isn't spoken for, but I'll come up with something."

B'Elanna nodded.

"See you at the briefing?"

"Sure."

"Love you."

"Love you, too."

Tom stepped nimbly around the many obstacles now in his path and reached the door. As he stepped out into the hallway, he shuddered. B'Elanna's "nesting" instincts hadn't kicked in with Miral until she was almost eight months pregnant. So far, everything about this pregnancy was different, and meeting Miral's needs in the meantime was adding to the strain. B'Elanna needed his support, but she also needed to be gently reminded of the reality of their circumstances. He would have given anything to be able to run this past Chakotay because he was reaching his wit's end.

At least you're not facing the end of the universe, he thought. But clearly life as he had come to know it was slipping farther from his grasp every day.

As soon as Commander O'Donnell arrived on *Voyager,* Captain Chakotay ordered all senior officers to the conference room. O'Donnell had brought his first, Lieutenant Commander Fife, and also had asked Url, who was already aboard, to join them.

"Lieutenant Kim suggested you have made some troubling discoveries about the planet," Chakotay said by way of opening the meeting.

"We have," O'Donnell replied. "Commander?"

Lieutenant Commander Fife activated the holographic display before them and instantly an image of the planet appeared. Simultaneously, significant data on its composition was listed on the room's large, flat panel display at one end of the table. O'Donnell stood before it as he began.

"This is a pretty young planet," he observed. "It was formed between two point two and two point five billion years ago. Life arose within the last five to eight hundred million years."

"That's hard to believe given the variety of life-forms it already sustains," interjected Lieutenant Patel, who specialized in xenobiology.

"I think the word you are looking for is unlikely," O'Donnell corrected her. "I am forced to conclude that many, if not most, of the life-forms living here now are not native to this planet."

"Then where did they come from?" Commander Paris asked.

O'Donnell paused to see if anyone else in the room knew the answer.

"The other planets," a young Betazoid Lieutenant suggested.

"Very good, Lieutenant . . . ?" O'Donnell asked.

"Lasren," the man obliged him. "Senior operations officer."

"You're the one working with Vincent?"

"Yes, sir."

O'Donnell continued. "About five hundred years ago, someone moved through this area, destroying every terrestrial world they came across and taking most of the usable metals and minerals they found. It seems, however, that they were not entirely without conscience."

"Is this planet some sort of conservation park or zoo?" Paris hazarded.

"More like an ark," Chakotay offered.

"That's my assessment as well," O'Donnell agreed. "They probably took more than two of each animal and plant, but small populations of millions of species were brought here. One would think, in hopes of allowing them to survive when their planets had been destroyed."

"So, what's the problem, Commander?" Chakotay pressed.

"I don't know if this was an experiment, a religious

observation, or guilt, but it was not well-planned," O'Donnell went on. "Thousands of species have already died out, and the rest will follow within the next hundred years. This planet can't sustain them as it is."

"Why?" Chakotay asked.

"A certain amount of inter- and intraspecies' conflict is normal for any ecosystem; healthy in fact. It assures that the strongest survive, and it weeds out the weak. That's not what we're seeing here. There is nothing natural about the speed with which life-forms are dying on this world. It's a question of balance. There is excess nitrogen in the atmosphere. This is due to a notable absence of bacteria. The few bacteria that exist are losing their battle for survival to vast varieties of fungi now dominating the largest landmasses. A number of herbivores no longer have sufficient food sources, and an even more alarming number of carnivores are being savaged by swarms of winged beetle-like organisms that flourish thanks to the fungi. This has also created a pollination problem. Insects and other animals that normally cover wide areas dispersing pollen are either dying or being forced into ever-smaller areas. As they go, so go the grasses, grains, and flowering plants. One species doing better than it should is some large herds of shelled creatures on several continents—they seem to like volcanic regions—that are releasing toxic quantities of carbon dioxide into the atmosphere, radically altering the acid levels of the ocean by creating fairly regular acid rainfalls. Larger populations of herbivores have already destroyed several forests, and if that process continues, the resulting loss of hundreds of other plant species will leave the herbivores without a food source.

"Long story short, too many life-forms that should never have been asked to coexist are now forced to do so. If left alone, they will mutually annihilate one another. If someone meant to save them, he failed spectacularly," O'Donnell finished.

Chakotay said evenly, "What does that have to do with us?"

O'Donnell stared hard at Chakotay, blinking rapidly. Finally, he said, "You don't think this is the distress call we came here to answer?" he asked.

"How could it be?" Lieutenant Kim asked.

"Commander Fife?" O'Donnell said, turning to his counterpart.

"I've spent the last several days trying to understand the creation of the wave form technology that first contacted *Voyager,* hid this area of space, and ultimately chose to reveal it to us."

"As have we," Doctor Sharak said.

"And what have you concluded?" Fife asked congenially.

This simple act of professional courtesy by Fife seemed to stun and please Chakotay. He bit back a smile as Lieutenant Patel replied, "The doctor and I have concluded that they are not a naturally occurring phenomenon."

"Agreed," Fife said.

Patel went on. "Subspace is filled with wave forms, but to force any to consolidate, in the way the proctors and sentries have, requires massive amounts of energy, both to rupture subspace, limit the range of damage, and eliminate all other local waveforms, thus forcing the emergence of the entities we perceive as the various individual wave forms."

"You believe that differentiation between them is the wave harmonics?" Fife asked.

Patel and Sharak nodded.

"Once they are formed, however, we are not aware of how they become capable of collecting, retaining, and transmitting data," Sharak admitted.

"They learned," Cambridge suggested.

"They're not sentient," Patel replied.

"Perhaps not," O'Donnell agreed, "but use a tool often enough in a repetitive manner and it begins to show wear. It is altered on an atomic level by its use."

"But pounding a hammer and slowly wearing away its head doesn't teach the hammer to operate independently,"

Paris chimed in. "It just leaves you with a little less hammer every time you use it."

"Suppose these wave forms were used to collect information," Fife replied. "They pass through an object in normal space and retain an imprint of that object. That imprint can later be read by an appropriately tuned scanning device."

"But there's no willful transmission on their part," Patel argued.

"That depends on the scanning technology," Kim interjected, building on Fife's reasoning. "They could have been *trained,* so to speak, to seek out or cease their motion whenever they encounter technology capable of reading their imprints."

"They do seem to take a pointed interest in them," Chakotay said. "Which could suggest that their creators/operators were working from starships."

"They had at least three hundred years of practice, or training, before one of them ventured out to find us or someone like us who could help them," O'Donnell added.

"Were their creators the ones issuing the distress call?" Chakotay asked.

"I don't believe so," O'Donnell replied. "Whoever had the power to do this, to destroy these planets, to harness these wave forms, didn't want anyone following in their footsteps or discovering their handiwork."

"Hence the cloaking matrix," Seven offered.

"Yes," Fife agreed. "The matrix generators are essentially a complicated adjustment of the wave form properties. But as we've seen, they are no longer responding to the programming of their creators. The wave forms that populate this area seem to be acting on their own initiative now."

"One moment," Chakotay said. "How do we get from the creation of these complex devices to the devices caring about this planet? What was their purpose in bringing us here, and what is the connection between them and the planet?"

"I not entirely sure yet," Fife replied. "I don't know of a

starship that is capable of releasing the energy required to create these wave forms. I believe that technology has to be planet based and likely pulls its energy from a planet's core."

"Have you discovered evidence of this technology on the planet?" Paris asked.

"Not yet," Fife allowed.

"But the possibility of its existence suggests we might want to take a closer look, doesn't it?" O'Donnell asked. "Terrible to think about technology like that being weaponized and falling the wrong hands," he added with a subtle nod to Fife.

"You honestly believe that these wave forms see this planet as their birth place, know that the planet is dying, and want us to stop it?" Chakotay asked.

"In a nutshell," O'Donnell replied.

"But even if every single life-form on that planet died, the planet will still exist, along with the energies that were potentially used to create the wave forms. Why would they care about the life-forms on the planet?" Kim asked.

"The original distress call included words to the effect that they were 'unable to sustain as ordered'?" O'Donnell asked pointedly.

"But that could suggest any number of things. 'As ordered' could mean as per the last instructions they received from their creators," Kim suggested.

"Or it could mean as it was originally organized," O'Donnell replied.

"We'd be violating the Prime Directive if we interfere," Paris said evenly.

"I'm not suggesting that we do anything yet beyond confirming our hypothesis," O'Donnell said.

"How?" Chakotay asked.

"Old-fashioned leg work," O'Donnell replied.

"It's a tall order for our limited staffs," Chakotay noted.

"We don't usually shrink from those," the *Demeter*'s commander offered.

"No." Chakotay smiled. "We don't." He paused briefly, then nodded his assent.

"But . . ." Paris began.

"We're just *looking* for now." Chakotay cut him off. "We're not doing anything to interfere with the natural progress of the life of this planet, nor are we running the risk of interfering with the development of any sentient life-forms. The questions raised so far are sufficient to warrant further investigation."

"And if this hypothesis is proven?" Paris asked.

"We'll cross that bridge when we get there," Chakotay replied. "Coordinate with Commander Fife and begin assignment of away teams," he ordered, clearly ending briefing.

O'Donnell had no idea what Chakotay would conclude once his suspicions were proven, which he was confident they would be. He had no qualms whatsoever about crossing that bridge, but he knew what it would cost Chakotay to do so.

Chapter Twelve

GALEN

For the first time since his arrival at Starbase 185, Axum slept. The Doctor had amended his treatment regimen and begun to inject into Axum small quantities of the catoms he had removed from Seven. Signs of improvement had been rapid and encouraging. The Doctor had continued the transfusions until Axum's catoms—supported and in many cases replaced by Seven's—had begun to replicate themselves and repair the physical damage. Rousing Axum from his coma had been uneventful, but the Doctor had not yet used a medical means to force him to full consciousness. He preferred to watch and wait, but he was certain that Axum was out of danger—*physical* danger at any rate.

Commander Glenn had proven herself to be both capable and extremely helpful throughout. She was a rare Starfleet officer, one who had completed both medical and command training. This combination made her the ideal candidate to lead the crew of the *Galen,* but the Doctor had only recently grown to appreciate her medical expertise. It was limited, thus far, only by her experience. But she possessed a keen mind and steady hand, and the Doctor did not doubt that over time, she would grow into a brilliant physician, assuming her command duties did not interfere.

The same could not be said of Doctor Mai, whose presence aboard the *Galen* had become wearisome. Her appreciation of nuance was limited, as was her patience. Mai had only begun to absent herself from the main sickbay in the last few days, since Axum's recovery had become assured. She had, however, left standing orders to be notified immediately should he regain consciousness.

Commander Glenn and the Doctor were seated on opposite sides of his desk. The commander was wolfing down her lunch—she often ate as if a phaser was pointed at her head. The Doctor was studying the developments in the catoms that had been transplanted to Axum. It had become an intently diverting and engaging topic of conversation.

The Doctor registered a smile creasing his holographic lips that elicited a chuckle from Glenn.

"Someone is inordinately pleased with himself this morning," she observed.

Glenn had become one person in whose presence the Doctor did not feel the need to sublimate his well-earned pride.

"I wouldn't have believed it possible had I not seen it for myself," he replied.

"Be honest," she chided him, "you still don't know exactly why it worked, do you?"

"I have several promising theories," he retorted. "I won't be able to test them further until Axum is fully recovered, at which point I will extract some of the catoms that were unique to him and compare them to those originally removed from Seven."

"You can't wait, can you?" Glenn asked.

"I will not proceed until I am certain that to do so will not jeopardize Axum's recovery," the Doctor assured her.

"It's a shame you never had a chance to take samples from Doctor Frazier and her people."

The Doctor shrugged. "I wasn't aboard *Voyager* when they were recovered, nor did I possess the ability to identify individual catoms at the time. A shame, though. I agree," he added. "It would have furthered my research considerably."

"Maybe we'll go back and visit them someday," Glenn offered.

"And ask them nicely to roll up their sleeves?" The Doctor grinned.

"After all *Voyager*'s done for them, it's the least they could do," Glenn replied.

"Perhaps," the Doctor agreed.

"I'm still puzzled by this Unimatrix Zero," Glenn said.

"How so?" the Doctor asked.

"What was it? I mean, it can't have been real?"

"Seven of Nine and Captain Janeway experienced it, and the Borg queen thought it a significant enough threat to warrant killing countless drones in order to destroy it," the Doctor replied.

"Yes, I've read the reports," Glenn said. "But I still don't understand how it was created."

"A random mutation," the Doctor said, "shared by one in a million drones."

"And every time they regenerated, they entered this beautiful, peaceful landscape and lived as individuals?"

"So the story went," the Doctor said.

"When they returned to consciousness, they were simply drones again, with no memory of Unimatrix Zero."

"Until we came along," the Doctor noted wryly.

"And destroyed their paradise," Glenn said. "That was thoughtful of you," she teased.

"The Borg queen really didn't leave us much of a choice." The Doctor shrugged. "It's telling, isn't it? The existence of Unimatrix Zero cost her nothing. But she still could not allow the drones a moment's freedom from the Collective."

"It made them less perfect," Glenn suggested.

"It made them less Borg," the Doctor corrected her. "But by forcing the issue, the queen's worst fear was realized."

"Unimatrix Zero was destroyed, but the drones containing the mutation were given the ability to experience their individuality while still being Borg," Glenn said. Glancing out the transparent window separating the Doctor's office from the sickbay, she sighed as she considered Axum. "Looking at him now, do you think it did more harm than good?"

"We gave those Borg a fighting chance to mount a resistance from within the Collective," the Doctor replied flatly.

"One or two at the most, on any given Borg vessel?" Glenn countered. "What resistance could they have offered, so hopelessly outnumbered?"

"One of them, a Klingon, took control of his vessel and helped *Voyager* rescue our lost away team during the conflict. If the reports of first contact with the Caeliar are accurate, it seems that much of the credit for the Borg's ultimate transformation is due to Captain Erika Hernandez. I wouldn't underestimate the power of one, even against the Borg," the Doctor replied.

"Seven's report indicated that Axum was located on a ship in the Beta Quadrant," Glenn said.

The Doctor nodded. "Which makes his presence here less of a mystery. Obviously he escaped his vessel, probably just prior to the Caeliar transformation."

"But why did he . . . ?" Glenn began, but paused, as if unable to speak of the horrors he had inflicted upon himself.

"I don't know," the Doctor replied gently. "But soon enough, we'll have the opportunity to ask him."

"Seven described him as a leader in Unimatrix Zero. She said that they developed a personal connection. Do you think it was more than that?" Glenn asked.

"I don't know," the Doctor replied. "To be honest, I have no idea what qualities in any individual Seven might find attractive. Her *personal* life is not my concern."

A puzzled glance flickered across Glenn's face, but before the Doctor could question her further, they were interrupted by the entrance of Doctor Mai. She was followed by a human man, likely in his eighth decade of life, and a much younger Trill female who wore the uniform of a Starfleet doctor.

"Has there been any change in the patient since your last report, Doctor?" Mai asked. That musical quality to her voice the Doctor had initially found pleasant had soured.

"Had there been, I would have advised you at once," the Doctor replied. Rising from his desk, he added, "Who are your companions?"

"Allow me to introduce Doctor Greer Everett, a fellow at the Federation Institute of Health, and Doctor Pauline Frist, Starfleet Medical," Mai replied.

Hands were shaken all around before the Doctor said, "You've both come a long way. How can we be of assistance to you?"

"Turn over all of your research into the Caeliar catoms, including the work you have done on Seven of Nine," Everett replied. "Doctor Frist and I will require a briefing as soon as possible on Seven's case in particular."

"Seven of Nine is my patient," the Doctor said, unfazed. "All of her records are protected by doctor/patient confidentiality." As he said these words, he caught Commander Glenn's response out of the corner of his eye. Her eyes were wide, and she was shaking her head back and forth almost too subtly to be noticed.

Doctor Frist immediately offered a padd to the Doctor, saying, "Here you will find direct orders from your superior officer, the chief of Starfleet Medical, to comply with all of our requests, Doctor."

"My commanding officer is Commander Glenn," the Doctor said, nodding toward her, "currently assigned to Project Full Circle. In the absence of a fleet commander, she takes her orders from Admiral Kenneth Montgomery, who is supervised by Admiral Leonard James Akaar," the Doctor replied. "Are their names appended to that request, Doctor Frist?"

"Starfleet Medical's authority in this case supersedes theirs, Doctor," Frist replied evenly. "Your position as a chief medical officer also obligates you to follow Starfleet Medical's orders when you receive them, even if they directly contradict the standing orders of your superiors at Starfleet Command."

"And the Federation Institute of Health?" the Doctor asked. "That's a civilian authority."

"Our charter from the Federation Council gives us wide latitude when the public health is threatened," Everett replied. "We are collaborating with Starfleet Medical with the assent of the Federation Council and the office of the President of the Federation."

Momentarily dumbstruck, the Doctor could not immediately locate a loophole.

"Excuse me, I need to verify these orders and your authority," the Doctor said. "In the interim, Commander Glenn can brief you on our patient's progress."

"Thank you, Doctor," Frist said, clearly certain that he would come to his senses soon enough and grant their request.

For his part, the Doctor had absolutely no intention of ever complying.

SAN FRANCISCO

Admiral Kathryn Janeway knew immediately that something was wrong. An emergency hail from Starbase 185 had awakened her in the middle of the night.

"Doctor?" she asked.

"Can Starfleet Medical order me to provide all of Seven of Nine's personal medical records to them, even those that she specifically requested that I classify?" he demanded.

Janeway paused to consider the question. Finally she replied, simply, "Yes."

"But," the Doctor immediately objected.

"Under certain circumstances they have the authority to suspend doctor/patient confidentiality," she clarified.

"What about the Federation Institute of Health?"

This question raised further alarms and opened several

new avenues of internal inquiries to her, but Janeway replied, "Depends on who is asking."

The Doctor took a few moments to read the orders in their entirety. Once he finished, Janeway was certain of one thing: this was not a casual inquiry. Someone very highly placed had a question or a problem and information only the Doctor could now provide was essential to his or her work.

"In this case, yes," Janeway confirmed.

"But Seven isn't even a Starfleet officer!" the Doctor shouted on a whisper.

"They're in the next room, aren't they?" Janeway realized.

The Doctor nodded, then continued with more composure, *"Seven never wanted to become an object of study. She has given me permission to share my work on her catoms with only a select group of people she trusts. I cannot betray her confidence."*

Janeway's response was measured. "Seven is a citizen of the Federation. Her request for confidentiality bars you from sharing her personal information with anyone *except* your superior medical officers. They, at their discretion, are also obligated to share that information with Federation civilian authorities. But, Doctor, Seven is well aware of this. Granted, she probably did not foresee these developments, but she cannot fault you for following the orders you have been given by a rightful authority."

"I won't do it," the Doctor insisted. *"I can deactivate my program at will."*

"You're willing to die over this?" Janeway asked, incredulous.

The Doctor wavered. *"I could deactivate myself until they realize I won't comply,"* he suggested. *"An act of conscientious objection."*

"The moment you reactivate your program, you will be subject to a court martial," Janeway advised.

"I never asked to join Starfleet," the Doctor said. *"I never had a choice. I could resign my commission."*

"Then you'll likely face charges from the civilian authorities for willful obstruction of an investigation," Janeway countered. "Not to mention showing a most callous disregard for the organization under whose guidance you were created and have for so many years thrived."

"Do you honestly think I should do this?" the Doctor asked, exasperated. *"Do you care so little for Seven's privacy?"*

"Please, don't be ridiculous," Janeway replied. "Doctor, Starfleet Medical is not your enemy. This isn't someone's idle curiosity you're being asked to satisfy. Nothing crosses the desks of the officers who wrote those orders that doesn't have severe and possibly devastating implications for the entire Federation. This isn't about Seven. Something else is going on. I am certain that were she available to provide the information herself, or to release you from your obligation to protect her, she would do so without hesitation." After a moment's pause to let this sink in, she asked, "What happened out there? Who was the patient they wanted you to treat?"

"Another Borg drone transformed by the Caeliar but who clearly wished to remain outside the gestalt," the Doctor replied, *"and an old acquaintance, unless I'm mistaken."*

"Who?"

"Axum."

Janeway searched her memory until the realization hit her. "Seven's Axum? The man I met in Unimatrix Zero?"

"Unless the Borg had more than one drone designated as Five of Twelve, Secondary Adjunct of Trimatrix Nine Four Two," the Doctor replied.

"Does he remember us?"

"He's not conscious. His injuries were extensive, and he is only now showing signs that he will recover. But I'll ask him as soon as I have the chance. Shall I pass along your regards?"

Janeway nodded through a withering glare. "Please do. Follow the orders you have been given, Doctor. If Seven objects, I'll talk to her."

"She's not going to blame you, Admiral."

"She's not going to blame you either, Doctor. Keep me advised. Update me as soon as you know more."

Reluctantly, the Doctor nodded, then ended transmission.

Janeway struggled to put together the puzzle, but she was missing too many of the relevant pieces. She understood the Doctor's reluctance. But she also knew that to fight this was to court damnation in the eyes of her superiors. The case was cut and dried. There was no room to question or refuse. This wasn't an illegal order. There were better ways to handle this than forcing a doctor to break his patient's confidentiality. Many would have hated the idea as passionately as the Doctor did, but the law was clear on the subject. The only challenge was geography. Had Seven been in the Alpha or Beta Quadrant now, she could have been called in for an evaluation that would likely have revealed all the Doctor was about to tell them. In her absence, his records would have to suffice.

For now.

The list of things Janeway was worried about had just grown longer.

GALEN

The Doctor took a few minutes more to consider his options. Unless they accessed his matrix directly, which he did not put past them, they could not read all of the records he possessed about Seven. Until they were willing to provide him with more data as to why this breach of her privacy was necessary, he could withhold whatever data he chose. Of course, Axum's recovery would belie his feigned ignorance.

Harder to pinpoint was the source of his discomfort with these orders. Seven was a colleague as well as a patient. They had known each other for much of the Doctor's existence, but he believed his reticence to disclose what was being requested would have been as firm were the subject any of his current or past patients. It was the principle that troubled him.

Wasn't it?

Each time he dug into his long-term memory files for a more vivid reason to refuse the order, intense waves of comfort washed through him. The effect was almost what he imagined narcotics might temporarily provide to organic beings.

He had not resolved the dilemma when Glenn called to him.

Hurrying to the sickbay, he saw her standing beside Axum. He was clearly stirring, and the upper portion of the bed had been slightly elevated so that he might rest in greater comfort while still communicating with some ease.

Doctors Mai, Everett, and Frist were keeping their distance. The Doctor saw fear on their faces directed toward Axum, a clear indication of how parochial their thinking was.

The Doctor moved briskly past them to Axum's side. He immediately checked his vitals, and when he saw nothing troubling, glanced at Glenn. She was studying Axum's face intently, and the Doctor noted that she had taken what remained of his left hand in hers, clearly hoping to comfort him with the simple power of touch.

Finally, Axum opened his eyes, fearful, but still too weak to act on that fear. Only once his gaze settled on Glenn did he seem to relax.

A sound croaked from his lips. The second time he made the attempt, the word was clearer.

"Annika?" he asked.

It was the first time the Doctor had noted any physical resemblance between Glenn and Seven. Both were graced with pale skin, pleasing physical features, and long blond hair, though Glenn's had more red in it. He would never have confused the two. Obviously this was wishful thinking on Axum's part.

"No," Glenn replied kindly. "I am Commander Clarissa Glenn of the Federation *Starship Galen.* Are you Axum?"

Eyes that had been filled with hope were suddenly brimming with tears. Axum's face contorted with pain as he closed them, nodding affirmatively.

"You are safe here," Glenn continued. "You suffered great physical trauma, but the worst of your injuries has been healed. We want to help you."

"Help? Me?" Axum said bitterly. "I don't want help. I want to die in peace. Why will none of you allow me to die?"

"Please," Glenn continued, her voice like warm silver, "we believe we know some of what happened to you. You were Borg?"

"An abomination."

"A victim," she countered kindly. "You were one of the few who regularly accessed a place called Unimatrix Zero?"

Axum nodded, but he now seemed almost as interested as confused. "Were you there, too?" he asked.

"No, but we know Seven of Nine, Annika," she corrected herself quickly. "We know she knew you there. We know that once it was destroyed, you retained memory of your individuality while still a drone."

"It made no sense," he cried out in desperation.

"You escaped?" she asked.

Axum's eyes grew suddenly cold. "I tried to hide. They attacked me. I defended myself. I was not one of them. But I could still hear them."

"You did what anyone else in your place would have," Glenn insisted. "You survived, that's the important thing."

"But Annika didn't," he said.

"Yes, she did," Glenn said. "She is a member of our fleet, though our ships are temporarily separated."

"I thought she was dead. There was a moment after I escaped when I could see, could *feel,* all of them. I wasn't afraid. But she wasn't there. Why wasn't she there if she wasn't dead?" he demanded.

"That moment was one of transformation," Glenn explained. "The Borg was unintentionally spawned by the Caeliar. The Borg, as you knew them, was absorbed by the Caeliar gestalt several months ago. But some, like Seven, chose to remain outside that community. You made the same choice?"

"If she wasn't there, I wasn't going," Axum replied simply. "Please, please take me to her," he asked, his anxiety increasing.

"We will," the Doctor said, stepping in. "I promise you, we will. For now, you need to rest." The Doctor quickly retrieved a hypospray and injected it into Axum's neck. Within moments he had relaxed into unconscious release. Facing Glenn, the Doctor added, "You did well, but I don't know how much information we should force on him right now."

She nodded wistfully. "You're right. He's going to need more than us soon. We need a trained counselor to help him come to grips with all of this."

"You'll do in a pinch, Commander," the Doctor assured her.

"You shouldn't have lied to him," Doctor Mai spoke up, now daring to step a little closer.

"Lied?"

"This man will not be returning with you to the Delta Quadrant, now or ever," she insisted.

"It is my belief that seeing Seven of Nine and communicating directly with her will be critical to his recovery," the Doctor said. "You want him restored to full health? There's only one way to do that. And he's hardly our prisoner. Is he?"

"We'll leave his ultimate dispensation to higher authorities, but for now, he is a former enemy combatant whom we have taken into custody," Doctor Frist replied. "Now, without further ado, Doctor, you owe us a briefing."

The Doctor could not help but continue to struggle with the warring directives within him. He was programmed to follow orders. But he also understood that by following them, he was betraying something essential that existed beyond the parameters of his matrix.

The problem was, he could not name that essential thing.

Chapter Thirteen

THE ARK PLANET

"What the hell are those?" Tom Paris asked softly.

"Give me a minute," Kim replied, aiming his tricorder at the closest distortion, hanging as if suspended by invisible wires fifty meters in front of him.

"Lieutenant Kim!" a sharp command reverberated through the helmet of his environmental suit, halting him instantly in his steps. Looking down, he realized he had crept forward in his zeal to analyze the phenomenon before him, and he had come perilously close to the brink of the ledge on which he, Paris, and Lieutenant Commander Fife were standing.

"Sorry," Kim said, stepping back and adjusting his aim. "Thank you, Commander."

"You're welcome, Lieutenant," Fife replied, his tone clear. *Please don't get yourself killed.*

"Why don't we all move back toward the doorway?" Paris suggested.

Until now, the doorway, or what remained of it, had been the only indication on the planet that any sentient humanoids had lived here. More than a week of painstaking analysis had yielded no other artifacts, fossils, or hints of past technology that could account for the creation of the wave forms. Portable scanners had been deployed and had penetrated ten kilometers below the surface. While thousands of cavern formations were present, nothing unusual was discovered.

As soon as Kim had begun to believe that there might

be nothing to see, that feeling had provided the insight he needed. Whatever they were seeking, if it was present anywhere on or below that planet, was cloaked. Seven had retuned the sensors and finally detected a series of underground caverns at the planet's southern polar region. Once a number of away teams had been dispatched to the area, the much smaller cloaking field, like its counterpart around the system, had been lifted. The wave forms were clearly not willing or able to communicate directly with them, but they were obviously following their efforts. Kim had taken this development as permission to explore further.

The caverns had been thoroughly mapped, several leading to dead ends as deep as twenty kilometers down. Some might have been naturally occurring, but many showed telltale signs of construction. All of them had been sealed by innocuous-looking piles of indigenous rock. Digging began at the most stable, ultimately granting them access to the vast open cavern. The remains of a heavy metal door embedded several meters into the rock face was the cavern's only discernible access point. The tunnel leading to it had been sealed almost two kilometers above this area; whoever had left it had not been concerned that it would be discovered. It led to a vertical shaft more than two thousand meters wide that extended to a depth of sixty-five kilometers to the planet's mantle. Often such a geological feature would have had a natural crater at its peak, but several kilometers overhead, the solid rock had sealed it from exposure. Numerous carefully placed vents, also not naturally formed, allowed for the continuous pressure release to ensure the stability of the formation.

What lay beyond the ledge looked like small stars suspended in the darkness above, and below and emitted the only ambient light in the shaft. After a few minutes of analysis, Kim found he could answer Paris's question.

"They're aborted wave forms," Kim finally said.

"How can we see them?" Paris asked.

"They cannot completely emerge from subspace," Fife

replied. "They're trapped. But where they intersect with the shaft's atmosphere, the electromagnetic reactions are producing light along the visible spectrum."

"Something went wrong in their creation," Kim theorized. "They should have emerged fully formed from subspace. These are the ones that didn't make it."

"Is this a graveyard?" Paris asked.

"No, it's the birth canal," Fife suggested.

Fife looked up and Kim followed his gaze. Several kilometers above, fifty meters of solid rock separated this cavern from the planet's surface. Tuning his tricorder, Kim analyzed the walls of the cavern.

As his companions followed suit, Kim saw the initial results, and his breath caught in his chest. The raw geothermal energy focused by the shape of this cavern and its location at one of the magnetic poles made it an ideal place, perhaps the only place on the planet capable of harnessing the energy required to rupture subspace and create the wave forms.

"The radiation levels in this chamber are off the charts," Paris noted.

"Now, aren't you glad we're in environmental suits?" Kim teased. In truth, the ambient temperature had demanded it, but that didn't mean Paris had agreed to the suits without complaint.

"I think you're right," Kim finally said. "This is where they were born."

"How did they get out?" Paris asked.

"They can move through shields and our ships at will," Kim chided him. "I'm sure they can handle solid rock."

"But where is the technology that created them?" Fife demanded. "Apart from that door, there is absolutely no trace of anything that could account for it."

Kim shrugged. "Maybe whoever did this took it with them when they left. Or maybe they just shoved it off the edge of this cliff and let the mantle melt it."

"Is there any chance *this* was the problem the wave forms

wanted us to solve?" Paris asked hopefully. "Was this the reason for their distress call?"

Kim considered the question. "There's nothing we or anyone else could possibly do here. It's not like they can feel pain. They are aberrations but of no harm or use to anyone, including the fully formed proctors and sentries."

"That's not what I wanted to hear," Paris said.

"I know," Kim agreed.

DEMETER

Against his better judgment and over the stern objections of Commander Fife, O'Donnell had chosen to move to the second phase of his research: bringing a few of the native species on board for closer study. At the very least, Atlee had asked that O'Donnell use holographic re-creations of plants and small animals he wished to analyze, but the idea was repugnant to the captain. How much of his ability to find unique and often unprecedented solutions to a problem was a result of tactile interaction and how much was drawn from the fires of his neurons, he might never know. But O'Donnell trusted real dirt. It couldn't lie.

The specimen now pacing the containment field in airponics bay four was a four-legged carnivore with thick, matted, yellowish gray fur, wide green eyes, and a long snout. Its teeth were sharp, but several critical ones were missing, suggesting that it had attempted to consume some of the hard-shelled reptiles that shared its habitat on the surface. Hunger did terrible things to the living, sentient or not, and the creature's desperation was palpable—as was its disdain for captivity. From time to time it lunged at the containment field. O'Donnell had made certain the field did not release a charge that would injure the creature, but it could not be pleasant to run into it head on, again and again.

O'Donnell was certain Alana, his wife who had died after a disastrous miscarriage, would have loved this poor guy.

He was a fierce predator but had the ill luck of standing less than half a meter high. A fully grown adult, he wasn't much larger than a domesticated lap dog. Cursed though he was, by the same forces that had doomed the planet, he would fight to his last breath for his continued existence. O'Donnell couldn't help hoping he would live to see many years more of that battle.

"What shall we call him, dearest?" O'Donnell asked of the empty lab.

Silence. For a split second O'Donnell wondered if he had done something to earn her displeasure. In the past, he had been unable to hear Alana, in his mind, when he strayed too far from his best self. While some might consider conversing with a dead person a sign of mental instability, for O'Donnell nothing could be farther from the truth. Alana had always been his best counselor, and he'd seen no reason to abandon her wisdom when she died. As long as he could hear her, all was right with his universe.

There are obvious similarities to lupus monstrabilis, Alana finally replied.

O'Donnell smiled to himself. "I was actually thinking of a name."

You could go with "monster" for short.

"You don't think he'd find that offensive?"

It makes him sound tougher than he is. He'd like that.

"Monster it is," O'Donnell agreed. He transported a small dish filled with a protein compound into the containment field. Until now, he had provided Monster only with fresh water. It had taken some time to study his blood and digestive tract to determine the precise nutrient compound that would best accommodate his dietary needs. The good news was there were large, unchecked rodent populations a few hundred miles from Monster's territory that could serve as an acceptable substitute, should these two species ever have the chance to get to know each other.

"Come on, Monster," O'Donnell coaxed as the animal

retreated from the strange new dish in its cage. Its hunger won out, and after a few sniffs and licks, he ate greedily what O'Donnell had provided. The meal was followed by a few long, resounding bellows from his throat, undoubtedly meant to call to his pack, alerting them to sustenance.

"Good Monster," O'Donnell congratulated him. Sated, Monster temporarily halted his pacing and settled himself on his side to relax while he digested.

"I beg your pardon, sir?" a voice asked.

Looking up, O'Donnell saw Ensign Brill, one of his botanical specialists who had entered carrying several samples he was studying concurrently with his work on Monster.

"Any luck, Brill?" O'Donnell asked briskly, ignoring the ensign's question.

"Atmospheric nitrogen will have to fall below seventy-nine percent for these samples to have any chance, sir," Brill replied.

Nodding, O'Donnell replied, "I think we can do that."

"How, sir?"

"Stulhatan has been working on some new bacterial strains," O'Donnell answered.

"Six new herbivores were just transported aboard," Brill added. "Shall we bring them here?"

"Put them in bay three, and leave the new samples of graminoids for them. Let's make them feel welcome, shall we?"

Brill paused, then ventured, "Sir, why are we allocating so many resources to finding appropriate nourishment for these species?"

"Because it's what we do best," O'Donnell replied.

"Unless the Prime Directive is suspended in the case of this planet, we will never have the opportunity to make the necessary changes," Brill said.

"Even if it isn't, you're telling me you're not learning anything by studying these life-forms?"

"I am. We are," Brill conceded. "I just don't want to see you disappointed, sir," he added, reddening a bit.

"I never am," O'Donnell assured him. "Now go get those herbivores some lunch, and let me know how they tolerate their new diet."

"Aye, sir," Brill said and turned to go. He had almost reached the door when he added, "He doesn't look much like a 'monster' to me, sir."

At this, O'Donnell chuckled. Monster seemed quite content now, rolled onto his side, licking his forepaws and running them over his snout. "You should have seen him a few minutes ago. He'd have killed you as soon as look at you."

"Good for him." Brill smiled.

Once Brill had left, O'Donnell considered lowering the containment field to test Monster's newfound complacency, but he opted against it. There were still too many of his brothers and sisters that needed help.

O'Donnell was going to be damned if he didn't make sure they got it.

"Did I read this right?" B'Elanna Torres demanded of Chakotay as she stormed into his ready room.

"Good afternoon, B'Elanna," Chakotay greeted her warily. He hadn't seen much of her in the last few weeks, but both her nerves and Tom's had seemed frayed lately, and he wondered if their recent domestic tranquility might be hitting a few bumps. He had also noted that she'd been spending more time in sickbay. There were no reports of a medical issue, but that didn't mean there wasn't one. Opting to tread carefully, he went on, "What exactly are you reading, Commander?"

"These are the metallurgic and mineral reports of the asteroid field surrounding the system," she replied, as if the cause for her disdain should have been obvious. Chakotay had scanned the reports, but nothing had caught his attention.

"See anything unusual in them?" Chakotay asked.

Torres handed him a padd and stood back, crossing her arms at her chest. He read the sections she had highlighted but failed to see what had piqued her interest.

"I give up," he finally said.

"The UV absorption patterns," Torres said, as if that should have clarified everything. When he continued to stare at her blankly, she went on, "Those are traker deposits."

"Really?" Chakotay asked.

"You still have no idea what I'm talking about, do you?"

"No, but I'm sure you're about to enlighten me," Chakotay replied, hoping his tone would set her more at ease.

"I already ran an ico-spectrogram to be sure," Torres said. "A number of the larger rocks out there have some significant deposits of dilithium."

That did it. Chakotay rose from his desk and moved around it to stand opposite her. "How much?" he asked.

"Enough to shore up our supplies for the next three years and then some. If we do this right, we could probably send some home the next time one of the fleet ships makes a run to the Alpha Quadrant. I mean, I know it's not the incredibly rare mineral it once was, but we know they're running short of everything back home."

Chakotay bowed his head, considering this revelation. The hopes he had nursed since they had left New Talax of proving the fleet's worth with this mission were not exactly coming to fruition. Finding a new source of dilithium in unclaimed space was certainly noteworthy, though he didn't know how far it would go toward burnishing the fleet's record thus far in the Delta Quadrant. Still, a discovery like this was a step in the right direction, if a complicated one.

"What's the problem?" Torres asked when he did not immediately send her off to begin collecting dilithium.

"The proctors and the sentries," he replied.

"The planets these rocks used to be a part of are long gone," Torres said. "Why would they care if we make use of them?"

"I don't know," Chakotay replied. "We still don't know for sure why they brought us here. *If* the planet is the source of their distress, I don't know if we're going to be able to help them. I also don't know if they are still acting on the orders or programming their creators left them. This entire area of space was hidden until they decided to show it to us. All we've done thus far is study the area, and they've seemed content to allow us to do so. Extracting dilithium from these fragments takes us from passive to active interference in their space. We can't ask for permission. They might not care, but they might, and if they do, their retribution could be swift and dangerous."

"How about a small test?" Torres asked.

"What are you proposing?"

"I'll go out in a shuttle and collect a few small samples. That will allow me to confirm the crystal's purity. And if the wave forms take issue, we'll have our answer."

Chakotay had to concede it was a reasonable risk. They already had several tactical responses at their disposal to deal with any attack by the wave forms. But he couldn't shake the feeling that he was about to trespass against the wave form's trust. And there was one other consideration.

"We've got a dozen away teams on the surface right now. We need to stay in orbit to facilitate emergency transports if necessary. But I'm not comfortable sending a shuttle too far out for us to render aid if the wave forms do take offense."

"The *Demeter* can cover the transports," Torres suggested. "The shuttle mission will take twenty minutes at most, and I can't imagine that all twelve teams would need emergency evacuation. They're scattered all over the planet."

"One sample, very small," Chakotay finally agreed.

"I'll let you know as soon as I'm ready," she said, turning to go.

"No," he said, stopping her in her tracks.

"What?"

"Send Lieutenant Lasren and Ensign Gwyn. Brief them thoroughly on the procedure before they go."

"Chakotay, I can do this in my sleep," Torres said.

"Yes, you can," he said. "But part of my job is making sure they can, too."

"When did we suddenly become older and wiser?" Torres asked.

"Damned if I know." Chakotay smiled.

DELTA FLYER II

"What was Commander Paris thinking?" Ensign Gwyn asked as she gritted her teeth in frustration. The knobs and levers he had installed in the shuttle's flight control panel were cute, but apparently challenging to operate.

"I believe those controls were meant to provide the helmsman with a greater capacity to feel the ship's responsiveness," Lieutenant Lasren said after he confirmed that Gwyn's difficulties were not taking the shuttle off course.

"A standard panel is plenty responsive," Gwyn retorted. "I guess our first officer isn't one for subtlety."

"The long list of his accomplishments when he held your current post suggest otherwise," Lasren observed.

Gwyn favored him with a disgruntled sidelong glance, then dropped the subject as the shuttle came within range of the asteroid from which they intended to collect the dilithium sample. Kenth Lasren was Betazoid, though he rarely used his empathic abilities unless asked to do so by a superior office. Having studied and served for so long with species that did not share his gifts, Lasren thought it rude to violate their personal space without invitation. Aytar Gwyn, for all she questioned Commander Paris's appreciation for subtlety, would never have won any awards in that category either. To assess her mood on any given day, all one needed to do was glance at the color, cut, and arrangement of her hair. Today she wore medium-length spikes of almost midnight blue. Everything about them said "stay away."

But the shift in her concentration was so abrupt, Lasren found himself reaching out with his heightened senses automatically. One moment she was all playful banter and the next she entered some state where all that existed was her and the ship she was flying. Lasren had never before sat beside her while she was flying, and he had never seen this change. He wondered if it was something she had learned. Searching more deeply, he saw the truth; it was automatic, as effortless as breathing to her.

No wonder she's such a good pilot, he realized.

"You want to catch dinner when we're done here?" Gwyn asked brazenly.

Now that she had maneuvered the shuttle to its optimal position for the dilithium extraction, she was back and had obviously sensed his empathic intrusion. Chiding himself internally for forgetting that she was also a low-level empath, given her Kriosian heritage, he replied, "I apologize for that. I was curious about . . . I . . . uh . . . should have just asked."

Gwyn turned to him again and winked playfully. "Curiosity's not a crime, Lieutenant." As he felt himself reddening slightly, she added, "We're in position."

Lasren double-checked his operations panel and said, "Ready to begin extraction."

"Transporters online and standing by," Gwyn said.

"Target acquired. Sensors confirm traker deposit at depth of eighty-six meters. Activating phase-pulse on my mark . . . three, two, one . . . mark," Lasren said.

The procedure Commander Torres had outlined to him was not difficult to execute. Slight modifications to the shuttle's weapons systems and sensors had been required. She had guided him through the process twice before clearing Lasren to launch, and he was determined to follow the fleet chief's instructions to the letter.

A short series of phase pulses would vaporize the area around the deposits. Sensors were locked onto the dilithium, and transporters would remove the sample as soon as the surrounding rock had been eliminated. The transport would be Gwyn's job. Lasren would have to make sure the confinement beam remained stable, to avoid damaging the crystals during transport.

After a few moments of silence, Lasren said, "Transporters have a lock."

"Initiating transport," Gwyn said.

The moment the words left her lips, the shuttle rocked violently beneath them.

"Aborting transport," she said automatically as she redirected her attention to the navigational sensors.

"We have company," Lasren confirmed.

"Two sentries have emerged from subspace and are approaching our position," Gwyn said. "I'm getting us out of here, Lieutenant."

"Works for me," Lasren agreed, then tapped the communications controls. "*Delta Flyer* to *Voyager.* We have a problem."

"We see them. Don't worry," Chakotay's assured voice said.

DEMETER

Commander Liam O'Donnell was about to congratulate Ensign Brill for his work in bay three. Suddenly, four different species—two docile, medium-sized *ungulates,* a juvenile *cervidae,* two winged creatures reminiscent of the Terran *Anser* genera, and a frisky, rather large iguana he would have sworn was a *Pumila,* simultaneously ceased their grazing and began moving through their containment areas as if they were trying to flee an approaching predator.

Before O'Donnell could begin to understand this reaction, a loud, sharp growling howl met his ears, clearly coming from bay four down the hall.

Monster? he thought.

Acting on instinct, O'Donnell moved to one of the lab's microscopes where bacteria native to the "ark planet" was undergoing analysis. He immediately noted an increase in cellular activity.

"What the hell is going on out there?" he bellowed.

THE ARK PLANET

Commander Tom Paris had been ready to leave the cavern an hour ago. He'd seen all he cared to of the wave form's birthplace, but Kim and Fife were like kids in a candy store; there were so many possibilities and nothing but time to test them.

Then the first tremor hit.

Kim and Fife were brainstorming about the alien technology that had failed to bring the wave forms fully into being when the ground shifted subtly, and both automatically moved closer to the doorway.

Loose dust began to descend from above as Paris said, "We're leaving, gentlemen."

Swift assents were their only response.

Once the tunnel that led to this cavern had been cleared, Paris and his team had transported down directly from *Voyager.* They had brought portable pattern enhancers and set them up near the doorway to facilitate their return.

They were five meters from salvation when a loud crack from above caused Paris to automatically reach for the backs of Kim and Fife's environmental suits. He was able to pull both of them clear before the rocks began to fall. They retreated as far as they could, avoiding the edge of the plateau, and watched in dismay as the doorway that had been their only exit caved in, burying their transport enhancers along with it.

"Paris to *Voyager*," the first officer called, activating his suit's comm system.

When he got no immediate response, Kim and Fife tried as well with no better luck.

"They can't get a transport lock on us now anyway!" Kim shouted. The cavern sounded as if it was about to tear itself apart.

"Then we dig," Paris ordered over the cacophony. Moving back toward what had been the doorway, he reached for the closest rock and heaved it out of the way.

Fife was beside him, grunting with strenuous effort when Kim said, "Tom."

"Dig, Harry!" Paris ordered again.

"Tom," Kim said more urgently, and his tone forced Paris to turn and follow his best friend's gaze.

From below, several small wave forms had emerged from the darkness and were making their way directly for the away team.

"I thought you said the wave forms in here couldn't emerge from subspace!" Paris shouted at Kim.

"They can't," Kim shouted back. "These are different."

"Where did they come from?"

"Somewhere down there!" came Kim's exasperated response.

"Which kind are they?" Paris asked, simultaneously feeling the ground beneath his feet disappear.

Kim started to answer, but as the wave forms enveloped them, his and Fife's screams overloaded the suit's comms.

VOYAGER

Much of the time spent on a starship was routine, if not dull. Then, there were moments like this one where everything seemed to go wrong at once.

Lieutenant Waters, who had taken Lasren's place at ops, advised Chakotay the moment the eruption of the sentries was detected near the *Delta Flyer II*. Kim had hand-picked Lieutenant Aubrey to man the tactical station, and Ensign Gleez, the gamma shift flight controller, had the helm.

Commander Torres had insisted on monitoring Lasren and Gwyn's work from the bridge and currently sat at Chakotay's right hand. The moment the sentries appeared, she cursed softly.

Not truly surprised by this eventuality, Chakotay ordered, "Helm, set course four-four-one mark eight and engage. Full impulse. Aubrey, prepare to vent tetryon plasma. Ops, do we still have a lock on the *Flyer*'s crew?"

"Aye, sir," Waters said from ops.

"Get them out," Chakotay ordered.

The sentries were still five thousand meters from the *Delta Flyer II* when Waters advised, "Transport successful, sir."

"Aubrey?" Chakotay asked.

"We'll be in position to vent plasma in forty seconds, Captain," Aubrey said evenly.

"Captain, I'm receiving a transmission from *Demeter*," Waters said.

"What's the problem?" Chakotay asked.

"The away teams have come under attack by the creatures they were studying and are requesting emergency transports. They need *Voyager* back in orbit as soon as possible."

"They can't handle the transports?" Chakotay demanded.

"They can't get a lock on team six. There was a cave-in, and they lost the signal from the pattern enhancers."

"Team six?" Torres asked.

"Commanders Paris and Fife and Lieutenant Kim," Waters clarified.

The engineeer was on her feet in an instant and moving to Waters's station. "Open a channel to *Demeter*," she ordered briskly. "I need to speak to the transporter officer."

"Venting tetryon plasma," Aubrey reported.

Chakotay watched as the sentries distorted and then retreated back into subspace. He could hear Torres's exchange with *Demeter*'s transporter officer.

"Captain, there's another . . ." Aubrey said.

A sentry appeared on the viewscreen within less than two thousand meters of the shuttle.

"What's its trajectory?" Chakotay asked.

"It's heading for the shuttle," Waters replied.

Why? Chakotay asked himself. The attempt to remove the dilithium had ceased the moment the first sentries were detected. The shuttle no longer posed any threat to them or the asteroid. Was this a show of force, or was it simply trying to punish them for their transgression?

Much as Chakotay hated to take action against the wave forms, he also wasn't content to allow them to destroy one of the most advanced shuttles in the fleet.

"Aubrey, target the sentry and fire tetryon pulses."

As soon as he had spoken, however, a new wave form appeared between the shuttle and the sentry.

"The sentry is slowing, sir," Waters advised. "The new wave form is a proctor."

"Hold your fire," Chakotay ordered.

It appeared that the sentry would pass the proctor, but as it approached, the proctor began to expand as if it intended to swallow the sentry whole. Before they made contact, the sentry ceased its motion, though its EM discharges appeared to increase in intensity. The proctor held its ground, and seconds later, both vanished from the main viewscreen.

What just happened? Chakotay wondered.

Torres's voice sliced through the air. "Listen to me," she said. "Forget the pattern enhancers. Set your sensors for optimum mineral resolution and scan for calcium phosphate."

"I'm sorry, Commander, but our sensors can't penetrate the magnetic field," the unfortunate transport officer replied.

"You need more power," Torres said, doing her best to control her temper. "Take it from all non-essential systems. Do it now," she ordered.

"There's too much interference," the officer insisted.

Torres's eyes met Chakotay's, and they spoke volumes of the pain she clearly wished to inflict upon the transport officer. "Captain," she pleaded.

"Gleez, best possible speed to the planet," Chakotay ordered.

"En route," Gleez confirmed. "We'll be in range in four minutes, sir."

The engineer shook her head slowly. She obviously didn't think it wise to wait that long.

Before Chakotay could reassure her, Waters advised, "Captain, incoming transmission from Commander O'Donnell."

"Onscreen," Chakotay ordered.

O'Donnell's face was set in grim lines, and his eyes were blazing. *"Did you just send a shuttle to collect something from a nearby asteroid?"*

"Yes," Chakotay replied coldly. "But that's not our priority right now. We have a team trapped underground at the planet's southern pole and we need to get them out."

"Transporters aren't an option without the pattern enhancers," O'Donnell said.

"If you would . . . !" Torres began.

"Commander Torres!" Chakotay cut her off sharply. "Can you send another team down with enhancers?"

"There's a seismic event under way in that area," O'Donnell replied. *"And we've still got four other teams under attack we need to retrieve."*

"Why so many?" Chakotay asked.

"You didn't think the wave forms would mind when you sent that shuttle out?" O'Donnell asked, incredulous.

"I considered it," Chakotay replied.

"We already know this entire area of space is one vast interconnected ecosystem," O'Donnell reminded him.

"And now we know they value every bit of it as much as they seem to value the planet," Chakotay said. "It was a calculated risk."

"It's not just the wave forms, Captain," O'Donnell said. *"All of the life-forms native to the planet displayed erratic otherwise unexplainable behavior, as did every life-form we were studying on the surface."*

"Captain O'Donnell," a voice called from *Demeter*'s bridge.

"What is it, Lieutenant Url?" O'Donnell asked.

"We have incoming."

"Incoming what?" O'Donnell asked tersely.

"It's hard to say, sir. Sensors show three life-forms in environmental suits. But they're not moving under the suit's power. They're rising out of the atmosphere."

"Can you get a transporter lock now?" Torres asked through gritted teeth.

"They are each surrounded by a unique EM field. It's scattering the targeting sensors."

"Move to intercept," O'Donnell ordered immediately.

Chakotay watched as *Demeter*'s bridge began to shake. O'Donnell seemed to take the incident in stride, looking up as the disruption continued, perhaps wondering if the overhead of the bridge was about to come crashing down on him.

After a few seconds that felt like a lifetime, the motion ceased.

"Report," O'Donnell said.

Url's voice replied, *"They entered the ship, sir, and the EM field released them. Commanders Fife, Paris, and Lieutenant Kim are in our cargo bay. Medics are on the way."*

"Are they alive?" Chakotay asked.

"Aye, sir," Url replied.

Grateful beyond words, Chakotay merely nodded. Torres stepped clear of ops and sat down hard on the low step separating the upper ring of the bridge from the command well, her face resting in her hands as she tried to slow her breath.

"When you reach orbit, why don't you come aboard, Captain?" O'Donnell offered. *"We've got a lot to talk about."*

"Agreed," Chakotay said, "once we retrieve our shuttle. *Voyager* out. Ensign Gleez?"

"Altering course now, Captain," Gleez said.

Chapter Fourteen

UTOPIA PLANITIA

"Commander Drafar, how nice to see you again," Admiral Janeway said, extending her hand to the Lendrin captain of *Achilles* and craning her neck upward to meet his eyes. He was actually taller than Admiral Akaar, and Janeway didn't think that was possible.

"And you, Admiral," he replied, skillfully hiding the surprise he must have felt when he received her orders.

Turning to a *Voyager* comrade, Janeway extended her hand to Lieutenant Vorik. She had seen him at the memorial service, but they had not spoken. "Hello, Vorik," she said warmly.

The hand that grasped hers was cold, but his voice was colder. "Admiral." He nodded, clipping the word to two harsh syllables.

Janeway was surprised at this. Although they had never been close, she had followed Vorik's progress in *Voyager*'s engineering section and felt the same proprietary regard for him as for all who had served under her in the Delta Quadrant. She could have been misreading Vulcan discipline for anger, but she didn't think so.

Letting it go for now, Janeway turned to Captain Regina Farkas, the only reunion she had anticipated with any trepidation. "Captain Farkas, you're looking well."

"Thank you, Admiral," Farkas said, taking her hand firmly.

Janeway read considerably less anger than she had expected, along with a healthy dose of curiosity.

"If you will all follow me, I'll explain your orders," Janeway said, leading the trio down a long flight of stairs to the holding area, a vast space of necessity, given what it housed.

When they had settled themselves in the dimly lit area, Janeway said, "Computer, maximum illumination." The computer acknowledged the order with a trilling beep and soon the room was aglow as light reflected off and gently caressed thousands of pieces of starship, only a few large bulkheads still intact.

"Captain, Commander, Lieutenant, meet the *Vesta,*" Janeway said.

Drafar and Vorik exchanged confused glances, but Farkas's eyes met hers with approval.

"What's left of her," Vorik said softly.

"Obviously, she has seen better days," Janeway acknowledged. "The *Vesta* was the test ship for the class now named in her honor—the first Starfleet vessels equipped with combined warp and slipstream drives."

"If memory serves, she was decommissioned after her test runs were complete," Drafar noted.

"She suffered many well-earned bumps and bruises," Janeway said, "a fate not uncommon for trailblazers. At the time, when Starfleet's resources were more plentiful, it was decided that she would best serve our future as a template for *Quirinal,* among others."

"She'll never fly again, Admiral," Vorik said, clearly sensing where this was going.

"Sure she will," Farkas corrected him.

"The Full Circle fleet cannot safely complete its mission in the Delta Quadrant with the resources left to it, and Starfleet does not currently have the resources to build a *Vesta*-class ship for the mission. Apart from Commander Torres," Janeway continued, "the crew who resurrected *Quirinal* are here in the Alpha Quadrant and have now been assigned to extend the same courtesy to the *Vesta*. I believe what you did once, you can do again, particularly when you have the resources of Utopia Planitia at your disposal. We can rebuild the *Vesta*."

"How long do we have to accomplish this task, Admiral?" Drafar asked.

"Four weeks," Janeway replied.

"It will take at least ten weeks to bring her up to current specs," Vorik replied.

"Four weeks," Janeway countered. "Five, if you wish to disappoint me."

"Four would be better," Farkas insisted.

"Captain?" Janeway asked.

Farkas said nothing, but her reply was clearly written all over her face. *When we're done here, Admiral.*

Janeway nodded her understanding. "Commander Drafar, you will lead the reconstruction efforts. Assign your people as you see fit, and feel free to pull crew from Captain Farkas and Lieutenant Vorik."

"You'll want to get Bryce down here yesterday," Farkas noted.

"Agreed," Drafar said.

"I'll expect a complete schedule in six hours," Janeway added. "I'll be returning to Earth tonight but available at any time to address any issues that might arise."

"Understood, Admiral," Drafar said.

"Aye, Admiral," Vorik added.

"Thank you, gentlemen." Janeway smiled. "Captain, walk with me?" she ordered Farkas.

"Of course, Admiral."

In the weeks that had passed since their last conversation, Regina Farkas had done some thinking. Satisfied that Kathryn Janeway would never again command a starship, let alone the Full Circle fleet, her ire had cooled, and she wondered if she had been too hard on the admiral. While it was true that the actions of the future Kathryn Janeway were beyond the pale, *this* Admiral Janeway was not that woman. Farkas had been granted more time than usual between postings to consider her past, present, and future. She wondered if in some alternate time line, some other version of her might have made similar choices. She hoped not. She also hoped that Command would find a way to keep her crew together. It was not lost on her that Kathryn Janeway had been the first one to take any meaningful step toward setting that situation to rights.

I bet much to Ken Montgomery's chagrin, she thought with an inward smile. The poor man had been forced to watch helpless as a mission under his purview had gone from bad to unthinkably bad, when the Federation needed to hear good news. Farkas didn't envy him. The truth was, Montgomery didn't have a lot of good choices when it came to the future of the Full Circle fleet, but that didn't mean it wasn't his responsibility to get off his ass and pick one. Farkas knew she had ridden him hard and that she wasn't the only one. And she'd been pleased when the commander in chief had stepped in and eliminated a few options from the table. But now that she'd gotten her wish, she wondered if her grief hadn't temporarily blinded her to some of Janeway's strengths. Her anger over the losses of *Quirinal, Hawking, Esquiline,* and *Curie* had been all-consuming. It had caused her to wonder if perhaps it wasn't time for her to take her oldest friend, Doctor El'nor Sal's, advice and finally retire.

When she'd seen Admiral Janeway's orders, Farkas's first thought was, *why has she been allowed to give them*. Her second was to kick herself for not seeing the elegance of the solution Janeway had concocted. She wasn't ready to forget the price they'd paid for Janeway's past decisions. But she understood the necessity of forgiveness. Without it, life's promise was too easily mired in pointless regret. She hadn't yet extended that forgiveness to the admiral, but she certainly felt herself being beckoned in that direction.

When they reached the platform leading back to the

observation room, Farkas asked, "Once the *Vesta* is ready to fly, who's going to command her?"

"I'd have thought that would be obvious, Captain," Janeway replied, "unless you've already made other plans?"

"Oh, I'll take her." Farkas smiled. "Thank you, Admiral."

"You'll be free to bring with you as many of *Quirinal*'s people as you like, and I hope the crew recovered from *Hawking* and *Curie* as well."

"It would be an honor. We'll still be short a hundred," Farkas noted.

"We may not be able to bring the *Vesta* to full capacity, unless you want to pull some cadets out a year early."

"No," Farkas said. "I think part of our problem, the first time out, was lack of experience in key positions. Let's not make the same mistake again."

"Agreed," Janeway said. "I'm wondering why you were so intent on pushing Drafar and Vorik?"

"They're engineers; they're not happy unless the deadlines are impossible," Farkas quipped. "But that's not the primary reason."

Janeway turned to face her. "What is?"

"Are you acquainted with Lieutenant Varia at Pathfinder?" Farkas asked.

"No," Janeway replied.

"They've reported several disruptions to our long-range communication relays in the Delta Quadrant over the last few weeks," Farkas said. "Admiral Montgomery has been advised but thus far doesn't think this is cause for undue concern."

When Janeway's eyes widened in response, Farkas realized that this was news to her. Interesting that Ken Montgomery was clearly keeping her out of the loop. Something else had obviously been driving Janeway when she decided to resurrect the *Vesta*. *The desire to prove herself worthy of command of the fleet,* Farkas presumed.

"Do they have any idea what's causing these disruptions?"

"Ten percent of the relays we first dropped have now gone dark," Farkas replied. "It is impossible to tell from here whether they were sabotaged or just suffered from some technical glitch. *Voyager* and *Demeter* are out of range, so they can't provide any intelligence. Pathfinder is now in danger of losing contact with New Talax if any more relays go down. *Somebody* needs to get out there sooner rather than later and find out what's going on."

Janeway nodded somberly. "You think there's any chance that with your people's help, Drafar can get the *Vesta* spaceworthy in less than four weeks?"

"Impossible they can do; *beyond reason,* probably not," Farkas replied.

"Damn," Janeway said softly.

"What about the *Galen*?" Farkas asked.

"They were called to Starbase 185 and are still there," Janeway replied. "But if the relays have come under attack, it's not prudent to send the *Galen*."

"No," Farkas agreed, then asked, "When *Vesta* goes out, will *Achilles* go with her?"

"I don't know," Janeway replied honestly.

"You got this approved through Admiral Akaar?" Farkas ventured.

Crossing her arms at her chest, the first sign of defensiveness Janeway had shown since she arrived, she said, "Is that a problem?"

"No," Farkas said. "But for all the flack I gave him, Montgomery never stopped defending you, at least initially. I'm not sure why you'd go out of your way to intentionally piss him off by going over his head."

Janeway sighed. "I don't have time for politics, posturing, or red tape. Until Command sees fit to assign someone to lead the fleet, I'm going to do everything in my power to see that its needs are met. If that means toes get stepped on or egos get bruised, so be it. Nobody else is making this a priority. You've been on leave for a month. That's a criminal waste of personnel. If I do nothing else before Montgomery or Akaar chains me to a desk, I will see to it that my people are given the best possible chance to complete their mission."

"*Your* people?" Farkas asked.

"Yes," Janeway said simply.

This wasn't arrogance, Farkas thought, stunned by the revelation. She'd long ago decided that arrogance had been the admiral's greatest sin. *What else but an unhealthy level of self-regard could possibly drive anyone to believe they had the right to alter history for their own convenience?*

Pain, Farkas realized. *Loss. Regret. And too many years spent wishing she'd done better by those who had trusted her with their lives.*

The admiral didn't think too much of herself. She thought *too little* of what she had accomplished. Whatever internal scale Janeway used to weigh her achievements, they were measured against a deep and abiding love for her crew. The risks that came with exploration were too great for most starship captains to allow that kind of attachment. It was the quickest path to heartache. Yet, the fearlessness with which Janeway embraced it, even now, was astonishing. Clearly, it could lead even the best intentioned into trouble. Farkas had rarely crossed that line, but Janeway had probably long since ceased to even acknowledge its existence. In some, it might be evidence of inappropriate need. In Janeway, it might be the source of her formidable strength.

Farkas felt her lips curving upward. Kathryn Janeway had her issues. But she wasn't here trying to save herself or her position. Her only concern was protecting the fleet. That was something Farkas could respect.

"I suspect we have a great deal in common, more than you'd like to admit," Janeway had said the last time they'd spoken.

Farkas hadn't believed Janeway until now.

STARBASE 185

"When will I be well enough to begin our journey to the Delta Quadrant?" Axum asked.

Commander Glenn did her best to keep her face neutral. It was a skill that Glenn had always wondered if she has mastered.

Over the past three days, the Doctor had begun to educate Doctors Mai, Everett, and Frist about the nature and capabilities of the Caeliar catoms. Glenn had focused her attention exclusively on Axum. The Starbase had no counselor, and Mai had refused to request one from Starfleet Medical. For Glenn, this was all the confirmation she needed that Axum would remain here only as long as it took for him to recuperate sufficiently for transfer, likely back to Earth. While it was obvious that whoever was calling the shots wanted Axum alive, it was unclear that a complete recovery was essential to his purposes. Glenn had also learned that the worst of the traumas Axum had suffered had not come from his hasty and horrific efforts to remove his Borg technology. It had begun the first moment he awoke on a Borg vessel with the full memory of his life and Unimatrix Zero.

Clarissa Glenn understood why Seven and Captain Janeway assumed that armed with self-knowledge the drones would have been capable of mounting a resistance. The actions of Korok, the Klingon drone who had gained control of his vessel would have given credence to this belief.

But that had not been Axum's reality. The only thing that made life as Borg drones possible for the assimilated was their ignorance of their past lives. Nestled within the Collective's firm embrace, they had known nothing but the rightness of their actions, the nobility of their form, and the quest for perfection.

To awake from that existence alone, but with the constant presence of millions of others within one's mind, would have been terrifying. They had mounted a resistance from within Unimatrix Zero, but there, they were in control. In the Unimatrix, the drones could manipulate their physical appearance at will. They couldn't die unless their real bodies were destroyed. All things were possible there. Not so in the world in which they found themselves upon awakening.

Axum hadn't buckled under the psychological strain overnight. For years he had kept his identity secret from the others aboard his scout vessel. He had carefully planned and executed several small disruptions to the ship's operations, hoping they would provide him with the means to escape. Then his ship had encountered a small colony, deep in the Beta Quadrant, and had been ordered to assimilate it. That action his conscience could not abide. To survive, however, he had no choice.

Even after those dreadful days, he had struggled to maintain his equilibrium. While executing another small act of sabotage, Axum had been discovered, and a battle had ensued. Fighting for his own life—killing several other drones he could not help but think of as victims, like himself—Axum managed to make his way into an escape pod and trigger the destruction of the vessel as he fled. He immediately set course for the nearest safe haven, a Federation starbase, but it would be a journey of months he was facing alone.

His actions had not escaped the notice of his vengeful queen. She did not trouble herself to dispatch a vessel to retrieve him. And she could not force him, freed as he was, in a sense, to destroy his ship. So, she had chosen to make his last days as a drone as painful as possible. For what felt like years, but had in fact been several weeks, she had been a constant presence in his mind. She had tormented him with visions of his actions as a drone and the progress of the Borg as they attacked the Federation. She assured him that as soon as any Federation craft or base found him, he would be instantly destroyed.

The queen had broken him, driven him to the frenzy that had led him to the only action he could take. He must remove her from his mind by force.

The extractions began.

The process of recounting these events to Glenn had been therapeutic for Axum. He had gained strength daily, and she had chosen to remain by his side long after her duty shifts ended. The commander had chosen not to contradict his belief that as soon as he was recovered, he would be reunited with Annika. In truth, this was the only future that mattered to him.

Glenn feared that to reveal what she believed to be his more likely future would thrust him back into a deep despair. For now, Axum waded in the shallows, still tormented, but grasping for the life of which he dreamed and trusting Glenn implicitly. She didn't know what a trained counselor would do right now, but she knew what she *had to do*: no further harm.

"It will be several more days," Glenn replied, taking his disfigured hand in hers and squeezing it gently.

"Good," he said with an assured smile. Even through the vivid scars etched across his face it was easy to see now how handsome he must have once been. "I didn't believe you when you first told me Annika was still alive. But now that I know she is . . ."

"What do you mean?" Glenn asked.

Another smile, this one more distant. "I *know,*" he said simply. "I feel her again. She is still part of me, the best part of me."

Glenn nodded, trying to reassure him. How much of the sensation he described was real and how much a product of the catoms that had been transplanted into him was an open question. If it strengthened his will to survive, it could only be a good thing.

The commander truly wished that she could convince her superiors that they were not living up to Federation ideals by using Axum as they clearly intended to. She knew the Borg Invasion and the merciless way they had pursued all-out war against the Federation had many in Starfleet questioning if those ideals lead to the invasion.

But Glenn, who had lost friends and family to the Borg, saw Axum not as a monster. She saw a man who had fought as best he could and now needed help. Unfortunately, Captain Jax Dreshing, the starbase's commander, still quoted regs when pressed on Axum's official status, no doubt coached by Doctors Everett and Frist.

Glenn had never before in her young life, as a Starfleet officer, encountered a situation where her oath demanded she sublimate her beliefs. It was a disturbing place in which to find herself and one for which there was no clear remedy.

"The Doctor's work clearly demonstrates that intermingling catoms from distinct individuals does not render them inoperative or damage them in any way," Doctor Everett argued.

"It's one case, Everett," Mai said. "And in this case, the catoms had reverted to a neutral state prior to the transfer."

"It's also worth noting that in C-1's case, he already possessed catomic technology within his body. This does nothing to shed light upon the possibilities of rejection in individuals not already predisposed to accept the catoms," Frist added.

The Doctor had followed much of the previous hour's discussion with the minimal amount of attention required. It had taken this long to make them understand both the established abilities and limits of catoms. What flights of fancy they were now enjoying or their relevance to Axum or Seven he could not imagine, but he was struck again by Frist's insistence on referring to his patient as C-1. It was more insulting than using his Borg designation.

"Catoms are not transmittable by any means we have observed other than direct injection," the Doctor interjected. "*Axum's* initial catoms were transformed matter. They replaced his former Borg technology. How much of their inability to completely restore him to health was due to his physical injuries prior to the transformation and how much might be credited to his mental state at the time we cannot ascertain to a certainty. But you can't 'catch' catoms like you would contract a viral or bacterial infection."

All three grew strangely quiet at this, staring at him intently. Something in the fear that followed each of them like a specter caught the Doctor's full attention. They were not speculating idly. They were not considering hypothetical uses for catomic technology. Admiral Janeway had insisted that something more was at stake here. For the first time, the Doctor gave serious consideration to what that *something* might be.

"Has a case been discovered of an individual who is not a former Borg containing catomic technology?" the Doctor asked directly.

The three glanced at one another, clearly wishing they were telepaths. It was Doctor Frist who turned to the Doctor and said, "Possibly."

"I'd like to review that file," the Doctor said immediately. What they were suggesting was extremely unlikely, and if their previous work with whatever case they had encountered had been as ham-handed and ill-informed as Doctor Mai's initial evaluation of Axum, this might well be a simple case of misdiagnosis.

Frist took the padd she was using to take notes on the Doctor's reports and began to pull up a series of files. She passed the padd to him across the *Galen*'s conference table saying, "What you are about to see does not leave this room, Doctor."

Agreeing, the Doctor began to read. In less than a minute he had absorbed the contents. He spent three more minutes pretending to finish reading while he processed the data and searched his diagnostic subroutines for conclusions beyond those already accepted. Finally, he asked, "How many people know about this?"

"Beyond those present here, fifty. The patients have all been quarantined. Starfleet Medical and the Federation Institute of Health have made eradicating this plague their highest priority," Frist replied.

"You have more than ten thousand cases referenced here," the Doctor replied. "Their families aren't curious about what's happened to them?"

"We're talking about three worlds that saw heavy fighting during the Borg Invasion, Doctor," Everett replied. "The damage to all three from Borg weapons was intense, and in each case, Borg vessels were destroyed in orbit. Debris from those vessels would have been found on the surfaces even before the Caeliar transformation. There is no way to know how many of our patients might have come in contact with debris that was once Borg but *then* dissolved, or how, exactly, they came into contact with Caeliar catoms."

"Three worlds," the Doctor said, "Aldebaran, Coridan, and Ardana; do they have anything in common apart from Federation membership and the devastation? Weren't several other planets attacked? Have you found any cases of this disease on those worlds?"

"We're in the process of checking, Doctor, but it is an arduous task, given the state of these worlds and our limited resources," Everett replied. "For now, the infection seems isolated to these three worlds, but that could change. Ardana was the last to report cases, but the massive civil unrest that has troubled them since the invasion could account for the time delay in reporting the infection's progress there."

"Do you have evidence to confirm that catoms have been found in these victims?" the Doctor went on.

"Why do you think we were so eager to see your research, Doctor?" Frist asked bitterly. "You are the first to visualize a catom. Your work will make ours much easier. Now we know what we're looking for."

The Doctor shook his head. "I understand your alarm. Any infection that spreads this quickly is a dire threat. But your conclusion—that somehow these people were *infected* by catoms left on their world in the form of transformed Borg debris—just seems impossible."

"Why?" Frist asked.

"The Caeliar were better than this," the Doctor replied, frustrated that he could not immediately find a better way to phrase his incredulity. "They wanted us to know as little as possible about them after they left. As soon as this station was detected, Axum's ship transmitted a virus here to erase all records from sensors. The catoms provided to Seven and Axum are extremely limited in their capabilities. They are the palest possible reflection of the wonder that is a Caeliar. The Caeliar's intention, when they did what they did, was clearly to eliminate any threat posed by the Borg. Why would they replace it with one of their own?"

"They may have been, good Doctor," Frist replied, "but they weren't gods. Who is to say that their technology wasn't somehow damaged or mutated in some way when it came into contact with these worlds, all of which were exposed to high energy and some exotic weaponry just prior to the transformation? They could not possibly have prepared these catoms for every conceivable interaction prior to their dispersal on these worlds."

"They perfected catomic technology thousands of years ago," the Doctor said. "They shouldn't have *had* to."

"The fact remains that thousands of people have already succumbed to this illness, Doctor. We can't identify the infectious agent. If it continues to spread, within months, hundreds of thousands will die," Everett reminded him.

"Over sixty-three billion died in the Borg Invasion. Adding a few million more is unacceptable, Doctor," Frist said. "We must do all we can, as quickly as possible, to end this new threat. If, as you suggest, the catoms were not the cause, they may be the solution."

The Doctor did not believe that the path they were following would yield the results they sought. His work with Seven and Axum's catoms had shown him the elegant simplicity of the technology. Nothing he had seen suggested anything but the most benign of intents from the Caeliar. It was possible that this was an unforeseeable result of catomic interaction, but the Doctor could not accept this premise. If he was to add anything meaningful to the discussion, he would need to evaluate some of these patients for himself. Further, he was certain that the work of using catoms beyond the purposes coded into them by the Caeliar was going to take years if not decades to develop. None of the individuals currently suffering from this plague was going to survive that long. Other options must be found.

"I am happy to make myself available to assist you in any way going forward," the Doctor said. "You have all of the information you requested regarding Seven and Doctor Frazier's people. You also have access to everything relating to Axum. I understand your reluctance to release him, but I want to go on record, even in light of this development, and state that I believe that to allow him to reunite with Seven of Nine is in his best interest and will likely be the only thing that might ensure his recovery. I could continue to monitor him and provide you with all of my findings, even in the Delta Quadrant. As you know, the Full Circle fleet has the capability to interact directly with the Alpha Quadrant."

Doctor Mai shook her head in disbelief. Doctor Frist was more diplomatic. "I will take your recommendation into account, Doctor. If the data you have provided yields substantial results in the short term, it is possible we will reevaluate the necessity of keeping patient C-1 closer for observation and further tests. Your participation in our work ends here. We thank you for your efforts, but your current assignment with the Full Circle fleet is too valuable for you to be spared to further assist in our efforts."

"You can't be serious," the Doctor said, aghast. "You need the best minds in the Federation working on this right now."

"I assure you, they are," Doctor Frist said evenly.

Chapter Fifteen

DEMETER

Demeter's briefing room could seat six comfortably. When Captain Chakotay had come aboard accompanied by Counselor Cambridge and Seven of Nine, Lieutenant Url had suggested moving the scheduled briefing to one of *Demeter*'s larger airponics bays. However, those were crowded with numerous life-forms from the Ark planet, all of them displaying varying degrees of distress. The briefing room was the only viable option.

Chakotay sat opposite Commander O'Donnell. Commanders Paris and Fife, along with Lieutenant Kim, who were all shaken, but physically unharmed, sat with them, and the remaining chair at the table was filled by Seven. Url stood near the table, ill at ease. Only Cambridge, who stood with his arms crossed leaning against a port, seemed truly comfortable with the arrangement.

"If there aren't any objections," Chakotay began, seizing control of the briefing, "I'd like to hear from Commander Paris's team." Turning to Paris he said bluntly, "What the hell happened down there?"

Paris still seemed disconcerted. His normally ruddy complexion was ashen, and he held his hands before him on the table, fingers firmly interlocked. "We were studying numerous distortions we discovered in the cavern. Lieutenant Kim and Commander Fife can speak their theories, but conditions were nominal until the tremors began."

"What did you find there?" Chakotay asked.

Fife nodded to Kim. "You go ahead."

"The cavern contained hundreds of subspace distortions; wave forms that were never able to completely emerge from subspace. We believe that many if not all of the wave forms that are now protecting this area of space were born there. The cavern is a perfect channel for the energy required. However, the technology used to fracture subspace and cause the wave forms to cohere was not found. We theorize it was destroyed before its creators left the planet," Kim reported.

"What caused the tremors?" Chakotay asked.

"The emergence of three fully coherent wave forms, proctors I believe, who rescued us," Kim replied.

"And did you do anything to precipitate their actions?"

"No, sir," Kim said.

"When did the tremors begin?" Chakotay asked.

"Sixteen zero five hours," Url replied. "We maintained transporter lock until the disruption began and the enhancers were lost."

"According to my readings, the seismic disruption on the surface began within seconds of the emergence of the sentries who moved to intercept the *Delta Flyer,*" Seven noted.

"As did the change in behavior of all of the life-forms we were studying aboard *Demeter,*" O'Donnell added.

"That's also when we began receiving reports that the other away teams were coming under attack," Url said. "We recovered all of the away teams, apart from team six, in quick succession."

"We're all on the same page then?" O'Donnell asked.

"I'm just now opening my hymnal sir," Cambridge replied. "Which page, exactly?"

O'Donnell favored the counselor with a withering glance. "When the shuttle team tried to extract dilithium from the asteroids, the response was immediate: an attack from sentries, the removal of Paris's team from their location by three proctors, and visible disruption to every living thing native to the planet."

"So you have concluded that because these events occurred in such close proximity, they must be related," Cambridge noted.

"Simplest explanation usually the right one and all that," O'Donnell said.

"When it comes to the actions of the sentries and proctors, I see your point," Cambridge allowed. "But when it comes to the life-forms, I'm afraid that's a harder sell. You're talking about hundreds of discreet organisms on the surface of the planet and on your ship. How did they receive the stimulus required to account for their behavior at the same time?"

"Have you ever sat outside at night, listening to the choruses of hundreds of life-forms going about their business, only to hear absolute silence suddenly descend just before a storm breaks?" O'Donnell asked.

"I'm not much of an outdoorsman," Cambridge admitted.

"Counselor," Chakotay cautioned him softly.

"All of the space that was once shrouded by the cloaking matrix is a vast interconnected system," O'Donnell said simply.

"Many life-forms are sensitive to subtle shifts in magnetic energy, including those that herald the onset of a change in the weather. But that is determined by their proximity to that energy. You're saying that an invisible connection binds all of them, regardless of their location?" Seven asked.

"Yes," O'Donnell replied.

"Something that none of our sensors detected?" Chakotay asked.

"I believe our senses just did," O'Donnell replied.

Kim jumped up from the table and grabbed his tricorder. "Stand up, Tom," he requested.

Paris obliged him and Kim completed a quick scan. He then turned to Fife. "Commander?" he asked.

Fife rose and Kim repeated the scan. He turned the device on himself. While they resumed their seats, Kim studied the results. "It's minimal, but it's there."

"What is?" Seven asked.

"Residual EM readings," Kim replied.

"What?" Paris asked, clearly concerned.

"Don't worry, Tom," Kim said. "All of the wave forms operate in the same way. When they surround an object, they effectively pull it partially into subspace. They create small subspace bubbles around the effected area, thereby easing their progress as they move through solid matter but also protecting whatever they scan."

"While in subspace, without shields, our ships would have been exposed to several forms of exotic ratiation," Seven agreed. "The subspace bubbles shielded us from its effects."

"Yes," Kim agreed.

"But there no were no 'bubbles' around us when they took us," Fife interjected. "They had their characteristic oval shape as they moved toward us, but that dissipated when we came in contact with them."

"Your eyes were open?" Paris asked incredulously.

"You can't do the same with a living organism," Kim said. "The wave forms protected us, moved us safely through solid rock and then the planet's atmosphere, but they did so by altering the subatomic essence of our environmental suits. They actually merged with the suits, bringing us briefly into subspace. Traces of the effect are still present in our skin, but not at dangerous levels."

"Will it dissipate over time?" Paris asked.

"Yes. We were treated with hyronalin. All evidence of our exposure will be gone within the next few hours," Kim replied.

"No wonder," O'Donnell said softly.

"Commander?" Chakotay asked.

"One question unanswered thus far was: How did the

people responsible for transporting the life-forms to the planet do it?" O'Donnell replied.

"They obviously had ships," Chakotay suggested.

"Yes, but we're talking about millions of species. Those ships had to be busy destroying planets and harvesting their resources."

"They used the wave forms," Kim realized.

"They used the wave forms," O'Donnell echoed in agreement.

"Even if that was the case, and the act of transporting them left some residual electro-magnetic energy within the life-forms initially brought to the planet, that was several generations ago," Seven countered. "The creatures we are studying are not the same ones brought here, except perhaps in the case of a few extremely long-lived species."

"What if the wave forms' work didn't end with the initial transports?" O'Donnell asked.

"They've watched the progress of the planet, witnessed the significant decline in species, and are still trying to save them," Chakotay said.

O'Donnell said, "When their efforts did not succeed, they went looking for help."

Silence descended briefly on the room as everyone considered the implications.

"Why didn't they go to their creators?" Cambridge asked.

"Maybe they did but didn't get the response they wanted," Kim replied.

"You would think that anyone who went to the trouble to create these wave forms and use them to save these species would have cared when they learned of the planet's status," Paris insisted.

"You would, wouldn't you?" O'Donnell agreed. "But the evidence now before us suggests they didn't or couldn't do anything to change the planet's current circumstances."

"But we can," Fife said softly.

"Absolutely." O'Donnell shrugged.

"You're talking about a complete reorganization of an incredibly complicated group of ecosystems," Cambridge pointed out. "We'd have to relocate hundreds of populations, create thousands of bacterial life-forms and several new botanical ones from scratch, and do a fair amount of terraforming."

"And on the seventh day, we'll rest," O'Donnell said cheerfully.

"We can't do that," Kim said simply.

"We're not *allowed* to do that," Paris corrected him gently.

"The Prime Directive prohibits us from interfering in the natural development of any pre-warp civilizations," Chakotay said evenly.

"When a sentient, warp-capable species makes contact with us and asks for our help, we are free to consider their request and proceed as we see fit," O'Donnell said. "Many such species have made similar requests of the Federation, and we've assisted them, even when they faced ecological disasters of their own making."

"The wave forms aren't life-forms, and their sentience remains an open question," Seven countered.

"Maybe," Chakotay said.

"Captain?" Paris turned on him, surprised.

"After we attempted to extract the dilithium and the sentries emerged, we immediately ceased operations and transported the shuttle crew to safety. We also neutralized those sentries. Shortly, another emerged, on course to destroy the *Delta Flyer.* Before it came within range of the shuttle, a proctor emerged and stopped it. The proctor placed itself between the sentry and the shuttle, and after a few moments, the sentry dispersed and the shuttle was left intact," Chakotay said.

"The proctors saved us, too," Kim added.

"Do you believe the proctors and sentries can read our minds?" Cambridge asked. "Why would they protect us? We haven't taken any action suggesting we are going to help them."

"Some of us might have," Fife observed, glancing toward O'Donnell.

"The proctor wave form *Voyager* contacted did make some sort of telepathic connection with Admiral Janeway. It disabled her, but when she awoke, she was certain that its intentions were benign. It communicated something to her, even though she couldn't quite understand it," Chakotay said.

"And it dumped more data than we could understand into our computers," Kim added. "It's possible that the wave forms are capable of interpreting our neurological patterns in some fashion."

"I agree," Chakotay said.

"Have you made a decision?" Paris asked.

"I'd like to speak with Commander O'Donnell alone," Chakotay replied. "Can we have the room?"

Commander O'Donnell stood and crossed to the briefing room's single window that afforded him a view of the Ark planet. It should have been a lovely blue orb, not unlike Earth. Water was plentiful, though the landmasses were larger than his homeworld's. The haphazard arrangement of its life-forms, however, left much of it shrouded in sickly wisps of yellowish haze. O'Donnell wished nothing more than to take a deep breath and blow them from the atmosphere, revealing the jewel beneath in all of its glory.

The commander believed Captain Chakotay shared this wish, but something prevented him from acting on it. As always, Alana sensed his turmoil and sought to ease it.

He wants to agree with you, darling, Alana advised.

Then why hasn't he?

He's afraid.

Of what?

"Commander?" Chakotay asked, ending the conversation.

Chakotay remained seated at the table's head. O'Donnell moved to the seat at his right hand.

"You know we can do this," O'Donnell began.

"Yes," Chakotay agreed.

"And you know we should."

"Then what?" Chakotay asked.

O'Donnell paused, wondering if he understood the question. "And then we take our lashes like good little Starfleet officers and move on."

"*If* we do this," Chakotay said, "we could be breaking the Prime Directive."

"There's a case to be made that the actions of the wave forms, including their original distress call, make the Prime Directive irrelevant," O'Donnell replied.

Chakotay considered this in silence, then replied. "They ask for help. We answer. We reorganize an entire planet to assuage whatever guilt or programming glitch is driving them and then they bring their cloaking matrix back online and we resume our mission having expended thousands of man hours and vast resources saving a planet that somebody else ruined for their convenience. There's no technology left down there to help us understand how those who created the wave forms did what they did. There's nothing more for us to learn here."

"And?" O'Donnell replied.

"Why are we doing this again?"

"Sir, it's the right thing to do."

"You believe the wave forms are still working to restore the planet to health. Why not teach them how to do that on their own?"

"Give a man a fish or teach him to fish?" O'Donnell asked.

Chakotay turned to look at the Ark planet. "We know how to heal this planet. If we could teach the wave forms what they need to know in order to do this work, what's to say they might not use that knowledge to do some good of their own in the future. We know they can travel beyond this parsec. And who knows how many worlds out there might be in need of such assistance?"

"If we could communicate with them, that might be a

possibility," O'Donnell replied, "but we can't. We're assuming a fair amount here based on their actions, but we don't know how detailed their understanding is of what's causing the planet's death. If their primary purpose was transporting life-forms and hiding them from the rest of the galaxy, it might take longer than our lifetimes to introduce them to the finer points of terraforming, let alone genetics."

"Maybe that should be our focus," Chakotay replied. "Offering assistance to the wave forms that asked for our help is not beyond the bounds of our mission. Solving their problem for them, just because we can, is over the line."

"Which line is that, exactly?" O'Donnell asked, rising from his chair and taking a step back. "Who the hell drew it?"

Chakotay's face hardened. "You're out of line, Commander."

"We were sent to expand our understanding of the galaxy. I'm sick of cleaning up the messes our superior officers make when they can't get along with the folks who share our galaxy. One bloody war after another. Billions of lives lost. It sickens the soul. Death is coming for this planet and every living thing on it."

"Death is coming for all of us, this planet included, whether we prolong its existence or not," Chakotay said.

"What if we save a species that flourishes and one day joins us out here? What if the wave forms can learn something by our example, if only that everybody traveling through space isn't out here to rape, pillage, and plunder for their own selfish reasons?" O'Donnell argued.

"The Prime Directive exists to remind us that we are not gods. We don't get to reorganize every world, every civilization, every existence out here in our own image," Chakotay reminded him.

"This isn't about a quest for perfection. We're not the Borg," O'Donnell insisted. "It isn't even about interfering in the progress of a planet moving through its natural life span. *Somebody else did this.* Somebody else already altered the fate of this world irrevocably. How does doing a better job than they did, actually allowing these life-forms to continue to evolve, fly in the face of the ideals of the Federation?"

"Right now, millions of Federation citizens are living in difficult and desperate circumstances," Chakotay said, clearly trying to remain reasonable. "The life-forms on this planet aren't sentient and may well never be."

"Does that make them less worthy of our efforts?" O'Donnell asked. "If Starfleet Command thought we were needed back home, that's where we'd be. They sent us out here. And as long as we're here, I think we should solve the problems that are put before us. If this is the last thing I get to do as part of Project Full Circle, I can live with that, Captain," O'Donnell said vehemently.

"When *Voyager* was stranded out here, we made a lot of choices that might not have been by the book, but our survival was at stake. The bar has been set higher this time around. We can't allow our emotional responses, our justifiable anger at what has transpired here, to blind us to our greater purpose. There's a lot of exploration we could do in the weeks it will take to help this planet. And when *our* superior officers ask me why I didn't use that time better, I can't tell them that I needed a win, that the horrors I've witnessed as a Starfleet officer created a moral imperative in me to balance the scales a little. I don't have the luxury of that kind of selfishness."

"Then I'm sorry for you," O'Donnell replied somberly. "I'm sorry you can't see that this is the only work worth doing out here."

Chakotay paused, allowing O'Donnell's accusation to sink in. Finally he said, "If we can find a way to communicate with the wave forms, to provide them with the information and tools they need, I'll allow it. If not, we move on."

At that, Chakotay rose and left the conference room.

VOYAGER

B'Elanna had read and reread the padd in her hand a dozen times. Certain that Tom would not return to their quarters until he'd been cleared by *Demeter*'s CMO and had briefed Chakotay, she'd bided her time, studying the events in minute detail. Each subsequent analysis confirmed her initial suspicions. The sick pit in her stomach, for once, had nothing to do with the son growing inside her.

When Tom finally entered, his strangely pale face glowed like an eerie moon in the dim lights of their quarters.

She was on her feet in an instant and in his arms. It was hard to tell who was trembling more, and their embrace did little to steady either of them.

Tom was the first to pull away, moving toward their bedroom. He paused at the threshold. "Miral?" he asked.

"She went down tonight without much of a fight," B'Elanna replied, her voice pitched low to keep it from betraying her.

Tom nodded. "I'm ready to join her. I need to . . ." he began.

"Tom?" she asked.

"What?"

"Are you . . . I mean . . . I . . ."

"What is it?" he asked, stepping toward her again.

"I'm sorry," she replied.

Tom paused, searching his memory. "For what?" he finally asked.

B'Elanna's eyes widened. *He must know by now.* Even if he didn't, he should hear it from her.

"It's my fault," she finally said.

Tom sighed, shaking his head slowly. "Honey," he began, "it's been a really hard day. Whatever you think you did, I forgive you. Let's go to bed."

"Whatever *I* think I did?" she asked with more heat than she'd intended.

Tom's shoulders slumped. "I didn't mean it that way."

"How did you mean it?"

Raising his head he said, "First thing in the morning, we'll fight as long and as hard as you want. But right now, I just can't."

"I don't want to fight," she insisted.

"Good," he said, moving again toward the bedroom.

B'Elanna wanted to follow. Instead, all she could do was face a rush of images, each more troubling than the last: hanging on to the 'fresher for dear life, destroying their replicator, her manic flurries of pointless activity. No wonder he didn't want to be around her right now. She was a mess and they both knew it.

B'Elanna moved to the sofa and sat, resting her face in her hands. She didn't know what Tom had decided until she felt him settle himself beside her and place a gentle arm over her shoulder.

"I'm sorry," he said.

"You don't have anything to be sorry for," she mumbled into her hands.

"I'm sure you were worried when you heard about this afternoon," he continued.

"Heard about it?" she demanded, her head shooting up. "I was on the bridge, trying to teach transporter operations to a . . ." She paused, biting back a curse. "I could have saved you, even without the pattern enhancers, but we were too far away, and that idiot on *Demeter* . . ."

Tom's face softened into a smile. "You take it for granted, B'Elanna, how good you are. You think it should be that simple for everyone. But it's never going to be."

"Don't smile at me like that," she replied. "I almost got you killed today."

"No, you didn't," he insisted.

"Weren't you at the briefing?" she demanded.

"Yes."

"So you know it was our attempt to extract that dilithium that caused . . ."

"Yes," he said. "It was Lasren and Gwyn on the *Flyer,* right?"

"You think Kenth Lasren talked Chakotay into attempting to mine an asteroid for dilithium?" she asked, incredulous.

Tom searched her face, clearly at a loss. "I don't know," he finally replied.

"*I* was the one who told Chakotay about the dilithium. I asked to take the shuttle out to collect the sample. It was *my* idea," B'Elanna said, her voice thick.

Finally, the light dawned. Tom sat back, taking it in.

"Okay," he finally said softly.

"Okay?"

"Yeah." He shrugged.

"Okay?" she asked again.

"What do you want me to say?" he said. "Please don't do it again? You didn't know. You couldn't have known."

"This isn't a game, Tom," B'Elanna insisted. "This isn't just you and me anymore."

"You think I don't know that?"

"It's easy to forget," she said. "I did. For almost two years while I was building that shuttle and running as far and as fast as I could, I forced myself to think about the fact that we might not make it. We might never see each other again. I had to be strong . . . for Miral."

"You gave up on us?" he asked softly.

"No," she said. "*Never.* But I didn't want the worst to take me by surprise. I wanted to be ready for it."

"I never did that," Tom said.

"I know." She smiled faintly. "I grew up without my father. I never wanted that for Miral, but I told myself we could handle it. We were warriors, we would be fine; all the things my mother used to tell me.

"Three months ago, all those fears went away. You found

us. You saved us from a life I had no idea how much I hated. To see you with your daughter . . . how much you love her, how much she loves you . . . Now, the thought of losing you hurts me in places I didn't know existed. I can't see anything past it. Miral can't grow up without you. The baby . . . *never knowing you at all?* I'd *have* to go on living for them. But I would never be the mother they need. I don't know anymore where I end and you begin. I can't lose you. *We* can't lose you."

"Shhh," Tom whispered, taking her in his arms as B'Elanna felt herself slipping toward a darkness she'd never dared name. "It's going to be okay," he murmured softly.

No, it isn't, something more certain in B'Elanna insisted.

"A lot of people do this, B'Elanna," Tom said. "A lot of career officers raise families in worse situations than this one. We can do it, too."

"How?"

"I don't know," he replied honestly. "I just know we will."

"We were wrong to bring them into this," B'Elanna said softly. "It's not fair to them."

"I don't agree," Tom said. "This is what we were born to do. We're our best selves out here. That's who they need to know. We're not leaving them back home where they'll never understand why we bothered to bring them into the universe if we didn't want to be with them while they were growing up. We're together and that's never going to change. We fought long and hard to get here. And there isn't a safer place they could be than with us."

"The entire multiverse almost ended right in front of us a few weeks ago," B'Elanna said. "How can you . . ."

"It didn't, because we were here to put a stop to it. I wouldn't want to be aligned with the forces of darkness and destruction, B'Elanna, because their track record against us stinks."

As B'Elanna sat back, a faint motion flurried across her belly. She immediately reached for her abdomen. Seconds later, the sensation came again.

"What?" Tom asked.

"Somebody's up." B'Elanna smiled.

Tom placed his hand over B'Elanna's. "It's too early for you to feel it," she said softly.

"Not for long." He smiled back.

Looking up at his face she saw absolute wonder. The terror was real, but so was this. Tom leaned down, resting his head gently in her lap. Wordlessly, she began to caress his hair.

"I should probably tell you . . ." she began, but stopped when she heard him begin to snore. As the stress and fear of the last several hours released her, B'Elanna laid her head back, allowing exhaustion to have its way with her.

What little sky was visible through the canopy of branches above was streaked with stars. The air was warm but not oppressive. The only ambient sound was the occasional trilling of a nocturnal bird, calling out for its mate.

Seven's companion lay beside her. Their skin was pleasantly moist where it touched. The peace of this moment was absolute. Nothing that had come before, nothing that would happen after could erase its perfection. Much as she wished to remain still, to stretch this moment out over eternity, deeper needs still churned within her. Knowing, patient hands sought her out, and she turned without hesitation to allow them to caress her. For a few moments she let them play over her as the need turned to hunger. Opening her eyes, she reached for his face, drawing his lips toward hers.

But his face . . .

Seven awoke, startled. The sweat pooling on her flesh and soaking the sheets met with the room's cool temperature and she shuddered violently. Reaching for a blanket, she expected to meet resistance. Hugh was less than generous in his sleep with the bedclothes, but she was already accustomed to it and could easily find the warmth she required from the heat of his body.

When her grasping fingers easily pulled the blanket over

her, she sat up. The stars outside provided little luminescence, but even in the dimness, she could make out the still figure of the counselor seated in a chair that had been pulled to the end of the bed. He wore a loose-fitting favorite robe, and from his ease she estimated he had been sitting there for some time.

"How was it?" he asked softly.

"To what are you referring?" she demanded. They had begun their relationship as counselor and patient, and over the course of that work, she had shared with him many of her most personal thoughts, feelings, and experiences. When they had allowed that relationship to change, her capacity for emotional expression through physical intimacy had been loosed, and she had marveled at how vulnerable she was to him. She could not now imagine any part of herself she had hidden from him, but he stared at her now as if reproving her for some great betrayal.

"I realize we haven't been bedmates for long, but in the early days you slept, when we found time for sleep, like the dead," Hugh replied. "That changed a few nights ago."

Seven felt heat rising to her cheeks and was grateful for the darkness around her. The dream from which she had just forcibly extricated herself was not the first of its kind. She'd lost count of them, as their frequency had increased, but his time line was accurate. She did not know why she had been reluctant to speak of the dreams. But some unspoken fear had cautioned silence, and unaccustomed to the experience as well as the fear, she had obeyed.

"Naturally, I flattered myself that you had, perhaps, wandered into my dreams," Hugh went on. "But that's not the case, is it?"

"You are the only man I have ever been with in this way," Seven said.

"But not the only man you have wished to be with?" he asked.

What he said was true, but it was not the cause of her

current agitation. It was so much more complicated; she wondered if it would be possible to make him understand and was momentarily irritated that she should have to.

"Have I not demonstrated enough fidelity to you, enough commitment to this relationship to satisfy your insecurities?" she replied.

"Who's Axum?" he finally asked, deflecting her barb.

Chilled, Seven pulled the blankets over her shoulders as she brought her knees to her chest and wrapped her arms around them. The pain he was inflicting upon her now wounded something in the center of her body, and she needed to protect it.

"Have you been attempting to access my personal logs?" she asked.

"No," he replied. "You spoke his name last night in your sleep. The soft moans and writhing woke me, and the pleasure he seemed to be providing you made me wonder why you would have ever let him slip through your fingers." His voice was soft, but his tone reeked of accusation.

Why this revelation horrified her, she could not say. It seemed inappropriate to be embarrassed for actions of her unconscious mind, but her mortification at having unknowingly shared this, even with Hugh, was absolute. She had never before felt so naked in front of him.

"You have shared intimate relations with how many women before me?" Seven asked.

"Good effort," he replied briskly, "but hardly the point. You went into this with your eyes wide open. I never hid my past from you, but it seems clear you have not extended me the same courtesy."

"I didn't think it mattered," she said, unnerved by the honesty he had dragged from her. "It wasn't real. I don't even remember it."

Concern seemed to draw him to her. Hugh moved to the side of the bed and sat facing her. "What does that mean?" he asked more gently.

"I was Borg for eighteen years," Seven replied. "During that time, while I was regenerating, I entered a shared thought-space, a shared reality, with several other Borg drones that contained a mutation that had somehow created this alternate reality. It was called Unimatrix Zero.

"Axum was a man I knew there. Apparently for many years, he and I shared an intimate relationship. But when my regeneration cycle ended, I had no memory of that place or anything I did there. I would never have known once I was severed from the Collective had Axum not found me and asked me to help him and the drones who shared Unimatrix Zero. They had come under attack by the Borg Queen."

"What did you do?" he asked.

"*Voyager*'s crew tried many things," Seven replied. "Ultimately, we were left with only one option. Unimatrix Zero was destroyed, but the drones that once inhabited it were given the ability to retain the memories of their individuality while conscious.

"To be completely honest," she went on, "when I learned what Axum and I had shared, I was curious. But circumstances did not permit me to delve into our hidden past. I hoped that once Axum and the others were freed, we might find each other. But he was on a ship in the Beta Quadrant and *Voyager* was still deep in the Delta Quadrant."

A faint smile rose to Hugh's lips. "'Was ever woman in this humour woo'd? Was ever woman in this humour won?'" he said.

"I never lied to you," she said softly. "I could never have given myself to you in this way had I felt the need or desire to lie to you. When these dreams began, they were so vivid. I assumed that what you and I had shared had begun to unlock whatever subconscious memories I might have of Axum."

"Did you love him?"

"I must have," she admitted. "But what does it matter if I can't remember anything we shared?"

"Move over," he said.

When Seven remained still, he rose and moved to the other side of the bed and climbed in beside her. Hugh then placed an arm over her shoulders, and after a few moments, she relented, relaxing into his arms.

"You're probably right about the source of the dreams," he said softly. "I wish you'd felt free to share them with me sooner. It would have made the last few days easier. But it doesn't matter now. You're entitled, of course, to your own private fantasy life. It's my job to make sure you never want to meet anyone else there but me."

"You were angry with me?" she asked.

"I was nervous," he replied. "I didn't think to find competition for your affections quite so soon."

"Should you ever have cause to worry in that regard, you won't have to wonder," she said. "Pretense is a waste of time. You've already taught me that."

"Care to begin a new lesson?" he asked.

"No," she said. "I'm tired. I'd like to spend a little time alone."

Hugh tensed beside her.

"In my mind," she clarified. "You should also get some rest. Clearly I have already stolen too much from you in the last few days."

"There are medications I could suggest that would offer you a dreamless sleep."

"I'll take my chances," she said, turning over and settling her head on the pillow. Hugh did the same, his body nestled close to hers but refraining from attempting to embrace her. His breath had become slow and regular before sleep finally came for her again; and with it, another intensely disquieting dream.

"You have got to be kidding me," a soft voice came from over Kim's shoulder. Turning from the astrometrics lab's main viewscreen, he found Lieutenant Nancy Conlon standing at the door to the lab, her arms crossed before her.

"Hey," he greeted her.

"Didn't you almost die about ten hours ago?" she asked in disbelief as she moved toward him.

"I guess." He shrugged.

"Weren't you ordered to hit your rack as soon as that briefing ended?"

"Yes."

Opening her arms and looking around the otherwise empty lab, she said, "So what gives?"

"I couldn't sleep," Kim admitted, "too much to do."

Conlon paused, her face etched with concern. Obviously worried, she asked, "You want to talk about it?"

"About what?"

"What happened to you today?"

Kim chuckled involuntarily, which only seemed to confuse and concern her further. "When you've *actually* died more than once, coming close doesn't pack quite the same punch," he said.

"Okay," she replied dubiously. "Jaded wasn't a word I'd ever thought to use to describe you, Harry Kim." After a long pause she continued, "So, if it's not mortal dread keeping you up, what's the problem?"

Kim shook his head. "Chakotay's about to order us to move on," he said.

"How do you know?"

"He told me," he said. "Stopped by when he returned from *Demeter*."

"I thought he was seriously considering O'Donnell's plan," Conlon said.

"He did," Kim assured her. "But when you've got limited resources and a lot of space to cover, carving out a month or more for something like this doesn't make much sense. Maybe, if the last few months had gone better, he'd take the chance. But he can't risk doing anything that Command might question. To do this would guarantee that as soon as they receive our report, we'll be recalled."

"So what exactly are you trying to do?" she asked. "It doesn't sound like he's going to change his mind."

"The captain said the only way he'd consider staying was if we could find a way to communicate with the wave forms," Kim said.

Conlon's jaw dropped. "Unless it's to thank them for saving your life today, I'm not sure why we'd want to do that."

"The wave forms asked for help. Responding to their distress call and assisting *them* does not violate the Prime Directive."

"They want us to save that planet," Conlon began, then caught herself. "Doing it *for* them is crossing the line, but helping them do it, isn't."

"Right. And we can't do that if we can't talk to them. At this point I'm doubtful we can establish any sort of rudimentary communications, but it's worth a shot, isn't it?"

Conlon stepped back and thought for a moment. Finally she asked, "Why do *you* want to help them?"

Kim turned to look at her, his face solemn. "I know it's not our problem. I know the life-forms down there will never know the difference. But it bothers me. Someone tried to do right by those creatures. They expended resources to create the wave forms and used them to save the life they found out here. They just didn't put enough thought into their work. The Ark planet is like a memorial to mediocrity. A lot of the problems down there were easy enough to see coming."

"For us, maybe," Conlon suggested. "Starfleet has explored thousands of planets with countless different life-forms over hundreds of years. Maybe whoever did this didn't have our expertise or experience and just did the best they could."

"That doesn't make me feel better about abandoning them." Kim shrugged.

"The wave forms are a piece of technology, Harry; interesting, complex, and clearly stubborn technology, but they aren't sentient."

"They lifted that cloak and brought us here because they

thought we could help. They saved my life today. We're about to leave, and we can't even make them understand why. What if somebody else comes out here, somebody with our expertise and ability who isn't bound by the Prime Directive, and the wave forms don't even give them a chance because we've taught them not to bother?"

"What did you say?" Conlon asked softly.

"What if somebody else comes out here . . ." Kim began.

"No, the last part. We *taught* them . . ."

". . . not to bother," Kim finished for her.

"You're trying to figure out how to take that message you originally decrypted and turn it into a translation matrix. You want to make them understand *why* we're doing what we're doing. But they're not capable of that. They don't assign meaning or value to the data they perceive and transmit. They are simply following their original programming. They were assigned a function—protect this space and keep these life-forms alive—and they are looking for more data that will allow them to do that."

"They've already downloaded every bit of information contained in the databases of both of our ships, but that data is of no use them if we can't show them how to use it."

"I'm saying it's simpler than that, Harry. You're reaching for the stars when the moon will do."

Kim thought for a moment until it hit him. "They've got the raw data but no way to correlate it to the function they are trying to complete."

"So," she encouraged him.

"So we just need to give them the explicit instructions," Kim realized. "We need to tell them exactly what we would do for the Ark planet, and let them do it."

"It's not a perfect solution," Conlon warned. "There are going to be substances, probably even some simple life-forms they will require, that we will have to create and let the wave forms introduce to the planet. We may not be crossing the line Chakotay is so worried about, but we'll be dancing right up to the edge of it."

"Yes, but as long as we're working *with* them, helping *them* advance their own abilities, I think he'll allow it," Kim said.

"Which just leaves one problem," Conlon said.

"How do we introduce that data to them? They eat our probes and the only subspace communication they responded to was the message they originally left with us," Kim replied.

"Right," Conlon agreed.

After a moment, Kim asked, "Any ideas?"

"Not yet," she said, "but I just started working on this. Give me a few minutes." She smiled and moved to the data terminal beside him.

Unable to repress a wide smile, Kim said, "You don't have to do this now. It is the middle of the night."

"And not at all what I hoped we'd be doing with our off hours," Conlon said, "but don't ever let it be said that Harry Kim didn't know how to show a girl a good time."

Kim chuckled, then paused. "Wait . . . did somebody actually say that?"

"Take it easy," she said slyly. "We have work to do."

Chapter Sixteen

SAN FRANCISCO

Four days.

The volume of communiqués and files submitted for Admiral Janeway's review was staggering.

I'm not even on duty yet, she mused. It was terrifying to imagine what her desk would look like when she had been officially reinstated.

While away from Starfleet headquarters, Janeway had missed six scheduled appointments, three with Counselor Jens and three with other evaluators. The reminders for those appointments were at the top of her day's duty roster and flashed at her in vivid crimson hues.

A familiar voice greeted Janeway as she was moving to her replicator to create the first of what she assumed would be several cups of coffee to get her through the day.

"Good morning, Admiral Janeway," Decan said. Once again he had flawlessly executed a maneuver he had long ago perfected: entering her office and coming within a hair's breadth of her without her noticing. The slightly built Vulcan had been her personal aide a lifetime ago. She assumed that once she had died, Decan had been reassigned, but she was touched he had taken the time to stop by to see her.

"Decan." She smiled warmly, only then noticing that he carried a small tray upon which rested a carafe, a mug, and a padd. "If you aren't a sight for sore eyes," she added immediately.

"There are a number of matters I believe it would be prudent for you to prioritize this morning, Admiral," he said evenly.

Surprised, Janeway asked, "How is it possible you did not receive a promotion during my absence of the last fourteen months? I assumed that by now you would be running this place."

"Shortly after your memorial service I was promoted to full lieutenant and was assigned to the headquarters staffing offices. I have been tasked with fulfilling the personnel needs of many departments, including those of Project Full Circle," he said.

"So this is just you being nice?" Janeway asked dubiously.

"I have found no work since your departure as fulfilling as that I did by your side, Admiral," he said respectfully enough, though Janeway did not miss the slight Vulcan sarcasm, "and I believe I am capable of continuing to render necessary services to the staffing office while addressing your needs as well."

"That is most kind of you, Decan," she said, "but you need to think about your career, too. Coming back to my office has to be seen as a demotion."

"On the contrary," he said. "I have always preferred assignments where my capabilities were most effectively used regardless of the perceived stature of the assignment. When I was asked to consider candidates for the position of your new aide, none had the requisite experience or temperament."

"Temperament?" Janeway asked pointedly.

"Do you wish me to elaborate on that point?"

"No." She smiled.

"Excellent. On a personal note, I hasten to add that I believe I will enjoy the challenges presented when I return to your service once your new position as commander of the Full Circle fleet is approved and you are back on a starship."

When she did not immediately respond, he added, "I have always wished to travel."

"That might be a problem," Janeway admitted. "I have no reason to believe that position will be offered to me again."

"A few things have come to my attention in your absence, Admiral, that I believe you will find interesting," Decan said, apparently confident about her future. "I have taken the liberty of reviewing your status and activity logs while you were away, and based upon your actions, prepared follow-up reports."

Janeway nodded, poured herself a cup of steaming coffee from the carafe, took the padd from the tray, and sat. It was the first time she had felt normal at this desk, and it was entirely to Decan's credit.

"Go ahead," she ordered.

"Captain Drafar reports that work is well under way on the *Vesta.* The estimated completion date is twenty-six days from today."

"Good."

"Lieutenant Varia has filed a new report from Pathfinder indicating that twelve percent of Full Circle's relays in the Delta Quadrant are no long operational as of this morning."

"Damn," she said softly.

"Varia also states that the relays have not been utilized by *Voyager* or *Demeter* in nineteen days."

"Wherever they are, they're still out of range."

"That is the logical conclusion, Admiral.

"Julia Paris has filed a preliminary petition with the Federation's Family Court for a hearing on the matter of her granddaughter's current custody. It will be assigned to the Twelfth District, but a hearing date has not yet been scheduled."

"I need to . . ." Janeway began.

"I have already prepared a rough outline of an amicus brief for you to file with the court," Decan advised, "and scheduled a meeting with civilian legal counsel specializing in custody issues. It is highly likely the court will order formal mediation prior to scheduling a hearing."

"Thank you."

"Several recent reassignments of medical personnel both from Starfleet Medical and the Federation Institute of Health might also be of interest. They suggest a concentration of efforts on three Federation worlds: Aldebaran, Coridan, and Ardana. Each of those planets saw heavy fighting during the Borg invasion, and if civilian reports are to be believed, a new, deadly illness has struck those worlds. Neither Starfleet Medical nor the Institute will confirm at this time. All official reports relating to medical issues on those worlds were classified several months ago. I have requested clearance for you to view them."

"The civilian reports . . ." Janeway began.

"I have aggregated all of the relevant articles for your review, some from decidedly unsavory media sources, but when considered in light of official actions are certainly suggestive," Decan clarified.

"You've been busy these last few days, haven't you?" Janeway asked.

"It is my preferred state of being," he reminded her. "Two of those transfers are now stationed at Starbase 185. I inferred that the issue might be of interest to you and *Galen*'s CMO."

"You inferred correctly," Janeway said approvingly.

"Your mother has left three messages, one each day since your departure from Earth. She would like you to contact her at your earliest convenience."

"Thank you."

"You will find among your prioritized files the record of Admiral Hiro Lin Verdell. I do not believe you have yet taken time to review it."

"I haven't. But, I need to."

"Captain Regina Farkas requested the same file for transmission to her personal database shortly after you departed Utopia Planitia."

"Did she?"

"Yes. I have taken the liberty of rescheduling your evaluations with Counselors Thrivven, Waxser, and Stilten."

"And those are?" she asked.

"Each of them specializes in unique testing procedures, all of them routine and standard when an officer has been captured, severely injured, or exposed to intense trauma."

"Those are going to be multiple choice tests, right?" she asked.

"I believe they also include neurological scans while evaluating visual stimuli," he advised.

"Terrific."

"Finally, I must apologize for not seeing sooner to one personnel assignment you must have found most inadequate. The initial request was not forwarded to my attention as it should have been, but I have rectified the error and hope my new selection will meet with your approval."

"Which assignment?" Janeway asked.

"Your primary counselor," Decan replied. "Counselor Jens's patient load was already too full to adequately accommodate you. I have secured another to complete your personal review who does not suffer from his limitations."

"Decan," Janeway replied seriously, "I could hug you right now."

"Please, Admiral," he began.

"Obviously, I won't. But I could. You have been missed."

"As have you, Admiral," Decan replied.

The office was unlike that of any counselor's Janeway had ever visited. Most favored decorations in soft, neutral tones and utilitarian chairs. The admiral had no idea what hues the walls of this space might have been. Vivid colors assaulted her from every direction: greens, riotous pinks, lavenders, and delicate shades of white. A vast and varied collection of ornamental plants and flowers sat atop nearly every available surface and covered many of the walls in long leafy tendrils. Although Janeway could not place the source, the sound of gently trickling water could be heard. The effect was not dramatic enough to create the illusion of being outdoors or in a botanical garden, but she was immediately conscious of a sense of vibrant, churning, beautiful life. The fragrances of the various plants were somehow muted.

A woman of average height with long, thick white hair that was pulled into a wild, uncooperative ponytail and who was wearing a light gray smock over her uniform turned gingerly from tending to a large orchid to greet Janeway as she entered. Hers were the most vivid violet eyes Janeway had ever seen. Many fine lines and deep crevasses across the counselor's face revealed her age, likely in her eighties.

"Admiral Janeway," she said, crossing to her and offering her hand. "It is a pleasure to meet you. I am Commander Rori Austen."

"Do you prefer commander or counselor?" Janeway asked.

"Counselor, since you asked," Austen replied. Her hands were warm and soft but her grip was solid. "And you?"

Janeway hesitated. She had every right to request to be referred to by her rank. It would be interesting to see what Austen settled on without prompting. But as she paused, she was struck by the wariness with which she approached the simple question. At some point in the last few weeks when confronting these strangers who held her future in their hands, she had begun to look for hidden meanings that might be wrought from every choice she made. She was reduced to overthinking her name. It was so unlike her as to be completely unnerving. Refusing to play the game into which she had been thrust, Janeway still wondered what the right answer to Austen's question might be.

It had to stop.

"Kathryn," she finally replied.

"Kathryn it is," Austen said with a cordial nod.

"Your office is lovely," Janeway noted.

"Thank you," Austen said with a wry smile. "Would you care to sit?" she asked, gesturing to a cushioned chair that rested beside a small table upon which stood a transparent pitcher of water, a single glass, and a tissue dispenser. A similar chair was opposite the table, and Austen moved to make herself comfortable, removing her smock and hanging it on a small metal rack located just next to the door before settling in.

Ignoring the padd on the table before her, which likely contained Janeway's records, she began, "I have already reviewed Counselor Jens's notes on your first sessions as well as your permanent file. I know you've only been back with us a few days. How are you adjusting?" She folded her hands in her lap. Her voice was warm and rich.

"Well enough, I suppose," Janeway said. "I realize this time has been given to me to address the deeper issues surrounding the significant traumas I have recently endured. But I haven't had much opportunity to do that. It seems everywhere I turn something is on fire and I need to put it out."

"Is there a reason you are assuming personal responsibility for these things you believe are *on fire* rather than allowing others to deal with them while you take some time for yourself?"

"It's what I do," Janeway admitted. "People put problems in front of me. I solve them. An occupational hazard, I suppose."

"I see."

Janeway paused, waiting for more, but Austen sat calm and composed, her eyes betraying a slight twinkle. Where Jens had been filled with useless questions, Austen seemed content to allow Kathryn to rustle into the weeds on her own.

"I have spent a little time with my family," Janeway offered.

"How did that go?"

"It's complicated," Janeway admitted.

"Is that usually the case?"

Janeway smiled in spite of herself. "My mother is always wonderful. She takes the good without dwelling on the bad. She accepts me as I am and never asks me to be anything else." She paused. "My sister is a different story. There's a lot of love there, but you have to go pretty deep to find it sometimes."

"They must have been relieved to learn that you weren't dead," Austen said.

"Yes," Janeway said, and nodded. "But Phoebe, my sister, assumed that my career with Starfleet would be ending when I returned and was very upset to learn that she was mistaken."

"Hmm," Austen said, looking away briefly to add this information to whatever mental picture she had of Janeway.

"She's a civilian," Janeway offered. "She doesn't understand our calling."

"Is that what this is?" Austen asked.

"For me," Janeway said, then ventured, "not for you?"

"It's an interesting choice of words," Austen replied, ignoring the personal question.

"How so?"

"If one is *called* to something, that implies that they lack the ability to exercise their own will in making a determination about whether or not to answer that call. I suppose it's possible that one might answer 'no,' but obviously you didn't."

"My father served Starfleet. I grew up adoring him and wanting to please him and living for the day I would follow in his footsteps. For me, there was no other path."

"It's a big universe, Kathryn. There are as many paths as you dare imagine."

"But only one that would give me the chance to see that universe up close," Janeway said.

"You had no choice?"

"Not if I wanted fulfillment."

"There are many civilian organizations engaged in exploration of the stars," Austen suggested.

Janeway paused. "Are you trying to soften up some ground here?" she asked. "Do you know something I don't about my future prospects with Starfleet?"

"No," Austen said, and Janeway believed her. "But you

have spent almost every moment since your return behaving as if the Full Circle fleet is already yours, and I'm not convinced that you are certain about your future prospects with Starfleet either."

"I have no idea what you're talking about," Janeway retorted sharply. "Like everybody else, I serve at the pleasure of my superior officers."

"You've been issuing orders beyond your purview," Austen said.

"I was given clearance to do so by Admiral Akaar."

"That was Picard's advice, right?" Austen asked.

Janeway felt her cheeks begin to flush.

"It sounds like him anyway," Austen clarified.

"As long as my status remains undetermined, the lives of people I care very much about are in danger," Janeway said evenly. "They have needs, and no matter what Command ultimately decides, I will see that they are met."

"That's not your job right now."

"I can't abandon them."

"They're not children, Kathryn. They wouldn't be out there if they hadn't proven they can take care of themselves."

"The needs I'm talking about are uniquely addressable from my current location."

"And in due time will be handled," Austen assured her. "But your task right now is to set their needs aside and tend to your own."

"My needs aren't that great," Janeway said. "I can do both. And if I can't, theirs come first. Anything else is just selfishness. I owe them better than that."

"You don't get to be selfish sometimes?"

"Not in the line of duty."

"Right now, your commanding officers are *ordering you* to be selfish. Instead you are focusing all of your attention on the needs of those you once commanded. You justify it by telling yourself you have no other choice."

Janeway drew in a sharp breath. Refusing to rise to Austen's bait, she took a few more slow, measured inhalations. "I don't know what else to do," she finally admitted.

Austen nodded thoughtfully, then said gently, "Of course you don't. Survival of trauma demands that you carve out a comfort zone from which to continue operating. That's all you're doing here."

"There's nothing comfortable about my life right now," Janeway retorted. "My responsibilities haven't changed, but I am now denied the power required to meet them. Everywhere I turn, one person after another is telling me that my past choices make me unfit to continue wielding that power."

"Power is never taken from us. It is only given away," Austen said softly.

"Why would I do that?" Janeway demanded.

"Either you have internalized others' opinions, or you agreed with them to begin with."

"I can command the fleet," Janeway insisted. "I have made mistakes, but I've learned from them."

"Painful mistakes?"

"As opposed to . . . ?"

"And when you say you have learned from them, what does that mean?" Austen asked.

"It means that I accept full responsibility for those choices and will use the knowledge gained from their consequences to make better decisions in the future."

"Accepting responsibility isn't the same thing as acceptance."

"I don't see the distinction," Janeway said.

"Apparently not," Austen agreed.

At this, Janeway rose from her chair. It was her nature to fight battles on her feet. "I don't know what your regrets might be, Counselor, or how complex the issues are that come across your desk on a daily basis, but commanding officers don't get to make easy calls. Nothing brought to our attention has a simple answer. We're forced to wade through the gray areas of this existence. We use our best judgment, knowing that the lives of our crew may be lost either way, and we are often forced to choose between the lesser of evils. When consequences are revealed to have been even more devastating than we had calculated, we accept it and move on because tomorrow another group of equally unpleasant options will be laid before us for consideration."

"What do you do with all that guilt?" Austen asked.

"Live with it," Janeway replied.

"But each time you are faced with a new decision, you have your past experiences to guide you," Austen said. "That should free you in a way. The more wisdom you collect over time, the easier it must be to confront even the most challenging issue."

"It should."

"But for you, it isn't, or you wouldn't be so reluctant to face this."

"What am I refusing to face?"

"Your power. Your control. You pretend to grasp for them with one hand while tossing them away with the other. You don't believe you can do this job, or you wouldn't be fighting so hard to convince yourself and everybody else that you can."

"I'm damned if I do and damned if I don't," Janeway said.

"So again you have no choice?"

"I can't run away from the only life I've ever known, the only course that has ever brought me any true happiness."

"Altering course isn't the same thing as retreating. Sometimes it is a tactic devised to allow you to regroup and return stronger."

"You're saying I need to get a hobby?" Janeway demanded.

"You need to tell me what you're so damned afraid of. You recently spent a great deal of time with an incredibly advanced species witnessing your life in every conceivable time line. Something you learned has you spooked."

"I don't know how familiar you are with quantum physics or temporal mechanics, but in essence, each individual time line is the product of a point of divergence," Janeway explained.

"Don't they all have some common point of origination?"

"It's not that simple."

"Are you sure?"

"Yes."

"Then what are you afraid of? You're not responsible for the actions of alternate versions of you. You're on your own unique path. The information you have received as a result of this extraordinary gift will be added to everything else you know, and it will be easier to avoid mistakes in the future as a result."

Janeway's heart began to pound harshly in her chest. She moved again to the chair and sat, willing her heartbeat to slow. "It will," she said softly. "It will."

"Or it won't," Austen suggested, "because the truth is, whatever you saw that terrified you so, lives in you, too. You can't avoid it. It is beyond your control. What if you have no choice?"

"I won't go down that road," Janeway insisted. "I won't be *her.*"

"Who?"

"The worst possible version of myself; the one who decided her life was so unbearable, she had to alter time to change it. She couldn't live with her choices. I will live with mine."

"Maybe it was the living with them that brought her to that point," Austen suggested. "Accepting responsibility, absorbing all the pain of the consequences of our choices isn't the same thing as acceptance," Austen said.

Janeway felt tears begin to burn her cheeks. The last time she had confronted the pain Austen was digging furiously to unearth was the moment her godson had seen fit to return Chakotay to her from the Omega Continuum. The tension of too many days operating in crisis mode had snapped her control, and she had dissolved into a mass of shuddering, violent spasms of agony. Once they had passed, Chakotay had gently taken her into his arms and held her. As her new life became reality, the horrors she had endured were buried in darkness she refused to contemplate. The darkness rose now, forcing her to realize that *buried* was not the same as *gone*.

"What do you want from me?" Janeway blurted out.

"Don't," Austen began gently, "*don't* add me to the list of those you feel you must carry. I don't want anything from you."

Janeway sat, terribly cold and completely alone in the churning center of a maelstrom as her past assaulted her. Images rose too quickly for her to catch them before they transmuted into others, each more sickening than the last; a tiny dank cell echoing with the sounds of Owen Paris screaming, a shuttle sinking beneath an icy lake, an alien array exploding and severing her completely from the life she had known, the first Borg cube she had encountered, the face of Tuvix standing on a transporter pad, the face of Noah Lessing pleading for his life as alien screeching echoed all around her, the face of her godson's mother vanishing as Janeway felt the violent river of Borg technology pouring into her veins, her death replaying over and over across eternity, and the absolute annihilation Omega had promised.

Janeway had no choice but to let them come, to wash over her, wave after wave, conscious that soon, they would suffocate her.

Terror counseled her to find her feet and run as far and fast as she could. Austen's kind face kept her rooted to her chair.

As she gulped for what she thought might be the last breath of air available in the room, another memory rose alongside these horrors: the face of her future self, etched with sadness so deep, Janeway could hardly bear to witness it. She had come to help, to give Captain Janeway the wisdom to avoid her mistakes, and in doing so, compounded them. Her counsel had brought Janeway—and those she loved—immediate relief, an end to their trials, but at the ultimate price of billions of lives, not least among them, Q's. Her shortsightedness had almost brought the entire multiverse to oblivion. *That* Admiral Janeway had chosen to die so her younger self and crew might live, but had that been a noble sacrifice? Or was it her only escape from pain she no longer knew how to endure?

How could anyone shoulder that burden alone? How could anyone absorb that much pain, suffer so deeply, and choose to continue? What would Janeway do when the deep, dark holes in which she buried her pain were full to overflowing?

"I didn't see it," Janeway murmured through trembling lips. "How could I not see it?"

"See what?"

"She came to bring us home. If I refused her help, Seven and many others would die. Tuvok would go mad. Chakotay . . ." she began but couldn't even complete the thought. "That future horrified me, but despite everything I knew to be right, fear won. I went along with her. I helped her. How did I not see that *she* was the problem?"

"Forgive her, Kathryn," Austen said softly. "Forgive yourself."

"I can't," Janeway replied through her tears.

"Then risk becoming her."

"I can't," Janeway insisted.

"Of course you can."

"How?"

"*Let go,*" Austen said simply.

Those words reverberated through her as surely as they had only weeks ago when she had found herself in the Q Continuum. A voice had beckoned her again and again to *let go*; a voice she had ultimately ignored because the peace it offered could only be purchased with passage to oblivion. The power of that voice had been beyond any Janeway had ever known and the eternal rest it promised would surely be hers when her work was truly done. She had never considered the possibility that such peace could accompany living.

Struggling to make sense of this, Janeway watched as her own imperfect past collected itself in the center of her being, a throbbing, pitiful mass of living regret. She knew only one way to deal with it and with all her might tried to force it into a dark corner from which its torments might be bearable. As long as she kept busy, it was easy enough to ignore.

Suddenly, she saw herself once again, standing before a mirror, just as she had in the Q Continuum when her body had been collected from cosmic dust and made whole. Before her the outlines of a woman were visible, the contours of her body a rough approximation of Janeway's own. But this woman gave off her own illumination, an almost blinding light. Janeway stared at her, not in the mirror, but *as* the mirror. All she had ever been, or would ever be, gazed silently at her, quietly demanding recognition.

That woman turned her gaze to the churning mass in the center of Kathryn's being and said softly, "*Go.*"

"*Go,*" Janeway whispered.

Her stomach rebelled but she persisted. Closing her eyes, Janeway allowed that mass to begin to rise. How something so heavy could be lifted with no more effort than that required to move a feather, she did not understand, but she refused to question it. It passed through her heart, her mind, and finally hung above her like a storm cloud.

"Go," she said again and exhaled, and as she did so, it began to disperse. Soon enough it vanished into nothingness. She looked again for the mirror, but it was gone. She was alone.

She felt . . . *whole.*

She expected to feel cold and empty. Instead, opening her eyes, she discovered a strange, almost heady sense of calm, not unlike that which accompanies vigorous exercise.

Austen smiled and waggled a finger toward her face. Janeway retrieved a few tissues and wiped away the last of her tears.

"I'd like to never do that again," Janeway said softly.

"You won't have to," Austen assured her, "not like this. Once you get the hang of forgiveness, it becomes a habit.

It isn't what we lose that defines us. It's what we refuse to release."

Janeway chuckled. "Just before I left the fleet, Chakotay tried to tell me that my life now could be a blank slate. But I couldn't feel that until now."

"It's good, isn't it?"

"It's better than good," Janeway replied. Sitting back, she asked, "How did you do that?"

"I didn't do anything."

Janeway smiled wryly. "Thank you, just the same."

Admiral Kathryn Janeway wasted no time. She returned to her office and collected all of the data she and Decan had compiled about various issues relevant to her command. She left explicit instructions for Decan, knowing he would follow them to the letter.

Walking down the hall to Verdell's office, she was pleased to find him otherwise unoccupied. Janeway sat with him for a little more than an hour, summarizing her primary concerns and offering him all of her data. She advised him to seek out and utilize Decan to the full extent of his abilities.

She wished him well.

By early afternoon, Janeway reached her mother's house in Indiana. Gretchen was, of course, delighted to see her.

Over several pots of warm tea, they chatted long into the night. In the wee hours, she fell pleasantly exhausted into the bed in what had been her childhood room and enjoyed the first dreamless sleep she could remember in years.

She awoke late the next morning and joined her mother, who was already busy in the garden. Apart from her final required evaluations, which turned out to be kind of fun as they no longer mattered, and a few pleasant follow-up appointments with Counselor Austen, she did not return to San Francisco, nor did she continue to follow the progress of the fleet.

Chapter Seventeen

VOYAGER

The astrometrics lab was packed with anxious officers. Seven and Lieutenants Harry Kim and Nancy Conlon stood at the room's main data terminal finalizing their preparations. Behind them, Commander O'Donnell, Captain Chakotay, Commander Paris, and Counselor Cambridge stood with their eyes fixed on the lab's viewscreen. Kim maintained an open channel with Ensign Gwyn at the helm, just in case the ship needed to move quickly. But in his heart, he knew they wouldn't. He also had a secondary channel open to an away team on the surface consisting of Commander Fife and Lieutenant Lasren.

It had taken Kim, Conlon, and Seven, working in close consultation with Commander O'Donnell, two days to devise a means to teach, or more specifically, to add to the wave forms' current programming parameters. The first problem had been finding a way to bring the proctors into normal space at will. The sentries' attention they knew how to get, but the sentries did not suit their needs. Conlon had suggested replicating small items that might pique the proctor's curiosity that were not already present on the ship. Everything within the ship had already been scanned and would therefore be ignored as non-threatening. O'Donnell had suggested using simple unfamiliar life-forms safely housed in probes. Seven had been the one to suggest the infinitely simpler course. A few hours of experimentation with harmonic waves designed to disrupt subspace revealed a simple frequency that forced the wave forms to emerge. This action occasionally alerted several sentries, and the process was refined until only proctors were summoned.

At that point, Kim was ready to provide the proctors with rudimentary data, but Seven had refused, pointing out that they were training these creatures and should proceed slowly. Two days and dozens of tests later, they could summon the proctors at will and were ready to begin giving them more complicated tasks.

They had begun by sending out several newly developed probes. The casings were standard, but they had been designed to transmit only on the appropriate frequency. The proctors were instructed to move to a specific coordinate, then to move between a series of coordinates, to bring the probe to a designated location on the planet's surface. Finally, the proctors were to move a small population of Monster's pack to a new habitat five hundred kilometers from their present range. Once the wave forms had grown accustomed to this method of data transmission, they seemed impatient for more. Over the past twenty-four hours, several proctors had emerged, uncalled, from subspace and came near *Voyager* and *Demeter*'s position as if hoping that by showing up, some task might be assigned to them.

Thus far, all of the tests had demonstrated unequivocally that the wave forms were capable of following instructions. Today's test was the only one that mattered, though. It was the first test that crossed the line from the wave forms doing the work required to providing them with material that they would not otherwise be able to create. They were moving into rudimentary terraforming, and if the proctors could not grasp or accomplish what was required, everyone's hopes for the planet were going to have to be rethought.

True to his word, Chakotay had not hindered the team's

efforts nor placed any time restriction on them as long as the proctors continued to demonstrate progress. He seemed as anxious as the team that this final test should succeed.

O'Donnell had synthesized a new bacteria: one that needed to be delivered to an arid region of the planet. It was designed for its specific climate, but in order for it to thrive, it would need a little encouragement. This meant that the proctors would have to alter local weather patterns, a more complicated but not impossible task. It was new territory for all of them, and Kim's breath stilled as everyone in the lab watched the probe's launch from *Voyager.*

"Look at 'em go," Conlon said softly as a number of proctors raced toward the newly ejected probe. As soon as one surrounded it, the others that had attempted to reach it first ceased their motion but remained nearby.

"Come on," Kim added under his breath. Phase one required that the first proctor to intercept the probe realize that it had to share the data provided with other proctors. This was a task no proctor could perform on its own. He smiled with relief as the wave form elongated its shape enough to allow its edges to touch several of those who had lost the race.

"Is that supposed to happen?" Paris asked from the back of the lab.

"It is," Kim replied. "They're sharing the information."

"As long as you're sure," Paris said softly.

Moments later, the probe was speeding to the surface of the planet, safely contained within the first proctor, and six others followed its course.

"*Voyager* to Commander Fife," Kim called over the comm. "You should be able to detect the arrival of the probe."

"Confirmed," Fife replied, all business. *"We are reading the probe's telemetry and confirm it is on course."*

"Man, those things can move." Lasren's voice came softly from the background of Fife's open channel.

A light chuckle came from Conlon at Lasren's enthusiasm.

A few moments later, Kim said, "Fife, report."

"The probe has passed through the upper atmosphere and is slowing. It has now reached optimal orientation for dispersal."

"Are the pods opening?" O'Donnell asked.

"Aye, sir," Fife replied.

O'Donnell moved to Kim's side and clapped a congratulatory hand on his shoulder.

"They did it," he said softly.

"The proctors have demonstrated the acquisition of a new skill," Seven allowed, "but the harder task remains undone."

O'Donnell shook his head at Seven, a gentle smirk on his lips as he replied, "Oh, ye of little faith."

"The pods have been released, and the contents are being distributed among the seven proctors who received the data," Conlon reported, bringing everyone's attention back to the lab's viewscreen. It displayed different views of the plain where Fife and Lasren's shuttle had landed. The shuttle's sensors would provide the clearest data about the test and its readings were instantaneously transmitted to *Voyager.*

The probe floated several meters above the surface. The pods containing the necessary bacteria had been transferred to seven discreet proctors, and their gentle back and forth motions suggested they were releasing the contents of the pods in a perfect dispersal pattern.

"Now comes the really hard part," Conlon reminded Kim.

Turning to address the group, Seven said, "We have now reached a new level of complexity in terms of programming the proctors. If they clear the final hurdle, we can safely assume that they will be capable of performing all of the functions required to revive the Ark Planet."

"I still say we're nudging the letter of the law toward maximum tolerance," Paris said dryly.

"It may not matter," Conlon interjected, her gaze fixed on the screen where from every angle the landscape appeared to be as hot and dry as ever.

"The last phase of this test is the most difficult," Kim

pointed out. "It may take several hours for us to determine whether or not the proctors can successfully alter atmospheric conditions to the necessary configuration."

"Can the bacteria survive that long?" Chakotay asked.

"Almost," O'Donnell replied.

"If you'd prefer not to wait, I can . . ." Kim began.

"Fife to Voyager, *"* Fife's voice called from over the comm. *"Ambient temperature is falling."*

"How much?" Kim asked.

"Two degrees in the last four minutes," Fife said.

"A good sign." O'Donnell smiled at Kim.

Everyone remained silently engrossed for the next few minutes watching, clearly worried that speaking might break the spell the proctors were casting in the atmosphere above the planet.

It was Paris who ended the silence. "I'll be damned," he said softly.

Kim's smile broke into full force as everyone watched Fife and Lasren rush back to the safety of the shuttle to avoid a massive deluge that had just begun to fall from the heavens. He turned to Conlon, who temporarily abandoned protocol and grabbed him in a firm hug. Seven simply stepped back and nodded to O'Donnell.

After a round of boisterous applause, everyone in the room broke ranks to congratulate Kim, Conlon, and Seven. Kim watched as O'Donnell pulled Chakotay aside and did his best to separate their words from the ebullient chatter filling the lab.

"Well?" O'Donnell asked.

"You've made your point," Chakotay replied, extending his hand.

O'Donnell took it and shook it firmly.

"I take it we're going to be here awhile," Paris said.

"Everybody get comfortable," Chakotay said. "We've got six weeks of hard work ahead of us."

"And in the seventh, we'll rest?" Cambridge asked lightly.

"Somehow, I doubt it," Paris replied.

For the first time since their arrival in the wave form's system, Chakotay felt unreserved satisfaction. The work that Kim, Conlon, and Seven had done to establish communications with the proctors was outstanding. He no longer cared whether it could technically be construed as a first contact. It was an accomplishment worthy of their mission statement, and the fact that the Ark Planet would be revived was a bonus. His crew would be busy but not under constant threat and expending their efforts on work that all could take pride in.

This was a good day.

Most of the assembled officers were still in astrometrics, peppering Kim and the others with questions related to their specific work to come. Chakotay watched as Counselor Cambridge silently moved to the lab's door and left, a decidedly dour look on his face.

Curious and certain his crew had matters well in hand, he followed the counselor and caught up with him as he entered the turbolift.

The two men stood silent in the turbolift. Chakotay allowed the tension growing between them to become uncomfortable before Cambridge finally blurted out, "Six weeks?"

Offering the counselor his most amiable face, Chakotay replied, "Is that a problem, Counselor?"

"Of course not, sir," Cambridge replied. Chakotay did not believe him for an instant.

"Aren't you the one who told me that what this crew needed was a fairly long stretch of routine? *This* is about as close to routine as things get out here."

The turbolift doors slid open on deck four, which housed Cambridge's quarters. Chakotay considered continuing to the bridge, but he stepped off behind Cambridge at the last moment. They walked in silence until they had reached his door, when the counselor turned on Chakotay and said, "Is there a problem, sir?"

"You tell me."

"I have nothing to do," Cambridge replied.

"If boredom is your issue," Chakotay began.

Cambridge raised a hand to silence him and activated his door, motioning for the captain to precede him inside.

Chakotay was relieved to see Cambridge's personal space in relative order. He had seen these quarters in more shocking states and knew that their condition often reflected the counselor's own. Whatever was troubling Hugh had not yet reached crisis levels.

"Can I offer you something?" Cambridge asked as he moved to the replicator and ordered a synthetic scotch.

"I'll take some hot cider," Chakotay replied.

"Are you a hundred and fifty years old?" Cambridge asked as he dutifully fulfilled Chakotay's order.

"It's a little early in the day," Chakotay replied, accepting the steaming mug. "But I've got a fairly lengthy report to begin, so whatever this is, could we move it along?"

"I don't like this place much," Cambridge finally admitted. "I'm ready to move on."

"Because it's boring?"

"Because something more challenging will better focus the crew's minds," Cambridge replied.

"According to my first officer, the entire crew is performing at peak efficiency," Chakotay argued. "They just established contact with alien technology and are utilizing it to work a miracle. You don't think that's challenging?"

"For *some* of them, maybe . . ." Cambridge began.

"I've got waste reclamation conduits that could use a good scrubbing if you really can't find something useful to do," Chakotay suggested.

"Don't be absurd," Cambridge snapped.

"Then what . . . ?"

"Bloody hell, Chakotay," Cambridge said, "did Seven ever tell you about Axum?"

Chakotay was momentarily stunned by the question. With Cambridge, Chakotay usually found himself on the receiving end of wisdom. However, the counselor was clearly at a loss. It was hard not to revel, just for a moment, at this unexpected reversal. Had Cambridge's difficulty in asking not been so evident, Chakotay might have made him suffer a bit. Repressing a smile, the captain moved to the chair Cambridge normally occupied for counseling sessions and sat.

Cambridge shook his head but followed Chakotay's lead, taking the "patient's" seat opposite him.

"She did," Chakotay finally replied.

"When you and she . . ." Cambridge said then cleared his throat, obviously uncomfortable addressing this. Years earlier, Chakotay and Seven had a brief romantic relationship that had long since deepened into friendship. It was inappropriate for the counselor to ask his captain for personal information, and they both knew it.

"We spoke about him before we were involved," Chakotay clarified. "I was there when she was first brought back to Unimatrix Zero. It was a confusing time for her. And I also spoke at great length about the place with Kathryn."

"Do you believe Seven still harbors unresolved feeling for him?" Cambridge asked.

"You're not asking as her counselor?"

"Of course not."

"Then you need to discuss it with her," Chakotay said gently.

"I have," Cambridge bellowed. When he had calmed himself he went on. "As best I can tell, she is withholding nothing. Seven claims they were involved in that fairyland they shared during regeneration but that she has no memory of the relationship. She'd put it so far behind her, it never even came up in our counseling sessions."

"How did Axum come up?" Chakotay asked innocently.

Cambridge turned away; Chakotay realized he didn't want to answer that question. "She's dreaming about him," Cambridge finally said softly. "She speaks his name in her sleep."

"Hugh, I really can't hear this," Chakotay said. "It is disrespectful to Seven."

"Don't you think I know that?" Cambridge said bitterly. "If I had anywhere else to turn, I can assure you I would."

Chakotay believed him. The situation was further complicated by the fact that someday, he might find himself on the other end of this conversation regarding him and Kathryn. Not that Kathryn and Hugh had ever been intimate, but as the ship's counselor, there would be lines Cambridge could not cross either.

"I can tell you this," Chakotay said. "Seven doesn't lie. Have you considered the possibility that what you now share with her is simply awakening repressed memories and dreams are the safest way for her to deal with them?"

"Thirty-some odd years of counseling experience hasn't completely escaped me, Chakotay," Cambridge replied. "If that were the only possibility here, I'd be fine. It's the others that have me worried."

"Others?"

"Axum was Borg. He should have joined the Caeliar gestalt."

"Most likely," Chakotay agreed.

"But what if he didn't?"

"The only Borg we know of that refused the Caeliar's offer was in unique situations," Chakotay replied.

"Unique, like possessing a mutation shared by only one in a million Borg and aware of themselves as individuals apart from the Collective for several years *prior* to the Caeliar transformation?" Cambridge demanded.

"A fair point, yes," Chakotay agreed.

"I know how powerful the urge to join the Caeliar was. The pain it caused Seven to refuse is something I can't contemplate. Your reports on Doctor Frazier and her people show similar sentiments. The need to care for their children gave them the strength to refuse the Caeliar."

"Why would Axum refuse?" Chakotay asked.

"If perfection was all the Caeliar was offering, it doesn't hold a candle to Seven," Cambridge replied.

After a moment, Chakotay nodded. "If Axum remained outside the gestalt, how could he contact her now, even subconsciously? We've already seen the limits of Seven's catoms when it comes to telepathic communication. She lost contact with Riley when we moved a few light-years from their system. Tens of thousands of light-years is an impossible distance, isn't it?"

"Tell me you're not going to lose a little sleep tonight wondering that very thing," Cambridge replied.

"Hugh," Chakotay said. "Seven has shared more of herself with you, here in the real world, than any other man she has ever known. She would never treat that lightly. We're likely going to be out here for years. Build something that will banish all memories of her past."

Cambridge raised a wary eyebrow.

A ship-wide alarm sounded bringing Chakotay immediately to his feet. Tapping his combadge he said, "Captain to the bridge. Report."

"Sorry, sir," Waters replied. *"There was an overload in waste processing. It's already been locked down. The alarm was canceled on site."*

"By whom?" Chakotay asked. It was a procedure that required command-level clearance.

"Commander Torres," Waters replied.

Relieved, Chakotay started to sit again but thought better of it. *What the hell was B'Elanna doing in waste processing right now? In fact, why hadn't she been in astrometrics with everyone else a few minutes earlier?*

"Go," Cambridge said, joining Chakotay on his feet.

"If you need to talk more about this," Chakotay offered.

"I won't," the counselor said.

"Stop it!" B'Elanna shouted as the alarm trilled again.

"Warning. Processor XVB-Nine-One-One-Three cannot complete required function," the computer's maddening voice advised.

"I said . . ." B'Elanna began as she tried to force the support stretchers of the bassinet she had replicated past the interface and into the bowels of the matter reclamation system.

"B'Elanna?" a worried voice called over her shoulder.

"Warning," the computer began again.

"I just . . ." B'Elanna said, heaving with all her might until a pair of strong hands grasped her arms from behind and gently pulled her back.

"Leave me alone!" B'Elanna shouted, turning on her most unwelcome savior. When she saw it was Chakotay, her anger and intensity quickly vanished, replaced by mortification. "I'm sorry, Captain. I didn't realize it was you."

"What the . . . ?" Chakotay began, but paused as he got a good look at the item B'Elanna had been trying to force into the processor. He looked again at her in exasperated confusion. "Is this Miral's?" he asked.

"She hasn't been small enough to sleep in one of these for more than three years, Chakotay," B'Elanna chided him.

Chakotay's gaze then moved to the pile of other items B'Elanna had clearly intended for waste reclamation. They included a number of toys and devices only appropriate for an infant. Confusion turned to deep sadness.

"Were you pregnant again?" he asked softly.

"*Am,*" she said. "I am pregnant again."

He stepped back, releasing a huge sigh of relief. His face was soon lit with absolute jubilation. "Congratulations, B'Elanna," he said warmly. "That's wonderful."

"I'm sorry you had to find out this way," B'Elanna said. "I was going to wait a few more weeks, just until we were into the second trimester, before telling anyone."

"I understand," Chakotay said. "Obviously I won't say anything. But, Tom?"

"He knows," B'Elanna assured him.

"So . . ." Chakotay said, gesturing to the pile.

Placing her hands on her hips, B'Elanna shrugged. "I wanted to get a head start, figuring out how to balance what the baby is going to need with all the new stuff Miral needs. I've reorganized our quarters six times in the last six days. I know it's not your problem, but I don't know how four of us are going to make this work." With this admission, she felt tears rising to her eyes. Wiping her nose to head them off, she returned to the bassinet and tried to break off one of the end slats.

"Wait," Chakotay ordered.

"This was stupid," B'Elanna said. "We're not going to need this for months. I don't know what I was thinking."

"Come with me," Chakotay said.

"I can't just leave this here," B'Elanna insisted.

"That's an order, Commander," Chakotay said.

She dutifully followed him out the door and down the short hall to the turbolift. B'Elanna kept her head down, torn between embarrassment and frustration. When they entered the turbolift, she turned to him and saw him staring down at her, his face lit with joy. He placed an arm around her shoulder and said softly, "Don't worry. I've got this."

Intrigued, B'Elanna followed him out of the lift a few moments later into the halls of deck three. She was confused when he finally stopped at a familiar pair of doors. "What are we doing here?" she asked.

Chakotay only smiled as they entered the largest single living space B'Elanna had ever seen on an *Intrepid*-class. Once the door had slid shut behind them he said, "Welcome to your new quarters, Commander."

B'Elanna studied the layout of the space for a few moments. "This is the fleet commander's suite."

"It was designed to the personal specifications of Admiral Batiste. Afsarah hated it and would probably have had it reallocated in short order had she lived. Admiral Janeway will never abide its existence for her personal use alone."

The Starfleet officer in B'Elanna counseled her to tread carefully, but then, she had never been the best Starfleet officer. "Don't you think Admiral Janeway might want larger quarters?" she asked delicately enough, but not too delicately for her meaning to be unclear.

"I don't know what the admiral's plans may be upon her return," Chakotay began, "but whatever they are, they will not require a space this vast to accommodate her."

"Or you?"

"No," Chakotay assured her.

"You haven't talked about getting married?" B'Elanna asked frankly. *In for a meter, in for a kilometer,* she decided.

Chakotay smiled again, as if the thought pleased him to no end. "No," he replied. "There hasn't been time. We've had a lot on our plates, and there's no reason to rush anything."

"But you *are* going to marry her?" B'Elanna demanded.

Chakotay's face fell into more serious lines, and his eyes clearly commanded her to drop it.

"Chakotay?" B'Elanna said, unwilling to let it go.

"If I have my way, I will spend whatever is left of my life by her side," he replied.

"And you're absolutely sure she's not going to mind you giving away all of this?"

"It's my ship." Chakotay shrugged. "So, here are your orders, Commander."

"Orders?"

"For the next several weeks, *Voyager* and *Demeter* will continue to assist the wave forms in reviving the Ark Planet. You will delegate as many of your duties in that regard as you can. The majority of your time is to be spent transforming this space to accommodate you, Tom, Miral, and your new child."

"This pregnancy is killing me," B'Elanna finally admitted. "If I'm not nauseated beyond belief, I'm ravenous. Either I can't sit still or I'm completely exhausted. It's like there's no middle ground in my life anymore."

"Remind me of a time when you were comfortable in any sort of middle ground?" Chakotay teased.

"Thank you, Chakotay," she said more seriously.

"Come here," he said, opening his arms to her.

She accepted his embrace and rested her head for a moment on his chest. "I'm so happy for all of you," Chakotay said softly.

"Me, too," B'Elanna said as she pulled away. "But do me a favor?"

"Another one?" He smiled.

"Don't tell Tom. I want to surprise him."

"How are you going to do that?"

"I'm pregnant and half out of my mind," B'Elanna replied, "but I'm still *me.*"

Chapter Eighteen

INDIANA

"Kathryn?" Gretchen asked.

"Hmm?" Janeway said with less than half her concentration. Her eyes were fixed on a particularly large pumpkin that had been taunting her for weeks, and she had all but decided that today was the day. Tonight, there would be pie. For several days after, there would be spiced pumpkin bread. Her stomach rumbled pleasantly at the thought.

"Darling?" her mother said more urgently, and this time, Janeway looked to her right. Her mother knelt beside her, gardening tools at the ready as they planned their assault on the patch of fall vegetables in Gretchen's garden. Gretchen rose to her feet and stood with a hand shading her eyes, peering intently at the long road that led to the house. Janeway followed her gaze and was flabbergasted to see the form of a man in a Starfleet uniform making his way toward them.

It was difficult to identify him at first, but soon he came close enough for his blue science uniform and balding pate to settle the matter.

"Doctor?" Janeway called, coming to her feet.

Startled by her voice, the Doctor turned his steps from the path that led to the porch and quickly found the way that led to the rear of the property. "Admiral!" he called with apparent relief as he hurried toward them.

"I thought you said you wouldn't be disturbed," Gretchen said softly.

"It's all right," Janeway assured her. And it was. The last few weeks had been like no others in her life. They had done more than restore her spirits. They had rejuvenated her. Long hours spent doing simple things with her hands as she and her mother revisited their shared past had been a gift she'd never thought to give herself. Her mother was still a hard worker, but she so loved the work she did, it never felt like an obligation. Janeway felt the same about her profession, but it was extraordinary to have spent time reveling in someone else's garden. It was a complete change of pace. Days started and ended earlier, following the gentle rhythm of sunrise and sunset. Real weather had become a treasure. They'd had a bit of rain, but most days began cold, warmed nicely in the afternoon, and ended colder. The coffee Janeway had always cherished had been a substitute for lost energy. Hot decaf or tea at the end of a day of manual labor felt like a reward. The food they had eaten, fresh from the ground, was sublime. It filled her, nourished her, and satisfied her completely.

But Janeway knew that this all-too-brief respite was temporary. She sensed with each passing day that its end was coming. Rather than create undue anxiety, however, this knowledge had allowed her to live more fully in the moment.

Whenever Command finally got around to analyzing her evaluations and deciding on her next post, Janeway knew she would be ready to accept it. And most surprising of all, she no longer had a preference. She would happily go where she was needed most and allow the future to unfold on its own. Janeway no longer had the slightest bit of interest in shaping it, forcing it into a form she thought she could manage. This time spent away from Starfleet had taught her that seeking such control was a waste of time, if not a complete illusion, and that her energy was much better expended opening herself up to each day ready to accept whatever it brought. She fervently hoped that she could remember this wisdom when duty called and brought along with it the rigors of schedules, meetings, and reports.

When he finally reached them, the Doctor took a moment to peer at Janeway, bathed in the light of an Indiana autumn, and wonder at what he saw. The admiral had discarded her uniform and wore a simple, long brown tunic over timeworn canvas pants with several handy pockets. A kerchief was tied at her neck, helpful for collecting sweat and dirt, and her face was smeared with a fair amount of soil.

"If I'd known it was this bad," the Doctor said seriously, "I would have come sooner."

Janeway laughed deeply and opened her arms to him. "It's good to see you, too," she said as he accepted her embrace.

"Doctor," Gretchen greeted him a little warily.

"Hello, Mrs. Janeway," he said, extending his hand.

"What brings you all the way out here?" Gretchen asked.

"It is the only way to make contact with your daughter," he replied. "Since the mountain would not come to me . . ." he began.

"Some sort of emergency then?" Gretchen asked.

"When isn't it?" the Doctor answered. "I apologize for interrupting this . . . what is this exactly?" he asked.

"Gardening," Janeway replied. Turning to Gretchen she said, "I'd love something cold to drink."

Gretchen understood and resigned herself to acceptance. "Can he . . ." she began.

"No, thank you," the Doctor said.

As Gretchen trudged toward the back porch, Janeway said, "Don't you dare start on that pumpkin without me."

Gretchen favored her daughter with a knowing smile tossed over her shoulder as she opened the back door screen.

"I mean it, Mother," Janeway added.

"Admiral?" the Doctor asked, clearly puzzled.

"Let's take a walk," Janeway said. Something in her still wanted to keep Starfleet away from her newfound peace for as long as possible.

They hadn't gone far along a narrow path that led to the

apple orchard when the Doctor said, "Is this really how you've been spending your time?"

"Yes," Janeway said simply.

"Are you aware of anything that's been going on in your absence?"

"No."

"Do I need to scan you for possible alien possession or replacement?" the Doctor asked.

"No," she said. "I needed some time. So I took it."

"I expected to find you at Utopia Planitia when *Galen* arrived there," he said. "I've sent you several transmissions in the last few weeks, but received no responses."

"Decan didn't . . . ?" she asked.

"Decan," the Doctor repeated, menace in his tone, "has become an unmovable barrier between you and the rest of the universe."

"Good." Janeway smiled.

"For you, perhaps," the Doctor chided her. "Are you aware that the *Vesta*'s time line for completion has been extended by ten days in your absence?"

"No." Janeway shrugged. "Why?" she finally asked.

"I don't think Admiral Verdell and Commander Drafar are capable of speaking a cordial word to each other. Nor are he and I, for that matter. He is the textbook definition of noncommittal."

"The fleet is his responsibility," Janeway said. "If he's not getting you what you need, talk to Ken Montgomery."

"What I need is *you,* Admiral," the Doctor said heatedly.

They had reached a shaded line of trees, and Janeway placed a foot at the nearest trunk, resting an arm on a low-hanging branch. The question was there, waiting to be asked, but Janeway knew that to ask it was to bid farewell to the peace she had discovered here. She had already accepted that her reprieve would be temporary, but she was reluctant to part with it. Her affection for the Doctor, however, forced it from her lips. "What's going on?"

"Axum remained under my care for two weeks after we last spoke. It was all I could do on his behalf. His recovery was truly miraculous."

"Not with you as his doctor," Janeway said.

"When I could stall them no longer, he was taken from me, and no one will tell me where he is now. But I am certain he is not recuperating, as I was told."

"What else would he be doing?"

"They're using him, Admiral, as a test subject."

"I'm sure Starfleet Medical will want to study him, but it will be a painless process and certainly they will not harm him or do anything to jeopardize his recovery," Janeway said.

"I've spent more than three weeks with the doctors in whose tender care he now rests. His recovery is the last thing on their minds."

"What's the first?"

"I'm not supposed to tell you this," the Doctor began.

"Does it have anything to do with the sudden reallocation of medical resources to Coridan, Ardana, and Aldebaran?" the admiral asked.

"Then you know?"

"There were rumors before I left of an illness that has appeared on those worlds."

"More than an illness. Starfleet Medical and the Federation Institute of Health are desperate to find the cause and a cure for what they are calling a new plague: one they believe is caused by exposure to catomic matter."

"Is that even possible?" Janeway asked.

"I've seen their preliminary research, and I'm convinced it's completely impossible. But don't try and tell them that. I educated them as best I could. They confiscated all of my files on Seven and all of *Galen*'s on the fleet's interaction with Doctor Frazier's people. I even heard them discussing the possibilities of sending an expedition to Arehaz."

"To do what?" Janeway asked.

"They need more catoms to study, and there are only a few places to get them."

"If this is a medical emergency," Janeway said, "they're going to do whatever is required to end it. It's their duty."

"Our duty is protecting those who can't protect themselves. Or have my files regarding Starfleet principles been damaged?"

"They don't need our protection, Doctor. No one is going to harm them."

"I told them explicitly that Axum's recovery would be hindered the longer they refused to allow him to make contact with Seven. They didn't care. They haven't even convened a panel to consider his request for asylum. They have designated him an enemy combatant."

Janeway didn't want to admit it, but that sounded like overreaching.

"You're worried about Seven?"

"No more than the rest of them," he insisted.

Janeway shot him a look and was surprised to see that his apparent indifference was not feigned. "No one is going to allow Starfleet Medical or the Institute of Health to run roughshod over people's rights. It's just not how we do things," Janeway argued.

"I don't know how to tell you this, Admiral, but since the Borg Invasion, I'm not sure who's in charge of *how we do things* anymore."

"You need to apprise Admiral Montgomery of your concerns."

"Then you won't . . . ?" the Doctor began.

"You can always contact me here. I'll give you my direct access codes, and if Montgomery does not take appropriate action, I'll talk to him," Janeway agreed.

The Doctor stepped back, surprised. "I would have thought your regard for Seven would have stirred you to more direct action."

"Seven is a grown woman. She can and will make her own decisions. If catomic technology is somehow responsible for this new plague, I am certain she will want to do everything in her power to see it stopped." After a moment, she added, "I know how important Seven is to you. I think it's possible you are reading too much into this because it is tied to your feelings and fears for her."

Again, the Doctor looked confused. His gaze shifted from her eyes for a moment as a veil of calm settled over his face. He said simply, "Seven of Nine is no more or less important to me than any of those I have served with. I am actually more concerned for Axum. He needs to see her again. He suffered severe psychological trauma in the days leading up to the Caeliar transformation, and to deny him access to Seven is cruel."

Janeway was suddenly at a loss, wondering how much might have changed in the interpersonal relations of those closest to her while she was gone. Normally when the Doctor was engaged in this level of denial, there were obvious tells. He often protested too much. The Doctor had nurtured deep romantic feelings for Seven, and Janeway could not believe that those feelings, however long ago resolved, wouldn't have been tweaked by the reappearance of Axum.

Yet nothing in the Doctor's demeanor suggested that he regarded Seven as anything more than a fellow officer who might be in danger.

A new and troubling thought surfaced.

"Doctor," she asked, "when was the last time you ran a high-level self-diagnostic of your matrix?"

"Last month," he replied, "as usual."

"You might want to run another."

"Why?"

"I'm wondering if your long-term memory storage subroutines might be degrading."

"Why would you think that?"

"Humor me," she insisted. "In fact, don't do a self-diagnostic. Have Reg run it."

"Is that an order, Admiral?"

"Nope," she said. "It's a suggestion, from a concerned friend. For orders, you need to go through the normal chain of command."

The Doctor's shoulders drooped visibly. "I don't have much faith in my current chain of command."

"That might be part of your problem," Janeway said. "You are programmed to follow orders, but you came to sentience while reporting only to people you had already grown to trust implicitly. I wonder if you are having difficulty trusting those you report to now because you simply don't know them all that well."

"I have no problem trusting officers who have proven themselves worthy of that trust. The rest, I judge by their actions, and thus far, I'm not terribly impressed."

"Run that diagnostic anyway."

"What will you be doing in the meantime?"

"Gardening."

"You've changed, Admiral," the Doctor said, and Janeway thought she heard a hint of disappointment in his words.

"Not as much as you might think," she said. "But I'm working on it."

Chapter Nineteen

VOYAGER

Seven was freezing. She had wrapped herself in a blanket over her nightclothes and robe and tucked every bit of exposed flesh beneath that blanket as she perched on the sofa in her fully illuminated living quarters. She had ordered the computer to raise the ambient temperature by two degrees. But nothing helped.

She resisted the urge to close her eyes. She did not expect the dream to intrude again. But the intense cold she felt made Seven wonder if she might still be asleep. All of the stimuli she was receiving from her senses told her she was awake. *Of course, she could have sworn she was also awake when her body had been submerged in that frozen tub.* The memory sent a new chill shuddering through her.

The chime to her quarters sounded.

"Come," she called through chattering teeth.

Chakotay entered, his uniform fresh and his face weary.

"Thank you for responding so quickly," she managed to say.

Grogginess gave way instantly to concern. Chakotay moved quickly to her side and sat, asking, "Do you need the doctor?"

"I don't think so."

Chakotay reached a hand up, palm forward, to touch her forehead. She recoiled as if he had intended to slap her.

He registered surprise at her reaction at the same time she did. It had been unconscious, or subconscious, this visceral need to avoid the feel of another's hands on her.

"I just wanted to see if you were feverish," he said gently.

"I'm sorry," Seven said. "Please proceed."

Chakotay repeated the gesture slowly, resting his hand against her forehead. "I don't think you're running a temperature. But we should still get you to sickbay."

"No!" Seven insisted.

Chakotay considered her kindly. Finally, he asked, "Why not?"

"I had a dream," she said softly. "A nightmare."

"How long have you been awake?"

"Eight minutes."

"A physical response to a dream should fade more quickly than this."

"I know this doesn't make sense, but part of me feels like I'm still there."

"Where?"

"A lab, a research station, a sickbay," she said. "It is not a location I have any memory of visiting. But it was a Starfleet facility. There was a Starfleet Medical insignia on the door."

Chakotay nodded for her to continue.

"I was restrained. Several large tubes were connected to my body. I was on fire, inside. The burning was unbelievable. I was lifted from a biobed and submerged in a tank of freezing water." Seven paused as a new wave of shudders shook her. "Then I woke up."

"It sounds awful," Chakotay agreed. "Could this have been a memory?"

"Not mine," Seven replied. "I wasn't living this through my body."

"I don't understand."

"I wasn't the subject in the dream. Axum was."

Chakotay's eyes widened as he sat back, rubbing his palms on his knees. Willing his hands to stillness, he said, "How do you know that?"

"In the last few weeks, I have dreamed of him often. I never did before, not even after I lost him when Unimatrix Zero was destroyed. What would have been the point?"

"That's not how dreams work, Seven."

"Mine do," she replied. "Once I started dreaming, I found I usually had the ability to direct them."

"I never knew you could do that, too," Chakotay said, smiling faintly.

"I didn't know what to make of the dreams when they began. They were very . . ." She paused and finally settled on, "*personal*."

Chakotay nodded his understanding.

"They were also very pleasant, despite the fact that I began to feel that it was inappropriate of me to enjoy them while also sharing the company of Counselor Cambridge."

"I am sure you've discussed this with him," Chakotay suggested.

"Yes. But when I saw how much it troubled him, I stopped. I thought I could make them go away. I couldn't. There have been times during these dreams that Axum spoke to me. He promised we would be together again soon. He was so happy."

Chakotay's brow furrowed.

"He didn't speak to me tonight," Seven went on. "I don't think he even knew I was there. He just screamed, pleaded for them to stop."

"Who?"

"I don't know. I don't think he knows. When this dream began I was already inside his body. I saw the tubes, felt the burning . . ." She choked, unable to continue.

"It's going to be okay," Chakotay assured her.

"Axum is alive," Seven said, daring him to question her.

Chakotay shook his head gently. "Seven, given all we've

been through together, do you honestly believe I would doubt your word?"

"No," she said with considerably less force. "That is why I asked you to come here."

"We have no reason to assume he died before the Caeliar reclaimed the Borg. We also know it is possible for you to sense other former Borg who remained outside the gestalt through your catoms."

"Then he must be close," Seven said.

"*That* seems incredibly unlikely," Chakotay replied. "You said you saw Starfleet insignia in your dream. Out here, that is only our ship and the *Demeter*."

"There could be other Starfleet vessels in the Delta Quadrant. *Equinox* was here for years before we discovered them."

"After *Voyager* returned home, Starfleet logs were gone through in painstaking detail for any other possible ships lost to the Caretaker. There weren't any," he told her. "If there had been, our first priority when the fleet launched would have been finding them."

"Axum could have been found by a Starfleet vessel in the Beta Quadrant," Seven said.

"That seems more likely," Chakotay agreed. "But the rest is harder to understand."

"Why?"

"Suppose he was found by a ship: What you describe in this dream might be medical treatment he is undergoing that frightens him. He might be ill."

"He wasn't," Seven insisted. "He is being tortured."

"That's what doesn't make sense. Starfleet doesn't torture people, Seven."

She paused, staring at him coldly.

"Seven?"

"Yes, they do," she said.

"That's quite an accusation," Chakotay said.

Seven paused again, unwilling to revisit this memory but more unwilling to allow Chakotay to harbor such dangerous naiveté. "When *Voyager* returned and the Borg infestation was discovered, I was involuntarily subjected to questioning by someone hand-selected by Admiral Montgomery," she said. "Because I had been Borg, they did not trust me to tell all I knew. They used inappropriate, painful means to force the truth from my mind. Of course, I had already told them the truth."

Chakotay's face paled. "You never spoke of this to me."

"I never spoke of it to anyone," she said. "I was not prepared to bring charges against them, and as long as I was unwilling to do so, there was no point in advising you or anyone else."

"Questioned how?"

"My examiner was Vulcan," Seven replied.

"A mind meld?" Chakotay asked, horrified.

Seven nodded.

"You should have . . ." Chakotay began, his face reddening with rage.

"Once the crisis was resolved, I wanted to move on with my life. I did. Difficult as it was, it was nothing compared to what I suffered at the hands of the Collective. But even if Axum was found in the Beta Quadrant," Seven said, intentionally changing the subject, "my catoms do not allow me to make contact with others at great distance."

Understanding her desire to drop the topic, Chakotay observed, "Your catoms surprise us daily. We need to make contact with Command and ask them if Axum has been found."

"We're not leaving here for at least a month," Seven replied.

"No," Chakotay agreed. "So in the short term, you need help."

"What do you suggest?"

"Doctor Sharak. I know he isn't as well versed as our Doctor in your unique physiology, but he is a good physician. If nothing else, we might need to put an end to your dreams. A neural inhibitor would help."

"I can't abandon Axum," Seven said softly.

"You also can't help him if whatever he is enduring destroys you."

Seven nodded.

"And you need to work with the counselor."

"I can't."

"Seven, the fact that you and he have a relationship now does not change his duty to you and this ship. I will speak to him, but I don't think that will be necessary. He cares deeply for you, and that concern will guide him, no matter what."

"He will think I am betraying him."

"Even if he does, he will set that aside to help you," Chakotay assured her.

"He shouldn't have to."

"And you shouldn't have to live a life where your thoughts and dreams are not your own. You didn't ask for this." Chakotay took a breath and continued more calmly. "The hardest part of sharing yourself with someone else is when you realize that you are sharing everything: the good and the bad. If you care for Hugh, you have to share this, too, as honestly as you can, especially when it is terrifying. If you pull away now, you will be betraying him. You will be disrespecting his ability to put your needs first. He deserves better. And you will be jeopardizing your physical and mental health."

Seven nodded. At some point in the last few minutes, the cold holding her in its grip had begun to fade a bit.

"I'm ready to go to sickbay," Seven said.

"Good. Let's go."

As they moved to the door, Chakotay gently guiding her with an arm around her waist, she said, "As for the other matter, I do not want you to bring it up with Admiral Montgomery."

Chakotay's jaw tensed visibly. "We're going to solve one problem at a time. But if Montgomery ordered what you described, he has no place in Starfleet."

Seven knew further discussion would not be helpful at

this time. She agreed with Chakotay but also feared that Montgomery's moral lapse might be more common among Starfleet than Chakotay imagined. Seven had counseled the President of the Federation to create a weapon of genocide at the height of the Borg Invasion. She accepted with open eyes the lengths to which sentient beings of good intent could be driven when faced with annihilation. Admiral Montgomery was a complicated human, capable of both good and evil. Once his anger and disappointment had settled, she was certain Chakotay would understand.

Of course, when she allowed herself to remember Axum's terror, part of her hoped Chakotay wouldn't.

Once Lieutenant Kim had discovered the means by which the wave forms could be taught, his focus had become singular. Given the relatively short length of time he had to accomplish the task that change in focus was understandable. Lieutenant Patel had also shifted her attention to assisting Commander O'Donnell with the strategies he intended to implement on the planet, hoping to save as many of the species as possible. As soon as the programming phase of the project had begun, Doctor Sharak had been assigned no further tasks related to the proctors or the sentries.

The doctor was not entirely at peace with this turn of events. He was not insulted, merely eager to continue to assist his fellow officers. As a physician, he was content with his duties aboard *Voyager.* He had left his people—the Children of Tama, or *Tamarians,* as the Federation called them—to learn all about the Federation. He knew this would consume the rest of his life, that it would aid his people, expanding their understanding of the galaxy. Perhaps, his time was better spent observing the crew and cataloging their responses to the new stimuli they encountered. All of the races aboard *Voyager* were interesting and unique. They were worthy of his complete attention.

Lieutenant Kim had been thoughtful enough to continue

to send Doctor Sharak the daily reports on the proctor project. Sharak assumed that many would not have time to review those reports as they were lengthy and voluminous in technical detail. *He,* however, had plenty of time, and did not step out of sickbay until all of the available data had been analyzed.

A few days ago, a subtle change had been detected in the behavior of the proctors. At least, *he* had detected it. The various reports suggested that no one other than the doctor had made note of the change.

A number of proctors tasked with duties on the planet had begun to emit low-level subspace discharges once their work was complete. Those discharges were different from the ambient "noise" normally emitted from the proctors, but they had been dismissed. Doctor Sharak had asked Lieutenant Conlon if she could isolate the readings of the discharges; she had created a subroutine to accomplish this. Once isolated, the discharges appeared to contain nothing more than random data. It was as if the proctors were purging data they found irrelevant to their assignments, perhaps clearing the way for new information.

It had taken time to translate the purged data, but with help from Conlon, Doctor Sharak had finally succeeded. The data consisted of a partial visual record of the given proctor's daily task. However, it also included images that could only have been taken from *Voyager* and *Demeter*'s databases. They were astonishing in several respects. Usually the images were of particularly intense moments: the attacks on the ship by the Indign or the Tarkons; the destruction of *Quirinal* while partially trapped in the Omega Continuum; the destruction of *Planck*; snippets of the battle to save the Children of the Storm.

It was the consistency of these images that gave the doctor pause. They might be meaningless. There was no way to know how much data the proctors could hold or how much might need to be purged in order for new data to be accepted.

But Sharak had a unique understanding of the ways in which a complex creature might organize data. If all the proctors working to restore the planet had access to the same information as the others—if the data from the original scans of *Voyager* and *Demeter* had been immediately shared by the proctor that had completed it with the others—there could be a purpose in the data they were now discharging.

This night, Doctor Sharak's work was briefly interrupted by the arrival of Miss Seven and Captain Chakotay. He had listened while Miss Seven recounted her new experiences while sleeping. He dispensed an analgesic and light sedative and coded a neural inhibitor to limit her mind's ability to access her dreams. There was no way to stop someone from dreaming; as dreams were a necessary component of restorative sleep, it was unwise to even attempt. But there were many ways to limit the brain's ability to access those dreams, or *interpret* them in any meaningful way.

He had requested that she spend the remainder of the evening in sickbay so that he might observe her. Once she had fallen into a light sleep, Sharak had confided his concerns about this course of action to Captain Chakotay.

"If, as Miss Seven believes, these are not true dreams, but images from a telepathic link made possible by her catoms, it is likely that our efforts to diminish them will be unsuccessful," Sharak said.

"We can't do anything to disconnect Seven from her catoms," Chakotay noted.

"We don't even know which cells, or portions of cells, of her body are catomic in nature," Sharak pointed out. "And it is clear that the functions they perform are crucial to her existence."

"We'll know more in the morning," Chakotay said.

"I will advise you immediately if there is cause for concern," Sharak assured him.

Once the captain departed, Sharak kept a watchful eye on

Miss Seven's readings, but resumed his study of the proctor's discharges. He had almost completed an examination of this day's data when a series of images caught his attention. He replayed them several times as an intuitive sense of understanding filled him.

The images he isolated were familiar: a number of stout herbivores had been relocated to a distant plain on a new continent. That plain had recently been seeded with a new form of grass for their consumption. As one of the creatures found a small tuft of grass and began to eat hungrily, an image of the "mother" of the Children of the Storm releasing thousands of bright white new life-forms from her atmosphere exploded on the screen before him. This image was followed by several other herbivores finding a food source, and again followed by repeated versions of the "mother's" moment of comprehension.

Doctor Sharak worked hard to speak Standard, the language of the Federation. But often during times of emotional intensity, he found their language insufficient. This was one of those times.

"*Sokath, his eyes uncovered,*" Doctor Sharak said softly.

Tom Paris wasn't sure what had awakened him. His quarters were dark, and he was pleasantly warm under the bedcovers. Miral was sprawled across her own small bed in a nook off their bedroom, sleeping soundly in a tangle of blankets partially thrown off. Perhaps it was her absence that had pulled him from sleep. Usually by this time, Miral had squirreled her way between him and B'Elanna to finish out the night. In truth, he struggled with this. Miral was not the most accommodating co-sleeper. Her arrival usually included several swift gut kicks and theft of pillows. Errant arms were thoughtlessly flung over his face. But he also lived for the feel of that small little body snuggling into his own. These nights would pass too quickly; perhaps they were already drawing to a close. He would miss them. Of course when the new baby came, there wouldn't be room for another between him and B'Elanna. . . .

Where's B'Elanna?

Rambling half-conscious thoughts gave way to full alertness as Paris pulled himself up in bed and verified that B'Elanna's side of the bed was empty.

"B'Elanna?" he called softly.

When there was no answer, he girded himself for whatever fresh pregnancy hell this night had devised for him. At least nothing was on fire. That was a step in the right direction. A quick search of the fresher and their living room confirmed B'Elanna's absence. With no other obvious recourse, Paris asked, "Computer, locate Commander Torres."

"Commander Torres is not in her quarters."

Paris paused, wondering if he had heard that right. Obviously she wasn't in her quarters. That wasn't what he had asked.

"Computer . . ." he began again.

"Go back to sleep, Tom," the computer advised. *"B'Elanna is fine and does not wish to be disturbed at the moment. Good night."*

Paris laughed lightly. He loved that his wife's engineering skills were without equal. He loved that she could reprogram the main computer to deliver the response she would have given if she'd been there. But damn it, now he *had* to know where she was.

Tempting as it was to just go back to bed, a gauntlet had just been thrown down. He quickly donned a pair of uniform pants, activated Kula to watch over Miral, and left their quarters to find his wife.

A search of main engineering, the astrometrics lab, the bridge, and the mess hall came up empty. The holodeck was his next stop. Holosuite two was running, with one of his old programs no less, and he was certain he'd found her. Though what would ever tempt her to enter Sandrine's was beyond him.

Stepping inside, he found himself in a re-creation of a bar he had frequented in Marseilles. He had programmed it to include a number of characters he remembered or half-remembered, but none of those characters was present now. A solitary figure sat at the bar, topping off a short glass, setting ice cubes tinkling as he did so.

"Counselor?" Paris asked when he recognized the figure.

Cambridge turned to him with hard eyes.

"The doctor is out, Commander," he replied and punctuated it with a sip of something dark, and if the smell was any indication, not synthehol.

"What are you doing here?" Paris asked.

"I refuse to believe that even to someone of your limited insight that it is not blatantly obvious," Cambridge replied.

Paris shrugged. They weren't close. Paris didn't really like the man's manner or methods. But he had developed a grudging respect for the counselor's abilities, and Cambridge had served the crew well. As first officer, however, the well-being of the entire crew, including the curmudgeonly Cambridge, was Paris's responsibility. If this was going to be a long-term solution to whatever Cambridge was facing, Paris needed to know—if only to advise the captain that their ship's only counselor was not going to be functioning at peak efficiency.

More to the point, Paris knew what drowning one's sorrows looked like. He also knew it was a temporary reprieve at best. "Care to share?" Paris asked.

Cambridge turned to him in utter shock.

"Whatever you're drinking?" Paris clarified.

"Oh," Cambridge said. He considered the bottle, which was more than half full, and replied by reaching under the bar for another small glass and pouring Paris two fingers.

Bracing himself, Paris tried to prepare for the heat that scalded his esophagus as the whiskey went down. A few loud coughs cleared his throat as the effect reached his head and gave him an instant warm buzz. "Where did that come from?" Paris asked when he could speak again.

Cambridge smiled. "My private stock."

Paris coughed again. "Pretty good. Also probably useful if you need to scrub conduits."

Cambridge chuckled and finished off his own glass with none of Paris's apparent discomfort. As he started to pour himself another, Paris slid his glass next to Cambridge's.

"You're sure you can take it?" Cambridge asked.

Ignoring the insult and forgoing a recitation of the years he'd lost to worse than what Cambridge was drinking, Paris said, "You shouldn't drink alone in the middle of the night, Counselor. People always find out and it looks bad. Besides, most people come to bars because they want to share their misery."

"I came to this one to be alone."

"Where are the regulars?" Paris asked.

"They were obnoxious in the extreme. I deleted them."

Paris raised his glass and said, "To old friends, you will be missed." He took a generous swallow. This one went down much easier.

He turned to the counselor who was studiously avoiding eye contact. Paris felt a brief surge of pity for the man. It wasn't hard to guess what had brought him here. You didn't spend as much time in bars as Paris had without acquiring a keen eye for the sorrows people had come to drown. Everything about the counselor screamed "Trouble at home." Paris was well aware, along with the rest of the crew, that *home* these days for Cambridge was with Seven.

The first officer was surprised. He had his doubts about the counselor but didn't figure Seven for a casual fling. When he'd learned of their budding relationship, he'd hoped for the best, if only for Seven. But obviously, Cambridge wasn't up to it.

"Well, thanks for the drink, Counselor," Paris said, shuffling off the barstool and polishing off what remained in his glass.

"Commander." Cambridge nodded his dismissal.

Paris stopped just before the holodeck arch and turning, he asked, "You're sure this is how you want to handle this? You're just going to give up?"

The look Cambridge shot him was equal parts confusion and warning.

Paris retraced his steps. "I don't know what you did, or if it's even fixable at this point, but there isn't a man who has ever laid eyes on Seven, let alone gotten to know her even a little, that wouldn't toss his mother out an airlock to be in your shoes right now."

"My personal life, Commander . . ." Cambridge began.

"Please," Paris cut him off, "there are a hundred and forty-seven people on this ship. It's too small for secrets. And it's not like you and Seven have gone to great lengths to hide your relationship. I thought the Doctor was going to suffer a catastrophic cascade failure right before my eyes when he asked me if I was aware." Stepping closer, Paris continued, "When the universe offers you someone like Seven, you don't let go. You fight like hell to keep her."

"Perhaps *you* do," Cambridge retorted sharply.

"I do," Paris replied. "My marriage is far and away the best thing I haven't yet found a way to screw up. But I earn it, every day. If I'd let any of our early miscommunications end things between me and B'Elanna, I wouldn't have found you here tonight. You'd have found me."

"Despite what you might think, Commander, *this* is not my doing," Cambridge said.

"The part where you're sitting here drinking instead of facing whatever this is head-on sure is," Paris shot back.

"I beg your pardon."

"Don't beg mine. Beg hers."

"I can't fight a ghost, Commander," Cambridge blurted out and clearly immediately wished it unsaid.

"A what?" Paris asked, wondering where the hell that had come from.

"Never mind," Cambridge said, turning away.

"There hasn't been anyone else," Paris insisted. "I know the Doctor did his damnedest, but that never came to anything. Unless she met someone on Earth . . ." Paris trailed off.

Cambridge simply shook his head slowly.

"Well the *Borg* don't . . ." Paris said, but caught himself. "Wait . . . what was his name?" Paris asked softly.

Cambridge turned to him, his face stone.

"Actel . . . Axel . . . Ax . . . something . . ." Paris said, trying to force a little clarity into his pleasantly sluggish brain. "That place we liberated . . ."

Cambridge turned away and Paris got the picture.

"You know what?" Paris said. "You're right. Stay here. If you can't handle a memory, I don't know how your fragile ego will endure spending the rest of this mission, let alone your life, with a woman like Seven. She's never going to lack for willing suitors."

"That's enough, Commander," Cambridge said.

"Axel . . . Axum!" Paris said, finally finding the name. "*Axum* is long gone. He's probably in Caeliar heaven right now along with the rest of them."

"Were you absent the day we discovered an entire group of former Borg who remained outside outside the gestalt by choice?"

Paris hadn't remotely considered the possibility that Cambridge's "ghost" might actually exist. But the counselor was right. And Paris would bet anything that if Axum was alive, the first person he'd come looking for was Seven.

"I retract my earlier advice," Paris said seriously.

"As well you should."

"The second part . . . not the first. Axum might have been her first love. He might have part of her heart forever. But she's a different woman now, and that woman *chose you*. You've got the upper hand because you're *here*. If you still want her, fight for her. If you're not willing to do that, you don't deserve her."

Using the counselor's methods on him felt good, but Paris

suspected that was the whiskey talking. Paris wasn't looking for payback. He needed to keep his crew happy. The pain of losing Seven could last a long time. Paris figured that could be avoided if Cambridge stepped up.

Cambridge rose from his barstool and crossed to him. Paris braced himself for a punch.

"You're right," Cambridge said softly.

When Paris returned to his quarters, B'Elanna was snoring softly on her side of the bed. Had he not been so concerned that she needed her sleep, Paris would have roused her and demanded an explanation for her absence. As it was, he simply laid down beside her, allowing the heat of her body to quiet him and the whiskey to lull him back to a deep sleep.

When Hugh Cambridge found Seven's quarters empty the following morning, he was concerned. That concern turned to outright terror when the computer advised him she was in sickbay. He entered to find her awake but under the doctor's care. Sharak was willing to fill him in on her medical details; as ship's counselor it was his purview. However, Cambridge wanted to learn what had brought her here from Seven's lips. Politely asking the doctor to excuse them, he settled himself on a stool beside her biobed.

"Before you say anything, I need to tell you something," Cambridge began.

"Proceed."

"I will always care about your happiness. Whether you find that happiness with me or elsewhere is immaterial. Please forgive me if I have given you any other impression."

Seven searched his face then reached for his hand. It took every ounce of self-control he possessed to resist the urge to bring it to his lips. Instead, he squeezed it gently.

"Is it your intention to end our romantic relationship?" Seven asked.

"No," he replied. "But if it is yours, I will accept it."

"It is not," Seven assured him. "But as you must suspect, matters have grown considerably more complicated."

"Tell me."

"Axum is alive. He has been communicating with me through our catoms. I don't understand how that is possible. What I do know, is that he is in danger."

"Then we must help him," Cambridge replied.

Seven nodded, smiling faintly.

That smile eased Cambridge's heart, even as it sliced it cleanly in half.

Chapter Twenty

SAN FRANCISCO

When Kathryn Janeway arrived in Admiral Montgomery's office, the room's temperature was decidedly chilly. This morning, Decan had made his first contact in a month. The Vulcan had advised her that Montgomery had asked to see her at fifteen hundred, local time.

Despite this, Janeway had enjoyed a pleasant lunch with her mother and helped her get things under way for dinner. They were expecting guests that evening. Initially she had been unwilling to allow anyone to trespass on her newfound happiness. As time wore on, she found herself looking forward to reconnecting with a few old friends. Tonight, she would see Mark Johnson and his wife for the first time since her return to Earth.

Now, she belived that Ken Montgomery would tell her that she had been assigned to a desk at Starfleet Command. She expected the dinner would help her accept the disappointment this meeting was sure to hold. She was ready to hear it. Janeway knew that all she had gained, in the last few weeks, would not be lost. She knew that Chakotay would look after their people as well as she would have. The pain of Command's choice would have been impossible to take six weeks ago, but no longer.

She was ready to accept it.

"Good afternoon, Admiral," Montgomery greeted her. He

did not rise from his desk or offer his hand. He simply stared at her solemnly.

"Admiral," Janeway said.

Coming right to the point, Montgomery said, "I completed my review of your evaluations yesterday and passed along my recommendation regarding your permanent assignment to Admiral Akaar. He concurred with my findings."

Janeway could tell he expected her to ask what those were. But she was in no hurry to hear them.

"It is the opinion of your counselors that dying and being resurrected has done no permanent mental damage to you. Some went so far as to suggest that it might have been the best thing that ever happened to you."

Janeway smiled at that. It sounded like Austen. "I wouldn't recommend it for everyone, sir."

"No," Montgomery agreed and continued, "but as it stands now, there is nothing preventing you from returning to active duty."

"I see."

"The issue at hand is what that duty should be."

Janeway nodded.

"I have reservations about placing you in command of the Full Circle fleet."

This was no surprise.

"I half expected when you arrived that you would immediately demand to be reinstated. Instead, you started acting as if you had been. You ignored the chain of command. You sought the counsel of everyone but me. You continued to intervene in the lives of your former crew. And in the process, you confirmed my worst fear about having you in command of the fleet."

Janeway took a moment to wonder if all of this might have been avoided had Counselor Austen been her first meeting. Jens had been Montgomery's choice. Cambridge's words came back to her. Montgomery had expected her to fail.

"What is that fear, Ken?" Janeway suddenly asked. She didn't expect he'd answer, but she was genuinely curious.

"That you are incapable of following orders."

This was a surprise, and Janeway allowed the shock of it to settle before she responded.

"I have always prided myself on being a model Starfleet officer," she finally said. "I have tried to uphold our principles. When faced with complicated judgment calls I try to err on the side of restraint. I place the needs of those I command far above my own."

"Or Starfleet's?" he interrupted.

"Never," she replied softly.

"So when you roped Captain Picard into allowing Commander Data to assist you in illegally removing Seven of Nine, Cadet Icheb, and your EMH from detention to illegally gain access to *Voyager,* that was in Starfleet's best interest?" Montgomery asked.

"Ken, I did everything in my power to convince you to let us help. You turned condescension into an art form as you ignored my requests. You left me no choice but to take the actions I did, and as it happens, I was proven right," Janeway countered.

"Eventually. But you had no idea what Covington was up to when you took those actions. They were about Seven of Nine."

"Who was instrumental . . ." Janeway began.

Stopping her, Montgomery continued, "When you allowed Captain Chakotay to forego his mission to Kerovi in order to save the life of Miral Paris, that was in Starfleet's best interest?"

"I was . . ." Janeway said.

"When you chose to personally investigate that Borg cube when any of a number of our scientists would have done as well, that was in Starfleet's best interest?"

Janeway paused. Montgomery's first case against her was almost entirely without merit, but the next two were closer calls. Her choice to allow Chakotay to pursue the Warriors of Gre'thor had cost Starfleet the ability to interrogate a Changeling infiltrator. Her choice to investigate the Borg cube that had assimilated her had been made primarily to prove that sending *Voyager* back to the Delta Quadrant to further investigate the Borg was unwarranted.

"I see your point," Janeway acknowledged. "But I also believe that my record demonstrates my devotion to Starfleet. We don't always see eye-to-eye, but when we work together, we serve the greater good."

"You still believe those choices were right because you could not have done otherwise and lived with yourself," Montgomery replied. "But you did not follow direct orders or standard protocols, nor did you err on the side of restraint. You made similar calls in the Delta Quadrant, but those were mitigated by your unique circumstances, and more latitude was granted in evaluating them. I don't give a damn about how you conducted yourself there. What you have shown since your return is that you answer first to your own internal sense of right, disregarding the authority of Command. It's not that I know exactly what you'll do out there. I *don't* know. You can lead, but the question is, *are you also willing to be led*?"

Janeway considered this seriously. It would never have occurred to her that she had not been led, if not by her superiors then at least by their shared ideals. But the picture Montgomery painted was too accurate for her to dismiss it.

A new thought occurred to her: If Montgomery had made his final decision with Akaar's blessing, what was this? Was he inflicting wounds just to pour salt in them?

"I will be led, whether I return to the fleet or not," Janeway replied. "So unless you're drumming me out of Starfleet, we're both going to find out."

"There are days I've wanted to," Montgomery admitted. "But I understand what a waste that would be."

"Why did you offer me command of the fleet in the first place?" Janeway asked.

"The Full Circle fleet has been one disaster after another," Montgomery replied bitterly. "I didn't see how you could do any worse than your predecessors."

"Leaving me out there saved you the trouble of confronting the fleet's issues?"

"More or less."

"Admiral Akaar didn't see it that way," Janeway guessed.

"He thought it was wrong to ask you to take up the post after all you'd been through. There were enough people raising hell to support his position, not that he needed it. I knew once he spent time with you, he'd see that you were too great a risk, and I expected he'd simply recall the entire fleet and we could put this exercise in futility behind us."

"You no longer believe in the mission of Project Full Circle?" Janeway asked, incredulous. "You're in *command* of it."

"It was Willem Batiste's idea," Montgomery replied coldly. "We all know now that he was *not* motivated by concern for the Federation. I'm surprised you still believe in it," he added. "You died trying to prevent it."

"That was before the invasion," Janeway replied, "before the Caeliar. Had I witnessed those events, I don't know how I would have felt. But the fact remains that the fleet has served with great distinction."

"Not from where I'm sitting. We have to secure Federation space right now with half of our usual resources. We all know exploration comes with acceptable losses, but we can't continue to sustain ones of the magnitude this fleet has endured. The whole thing was a bad idea."

Janeway was struck by the harshness of his assessment. But slivers of the truth shone through the cracks. "I'm not the problem," she said softly. "This is about you and your reputation. You don't want the Fleet on your record. And until a few months ago, nobody was paying attention, were they? Not with so many pressing concerns closer to home. Then things went seriously sideways, and your first instinct was to pass the buck. You wanted to shift the blame to me. But Akaar wouldn't let you. You're in his crosshairs right now, and as the fleet goes, so goes your career."

"Akaar retains enough naïve arrogance to believe that the price of exploration never outweighs its potential. There's a case to be made that had the fleet not been out there two months ago, we wouldn't be having this conversation right now. Omega would have ended everything. But with that crisis behind us, it's hard to justify leaving them out there. When he brought you back, I was sure the rest of the fleet would follow in short order."

"Why haven't they?"

"The *Vesta* will be ready to launch in less than a week. That was your doing. It was an inspired call. Some of your detractors have had a change of heart, and you've received considerable support from others who have taken an interest in the issue. Your counselors have filed glowing reports. And you surprised both of us by stepping back and letting other people do their jobs. I didn't know you had that in you."

"I didn't either," Janeway replied mirthlessly.

"It proved to us beyond a shadow of a doubt that you are the only officer we have right now who should be in command that fleet."

"Excuse me?" Janeway replied, certain she hadn't heard him right.

"Verdell's a good man, but he's made a complete hash of the reconstruction efforts. He's been flying a desk too long to understand how things work out there. Akaar saw that. There is no one else who can be brought up to . . . " Montgomery stopped himself. "We need answers about those comm relays sooner rather than later."

"So I'm the bottom of the barrel?" Janeway asked pointedly.

"Don't be ridiculous," Montgomery said. "You are a calculated risk."

"I'm returning to the Delta Quadrant?" Janeway asked, unable to believe the words she was saying.

"Assuming you and I can come to terms regarding a few outstanding points of contention," Montgomery said.

"And those are?"

"First, there is the issue of fraternization."

"I beg your pardon," Janeway replied.

"Are you currently engaged in an intimate relationship with Captain Chakotay?" Montgomery asked.

"Throw all the stones you like at my professional choices, Admiral," Janeway warned, "but take care with my personal ones. I won't be held to a different standard than my peers."

"Your peers?"

"The captain of the flagship is married to his CMO. *Titan*'s captain is married to his ship's counselor. There's Admiral Shelby and Captain Calhoun . . . Didn't Picard officiate when they got married?"

"The operative word there is *married*," Montgomery replied.

"Before those relationships were made official, there was no fraternization going on?" Janeway asked. "What century is it again?"

"I'm not judging you, Kathryn," Montgomery insisted.

"Really?"

"If a relationship develops between two people within the same chain of command, it often results in complications that are distracting for the crew. If you expect to lead the fleet, including Captain Chakotay, you will be required to maintain more than a modicum of propriety until such time as your relationship becomes public and official. At that time, your superior officers are permitted to decide if the nature of that relationship presents problems for the crew. In each of the incidences you cite, those evaluations were made. You will be accorded the same treatment as your peers."

"Let me think, where did I leave the keys to that chastity belt?" Janeway said.

"I'm serious, Admiral."

"I agree with you, under most circumstances," Janeway

said. "But there are clearly incidences of fraternization that have not led to the wholesale disruption of operations. I know that the nature of my relationship with Captain Chakotay and the deep friendship on which it was founded will ensure that it does not compromise my ability to serve as his commanding officer."

"Nevertheless," Montgomery went on, "quarters have been prepared for you aboard *Vesta*. For the duration of the fleet's presence in the Delta Quadrant, you will maintain those quarters. This is a direct order."

Janeway considered the order. "That's actually not a bad idea. If we decide to marry?" she asked.

"Do me a favor and don't, at least not for a while," Montgomery said. "I'd hate to miss the ceremony," he added semi-seriously.

"We'll make sure your invitation doesn't get lost." Janeway smirked. "Is there anything else?"

"Starfleet Medical has requested that Seven of Nine be returned to Earth as soon as possible," Montgomery said.

Given the Doctor's recent reports, this was not surprising, though Janeway had held out hope until now that it would not come to pass. Montgomery continued, "There is a medical emergency on three Federation worlds; almost a hundred thousand additional lives have been lost. Starfleet Medical fears that count could triple."

Janeway looked up abruptly. "*Triple?*"

Montgomery nodded grimly. "We need all hands on deck on this one, and Seven's an invaluable resource for their research."

"She's also invaluable to the fleet," Janeway said. "But, when she is apprised of the circumstances, I'm sure she'll want to comply. The disease is catomic in nature?"

"So we believe."

Remembering the Doctor's concerns, she chose her words carefully, "I assume that once she returns, Seven will immediately be reunited with the patient from Starbase 185 known as Axum?"

Montgomery leaned back, clearly frustrated. "Your former EMH doesn't know when to keep his mouth shut."

"I share some of his concerns regarding Axum's recovery. The Doctor believes it is essential that Axum see Seven. You should also consider that while not a Federation citizen, Axum has rights. I'm sure once it's explained to him, he'll want to help us. I knew him briefly, and he seemed like a good man."

"This request is a deal breaker?" Montgomery asked.

"Yes," Janeway said.

"I'm going to take heat for it: agreed. You also need to tell the Doctor to stand down."

"If I can assure him of Axum's well-being, and Seven's, he won't trouble you further," Janeway replied. "But given his expertise, I strongly suggest you keep him in the loop."

"Consider yourself so assured," Montgomery said.

"How are we going to arrange for her transport?" Janeway asked. "We have no idea where *Voyager* is, do we?"

"They haven't reported in," Montgomery replied. "I don't know if they're out of range or if the relays are the issue."

"We'll find out," Janeway said. "Will *Achilles* . . ."

"*Vesta* and *Galen* will join the fleet," Montgomery interjected. "As soon as the *Vesta*'s repairs are complete, *Achilles* will be formally severed from it. I know you might be able to use her, but she's more valuable to us here," Montgomery said.

"I understand," Janeway agreed, "but I don't want to make a habit of sending vessels back and forth for personnel transports. It's a drain on our limited resources."

"There is a slipstream-capable vessel stored on *Achilles* right now that was designed by your fleet chief, Commander Torres. You will return Seven to Earth on that vessel—I think it's designated the *Home Free*—and we'll get her back to you as soon as we can."

"You realize, Ken, the final decision has to be hers."

"You just said you were certain she would want to help."

"I am, but I cannot order her to comply. I don't have that authority, and neither do you."

"You do have the authority to refuse to allow her to remain with the fleet as a civilian advisor," Montgomery pointed out.

"I would never do that," Janeway cautioned him honestly.

"Make sure she understands that it is temporary and vital to the interests of the Federation."

"I'll do my best."

"Then there's the issue of the Paris family," Montgomery went on.

"Has the court . . ." Janeway began.

"The court has ordered mediation," Montgomery said. "Commander Paris, Commander Torres, and their daughter are ordered to attend."

"Really?"

"Julia Paris has a lot of friends in very high places. Should it come to her attention that Starfleet had the ability to bring them home, perhaps with Seven, and did not, they might hold Starfleet and the Parises in contempt."

"You're asking me to do without Seven, the fleet's chief engineer, and *Voyager*'s first officer indefinitely?" Janeway asked.

"Mister Paris brought this on himself. Tell Chakotay to promote whomever he sees fit in the interim, and you should also feel free to assign a new fleet chief if you think it's warranted."

All of her worst fears but one were now real.

"Admiral." Montgomery rose to his feet.

Janeway came to attention.

"Vice Admiral Kathryn Janeway, you are hereby ordered to take command of the Full Circle fleet," Montgomery said. "Your first priority is to investigate the damaged relays and determine the cause. Once done, *Vesta* and *Galen* will regroup with *Voyager* and *Demeter*. You will then arrange for the transports we discussed."

"Aye, sir," she said.

Montgomery extended his hand to her, and she shook it firmly. "And Kathryn?" he added, as he resumed his seat.

"Yes?"

"Going forward, I will be your first, and last, point of contact."

His tone chilled her. She honestly hadn't anticipated his anger.

"As long as you have our backs, Admiral, I will have yours," she assured him.

"Understood," he said.

When Janeway returned to her office, Decan was standing inside waiting for her. He was Vulcan, so he wasn't smiling, but she sensed his happiness nonetheless.

"How did you know?" she asked.

"How did I know what, Admiral?"

"That I would be given command of the fleet?"

"Admiral Montgomery is a small man who thinks in small terms. Neither you, nor Admiral Akaar, suffer from that failing. It was only logical to assume that ultimately, Admiral Montgomery's concerns would be given their proper, negligible weight."

"Admiral Akaar was the one who brought me home in the first place."

"Have you not found your time here beneficial?" Decan asked.

"I have," Janeway said.

"As he knew you would. Once Admiral Akaar realized he could not rely on Admiral Montgomery to make the appropriate choices regarding you and the fleet, he took that task upon himself. I knew the other likely candidates and did not doubt that once the admiral evaluated them, he would see that you were the best choice," Decan replied.

Nodding her understanding, Janeway said, "We have work to do."

"Obviously," Decan said.

"Does the Academy still place first years in posts within Starfleet departments?" she asked.

"It remains a core requirement for the final year of study," Decan replied.

"Do you know who selects and approves of those posts?"

"I do."

"Contact him immediately. I have a special request to make."

"Concerning which cadet?"

"Cadet Icheb," Janeway said.

Chapter Twenty-one

VOYAGER

As the familiar sensation of transport released him, Tom Paris heard his daughter squeal in delight and shout, "Daddy's here! Daddy, look!" Though he had promised B'Elanna not to open his eyes, even after the site-to-site transport from their quarters was complete, Miral's excitement made that impossible.

Tom took in the room; he had no idea where he was. Behind him was the door. To his immediate right was a large sitting area with a long couch that Miral was bouncing on. Across from it, beyond a small coffee table, was his antique television set. To his left was a small nook complete with data terminals where two could comfortably work. The far wall was banked by a long port. Below it, running the length of the room, was a shelving unit for storage. It was centered by a larger dining table than he was accustomed to. It could seat four and probably six with ease. The far right corner appeared to be a functioning galley, divided from the rest of the room by a short bar, behind which were a replicator and two properly vented burners. Even with all these furnishings, the room still had an open, airy feel to it. The center space could be used to create a variety of play spaces for the children to share.

The room had doorways on either side. Stepping forward and peeking to the right, Tom saw a slightly larger-than-standard bedroom and 'fresher. He then spared a glance at

B'Elanna, who was grinning at him from ear to ear as he crossed to the left-side doorway and found two small rooms, one obviously for Miral, as it already contained a number of her playthings, and another set up as a nursery.

Miral scooted past him into her room and shouted, "This is mine, Daddy!"

"I see that, honey," he said. Of his wife, he asked, "Did you tell Chakotay before you reconfigured this cargo bay for our personal use? Wait, didn't this use to be the fleet commander's suite?"

"It was Chakotay's idea," she said.

"Does he know something I don't about Admiral Janeway's plans?"

"Only that she would have hated these quarters," B'Elanna assured him.

"Is this what you've been doing when you were supposed to be sleeping?"

"Yes," B'Elanna admitted. "But it was worth it, don't you think?"

"It's amazing," he said. "I don't know what to say. You don't want the kids to share a room?"

B'Elanna shrugged. "We could always change it later. For now, it will be good for the baby to have his own space; less of a distraction for Miral. After that, he'll probably want his own room."

Tom nodded then caught himself. "His?"

B'Elanna's smile widened. "That's right, flyboy. You're going to have a son."

Tom felt his face flushing. He hadn't let himself think much about the baby's gender until now. He had become comfortable as the father of a daughter. *A son*? Much as he and his father had found their way back to each other eventually, he worried that his childhood had left him ill-equipped to parent a boy.

"Tom, you okay?" B'Elanna asked.

"I am," he said.

"We're going to be late for the briefing," she added.

"Right," he said, squaring his shoulders.

"Kula?" B'Elanna called, and the holographic Klingon nanny appeared. "I'll be back shortly," she advised the program.

The nanny nodded and entered Miral's bedroom.

"Miral, behave for Kula. We'll go to the holodeck as soon as I get back," B'Elanna added over her shoulder. "You ready?" she asked Tom.

Tom was and he wasn't. The new life he and B'Elanna were about to embark on was suddenly more real to him than it had ever been. It was terrifying, but in a good way.

"Yes," he said softly. "And honey?"

"Mmm-hmm?"

"Thank you."

"You're welcome."

Lieutenant Harry Kim stared in wonder beyond Commander O'Donnell at the main viewscreen of the astrometrics lab. What had once been a planet clouded in a sickly yellowish haze was now a bright world of blues, greens, and browns. As O'Donnell was busy explaining to the senior staffs of both *Voyager* and *Demeter,* the proctors had completed the final phase of their work, and the planet could now sustain approximately ninety-two percent of its life-forms indefinitely.

Looking around the lab, Kim saw the same pride and satisfaction he felt reflected on the faces of his fellow officers. The work had been long and arduous, but it had been worth it. They were about to leave one tiny planet a lot better off than it had been when they found it.

If he had any regret, it was that the proctors were not capable of understanding what Starfleet had done for them. The proctors had performed their functions brilliantly and had been given all the data they needed to continue to monitor the planet's progress and intervene if necessary. But it didn't feel like a first contact. The deeper connection, the exchange of ideas that was typical of a first contact wasn't possible. Kim didn't need to hear a "thank you." Still, he knew something about this mission would always feel unfinished for him.

Captain Chakotay was lavishing praise upon all assembled and admonishing them to pass along his sentiments. He thanked Kim, Conlon, Seven, Patel, and Commander O'Donnell. There had been plenty of tension between the ships' captains when this mission had begun, but it was behind them. After working together, Kim had decided that he genuinely liked O'Donnell and suspected that deep down, the commander was growing on Chakotay as well.

As the room began to empty around them, Doctor Sharak approached the tactical officer. "I would trouble you for a moment with your permission, Lieutenant."

"How can I help you, Doctor?" Kim asked, smiling at the formality with which Sharak often began personal interactions. Given the vast, and for a long unbridgeable gap between the way Tamarians and other humanoid species framed their language, it was still a marvel to Kim that Sharak could speak Federation Standard.

"I have been studying daily several unusual data purges the proctors have made during our work," Sharak began.

"Lieutenant Conlon mentioned it. Is there anything more you need?" he asked, wondering why it seemed to matter to Sharak.

"No," Sharak said. "Lieutenant Conlon was most accommodating. I simply wish to show you my findings."

"Sure," Kim said.

With a curt nod, the doctor moved to the lab's main data terminal. As he brought up the file containing his results, the image on the main viewscreen went dark. "Not all of the data purged by the proctors was retrievable," Doctor Sharak began. Having spent as much time as he had trying to decrypt the wave form's data process, this did not surprise Kim. "But this is an aggregation of images from the first week."

Kim watched the grainy display proceed. He recognized much of it. Sensor readings and visual images taken from the starships and shuttles that had facilitated the proctor's work were intercut with older images that could only have come from *Voyager* or *Demeter*'s databases. They appeared quite random. But the confluence of old data with current data was odd, and Kim had no idea what to make of it.

"I'm sorry, Doctor," Kim finally admitted. "I'm not sure what you're getting at here."

"Our first efforts on the planet were somewhat destructive in nature, were they not?" Sharak asked.

Kim nodded. "In a way. A lot of areas had to be cleared in preparation for seeding, and the progress of some of the more aggressive life-forms had to be curtailed."

Doctor Sharak paused the visual feed on an image of the *Planck* as it exploded in space. The question sprang immediately to Kim's mind: *Why would the wave forms have saved that image, or purged it?*

"They understood," Doctor Sharak said in answer to his unspoken question. "They knew what we were doing and expressed their understanding in terms they thought we would recognize."

The notion was so shocking it took Kim a moment to process it.

"These came later," Sharak continued, opening another file. Suddenly the images of life-forms on the planet roaming peacefully in their new habitats and finding nourishment were interspersed with images Kim understood: the "mother" of the Children of the Storm as he had last seen her, glowing white and shooting new and vibrant thoughts from her atmosphere.

Chills coursed over Kim's entire body.

"These came yesterday," Sharak continued.

Kim's heart stilled. The planet—as it now appeared, vibrant and lush—was intercut with the memorial service, when the white disc had exploded into being above the field at Federation Park and then slowly descended to rest in its ceremonial dish.

"Their thoughts are not like ours. They don't have words. They have data. But they clearly assign meaning to that data and can correctly interpret the correlation. They have mourned as we have mourned," Sharak said softly. "They are renewed as we are renewed by our efforts here." When Kim did not immediately reply, Sharak asked, "Do you not see?"

Kim turned to the nearly empty room. The person the lieutenant required, however, was still present.

"Captain!" Kim shouted.

The fleet had been set to depart for a series of coordinates almost twenty thousand light-years from their current position. The coordinates would put them within range of their subspace relays and allow them to transmit their latest reports and receive updated orders from Starfleet. Eager as Chakotay was to make that journey, he immediately agreed to extend their stay in the wave form's system. He wanted to find out if Doctor Sharak's theory was correct. Chakotay would have had second thoughts had Seven not demonstrated marked improvement since she began using the neural inhibitor. It would be a little longer until they might learn something about Axum, but she was no longer suffering daily torments.

All available personnel set aside everything else to pore over the data purges. More eyes discovered that individual proctors chose different images to express their understanding of the work they had been assigned. However, in every case, that understanding reflected in some way on their task.

Doctor Sharak was invaluable to this work. Where most could take an educated guess at the links between actions and images, the Tamarian could immediately grasp the essence of an image and translate it. Chakotay quickly realized that the data being returned was communicating more than information. Most often, the words Sharak would find to express the responses were emotional: anger, sadness, fear, distress, hope, or joy. Gratitude was there a few times, which seemed to please Lieutenant Kim inordinately.

Once Chakotay was confident that they had correctly translated all of the images the proctors had sent out, the next question was simple: Could communications be established with the proctors? Despite all their efforts, it soon became clear that any communication they might successfully establish, even now, would likely be incredibly limited.

They had settled on one question to ask of the proctors. As they prepared to open communications with the proctors, no one knew if they could make the wave forms understand that the data they would be receiving required a direct response.

Chakotay sat on the bridge, Commander Paris at his left hand and Doctor Sharak at his right. Counselor Cambridge stood next to the Doctor's chair. Lieutenant Lasren stood behind Lieutenant Kim at ops; Kim would be handling the transmissions to the proctors. Lieutenant Aubrey had Kim's post at tactical. Patel was at the bridge science station, Gwyn sat at the helm, and Conlon was on an open channel in engineering. Seven would monitor the attempt from astrometrics.

Commander O'Donnell's senior staff was at its posts on *Demeter*'s bridge. Half of *Voyager*'s viewscreen showed his face, the other, the area of open space that had become the central point for programming the proctors over the last several weeks.

"Lieutenant Kim?" Chakotay asked, eager to be under way.

"We're ready, sir," Kim replied.

"Go ahead," Chakotay ordered.

As Kim harmonized the subspace frequency standard to the proctors, a single wave form gracefully erupted from subspace and held its position, awaiting further data.

Doctor Sharak stared at the monitor in the arm of his chair. The universal translator did not have sufficient data to translate the proctor's "language" as well as the doctor could.

Sharak uttered a soft snort as a series of images began to flash on his screen.

Turning to Doctor Sharak, Chakotay asked, "What are you seeing, Doctor?"

"It is impatient for data," Sharak replied.

"Let's not keep it waiting, Harry."

"Aye, sir."

The first transmission would be simple: an indication that the ships were prepared to depart. The response was immediate.

"The work is complete," Sharak translated. "The planet will be sustained."

"So far so good," Chakotay said and smiled.

"Wait," Sharak said, pausing as he studied a new series of images before him.

"What is this?" Sharak asked of Chakotay as he froze an image on his small screen.

"That's the *Delta Flyer* trying to extract dilithium from one of the asteroids," Chakotay said.

"And this?" Sharak asked, indicating a new image.

"The moment when a proctor kept one of the sentries from destroying the *Flyer,*" Chakotay replied.

"Yes," Sharak said. "They wish to compensate us for our efforts. Is payment required?" Sharak asked, clearly translating for the proctor.

"Not at all," Chakotay assured him. "Harry?"

"Transmitting response," Kim said.

A few moments later Sharak said, "You will not meet with resistance should you choose to proceed."

"Now they tell us," O'Donnell quipped from the main viewscreen.

Laughing lightly, Chakotay said, "Harry, our question?"

"Transmitting request now," Kim answered.

The "request" was simple. It was an image of the fragment of hull containing the words WORLDS OF THE FIRST QUADRANT. Again, the response was immediate.

One destructive image after another filled Sharak's screen; Chakotay thought he understood the proctor's answer.

"I don't think the Worlds of the First Quadrant are too popular around these parts," the captain offered.

"Wait," Sharak counseled, "there is more to it than that."

Chakotay looked up at Kim, who was also studying the response at Lasren's station.

"Lieutenant Kim," Doctor Sharak said, "please resend the same transmission."

"Resending," Kim replied.

A number of different proctors emerged near the first and began transmitting their own data. It soon became more than Sharak could translate, and Kim took a few minutes to isolate the incoming messages, separating them for easier study.

Finally Sharak said, "They believe it would be dangerous for us to contact these 'Worlds.' They view them as hostile and aggressive. They are not like us."

"They don't know us very well," Cambridge observed softly.

"Give me a minute," Kim called from ops.

"What do you propose, Harry?" Paris asked.

"They need to understand *why* we want to make contact with these worlds," Kim replied.

"Proceed," Chakotay ordered.

After a few silent minutes, Kim said, "I've sent a new transmission containing data from several first contacts we've made."

"Did you tell them about the Tarkons?" Paris asked, obviously teasing.

"Captain," Aubrey called from tactical, "the proctor is approaching. A second proctor is moving to intercept *Demeter.*"

"We'll be all right, Chakotay," O'Donnell counseled calmly. *"They're not going to hurt us now."*

"Harry?" Chakotay asked.

"I don't know, sir. Their previous scans haven't done any

damage. Maybe they think they need more information than I'm giving them."

"They think *we* need more information," Sharak corrected him softly.

"The proctor has surrounded the ship," Aubrey advised.

Chakotay was about to order O'Donnell to prepare countermeasures should they prove necessary when communications with *Demeter* were lost.

"Everybody remain calm," Chakotay ordered. "This will be over in a few seconds."

"Scan in progress," Kim began, but then fell silent.

The tingling sensation Chakotay associated with the proctor's previous scan began but did not pass. Instead it intensified, along with a dull throbbing at the base of his neck.

Then the assault began.

Chapter Twenty-two

INDIANA

The last few days had been busier than any Janeway had experienced during her liberty. Apart from the numerous updates on the *Vesta*'s progress and recalling of all personnel from the *Quirinal, Esquiline, Hawking,* and *Curie* who had been assigned to the *Vesta,* and canceling the leaves of *Galen*'s crew; there were numerous personal matters to be settled.

She had labored over a response to T'Pel's message. Ultimately, Janeway had opted for a short one that communicated her understanding of Tuvok's wishes and her assurances that whenever he wanted to speak with her, she would be available.

A longer message had been sent to Julia Paris. Janeway had already filed a brief with the court regarding the custody issue, but she chose to make one final appeal to Julia. She did not believe it would be received in the spirit it had been intended, but her love for the entire Paris family, Julia included, demanded that she make the effort.

Janeway had chosen not to monogram the blanket for René Picard. Instead, she'd had TO A YOUNG EXPLORER embroidered on it. The card that accompanied it had simply read FROM A VOYAGER.

There was time for a final visit with Mark Johnson. Over coffee in a local café they had once frequented, Janeway had expressed her gratitude to him for personally informing Chakotay of her death. Mark had promised that the next time someone told him that Kathryn Janeway was dead, he was going to laugh in his face. She'd teased him that the third time might be the charm on that one, but he'd said he refused to believe it.

Finally, Janeway had sat down and composed a lengthy message to Phoebe. She had been invited over several times, but even on Janeway's last night, her sister did not make an appearance. Janeway had known she wouldn't. She knew too well the pain her sister refused to release. In her message Janeway suggested that Phoebe speak with Counselor Austen. Though Phoebe was not Starfleet, as a family member, she had the option of availing herself of Starfleet Medical's services, and Austen had said she would be pleased to speak with Phoebe were she so inclined. Whatever she chose, Kathryn had assured Phoebe of her understanding, love, and acceptance.

Her final dinner with Gretchen should have been a solemn affair—it wasn't. Both women were determined to make the most of every moment they'd been given, and they did so. Curling up before the fire in the living room after a light meal, while the dinner plates sat unwashed, they discussed frankly Janeway's hopes and fears for the future.

Gretchen had been pleased to learn of her deepening relationship with Chakotay and asked that she pass along her regards and an invitation to visit. Her mother had promised to keep tabs on Julia Paris. Though she did not know Julia well, Gretchen understood that she was commanded now by her pain rather than her mind. Gretchen also insisted that if the Paris family or Seven should require a place to stay when they returned to Earth, they contact her. Starfleet would offer them accommodations, but Gretchen could give them a home.

Their final embrace and parting words were filled with love and hope. The years that were about to separate them held no fear. Gretchen sent her daughter off, as she always had, with pride.

SAN FRANCISCO

When Janeway arrived that evening on the grounds of Starfleet Academy, she was directed to a private lounge to wait for the arrival of the cadets she had asked to see. They arrived within five minutes—both in uniform—entered the lounge, and stood at attention.

"Cadet Icheb, Cadet Wildman," she greeted them formally.

"Admiral," they replied in unison.

"At ease," she ordered.

Only now did wide smiles spread across both their faces. Naomi's was particularly vibrant.

"Come here, you two," Janeway said, opening her arms. Naomi Wildman beat Icheb there by a few paces and hugged her fiercely. Janeway returned the embrace with equal strength. Icheb settled for extending his hand and Janeway took it in both of hers, saying, "You're looking well."

"I am well, thank you, Admiral," Icheb said.

"I assume your studies are proceeding apace?"

"They are."

"Have you by any chance received your internship assignment for the coming semester?" she asked.

Icheb nodded. "I have. But I was considering speaking to my advisor about altering it. I was assigned to Starfleet Medical Research. I do not intend to pursue medical studies. I thought it might be a mistake."

"It wasn't," Janeway assured him. "I made the request, and I would consider it a personal favor if you would accept it."

"Of course," Icheb said. "Had I known, I wouldn't have questioned it."

"I'm leaving tomorrow to head back to the Delta Quadrant. Seven will likely be returning to Earth and will be working with Starfleet Medical for what I hope will be a brief time. I want you nearby, just in case."

"If there is anything you or she requires, please advise me. I will always comply."

"I know," Janeway said. "You're dismissed, Cadet. I need to speak with Cadet Wildman alone."

"Safe journey, Admiral," Icheb said, then turned to go with a smile and a wink at Naomi.

As soon as they were alone, Naomi seemed to withdraw a little, as if embarrassed by her earlier enthusiasm. Placing an arm around her shoulder, Janeway said, "Would you like to take a walk, Naomi?"

"Yes, Admiral," she said.

The Academy grounds at night were as lovely as Janeway remembered. She wondered who was responsible for them, as Boothby *must* be retired by now.

"Icheb told me as soon as he got back that you were alive," Naomi offered. "I couldn't believe it, but I knew he would never lie about something like that."

"There have been days I didn't believe it either," Janeway said.

"Did it hurt to be dead?" Naomi asked. It was an innocent, almost childlike question, but Janeway understood what she was really asking.

"No," she said. "But to be honest, I was never really dead. Not all of me. Or I couldn't be here now."

"Icheb said Q brought you back."

"Q saved all that was left of me after I was assimilated—in that way, Icheb was right."

"I'm so glad he did," Naomi said, looking up. "It was harder to live in the universe without you. It didn't seem like near as nice a place."

Janeway pulled Naomi closer, saying, "I'm glad, too."

"Thank you for forwarding Neelix's letters," Naomi added as they ambled down a manicured path edged with low-trimmed hedges toward the gardens.

"Have you prepared a response for him?" Janeway asked.

"Oh, yes," Naomi replied. "I intended to send them out through Pathfinder."

"In the future, you should contact a Lieutenant Varia at Pathfinder directly. I will personally take any letters you have ready to send now."

"Thank you so much," Naomi said and smiled.

"Icheb mentioned to me that you'd had a bit of a rough start here," Janeway said gently.

Naomi nodded.

"Is it getting better?"

Naomi shrugged. "Not really."

Janeway paused, knowing the impact her words had always had on this young girl and mindful that she must tread carefully.

"Naomi, why did you apply so early to the Academy?"

She paused in her steps. "I didn't think I had a choice. I had completed my secondary studies, and given that I always intended to enter the Academy, all of my advisers felt I should apply at once. I think maybe they thought I'd have a hard time getting in because I'm young."

"Apparently they were wrong," Janeway observed wryly.

"Yep. My mom applied twice before she got in. My dad took three tries. They couldn't believe it when I was accepted right away. But they were so excited."

"I know your unique physiology means that you mature faster than human children do. I have watched you for most of your life, amazed at your quick mind and determination to take on responsibilities far beyond most of your years," Janeway said. "But you don't have to be in such a rush to grow up. You always have choices."

"Starfleet is all I know," Naomi said.

Janeway paused and turned to face her, placing her hands on Naomi's shoulders. "I know," she said. "As someone who spent her youth dreaming of a life among the stars and then living that dream, I would never suggest that it is not a challenging and wondrous path to walk. But you've had a lot to absorb over the last few years. Your first home was *Voyager*. As soon as we got back there was your family, your father, new schools, new friends. It's a lot to handle for someone twice your age. And were it not for your Ktarian heritage, you would have had several more years to get comfortable with all of that change before starting at the Academy."

Naomi's face darkened a little as she pondered these words.

"I'm not saying you don't belong here, Naomi," Janeway continued. "Maybe you aren't happy here right now because the first year is hard for everyone, and life at the Academy is incredibly demanding. Or maybe you're not happy because you haven't given yourself permission to imagine that you could be doing anything else right now," she suggested gently.

"Like what?" Naomi asked.

"I don't know," Janeway admitted, "but the world, the galaxy, the universe, is really big and filled with interesting people doing amazing things. And not all of those people wear a uniform." She smiled.

"I don't want to give up just because it's hard," Naomi said. "If you had given up while we were still in the Delta Quadrant, I might never have had this chance. I might never have known my father."

"Making a different choice isn't the same thing as giving up," Janeway said. "Sometimes we're not happy because we aren't living up to our own expectations. But sometimes we're not happy because we're asking the wrong things of ourselves. Part of growing up is learning to tell the difference between the two. I don't ever want to see you run away from anything. But running *toward* something else is different. You'll still be eligible to enter the Academy for the next several years. If you decide to commit yourself to this life, you will find it difficult. But you need to know before you do that Starfleet is the *only* path you want to walk. I'm not sure what takes more courage: forcing yourself to do this now, or allowing yourself to imagine a different life that might make you even happier."

"Then you don't think I should stay?" Naomi asked.

"I think you should do what *you* want," Janeway replied with emphasis. "And more than anything, you should know that whatever path you choose to follow in your life, I will be watching with great pride. You don't have to be a member of Starfleet to have my love and respect, or your parents'. You had our love from the day you were born and earned our respect every day thereafter. Both will always be yours."

Naomi nodded. "Thank you," she said with a faint smile.

"You're welcome," Janeway said.

After a long pause, Naomi asked, "Is Seven going to be okay? Do you think I could see her when she comes home?"

"I don't know if that will be possible," Janeway said honestly. "But she will be fine. I promise."

Naomi nodded, but her face was dark again. "I hope so," she said softly.

So do I, Janeway added to herself.

VESTA

When Vice Admiral Kathryn Janeway materialized on the *Vesta*'s main transporter pad, Decan was waiting for her.

"Good morning, Admiral," he said.

"Lieutenant." She nodded crisply.

"All of your personal effects have been transferred to your quarters. Captain Farkas . . ." he began, but was interrupted by the entrance of the captain through the doors behind him.

"Admiral on deck," Farkas announced formally. At once, she, Decan, and the transport operator shot to attention.

"Good morning, Captain," Janeway said. "At ease." Though she appreciated the protocol, she wondered if Farkas was trying to impress her or establish her territory as soon as possible.

Separating her feet to formal "ease," Farkas said, "We are prepared to launch on your order, Admiral."

Janeway dismissed Decan with a nod, stepped close to Farkas, and said, "Are you ready?"

Smiling faintly, Farkas replied, "Always. There's an officer from *Galen* waiting in your office, and he is refusing to report back to his ship until he speaks with you, personally."

"The Doctor?" Janeway guessed.

"Lieutenant Reginald Barclay," Farkas said.

Puzzled, Janeway said, "Would you be so kind as to accompany me there?"

"Of course, Admiral," Farkas said.

Once they were en route, Janeway said, "I wish to address the crew formally, but it can wait until we're under way."

"Once we launch we're twenty-two hours from the first relay stations that have been damaged," Farkas advised.

"Noted," Janeway said.

Pausing, Farkas said, "Permission to speak freely."

Pleased that these words from Farkas no longer chilled her, Janeway replied, "You never need to ask, Captain. I know you still have your doubts about my posting, but in time . . ."

Farkas waved a hand. "I was spoiled rotten in the Delta Quadrant," she said. "Batiste was a cipher, but Captain Eden was a good fleet commander. Ten minutes in the company of Admiral Verdell reminded me how rare those are. I was too hard on you, Admiral. I was in pain; assigning blame was comforting. It was also too easy. I was using you so I could avoid looking at myself. Montgomery was using both of us and hoping to play us against each other. My anger was convenient for him. When I finally understood that he was just trying to cover his own ass I formally withdrew my objections. I hope you will accept my apology for unkind words spoken in anger. "

"Of course," Janeway said. "But I am curious."

"About what?"

"What made you realize what Montgomery was up to?"

"This ship," Farkas said honestly. "He should have thought of the *Vesta* long before you did. And a little wise counsel," she added.

"From whom?"

"Our CMO, Doctor El'nor Sal, is one of my oldest friends. She nearly slapped me silly when I told her about our first conversation. She reminded me that it was easier to judge than be judged and that if I thought *Ken Montgomery* was my friend, I needed a full psych workup. And then she suggested I read your record from the beginning. You don't do anything the easy way, do you?"

"No," Janeway agreed. "Just the best way I know how."

As they reached the doors to her new office, Farkas said, "I'll be on the bridge if you need me."

"Launch as soon as possible," Janeway said. "We have a lot of work to do."

"Finally," Farkas chuckled.

Lieutenant Reginald Barclay sprung to his feet when Admiral Janeway entered.

"It's good to see you, Reg," she said immediately. "I know you wanted to speak to me about something at the memorial and I brushed you off. I'm sorry. It did not reflect my general opinion of you or the seriousness with which I take your concerns."

"I know that, Admiral," he said.

"Sorry it has taken me so long to rectify that."

"Please don't give it another thought, Admiral," he said seriously. "You never need to explain yourself to me."

Janeway nodded graciously and moved to sit at her desk, gesturing for Barclay to take one of the seats opposite.

"I came because, well, first . . ." he began, hesitating as he clearly tried to order his unruly thoughts.

"Captain Chakotay advised me that you remain concerned about locating the hologram known as Meegan," Janeway offered.

"I do, but . . . well, yes, I do, Admiral," Barclay said, sensing an opportunity. "She is the most advanced hologram ever designed, and I'm not bragging when I say that."

"You created her with Doctor Zimmerman, correct?" Janeway asked.

"Yes, Admiral."

"Then she must be."

"There were, originally, eight Neyser entities stored as pure consciousness," Barclay continued. "One of them claimed Meegan, and she took the other seven with her when she made her escape. The shuttle she stole was retrieved by Ambassador Neelix. She replaced it with a mining vessel. I believe she chose that vessel because she intended to bury the other seven entities within the asteroid field around New Talax so that she could retrieve them later. *Galen* initiated a sensor sweep of the field before we departed. *Voyager* was to complete it after we left. I am eager to review their findings."

"I will see to it that those reports are forwarded to you as soon as we reach the relays," Janeway replied. "Finding Meegan will be a priority for me. I understand that you feel responsible for her, more so because you did not advise anyone before she left of her unique capabilities as a hologram. I appreciate any assistance you can provide in locating her, but the responsibility for that is not yours. It is now mine."

"Thank you, Admiral," Barclay said, nodding vigorously.

"We are getting under way, so if there's nothing else," Janeway said.

"Actually," Barclay said, rising to hand her a padd, "there is. *This* is what I came to show you, though I appreciate your consideration of the Meegan problem."

Janeway took the padd from him. "What is this?"

"The Doctor indicated that you wanted me to run a full diagnostic of his program. He is functioning within normal parameters, but the scan revealed the presence of a coded file I was unable to access."

"Unable?"

"It was encrypted. I could have broken it, but I chose not to. I have already trespassed on the Doctor's privacy, and I don't want to do so again."

"How are we going to figure out what the file contains?"

"It was specifically coded to be opened by your authorization only," Barclay said. "It was created one week after your encounter with the Omega Continuum, just after *Voyager*'s arrival at New Talax."

"Thank you, Reg."

When Barclay had reached the door he added, "Admiral, unless there's something in there that could do serious harm to the Doctor, I don't want to know about it."

"I understand," Janeway said. "You should consider the matter closed unless I have no choice but to ask you for further assistance."

"Thank you, Admiral."

Curious, but mindful of her priorities, Janeway contacted the bridge and ordered Farkas to launch as soon as Barclay was back on *Galen.* She had intended to watch the launch from the bridge but chose to remain in her office and study the file that had been designated for her eyes only.

It was a recorded message, but not from the Doctor. It was from his creator, Lewis Zimmerman. It was to advise Janeway of an alteration to the Doctor's program that Zimmerman had recently made at the Doctor's request. While the rest of the fleet's crew had gathered for the memorial service at New Talax, the Doctor had taken the opportunity to speak with his creator, and the alteration had been uploaded within a few hours.

The first time she listened to the message, its contents struck her with the force of a physical blow. The second time, she was able to find a few shreds of approbation for Zimmerman's actions. The odd comments the Doctor had made that had predicated her request for the diagnostic now made sense. It was also clear that he could continue to perform his duties despite the alteration. What was difficult to accept was the fact that the alteration was permanent, or it sounded like it would be so risky to undo that it might as well be.

It took Janeway several minutes to collect herself after closing the file. It took her several days to decide what to do with the information Zimmerman had provided to her.

Chapter Twenty-three

VOYAGER

It could have been hours, but the ship's chronometer reported it was less than ten minutes when Harry Kim returned to consciousness, lying on *Voyager*'s bridge. He took a quick physical inventory to assure himself that he was still in one piece. He assumed that the pounding in his head would diminish as normal blood flow was restored to it.

Looking around the bridge, Kim saw that everyone had been affected as he had. It was written on every face; relief, horror, and shock overwhelmed them. Seated beside the captain, Doctor Sharak was weeping softly.

"Status?" Chakotay called, breaking the silence.

"The proctors have retreated to subspace, sir," Aubrey reported.

"All departments are reporting status nominal," Kim advised from ops. "No injuries. No damage sustained."

"*Demeter* is hailing us," Lasren advised from over Kim's shoulder.

"Onscreen," Chakotay ordered.

One look at O'Donnell's face confirmed that *Demeter* had experienced the same thing.

"Everybody there okay?" O'Donnell asked.

"We're fine," Chakotay said.

"Those people . . ." O'Donnell began but obviously found it difficult to continue.

"Let's bear in mind that we've only seen the proctor's side of the story," Chakotay said.

"You think there's another side worth hearing?" O'Donnell asked.

"There usually is," Chakotay said.

Kim understood O'Donnell's disgust. What the proctors had just shown them was one of the most wanton, egregious abuses of nature Kim had ever witnessed.

How the World ships had arrived, the proctors did not know. There were dozens present by the time the proctors had been created from the Ark Planet technology. From birth, they were slaves to the will of the World ships, and for a very long time had moved through several star systems, ripping one planet after another to shreds.

Initially the destruction of life did not trouble the proctors. *Life* had no distinct meaning for them. Eventually, the proctors were used to transport individuals among World ships, and the impressions left by direct contact with life-forms had created an awareness of life as something distinct and precious among the proctors.

The proctors now understood that when they destroyed local planets as ordered, they were destroying *life* as well, and that troubled them. They tried to rebel. They did not succeed. World after world was destroyed, and countless wave forms were birthed to carry the materials ripped from them to the waiting ships.

The proctors finally achieved a small act of defiance. A new world was targeted for destruction. Billions of life-forms would be lost. The proctors understood these life-forms to be victims, like them. Several proctors broke free long enough to rescue some of the life-forms and move them to the only safe world they knew existed, the Ark Planet. This confused the World ships, but eager for *their* work to continue, the life-forms aboard did not interfere until the proctors had saved as many as possible. This process was repeated on every subsequent planet the proctors were programmed to destroy.

When the World ships had taken all they could, they prepared to move on. New wave forms were constructed—the sentries. Their programming was singular: hide the space the World ships had plundered and destroy anything that trespassed. Finally all evidence of the World ships' technology was taken from the Ark Planet and the ships departed.

Kim had known that many planets had been destroyed in this area. Living that destruction from the proctors' point of view transformed it from an intellectual exercise into a shared holocaust. But it was also clear that the people of the "Worlds of the First Quadrant," at least two distinct alien races, required the resources they had taken. By the time the ships departed, there were hundreds, not dozens. They had used what they had forced the proctors to take to build, or rebuild, their civilization. Lifted from the World ship's data banks by the proctors were images of alien worlds filled with life that had been the beneficiaries of this space's unwitting generosity.

The coordinates of that system were imprinted on Kim's mind as clearly as the images of the destruction the World ships had wrought.

Kim wished he didn't know any of this. It would have been easier to move on thinking they had done some good. That good was tainted now. While they had aided the wave forms tremendously and brought them a measure of solace, what was the point? Someone else could easily come along and undo what little good the Starfleet crews had accomplished or simply destroy the Ark Planet on a whim.

Was there any possible justification for the actions of these "Worlds"?

For the first time since the mission had begun, Kim wished he had kept his mouth shut during the initial briefing two months ago. He could have lived the rest of his life without knowing the truth the proctors had just revealed to him.

Every fiber of Chakotay's being screamed for justice. He wanted, no, he *needed* to confront these people with their transgression. Those who had achieved the ability to travel through space usually, but not always, did so with a certain amount of humility. Few in the history of space exploration had been so thoughtless or greedy; the Borg came to mind.

As much as he might want to, confrontation was not an option. *Voyager* and *Demeter* would not survive an encounter against the forces of the Worlds. Chakotay knew it was absurd to think they'd be disconcerted by an alien federation's moral outrage. There was always a chance that in the years that had passed since the World ships departed, they had met someone else's justice, but it was also possible that they had continued on their wanton path of death and destruction.

"Captain, if I may?" Fife asked from *Demeter*.

"Yes, Commander," Chakotay said.

"Our mission parameters clearly state that we are to investigate all potential threats to the Federation. The Worlds of the First Quadrant are surely one," Fife stated.

"We can't go in with phasers blazing," Chakotay said. "As much as I'd personally like to."

"We could listen to their side of the story first," O'Donnell suggested.

"And then we open fire?" Paris whispered to his captain.

"Commander Fife has a point," Chakotay replied. "It is certainly in the Federation's interest that we investigate this civilization."

"I'm not sure that 'civilization' applies here," O'Donnell noted.

"What we all just saw was the work of individuals who lived several hundred years ago," Chakotay said, reining in his anger. "Any representatives of these Worlds we would encounter today are not directly responsible for these acts. *But,*" he continued, "it would be foolhardy to risk making contact. We will set course for our previously designated rendezvous point and report our findings to Starfleet Command."

"I agree," O'Donnell replied.

"Ensign Gwyn, set coordinates for our previous rendezvous point, and bring the slipstream drive online," Chakotay ordered.

"We'll see you on the other side, Captain. Demeter *out,"* O'Donnell said.

The faint ambient light offered by the stars present on the main viewscreen vanished.

"Ensign Gwyn, belay my last order," Chakotay said immediately. "Harry, what just happened?"

"The cloaking matrix has just been restored, sir," Kim said.

"Why?" Chakotay asked, turning to Doctor Sharak.

"Sir," Aubrey reported, "long-range sensors are detecting two vessels. . . . No, make that five vessels approaching the nearest border of the cloak."

"Where did they come from?"

"I don't know, sir," Aubrey said.

"Seven to Captain Chakotay."

Hoping for a better answer, Chakotay replied, "Go ahead, Seven."

"Thirty seconds ago, a previously undetected subspace aperture opened approximately five million kilometers from the border of the cloak. The incoming vessels exited the aperture and are on an intercept course," Seven reported. *"At present speed they will reach us in four minutes, forty seconds."*

"Can we use the data astrometrics has already gathered to plot a safe slipstream jump from our present location?" Chakotay asked.

"I would not advise it, Captain," Seven said.

"Nor would I," Conlon concurred from engineering.

"Can we safely exit the cloaked area at maximum warp and avoid these vessels?" Chakotay asked.

"Only by traveling toward them," Seven said. *"Our previous scans of this sector are not precise enough to safely navigate at warp speed as long as the cloak is operational."*

"We didn't explore enough of the rest of this parsec once

we focused our efforts on the Ark Planet," Paris advised. "We can't run away from them at warp either."

"Red alert. All hands to battle stations," Chakotay ordered. "Harry, are they World ships?"

"Their configuration does not match anything we just saw, but that doesn't mean they . . . wait . . ." Kim said as he resumed tactical from Aubrey.

"Lieutenant," Chakotay barked.

"Our database has identified a single vessel," Kim reported. "Turei."

"Turei?" Chakotay asked in disbelief.

"I have a second match now, Captain," Kim continued.

"Who?" Chakotay demanded.

"Two of the ships are Vaadwaur," Kim said.

"That can't be right," Paris said.

"Can you confirm Turei and Vaadwaur life signs on those vessels?" Chakotay asked.

"No, sir," Kim said.

Chakotay turned to Paris. "We know the Turei traveled using subspace corridors that once were claimed by the Vaadwaur. It's not outside the realm of possibility that one of those corridors terminates at the border of the cloak. But what are they *doing* here?"

"The better question is why are they working together?" Paris said. "The last time we encountered them, they almost destroyed us trying to kill each other."

"We can identify three out of five ships. If the other two are World ships, maybe they've formed some sort of alliance," Chakotay ventured.

"Harry, have they entered the cloaked area yet?" Paris asked.

"They are fifteen seconds from the border," Kim said, "maintaining course and speed."

"They *have* to be accompanied by World ships," Chakotay reasoned. "Otherwise, what makes them think they can safely navigate throught the cloak?"

"Maybe they don't know about the cloak and assume they are entering a void," Paris said.

"They are not accompanied by World ships," Kim reported.

"How do you know?" Chakotay asked.

"The sentries are attacking all five vessels," Kim replied.

"On screen," Chakotay ordered. "And open an encrypted channel to *Demeter.*"

For a minute, it looked like the new arrivals had made a terrible mistake by entering the cloaked area. The sentries took them unawares. They were forced out of warp as their proximity to the wave forms disrupted their fields. The sentries attacked en masse, ripping at the alien vessels' hulls but failing to do severe damage.

"Captain Chakotay," O'Donnell said as Chakotay watched the approaching vessels begin their attack on the sentries. The red-alert klaxons blaring on *Demeter*'s bridge were added to the sound of *Voyager*'s, and in the interest of maintaining sanity, Chakotay ordered his silenced.

"We need to get out of here," Chakotay said.

"No argument, but where?" O'Donnell asked.

"We can navigate through the area at impulse. Set course one-nine-eight-mark-six and stay with us. We're going to put as much distance as possible between us and those ships. If the sentries don't finish them . . ."

But Chakotay could see that the ships had come with countermeasures prepared for the sentries. Several sentries were being disrupted by some sort of directed energy weapon. New sentries emerged to continue the attacks, but they were quickly becoming little more than a nuisance.

"They'll be back on course in a few minutes," Paris estimated.

"If the sentries keep it up, it'll slow them down some," Chakotay countered. "Helm, engage," he ordered.

"When they arrive, I'm assuming you'll do the talking?" O'Donnell asked, after ordering *Demeter* to follow.

"*Voyager* encountered two of these species before, but neither contact ended on friendly terms. I don't know if they're here for us. But even if they aren't, they're not going to be happy to see us."

"Understood," O'Donnell said. *"Mister Fife, you have the bridge,"* he ordered.

"If we are forced to engage, Commander Fife . . ." Chakotay began.

"We'll do ourselves proud, sir. Don't worry about Demeter,*"* Fife said.

"One of the alien vessels will be in range in less than thirty seconds," Kim advised from tactical. "They have adjusted their course to intercept us."

"Are they hailing us?" Chakotay said hopefully.

"No, sir," Lasren replied.

"Their weapons are armed," Kim added.

"Captain," Lasren and Jepel said from their respective ops stations aboard both ships.

"Go ahead, Lasren," Chakotay said.

"Two proctors have just emerged from subspace and are approaching our vessels," Lasren reported.

"Tell them to back off," Chakotay ordered, even as the familiar hum of being enveloped by a proctor sounded throughout the bridge.

"Too late, sir," Lasren reported.

"Transmit a message that they must release us," Chakotay said.

"Transmitting now," Lasren replied.

"Captain," Gwyn called from the conn, "I've lost helm control."

A sinking pit opened in Chakotay's stomach.

"Kenth?" Chakotay demanded.

"No response, sir," Lasren said.

"We're moving," Paris said.

"The proctor has taken control of the helm, sir," Gwyn advised.

"Where are we going?" Chakotay asked.

Dozens of images flashed over Sharak's screen. After a moment, he replied, "The proctors want to keep us safe. They think they can evade the hostile ships."

"They *think*?" he asked.

"The proctors only say that they will make the attempt," Sharak said. "They feel obligated to try."

"I'm not comfortable leaving this in their hands," Chakotay said.

"There is the frying pan and then there's the fire, sir . . ." Cambridge observed softly.

"What about *Demeter*?" Chakotay asked, cutting him off.

"We've lost communications, but they are surrounded by a proctor and are matching our course and speed," Lasren said.

"With the comm down, we can't hail the incoming ships, on the off chance this is just a terrible misunderstanding," Paris noted wryly.

"Do we still have control of our weapons?" Chakotay asked.

"Yes, sir," Kim said. "But firing through the proctor might not be possible."

"Can the proctors protect us from enemy fire?" Chakotay asked of Kim.

"Theoretically, yes," Kim said.

"We're about to test the theory," Paris noted as the incoming vessel finally came within weapons range and opened fire.

Chapter Twenty-four

VESTA

At Admiral Janeway's request, the *Vesta*'s reconfigured conference room had been designed to accommodate several meetings at once. There was a large oval table that ran along the room's far wall, beneath a bank of rectangular windows. It housed the newest holographic imaging displays at its center. Individual personal data screens also could be accessed at each of the twelve seats the table could comfortably hold.

There were also three smaller tables, each of which could seat up to six. It was a lot of space to designate for briefings, but Janeway had come to think of each of the four ships in her fleet as part of something greater. She could envision many times when representatives from each vessel might need to convene to discuss and exchange data, both in small groups, or as a large collection of officers.

Her first meeting in the briefing room consisted of only five officers; they sat at the room's large table where a three-dimensional display of the damaged relays was now visible.

Janeway sat at the table's head, along with Captain Farkas and *Vesta*'s chief engineer, Lieutenant Bryce. Commander Glenn and Lieutenant Barclay had joined them from the *Galen*.

Farkas had briefed Janeway regarding Lieutenant Vorik. He'd had seniority and would have been assigned as *Vesta*'s chief engineer. Vorik had refused to state a preference when asked directly if he would accept that post. "He would serve where Starfleet ordered him to serve," were his exact words. It was obvious to Farkas that the Vulcan had no desire to remain with the fleet. Two days prior to launch, Farkas had received Vorik's official transfer request and had granted it. Farkas had been pleased to have the problem behind her. Janeway had been less so, especially considering the imminent departure of B'Elanna Torres. Vorik might have served as a temporary replacement for fleet chief.

Captain Farkas had chosen a relatively inexperienced lieutenant, Phinnegan Bryce, as chief engineer. After listening to Bryce's initial report on the status of the relays, Janeway was more than comfortable with Farkas's choice. Bryce was young, energetic, and thorough. He possessed a keen and analytical mind. She liked him more the longer he spoke.

"The damage evident to these three relays is the most severe, but the same damage was done to all thirty-nine that are no longer operational," Bryce reported. "Initial scans reveal significant traces of ion particles."

"Was this a natural phenomenon?" Janeway asked. "An ion storm?"

"No," Bryce said. "But it was supposed to look like one."

Janeway had been prepared to hear that the relays had been damaged by sabotage, but the news chilled her nonetheless. "The damage we see here would have had to result from six separate ion storms all hitting the relay system at different points and all causing the same kind of damage.

"The relays perform regular scans of surrounding space and none of the undamaged relays report the presence of an ion storm. And the damaged relays are concentrated in areas significant to their overall deployment. We could lose twenty along any number of points in the string of relays and not risk our link to the Alpha Quadrant."

"Whoever did this was assuming we wouldn't come back to investigate?" Farkas asked.

Bryce nodded. "Or they're really dumb." Eliciting an

unexpected chuckle from Admiral Janeway, he added, "But I don't think so. From a distance it would have appeared that a few links in our chain of relays were malfunctioning prior to their complete loss. The damage was done slowly, over several months, to add to this illusion. But the relays targeted were critical."

Bryce shifted the holographic display to an image of the entire chain of relays stretching from the border of the Alpha Quadrant, where the *Vesta* was now located, almost twenty thousand light-years into the Delta Quadrant. The damaged relays were indicated by red flashes. The rest glowed a healthy shade of green.

"We haven't lost that much of our chain. But given the position of the damaged relays, we're a few weeks away from losing the entire system," Bryce concluded.

"Someone is trying to trap us out here without the ability to contact Starfleet Command," Janeway said.

"If we weren't here *now,* we'd be assuming we had months before risking losing the system, given how few were targeted," Bryce added.

"Do we have any idea who did this?" Janeway asked.

"No," Bryce said. "Deep space sensor reports show nothing; no ships, no natural phenomena, nada."

"I'm going to dispatch a few shuttles to recon the area," Farkas said. "Whoever did this might be watching to see the results of their handiwork."

"Agreed," Janeway said.

"Can we repair the damaged relays, or do they have to be replaced?" Janeway asked.

"Replaced," Bryce said.

"And upgraded," Lieutenant Barclay added.

Turning to address the officer who had spearheaded Project Pathfinder, establishing communications between *Voyager* and Command, Janeway asked, "How?"

"The shielding system of all of the relays needs to be

enhanced," Barclay said. "And while we're at it, I think we would do well to hedge our bets."

The display shifted again, now showing the innards of a single relay. Janeway immediately recognized the technology.

"Regenerative circuits?" she guessed.

"Yes, Admiral," Barclay said.

"How long will these modifications take?" she asked.

"We can have the damaged relays replaced within five days," Bryce said. "The upgrade will take at least two weeks. And that won't include all of the relays but enough to limit anyone's ability to take out the entire system in a similar fashion."

Janeway inhaled sharply. This was not what she wanted to hear.

"Admiral?" Farkas asked.

"Do we have any idea where *Voyager* and *Demeter* are?" Janeway asked.

"Their last transmission was sent from New Talax," Bryce said. "Eight weeks ago they departed for coordinates approximately forty thousand light-years from that location, and they have not transmitted any reports since then."

"Eight weeks without reporting in?" Janeway confirmed. Forcing her concern for half of her fleet down, the admiral reminded herself that she trusted Chakotay implicitly.

"Captain Farkas, Commander Glenn," Janeway ordered, "allocate all necessary personnel to repairing the relays. Utilize every resource at our disposal to speed the work. Keep a regular rotation of shuttles out there searching for evidence of whoever did this."

"Aye, Admiral," Farkas said.

"Yes, Admiral," Glenn said.

"If I may?" Lieutenant Barclay piped up.

"What is it, Reg?" Janeway asked.

"The shuttle operators should look for evidence of gravimetric displacement, excess tetryons . . ." he began.

"Or anything else that might indicate cloaked vessels," Janeway said and nodded. "See to it," she added to Farkas. "Dismissed."

Janeway waited until the room had cleared to allow her shoulders to slump and to indulge in a few minutes of worry about *Voyager* and *Demeter.* Eight weeks was a long time to go without reporting in. *But not unheard of.*

It didn't matter. Unless the relays were repaired and upgraded, the Full Circle fleet would lose contact with Starfleet Command at the hands of an unknown enemy. And *that* was entirely out of the question.

"They're fine," she said aloud to the empty briefing room.

Chapter Twenty-five

VOYAGER

For quite some time, it looked as if the proctors had matters well in hand. They easily absorbed the first volley of fire from the alien vessel and moved decisively to evade another direct hit. Once clear, they glided gracefully through the darkness, carrying *Voyager* and *Demeter* with them. Chakotay could not calculate their speed, but the feel of his ship beneath him put their velocity near maximum warp.

Their pursuers followed with difficulty. The sentries continued their attacks, unconcerned or unaware of their futility. The proctors had opened a wide lead on the alien vessels by the time faint pinpoints of light began to dot the main viewscreen.

"We're nearing the far edge of the cloaking field," Gwyn reported.

"If the proctors would release us, we could calculate a slipstream jump and execute it as soon as we're clear of the cloak," Paris said.

"We'd need a few minutes for our long-range sensors to sweep the area and plot our course," Chakotay said. "And we can't tell *Demeter* what we're planning. I won't risk leaving them out here on their own."

"We don't want the proctors to release us just yet," Kim said from tactical.

"Why?" Paris asked.

"There are fourteen additional ships, holding position, three hundred million kilometers to port," Kim said.

As Chakotay absorbed this development in silence, Paris said, "We're headed right for them, aren't we?"

"Yes," Kim replied.

"Can you identify them?" Chakotay asked.

"Two Turei vessels. One Devore attack cruiser," Kim said.

"The *Devore*?" Paris asked, incredulous.

"Who are the Devore?" Cambridge asked.

"Long story," Chakotay said.

"Will *they* be happy to see us?" Cambridge asked.

"No," the captain and first officer replied in unison.

"This makes no sense," Paris said. "Even if the Turei and Vaadwaur found a way to bury the hatchet, Devore space is thousands of light-years from theirs. Who invited them to this party?"

"Agreed, any alliance between these races is extremely unlikely, but we'll worry about that later," Chakotay said tensely. The armada now arrayed against his ships came into view on the main screen. Three were large, well-armed battle cruisers. The rest were smaller, but also armed to the teeth.

"Our pursuers have cleared the cloaking field," Kim advised from tactical. "They are moving to join the others. All ships have raised shields and armed weapons."

A loud burst of static spiked over the comm system followed by a harsh male voice punching through the interference.

"Federation vessel, you will not be permitted to approach the gateway to the Worlds of the First Quadrant. Any attempt to do so will result in your immediate destruction."

"What gateway?" Kim asked softly.

"This is Captain Chakotay of the Federation *Starship Voyager*," Chakotay began.

"I'm sorry, sir," Lasren interrupted him. "They closed the channel immediately."

"They just wanted us to know why they were about to open fire," Paris observed.

"They know us," Chakotay mused. "They addressed us as *Federation vessel.*" That was disconcerting. "And they think we're trying to reach the Worlds of the First Quadrant."

"The hail came from the largest unidentified vessel," Lasren reported. "Life-form readings on that ship are sketchy but do not match Turei, Vaadwaur, or Devore."

"Why are their comm systems working when ours aren't?" Cambridge interjected.

"These ships obviously know more about this area of space and the Worlds of the First Quadrant than we do," Chakotay said, thinking out loud. "They didn't hesitate to enter the cloaked area, they had countermeasures prepared for the sentries, and they have devised a means to cut through the interference generated by the proctors. They have us at a number of disadvantages right now."

"If we could tell them we have no interest in this gateway, maybe they'd . . ." Paris began.

"The Turei, the Vaadwaur, and the Devore?" Chakotay cut him off. "They're not just going to let us go."

"If the proctors can get us clear, they might lose interest," Paris argued.

"They won't." Chakotay studyed the evolving deployment of the alien armada. Thirteen of the ships were approaching *Voyager* and *Demeter.* Six held position several thousand kilometers to port. As the net drawing close around *Voyager* began to tighten, Chakotay realized that there was only one path that might lead to temporary safety.

"Five ships arrived at the far side of the cloaking field via a subspace tunnel," Chakotay said. "We know the home of the Worlds of the First Quadrant is thousands of light-years away. Somewhere out there, I'm betting close to the position of those six ships, is the entrance to another subspace tunnel."

"The gateway they don't want us to enter?" Paris asked. "Sir, you're not suggesting . . ."

"The proctors will never take us to the Worlds of the First Quadrant," Kim added.

"The proctors *must* know how to access it," Chakotay continued. "It's our only chance. Lasren, transmit a message to the proctors. Tell them we must enter that gateway."

A brief silence ensued before Sharak said, "They will not comply."

"Kenth, remind them what Omega did to our fleet," Chakotay ordered.

Another long moment passed before a single image appeared on Sharak's screen: a ring of fire.

"We're altering course," Gwyn reported from the helm.

"That's better," Chakotay said. "*Demeter*?"

"Matching our new course and speed," Lasren said.

"Captain, are you sure?" Paris asked.

With a grim smile, Chakotay said, "Not really."

The relatively smooth ride *Voyager* had enjoyed ended abruptly as four of the alien vessels broke formation and moved to intercept the Federation ships. Again, the enemy fire was absorbed by the proctors. Their weapons blazed in shades the computer interpreted as reds, blues, and greens. The firing forced a course change as the proctors tried to avoid impact. Although the proctors cut it closer than Chakotay would have wished, they quickly found a new path through the evolving chaos and continued to carry both *Voyager* and *Demeter* on separate courses toward their goal.

"We might just . . ." Paris began but was cut short by a sonorous boom rattling the entire ship.

The captain sensed a variation in the hum emanating from the proctor currently protecting *Voyager*. "Harry, report!"

"That was a torpedo, sir," Kim replied. "High yield. Without the proctor, our shields would have taken heavy damage."

"Was the proctor affected?" Chakotay asked.

"I'm reading intermittent fluctuations in its EM field," Kim said.

Chakotay looked back to the main viewscreen. The "gateway" might be closer than ever, but all nineteen ships were coordinating their movements, offering *Voyager* no direct route to its entrance.

"What's *Demeter*'s status?" Chakotay asked.

"Their proctor is keeping them clear of *Voyager*. Both proctors seem to be trying to divide the attention of our attackers. But *Demeter* has taken four direct hits," Kim said. "Their proctor is worse off than ours."

"Captain, this isn't going to work. We need to regain helm control and get out of here," Paris said for Chakotay's ears only.

"The proctors wouldn't have agreed if they didn't think they could get us through this," Chakotay said.

"That's a lot to take on faith," Paris said.

Another series of jolting shocks pummeled the ship. Chakotay estimated at least five direct hits on *Voyager* that time. The proctor's hum had become a high-pitched whine.

"Lasren," Chakotay said, "I want you to send another message to the proctor surrounding our ship."

"What's the message, sir?" Lasren asked.

Once Chakotay outlined his request, it took the ops officer a minute to compose the transmission, during which *Voyager* was tossed mercilessly about. This time, the proctor sent an immediate response. Chakotay turned to Sharak, who translated it with a grim nod.

"Helm, prepare to engage at full impulse. Set course away from the gateway, and let's hope most of our new friends decide to follow. Shields to maximum. Ready all weapons," Chakotay ordered, then added, "And ready the slipstream."

Five seconds later the whine disappeared completely and Gwyn said, "Helm is responding, sir."

Okay, Fife, Chakotay thought. *This is your chance. Take it.*

DEMETER

The moment Commander O'Donnell handed over *Demeter's* command, Fife wondered if O'Donnell would leave the bridge. He was pleased when the commander didn't. Instead, O'Donnell stood behind his chair, clutching its back to avoid being tossed onto the deck as *Demeter* began to draw its share of enemy fire.

It was a maddening experience for the young lieutenant commander. Four months earlier during the first combat Fife had seen in the Delta Quadrant, *Demeter* had been captured by the enemy and moved into their space. Fife had been consumed by his desire to free *Demeter* from the control of the Children of the Storm. That desire had blinded him to his duty to O'Donnell and *Demeter.* He was determined not to repeat his mistakes but was also absolutely unable to countenance this loss of control. It didn't frighten him, it enraged him. But Fife also knew that the proctor now surrounding his ship was its best defense against the attacking vessels.

"Lieutenant Url," Fife called to his tactical officer, "prepare to vent tetryon plasma on my order." He had ordered this countermeasure prepared weeks ago, to disperse the wave forms in the event of an attack.

"Sir, right now the proctor is the only thing that can protect us from those ships."

"Mister Fife knows that," O'Donnell cut Url off briskly. "Follow your orders, Lieutenant."

"Aye, sir," Url replied.

"Ensign Vincent, I want the comm restored. I need to be able to speak to Captain Chakotay," Fife said.

"Aye, sir," Vincent replied from ops, though both knew this was probably a futile effort.

"Ensign Falto," Fife called to the helm, "prepare to resume control of the helm as soon as the tetryon plasma is released. Make sure the slipstream drive is online and our rendezvous coordinates entered."

The next few minutes were a test of Fife's patience. The small ship shuddered and rocked as the proctor guided it through the hostilities. He wanted to give it the full benefit of the doubt. But he also wasn't going to allow it to lead *Demeter* to its destruction. Should it fail at an inopportune moment, *Demeter* would be sitting in the crossfire of several alien ships. They couldn't absorb the damage *Voyager* could. The weapons now pummelling his ship could likely destroy it with a few direct hits.

"Commander Fife," Url reported, "our proctor seems to be altering its strategy."

"How?" Fife asked, wondering if the high-pitched whine that now grated more annoyingly than the constant pounding of alien weapons might indicate that the proctor had sustained critical damage.

"I believe our proctor is coordinating its efforts with *Voyager*'s, and they are working to divide the attention of our attackers," Url said.

"Your point?" Fife demanded.

"We've altered course, sir, and are approaching *Voyager*," Url said.

"Why?" Fife asked, more of himself than his crew.

"Don't do anything until you know for sure," O'Donnell suggested.

Fife didn't want to trust O'Donnell's instincts, but they were usually correct. He held his peace, knowing that within moments he'd have an answer.

"Mister Fife, the proctor surrounding *Voyager* has released it," Url reported.

Good, Fife thought. "As soon as ours does the same, prepare to return fire and engage the slipstream drive," Fife said aloud.

Fife watched intently as the vibrant greenish haze that had surrounded *Voyager* was sloughed completely off but was immediately taken aback when it moved directly toward his ship.

"Url," Fife began but was paused by the firm hand of Commander O'Donnell pressing on his shoulder.

The second wave form surrounded *Demeter,* reinforcing the proctor already present, and the whine of its straining efforts diminished to a low, resonant hum. Fife's heart sank.

"Vincent, can we contact *Voyager*?" Fife demanded.

"No, sir," Vincent said.

As if rejuvenated, the proctors now encircling *Demeter* dodged and weaved gracefully through the oncoming attacks, increasing their speed.

Fife wanted to return fire before making a brisk escape via their slipstream drive, but it seemed that was not Captain Chakotay's plan. *Voyager* had just purchased *Demeter*'s survival, likely at the cost of their own destruction.

An orange ring of fire blossomed into existence in the center of the main viewscreen.

"Hello," O'Donnell said behind him.

"Report!" Fife shouted.

"It's a subspace distortion," Url said.

"Specify!" Fife demanded.

"It's an aperture, sir, leading to a subspace tunnel," Url clarified.

"To where?" Fife asked.

"Give it a minute and we'll both know," O'Donnell said.

VOYAGER

As the proctor released *Voyager* from its protection and moved swiftly to reinforce *Demeter,* Chakotay's mind stilled. Three massive impacts followed within seconds, jolting the bridge and overloading a few power conduits that belched sparks and fumes above his head. The rough lines of two enemy ships as they passed *Voyager* following their attack runs were briefly visible on the viewscreen but dissolved into the chaos of new phaser fire coming from three more vessels approaching from different vectors.

"Shields down to eighty percent," Kim reported.

"Maintain course," Chakotay said. "How many are in pursuit?"

"Eight," Kim said. "Four continue to engage *Demeter,* and the other seven are regrouping around the gateway."

Another resonant shock sounded through the bridge.

"Return fire," Chakotay ordered. "Show me *Demeter.*"

The small, graceful vessel that was now the fleet's best hope for surviving this encounter moved directly toward a circular distortion of vibrant orange and blue hues. A few of the nearest vessels were breaking off, but the rest were moving into position to form an impenetrable wall between *Demeter* and the now-visible gateway.

Chakotay did not believe that the proctors protecting *Demeter* would fail in their mission, but he also understood that the longer they were prevented from entering the gateway, the greater the odds that they would sustain more damage than they could endure.

Demeter's chances were better than *Voyager*'s as long as the proctors surrounded them. But he could not leave their fate to chance.

"Helm, bring us about. Set course for the ships blocking the gateway," Chakotay ordered. Chakotay expected a sharp rebuke from Paris but got none. Doing this was to all but ensure their destruction. To fail to do it was to risk the loss of both ships.

Gwyn followed her orders without hesitation, taking *Voyager* into a fluid dive and reorienting their heading while simultaneously evading most of the enemy fire. Chakotay smiled grimly. This told him something about those he was fighting. They'd been unprepared for the maneuver. They had decided *Voyager* was running scared.

They underestimate us, Chakotay thought and hoped fervently they would continue to do so.

A few glancing blows rocked the ship as they moved into a pocket of empty space. Their pursuers had overshot their target, but it wouldn't take them long to regroup and formulate a new attack pattern.

"Harry, target the three vessels closest to the center of the gateway. Fire torpedoes at will," Chakotay ordered.

Seconds later, *Voyager*'s phaser fire—a prelude to the main event—was focused on the three vessels. The shots were centered on the most vulnerable areas of their shields. Because the ships refused to move, the torpedoes that followed were able to penetrate the weakened shields. Six direct hits forced two of the ships out of formation while destroying the third completely.

"Evasive pattern Delta-six," Chakotay ordered, anticipating the fire about to target *Voyager* from the rear. Luckily, two vessels that had been gunning for *Voyager* managed to hit their allies instead, crippling one of them in the process.

"Chakotay, they're in," Paris said.

Satisfaction centered the captain again as *Demeter* slid past the blockade and glided effortlessly into the ring of fire. Once they had done so, the gateway vanished.

One less thing to worry about, for now.

The ship shuddered again as two direct hits on their aft shields pounded them mercilessly.

"Shields at fifty-five percent," Kim reported.

"Captain," Sharak said sharply.

Chakotay turned to face the doctor.

"Before it departed, the proctor transmitted a message I cannot translate," Sharak said.

Chakotay glanced at Sharak's small monitor and studied the long string of symbols and numbers. They meant nothing to him either.

"Was there a visual transmission to accompany it?" Chakotay asked.

"No," Sharak said.

"Transmit it to astrometrics," Chakotay said. "Seven, take a look at this transmisison and translate it, if you can."

"Understood," Seven replied over the comm.

Three more ships were closing fast on their position, and Kim scored a direct hit on the lead vessel, shearing off a single, rear-mounted nacelle. The ship spun toward a fiery end, taking out a smaller ship that could not avoid impact in time. The resulting shock wave ripped through *Voyager,* rattling Chakotay's teeth in his head as Gwyn tilted the ship upward and an invisible elephant briefly sat in his lap.

"Rerouting additional power to intertial dampeners," he heard Lasren report, and the effect diminished.

"The slipstream drive is ready, sir," Paris reminded him. "*Demeter* made it. We can find them later."

"I know," Chakotay said. He still remembered coordinates the proctors had first given them: the location of the home of the Worlds of the First Quadrant. It was a journey of approximately ten thousand light-years, nothing for their advanced propulsions system.

But Chakotay had no way of knowing how much time *Demeter* might have once they encountered the Worlds of the First Quadrant.

Never mind the fact that going to slipstream velocity in the middle of a battle was an untested maneuver.

"Captain," Seven called, *"I've translated the proctor's message. It's a harmonic resonance frequency. We can emit it from the main deflector."*

"What does it do?" Paris asked.

"The target coordinates coincide with the gateway's," Seven said.

"They gave us the key," Chakotay realized.

"Captain," Paris said, *sotto voce,* "we need to make repairs and find a better time to use that key."

Chakotay shook his head. "What about *Demeter*?"

"We're no help to them dead," Paris added.

"Then let's not die," Chakotay said as he made his decision. "Gwyn, resume course for the gateway. Reinforce forward shields. We have to protect the deflector dish at all costs."

"Eight ships have locked firing solutions on us," Kim said.

"Will our shields hold?" Chakotay asked.

"Only if most of them miss," Kim said.

Paris ordered, "Gwyn, go to full impulse heading one-one-nine-mark-three then execute all stop."

The flight controller complied so quickly and effortlessly it seemed as if it had been her idea. Seconds later a flurry of torpedoes and phaser fire erupted directly ahead of *Voyager*. A few badly aimed phasers managed to hit the shields but glanced off them.

"Full impulse, now," Paris ordered. "Course . . ."

"Got it," Gwyn said. The abrupt change in course and speed had flummoxed the enemy firing solution. She now had a very small needle to thread to avoid impact with the ships. Kim helped clear the path, targeting the only ship close enough to foil them with a full barrage of phasers. *Voyager* glided past it so close, Chakotay could see the alien script identifying it on its port hull.

"Deflector ready?" Chakotay asked.

"Aye, sir," Kim said.

As Gwyn brought the ship into alignment to open the gateway, the largest enemy vessel remaining moved to intercept. Kim targeted them immediately with a torrent of phasers and torpedoes, but their shields held.

The vessel returned the courtesy as six large forward-mounted phaser cannons rained fire on *Voyager*.

CIF TWELFTH LAMONT

"General Mattings, we have incoming," JC Eleoate reported.

The general sighed, shaking his head sadly.

They'll never learn.

"Time to intercept?" Mattings asked as he left the forward research station where he had been enjoying a pleasant conversation with EC Emm-its about his research year spent on Femra and returned to the heart of his ship's bridge, a circular data station situated between his armaments officer and *Lamont's* sensor technicians.

"They will exit the corridor in seventy-five clicks, General," JP Creak said.

"Let me see 'em," Mattings requested, and a visual of the doomed ship appeared on his main receiver. "Damn, but she's a pretty thing," Mattings said. "Where's she from?"

"The protectors have not transmitted a designation," Creak said.

"She's accompanied?" the general asked, surprised.

"By two of the ancients," Creak said.

"Two?"

"The integrity of both has been compromised. One is at thirty-seven percent, the other at sixty-one percent."

"Since when do protectors, even the old ones, operate in tandem?" Mattings demanded.

"Unknown," Creak said, "but the ancients are always unpredictable."

The general had thirty clicks left to decide the fate of the incoming vessel. It wouldn't have taken half that time had she not been so unusually configured.

Most of the ships that managed to breach the main stream and enter the flow were ungainly things, rude constructions of hulls and arms that announced their hostility at first glance. The ship now approaching did not. Her single elongated central hull was lithe and sleek, a little more than six hundred paces long, and looked as if it had been constructed by the hand of a sculptor. She glided like a bird without wings. Her propulsion array was distributed along two wide arcs that almost touched above and below the central hull, attached to it by long cylindrical pylons. They formed a halo around her as she approached, and though Mattings hadn't attended observations regularly in years, the image struck a reverent cord in him nonetheless.

What a shame, Mattings thought. But before he could give the order to open fire, JC Elioate said, "They are cleared, sir."

"The protectors transmitted current codes?" Mattings asked in disbelief.

"The initial transmission was out of date, but the reinforcing protectors native to the stream recognized it as friendly," Elioate said.

"All right," Mattings said, admittedly relieved. "Stand down weapons. Let's get ready to say hello."

VOYAGER

Gwyn did her best to evade the incoming barrage, but there was only so much she could do. Impacts sounded like deafening cannons, inertial dampeners struggled valiantly, but the concussive shocks threw many of the bridge crew to the deck, including Commander Paris, Counselor Cambridge, and Doctor Sharak. Chakotay felt a brief sensation of weightlessness but held fast to the arms of his chair. His right torso slammed into the armrest, and a burning pain shot up his right arm. The shock left him momentarily breathless, but he maintained his focus. Patel's science station exploded. Had she not already been facedown on the deck, it would have killed her. Smoke, fumes, fire-suppression systems, and emergency lighting set the scene for what Chakotay thought would be his last moments of life.

Chakotay looked over his left shoulder to see Lieutenant Kim still standing his post. "Harry?" Chakotay shouted.

"Shields are at ten percent, sir," he said.

It was better than Chakotay had expected. "Gwyn, set course away from the gateway. As soon as you have clear coordinates, engage the slipstream drive," he ordered.

"The deflector is offline, sir," Kim advised.

Without it, they couldn't use the slipstream drive. Or the warp drive, for that matter.

Gwyn had begun to execute a sharp port turn, showing the enemy ships approaching from the rear the long view of *Voyager's* port nacelles, and several of them took the opportunity to open fire on the easy target. Another series of jolts shook the bridge, and this time, Chakotay was surprised he was still alive to hear them.

At almost the same moment, however, a rolling wall of flame engulfed *Voyager* from her stern, illuminating the viewscreen briefly enough for Chakotay to see the full extent of the damage to the bridge in a chilling few seconds.

"Hull breaches on decks six through twelve," Lasren reported. "Force fields are holding."

As *Voyager* emerged from the flames, Gwyn was doing her best to outrun several large chunks of debris now following in its wake. Kim called, "The lead vessel blocking the gateway was destroyed, sir. I have ten, no twelve . . . make that twenty new ships emerging from the gateway."

"Helm, evasive," Chakotay ordered. The new arrivals had caught the attention of the remaining would-be attackers, and they scattered, ignoring *Voyager* completely as they moved to engage their new targets.

Chakotay allowed Gwyn to choose her own course as the battle raged around them. As Doctor Sharak tended to the injured, damage control teams began hasty repairs. The viewscreen showed the new vessels making quick work of what remained of the fleet that had attacked the Federation ships. One of the larger vessels and three small ones engaged their warp drives and managed to escape. The rest were easy pickings for the obviously disciplined and well-trained forces that now engaged them.

If those ships turned on *Voyager,* she could offer no resistance. Shields were all but gone, and their remaining torpedoes weren't going to make a dent against the newcomers. Chakotay might prolong the inevitable for a minute, two at the most. The best he could do was stand down and pray for mercy.

"All remaining enemy vessels have been destroyed, sir," Kim advised. "Most of the ships that came through the gateway are retreating back into it."

"Okay," Paris said, motioning Sharak aside and wiping the blood pouring from his lower lip onto his sleeve.

"The lead vessel is altering course to pursue us," Kim noted.

"Helm, bring us about," Chakotay ordered. "Take all weapons systems offline. Begin transmitting friendship greetings on all frequencies."

After another few painful seconds of silence, Lasren reported, "The vessel has identified itself as *Confederacy Interstellar Fleet Twelfth Lamont*. They are hailing us."

"Put them onscreen," Chakotay said.

"I'm Ranking General Mattings. You're Voyager?*"* the general asked.

He was humanoid, his skin a rich brown shade and deeply creased around his eyes and mouth. The eyes were large black ovals that protruded beneath a demi-lune bony ridge above them. There was no nose to speak of, but two large openings reminiscent of nostrils sat above thin lips. The most unnerving sight—apart from a crisp white uniform all but buried beneath straight lines of shiny metal geometric shapes, some encircled by red and purple ribbons—was his teeth: sharp points reminiscent of a shark's.

But Chakotay was prepared for Mattings's appearance. He had seen the faces of the general's ancestors in the transmission of the proctors on the Worlds of the First Quadrant.

Chakotay rose from his chair, suppressing a grimace, to face the general. He had to remind himself that he should greet them patiently and be open to hearing their explanation for the destruction their ancestors had wrought. The captain also had to remind himself that he had no idea what had become of *Demeter*, and their survival could depend upon how he handled this moment.

At the forefront of his mind, however, was the reality that this man now held *Voyager*'s life in his hands.

"I am Captain Chakotay of the Federation *Starship Voyager*," he replied. "We're explorers a long way from home, and we come in peace, seeking the Worlds of the First Quadrant."

Mattings chortled. *"That's what your Commander O'Donnell said as well."* After a brief pause he added, *"Can you make it back to the stream, or do you need a tow?"*

"Our systems have been badly damaged, but we can manage under our own power," Chakotay said.

"Then get a move on, Captain," Mattings ordered. *"I'll leave a few ships behind in case those bastards try again. They always try again. Idiot children, all of them. But you have been cleared to enter the stream."*

"By 'stream' are you referring to the subspace tunnel accessed through the visible aperture?" Chakotay asked.

"They're streams of a great river, son," Mattings said. *"And this one is the only access to the heart of the Confederacy of the Worlds of the First Quadrant. You say you come in peace. You were brought here by some of our most ancient protectors, and if they say you're good people, you are."*

"Protectors?" Chakotay asked. "You mean the wave forms?"

"You want to sit here all day playing with your gristle?" Mattings demanded, not unkindly.

"No, General," Chakotay said. He wasn't predisposed to like the man, but everything about him suggested he was a leader, a warrior, and maybe even an explorer, comfortable making contact with alien species. He was also worldly, if a little condescending. "Helm, set course for *the stream* and engage at full impulse."

"We'll have your back, Captain," Mattings replied. *"We'll talk again where the stream ends."*

"Understood. *Voyager* out," Chakotay said.

Chakotay turned to Paris. "What do you think?"

"He did not give us *Demeter*'s status," Paris said. "Obviously he spoke to O'Donnell. And they did defend us from those 'bastard children,' was it?"

"I'd hazard a guess that there are lots of folks out here

interested in entering that stream," Counselor Cambridge mused from the deck where he was now seated.

"So we're the lucky ones, then?" Paris asked.

"I hope so," Chakotay said. "If they wanted us dead, we would be."

"I hope we're being welcomed as fellow travelers and not taken prisoner," Paris said.

"We have to make sure *Demeter*'s still in one piece." Chakotay turned back to Kim, who stood his post, his face inscrutable. "Harry?" the captain asked.

"I have a good feeling about this," Harry said.

Paris laughed outright. "This morning you hated these people."

"*These people,*" Harry said with emphasis, "just saved our lives. Their ancestors were responsible for great wrongs, but so were ours. I'm curious to see who they are now."

"So am I, Lieutenant," Chakotay said, and smiled.

With that, *Voyager* cleared the gateway and entered the stream.

The journey was brief and reminiscent of the one *Voyager* had traversed along the corridors that had been claimed by the Turei. The first thing Harry Kim saw when they were again in open space was the sight of *Demeter,* beautiful and undamaged, but now free of the proctors who had brought them here.

The second was a sight that made the hairs rise on the back of his neck.

The stream ended in a system, warmed by a single G-class star. A blue-green gem of a planet hovered nearby, surrounded by at least two visible large space stations where several vessels were docked. Light traffic orbited the planet, and Kim surmised that Lasren was now busy cycling through the comm traffic.

The tactical officer smiled to himself. He'd seen a lot in the Delta Quadrant in over seven years of exploration. Numerous space-faring people had crossed *Voyager*'s path organized as empires, imperiums, collectives, cooperatives, and species. None of them had reminded him so viscerally, at least on the surface, of the Federation.

It troubled him to think of how this confederacy had come into being. But what they had built was promising at first glance. Kim had always appreciated how big the galaxy was. Today, however, it seemed somehow smaller.

Chakotay had only moments to take in the scene before the image on the viewscreen was replaced by the faces of Commander O'Donnell and Lieutenant Commander Fife, standing side by side on *Demeter*'s bridge. Fife was calm and professional. O'Donnell's eyes held a curious light.

"It's good to see you in one piece, Captain," O'Donnell offered.

"You, too," Chakotay said.

"Welcome to the Confederacy of the Worlds of the First Quadrant," O'Donnell said.

"Is it just this one system?" Chakotay asked.

O'Donnell shook his head.

"Have you encountered any hostility?"

"We're all friends here, apparently," O'Donnell said. *"Unauthorized ships that enter that subspace tunnel are destroyed on sight when they get here. But ships that come under the protection of the wave forms are not. The general indicated that no ship has been deemed worthy of the protector's attention in more than a century."*

"What happened to the proctors . . . I mean, *protectors*?" Chakotay asked.

"They dispersed almost as soon as we entered the system," O'Donnell said, his voice thick. *"I guess they took too much damage . . ."*

"I'm sorry to hear that," Chakotay said.

O'Donnell nodded, then continued, *"A delegation has been dispatched from the First World to meet us. We've been asked to hold our ships at these coordinates until the diplomats arrive."*

"We will comply," Chakotay said. "We need to begin making repairs in the meantime."

"Need any help?" O'Donnell asked.

"Any and all you can provide," Chakotay answered.

"I'll see to it."

"Mister Fife," Chakotay said.

"Yes, sir?"

"Excellent work."

"Thank you, sir," Fife said.

"Captain," Lasren called, "General Mattings is hailing us."

"On screen," Chakotay said.

"We're monitoring your ship-to-ship transmissions, Captain," he said by way of greeting. *"I expect that doesn't surprise you."*

"It doesn't," Chakotay said. "But we have nothing to hide."

"Good to know," Mattings said. *"Your official delegates will arrive shortly, but in the meantime, permit me to formally welcome you to our confederacy. Have you ever seen anything like it?"* he asked proudly.

"Actually," Chakotay said, "I have."

This seemed to surprise the general. After a moment he said, *"You know, the diplomats probably won't arrive until shift change. Protocol and all that. In the meantime, would you care to see the Twelfth Lamont? I'll cover your tab."*

"I would," Chakotay said sincerely. "May I bring a few of my officers with me?"

"As long as they don't carry side arms," Mattings said. *"I'll send a pod along to collect you."*

"Thank you. *Voyager* out," Chakotay said, trusting his gut and choosing not to reveal *Voyager*'s transporter technology. He was certain the Confederacy ships were scanning their vessels, but he was not going to do likewise until he was assured of his people's safety. Even passive scans might be considered offensive by the force of superior numbers at this stage of the game. Since Mattings had offered to send a ship, Chakotay could only assume that either they did not possess transport technology or they were keeping some of their cards hidden.

Chakotay turned to Paris. "Commander, you have the bridge. I want a full report on our repairs when I return. Bring any of *Demeter*'s crew over to assist repairs via shuttle. No transporters, and no power to them."

"Captain," Doctor Sharak, who was already treating the injured on the bridge, spoke up, "I have patients who will require transport to sickbay."

Chakotay looked to Paris, who nodded in understanding. "I'll take care of it, Captain. We'll have to do it the old-fashioned way."

"Good," Chakotay said. Doctor Sharak had scanned his injuries, repaired them, and administered an analgesic for the pain as they traversed the subspace corridor. But a clean uniform was definitely in order.

Turning, Chakotay smiled and added, "Counselor, Mister Kim, Mister Lasren, get yourselves cleaned up and report to the shuttlebay. You're with me."

Chapter Twenty-six

VESTA

Captain Regina Farkas sat at her ready room's desk as Commander Malcolm Roach, her first officer, stood at ease before her. Five months of service hadn't tempered the stern young man. He remained as crisp and tightly wound as ever. A stocky man of medium height whose width was from serious muscle he maintained in the ship's gym, Roach had just returned from one of the recon missions. They were awaiting the arrival of Admiral Janeway so he could make his report.

The doors of Farkas's sanctuary slid open, and the admiral entered, nodding briskly to both of them. She moved immediately to one of the two chairs opposite Farkas and said, "Take a seat, Commander, and tell us what you found."

Roach did as ordered, Farkas smiling inwardly at the pain it caused him to do anything that resembled relaxing in the presence of a superior officer.

"We had completed our scans of sector Three One Nine, confirming operational status of the relays there likely to be targeted according to Lieutenant Bryce's calculations. None of them has been damaged," Roach began.

"But you found something unusual?" Janeway coaxed.

"We did, Admiral," Roach said. "We ran discreet scans for anomalous readings and discovered a higher than expected concentration of tetryons. We altered course to investigate. As we did so, our scanners clearly picked up a cloaked vessel."

Janeway shot a glance at Farkas, who leaned forward over her desk.

"We hailed them. Something must have malfunctioned on their end. For twenty seconds, the ship decloaked, and we were able to perform a cursory scan. They re-initialized their cloak and set course away from the relays. As per our orders, we did not pursue."

"Very good, Commander," Janeway said. "We need intelligence right now, not casualties."

"That was my understanding, Admiral," Roach said.

"Any life-signs?" Farkas asked.

"Aye, Captain," Roach said. "There were four individuals present, but only one we could identify."

"Who?" Janeway asked.

"A member of the Voth species, Admiral," Roach said.

Janeway's eyes widened and her posture stiffened. "Anything else?" Janeway asked.

"No, Admiral. We have added the readings to our databases. All recon ships will now be on the alert in case they come across anything similar. Repairs and upgrades to the relays are due to be complete within the next two days."

"Thank you, Commander," Janeway said.

"Dismissed," Farkas added, and Roach rose gratefully and returned to *Vesta*'s bridge.

As soon as the door shut, Farkas said, "The Voth?"

Janeway stood, started to pace, and clearly thought better of it. Instead, she planted her hands on the back of the chair she had just vacated.

"If I remember correctly, they are not friendly?" Farkas asked.

"Not even a little," the admiral said.

"Are they local?"

"We encountered them three years into *Voyager*'s journey home. Their space is tens of thousands of light-years away. I honestly can't imagine how they could be *here,* nor can I understand why they would venture so far from home or who they might be working with. They were xenophobic in the extreme and aggressively territorial."

"Humanoid?" Farkas asked.

Janeway smiled bitterly. "Saurian. We uncovered compelling evidence that they originated on Earth millions of years ago. They considered that heresy against their doctrine. We were only freed from captivity when the scientist pursuing the research in question recanted his testimony."

"They captured your crew?" Farkas asked, surprised.

"They captured *Voyager.* Their technology was formidable," Janeway replied coldly.

"Well, I'd hate to waste time out here going up against amateurs," Farkas observed grimly.

"I just doesn't make any *sense,*" Janeway insisted.

"Bridge to Captain Farkas," came the voice of *Vesta*'s ops officer.

"Go ahead, Jepel," Farkas said.

"We've just received a subspace message from Voyager, *Captain. They are en route to rendezvous with us here and will arrive within six hours."*

Janeway stood upright and brought a hand to her mouth, which failed to hide her relieved smile.

"Acknowledged," Farkas said as she rose from her desk, then added, "What about *Demeter*?"

"Captain Chakotay's transmission includes a preliminary report on their recent mission. Demeter *is remaining at* Voyager*'s last coordinates pending review of the preliminary report."*

"Thank you, Jepel," Farkas said. "Farkas out."

"Okay," Janeway said, clearly rifling through the ever-shifting priorities she now held in her head.

"I'll advise you as soon as they arrive, Admiral," Farkas said.

"Thank you," Janeway said. "I'll want you, Glenn, and Chakotay in the briefing room as soon after as possible."

"It's been awhile since I actually looked forward to reading a report," Farkas said and smiled.

"Me, too," Janeway agreed.

Chakotay had been prepared to see the *Vesta* as soon as he received the transmission Captain Farkas had dispatched advising *Voyager* of *Vesta*'s current position and new rendezvous coordinates. He had not expected the magnitude of relief he felt when he first caught sight of her. Hard as it was to believe, she was actually a little larger than either *Quirinal* or *Esquiline.* During his conversations with General Mattings and the diplomatic delegation of the First World, Chakotay had done his best to communicate in broad strokes the capabilities and interests of the Federation. They seemed reluctant to accept his words, particularly the diplomats. "Why would any organization as vast as this *Federation* send such comparatively small vessels so far?" they'd asked. As soon as *Vesta* entered Confederacy space, Chakotay knew they would revise their assumptions.

Captains Farkas and Glenn were waiting with Admiral Janeway when he entered the briefing room. One look at Kathryn told him the time spent away had been good. Her normally fair skin was lightly tanned and her eyes were shining. She looked more like herself than she had when she departed for Earth and was clearly at ease in her new role.

"Welcome aboard the *Vesta,*" Captain Farkas greeted him, moving to shake his hand.

"She's a beautiful ship, Captain," Chakotay replied.

Kathryn communicated in a brief nod her relief and happiness in seeing him again but said crisply, "You've been busy, Captain."

"Wouldn't have it any other way," he said, and smiled.

"Let's get going. We have a lot of ground to cover," Janeway ordered.

"Yes, Admiral," Chakotay said, taking a seat between Farkas and Glenn.

"I've reviewed your initial reports," Janeway began. "It seems that distortion ring was a great deal more than met the eye. I commend you for your decision to focus on establishing meaningful and workable communications with them in regards to the Ark Planet."

"Thank you, Admiral," Chakotay said.

"And obviously your discovery of the Confederacy is astonishing," Janeway went on. "What are your impressions of them? What didn't you include in your formal report?"

Chakotay nodded, understanding the question. "They are an extremely complicated group of people," Chakotay began. "I had the opportunity to meet with several of their military officers as well as representatives from their diplomatic corps. Their Confederacy is older than the Federation, but smaller. Some fifty-three worlds are members, and six more have signed non-aggression pacts with them. They are fortunate to have found a corner of the Delta Quadrant relatively inaccessible to many space-faring species and don't seem interested in expansion. The organization of their society doesn't lend itself to growth."

"How so?" Farkas asked.

"Member worlds are represented in the confederate government on the First World and vote on all matters relating to the entire confederacy. Control is very centralized. They have their ways of doing things and aren't all that interested in incorporating new ways of thinking.

"Their military, and they view their interstellar fleet as such, is large and tasked with maintaining civil order as well as dealing with interstellar threats. Their technology is advanced in some ways, but I don't think they're on par with Starfleet. They don't possess transporters, replicators, or advanced propulsion systems like ours. They maintain a centralized system of currency, and trade is highly regulated.

"They consider most species that are not part of their

confederacy as beneath them, but they seemed impressed by what I told them of our Federation."

"That's troubling," Janeway noted.

"Not when you consider their origins," Chakotay replied. "The Confederacy was founded five hundred years ago by two species who had long been at war but found themselves equally powerless against the Borg. They fled their home-worlds, suffered great losses along the way, but eventually discovered a subspace tunnel leading to the system that is the home of their First World. They chose to extract resources from several large systems on the other side of what they call 'the stream' and worked for hundreds of years to rebuild what they had lost. Apparently those who discovered the first world assigned it religious significance, and there were edicts against disturbing the soil to build what they needed. It's both telling and unfortunate that those edicts did not extend to every planet they encountered. The technology they created—the wave forms—to harvest those resources they had no compulsion about taking eventually developed beyond their programming and became resistant. Ultimately the ancient ones, the wave forms *we* encountered, were abandoned, and the area of space was hidden by a vast cloaking matrix.

"Some of their history is troubling, but not necessarily any more so than ours. They like their place in the universe, if that makes sense," Chakotay said. "They don't allow outsiders to enter the stream, and any vessels that slip through are usually destroyed. We were a special case because we were brought there by some of the ancient wave forms."

"Have any outsiders petitioned for membership in the Confederacy?" Glenn asked.

"They recognize that most species from beyond the stream are simply too far away to be managed effectively. It would strain their resources to an untenable point.

"They are, however, very interested in learning more about the Federation."

"To what end?" Janeway asked.

"A formal alliance that included sharing some of our more advanced technology seemed to intrigue them," Chakotay said.

"What do we get out of it?" Farkas asked.

"A base of operations in the Delta Quadrant," Janeway said. "A powerful refuge closer than the Alpha Quadrant in the event communications are severed and a real presence beyond any we could establish with a small exploratory fleet."

"Precisely," Chakotay said.

"Bottom line," Janeway said. "Do you trust them?"

Chakotay considered his words carefully. "For the most part."

"All right," Janeway said. "I've already run your initial reports by Command. They have ordered us to return to the Confederacy to further explore the potential for diplomatic relations. But there are other matters to consider."

"Did you note the section of my report when I indicated that some of the vessels that attacked us before we accessed the stream were old acquaintances?" Chakotay asked of Janeway.

"I did," she said. "And we have a similar problem here."

"How so?"

"A number of our relays have come under attack in the last few months. We have discovered that the Voth are among those perpetrating the attacks."

Chakotay's jaw dropped. "The Voth?"

"I felt the same way when I read that the Devore had joined the Turei and Vaadwaur," Janeway said.

"An unlikely coincidence?" Farkas asked.

"Very," Janeway said. "Can you think of any explanation, Captain?" she asked Chakotay.

"The stream is one of many subspace corridors we already knew about. Perhaps in the absence of the Borg, other races have come across them and are beginning to utilize them," Chakotay said.

"As individuals, I can see that," Janeway said. "What

doesn't seem possible is their willingness to work together to accomplish anything."

Chakotay shrugged. "I agree."

"Clearly, they know the Federation has sent ships out here, and they don't seem happy about it," Janeway offered.

"Given our first encounters with them, that's not surprising," Chakotay said. "But could we possibly be seen as enough of a threat to warrant these preemptive strikes? And bear in mind, I don't think the Turei, Vaadwaur, or Devore were expecting to engage us out there."

"No, that was just a happy accident," Janeway said grimly.

"What do we do?" Chakotay asked.

"We have reinforced our relay system," Janeway said. "Should the attacks continue, we will have to deal with them. I was thinking of asking Neelix to do a little recon from time to time."

"I don't think the people of New Talax are ready to face the Voth," Chakotay said.

"Just to gather intelligence," Janeway said, raising a hand to forestall argument. "Obviously, I don't want Neelix or his people engaging anyone."

"If they get caught looking, they might not have a choice," Chakotay said.

"Pathfinder is monitoring the system as well," Janeway added. "They will keep us apprised of any activity they detect."

"From the Confederacy, we're twenty thousand light-years away from the relays," Chakotay advised. "Should we consider extending the system in that direction?"

"Why don't we wait and see how our early meetings go?" Janeway said. "If it looks like an alliance is possible, extending our communication system will become a priority."

"There might be more than one way to do that," Farkas added. "We don't know what the Confederacy might bring to the table."

"Good point," Janeway agreed. "*Vesta, Galen,* and *Voyager* will depart for the Confederacy tomorrow at zero seven hundred. There are, however, a few additional issues."

"Such as?" Chakotay asked, sensing a distinct negative shift in her demeanor.

"A medical crisis has emerged on several Federation worlds," Janeway replied. "Starfleet Medical believes the illness is due to exposure to Caeliar catoms."

Chakotay was taken aback. "Is Seven vulnerable?"

"No," Janeway said. "The plague is affecting inhabitants of worlds where Borg debris was transformed. There is no indication that those who were provided with catoms directly by the Caeliar are in any danger."

"The only people the Federation know of that have Caeliar catoms are Seven and Riley Frazier's people. How did the Starfleet Medical come to that conclusion?" Chakotay asked.

"Two months ago, Axum, a former Borg drone, was recovered by Starbase 185," Janeway replied. "He is currently being examined to enable our scientists and doctors to better understand catomic technology."

"Seven has been experiencing what she believes to be catomic communication with Axum," Chakotay said.

"How is that possible?" Janeway asked.

"I don't know," Chakotay said. "She described the examinations he is enduring as torture. Doctor Sharak inhibited her neural pathways to prevent these communications from causing serious trauma to her."

"The Doctor took over Axum's treatment at Starbase 185 as soon as the *Galen* arrived," Glenn reported. "In order to save his life, the Doctor provided Axum with a small number of catoms he had extracted from Seven. That could explain what Seven is experiencing, Captain. But I can assure you that while he was in our care, Axum was treated with compassion."

"I don't doubt that," Chakotay said, "but where is he now?"

"We don't know," Janeway said. "The Doctor expressed

concern from day one that Axum might be in some danger from those studying him. But I find that hard to believe."

"I don't," Glenn said. "They're terrified, Admiral. It's not that they want to hurt him, but they have no idea what they're dealing with, and they need answers yesterday."

"We don't abandon our most cherished principles for the sake of convenience, do we?" Janeway asked. "I know things have changed in the last year, but not that much."

"If Seven, the Doctor, and Captain Glenn all share the same concerns," Chakotay began, "I'd be hesitant to dismiss them out of hand."

"As would I," Farkas agreed. "People do incredibly stupid things when they are frightened. We need to do anything we can to help them cure this plague."

"Starfleet Medical has asked that Seven return to the Alpha Quadrant at once," Janeway said. "The choice will be hers, but I'm confident she will want to assist them."

"As am I," Chakotay said, "if for no other reason than to assure herself of Axum's well-being. But given her current medical issues, we can't send her back alone."

"We're not," Janeway said. "Julia Paris, Tom's mother, has petitioned the Federation Family Court for custody of Miral. The court has ordered mediation, and the Paris family has been ordered to appear."

For the first time in a long time, Chakotay remembered what panic felt like. "No one is taking Miral away from her parents," he said coldly.

"Julia needs to see her son," Janeway said. "I know he'll make her understand. We need to facilitate that meeting."

"Send Tom with Seven, but B'Elanna and Miral stay with *Voyager,* just in case," Chakotay said.

Janeway sighed. "The whole Paris family needs to appear."

"If we need to send B'Elanna and Miral back, we have to return to the Confederacy to do so," Chakotay stated. His gut assured him that Tom would see this his way.

"Why?"

"They're aboard *Demeter,* along with Counselor Cambridge and Lieutenants Patel and Lasren," Chakotay said, wondering how quickly Kathryn would see through his lie.

Janeway's eyes met his with obvious disappointment.

"That's a problem," Janeway said evenly.

This was a more complicated matter than Kathryn realized. He was confident that once they were alone, he could make her understand that.

"Seven and Tom will depart tomorrow," Janeway ordered. "We brought the *Home Free* to facilitate their transfer."

Chakotay nodded and added, "We should send the Doctor, too."

"No," Janeway said quickly.

Chakotay was shocked by how suddenly she dismissed the notion.

"Another officer from our fleet would be helpful to Seven, but the Doctor won't be going," the admiral continued.

"Begging your pardon, Admiral," Glenn interjected, "but the Doctor knows more about catoms than anyone else. He's the *obvious* best choice. We just need to make Starfleet Medical see that."

"I was provided with all available data from their current research, and the Doctor will be free to review it and expand upon it from here. But he's not the best choice to help Seven."

Chakotay found this hard to believe but also knew Kathryn wouldn't make such a statement lightly.

"What about Doctor Sharak?" Janeway asked. "He has treated Seven."

"Yes," Chakotay said. "But he's not the Doctor."

"Captain, my primary concern is for Seven," Janeway said. "With her help, I'm sure those already studying the plague will make significant progress. Doctor Sharak will accompany her, and Commander Paris will be close at hand should any of our fears appear well founded," she added, settling the matter.

"What does *Voyager* do in the meantime for a chief medical officer and first officer?" Chakotay asked.

"Can the *Galen* spare the Doctor for a few weeks?" Janeway asked Glenn.

"Yes," Glenn said.

Turning back to Chakotay, Janeway asked, "Harry is next in command?"

"Yes."

"Do you have any concerns about making him your acting first officer?"

"No," Chakotay said.

"Advise your crews accordingly, and be ready to depart at zero seven hundred," Janeway said, bringing the meeting to a close. "Captain Chakotay, if you'll remain?"

"Of course, Admiral," Chakotay replied.

Kathryn Janeway hadn't spent much time imagining what her reunion with Chakotay would be like. Such thoughts took her too far from the present, but once she knew that he was en route, she had indulged in idle speculation.

That speculation had not included the possibility that as soon as they saw each other again he would lie to her.

As Farkas and Glenn departed, Janeway sat. Clearly sensing her misgivings, Chakotay did the same.

"You left B'Elanna and Miral with the *Demeter*?" she asked pointedly once they were alone.

"It's good to see you, too," Chakotay said. "I trust the review process went well for you?"

"Computer," Janeway called, "are Commander B'Elanna Torres and Miral Paris currently aboard *Voyager*?"

Chakotay's eyes did not leave hers as the computer replied, *"Commander B'Elanna Torres and Miral Paris are not aboard* Voyager*."*

Janeway wanted to feel relief, but couldn't.

"Kathryn," Chakotay began, reaching for her hand.

She pulled it away automatically, not knowing what to do with her absolute certainty that Chakotay was deceiving her.

"This isn't a game, Chakotay. Tom has to do this right, or Julia will never accept that she's making a terrible mistake."

"He will," Chakotay argued.

"It will look like he's starting off in bad faith."

"I don't care what it looks like," Chakotay replied. "If there is the slightest chance that the proceedings end with Miral clinging to her mother, crying hysterically as a court official pulls her free and gives her to Julia, it's too much to risk."

"That won't happen."

"B'Elanna is pregnant again," Chakotay said.

"Ah," Janeway said, the light beginning to dawn.

"If you're wrong, having already lost Miral, B'Elanna then delivers another child that is also taken away from her."

Janeway shook her head, willing the thought from her mind.

"Tom and B'Elanna should have the final say. If they both want to go, fine. But if they see this the way I do, at least now we have options," Chakotay insisted.

"I don't need options, Chakotay. I need the truth."

"You need plausible deniability. I just gave you that."

"How?" Janeway demanded.

"You don't want to know."

"This isn't going to work," Janeway suddenly realized. "We're supposed to be in this together."

"We are," Chakotay assured her. "You honestly think I'm wrong?"

"It's not your decision!" Janeway said, her voice rising.

Finally, Chakotay stood. He turned and moved toward the door but stopped just short of the sensor.

"All fleet ships were programmed with a special protocol regarding B'Elanna and Miral when they rejoined us. Their identities are classified. *Voyager* is the only ship in the fleet where their comm signals read their actual names. When any other vessel inquires, they are listed as not present. I took a chance that B'Elanna had forgotten to revise the protocol."

He turned back. Janeway had risen from her chair but did not move to him.

She understood why Chakotay was doing this. A few years ago, she might have done the same. But there was more riding on every choice she made than he could possibly understand. The last few months had shaken her perceptions of Starfleet Command. It was a pettier place than she remembered. It pained her to imagine descending to the same level as officers like Montgomery. She knew what Akaar expected of her, and a deception like this would threaten all she had worked so hard to recover as well as the fragile peace she had hoped to build on.

But that didn't make Chakotay's fears easier to dismiss.

"Tell Tom and B'Elanna everything. It's their lives and their family. I'll trust their instincts about this, and yours," she added.

"Thank you."

"But so help me if this becomes a habit between us . . ." she began.

Chakotay smiled warily. "It won't." He stepped closer, asking, "What's wrong with the Doctor?"

Kathryn couldn't contain the grim chuckle that escaped her lips. "You don't want to know."

Chakotay's obvious curiosity was elevated to concern. "Kathryn?"

"You don't *need* to know," she clarified. "He is functioning within normal parameters. We'll be working closely with him over the next few weeks, and if I think there's a problem, I'll inform you. I'm not withholding this as payback. I'm respecting his privacy."

"Fair enough," Chakotay said. "We've prepared new quarters for you aboard *Voyager.* Ironically, I reallocated the former fleet commander's suite to the Paris family. I figured they were going to need it."

"They are," Janeway assured him. "But it doesn't matter. I've been ordered to maintain quarters aboard the *Vesta.*"

Chakotay started to ask her why, but seemed to think better of it. "I see."

"It won't be a problem," she assured him in a low voice.

"Welcome home, Kathryn," he said softly.

Chapter Twenty-seven

VOYAGER

"I'll kill her," B'Elanna raged.

"She's Miral's only living grandmother," Tom said, glad that he had sent Miral to the holodeck with Kula. "How does your mother not understand what we tried to do for *her*?"

"She's lost a lot lately, B'Elanna. She's in twenty different kinds of pain. This is what Mom's focusing on, but it's not her real problem."

"No, now it's mine," B'Elanna insisted. "She'll never see Miral again, and *never* lay eyes on her grandson."

"Let's not overreact," Tom said, struggling to maintain his composure. When Chakotay had told him of his mother's court filing, Tom had felt exactly as B'Elanna did now. But he'd soon accepted that it was *his* actions that had brought all of this on, and he'd felt a sliver of compassion for his mother. Clearly B'Elanna was not so inclined.

"Forget it," B'Elanna went on. "She's forty thousand light-years away. Starfleet isn't going to force us to go back there. When our tour ends here, we can stay, just like we planned. New Talax is looking better by the day. Hell, maybe the Confederacy could use a sharp pilot and a fantastic engineer."

"No," Tom said, his ire intensifying. "*We* did this to her. *We* have to make it right."

"All we did was protect her," B'Elanna shouted.

"But to do that, we lied to her. I almost lost my best friend over this, B'Elanna. I should have thought twice before telling my mom in a letter. It would have been different if we went to her together. She would have been so happy just seeing you and Miral. . . ."

"You are out of your mind," B'Elanna said. "Your mother has never known what to do with me. She tolerated me because she had no choice. *Now* she thinks she can take my children from me? Does she know nothing about Klingons?"

"That's enough!" Tom shouted. His anger was abruptly replaced by shame. The plan to guard Miral had been B'Elanna's, with a little help from the Emperor Kahless, but he had gone along with it. If he was being completely honest with himself, the injury to his mother by this should be laid at his feet.

B'Elanna crossed her arms at her chest. Her belly had finally started to swell slightly, and the sight of his developing son filled him with fierce protectiveness. Moving to his wife he wrapped his arms around her. "We'll get through this. Remember the Warriors of *Gre'thor*? Remember the *qawHaq'hoch*? Remember when they had Miral and we had no leads? This is nothing compared to that."

"No, it's worse," B'Elanna said, pulling back. "It's lawyers. They don't care about the truth. They care about Julia getting what she wants."

"We'll have representation, too," Tom argued. "But it won't matter. I can make my mother understand. She just needs to hear me apologize."

"Didn't you do that about a thousand times in that letter?"

"She needs to hear it *from* me."

"Then go," B'Elanna said, moving away from him.

"Alone?" Tom asked.

"Miral and I stay here until this matter is dropped. Period," B'Elanna said.

It hadn't been that long ago that B'Elanna had been terrified by the thought of living without him. That fear was obviously gone, mitigated by the far greater terror of living without her children. Tom understood, but that didn't make it hurt any less.

"Okay," Tom said softly.

B'Elanna looked at him, her face red and her eyes glistening with tears she would not allow to fall.

"I'll be back as soon as I can," he added.

"You're not leaving until tomorrow morning," B'Elanna said hesitantly.

"Harry's taking over in my absence," Tom said. "It will take me most of the night to bring him up to speed."

B'Elanna nodded. "I see."

"I love you, honey," Tom said, too late.

"I love you, too," B'Elanna replied.

Tom moved sluggishly to their quarter's door, half hoping that B'Elanna would call him back.

She didn't.

As soon as the doors slid open, Tom was greeted by the sight of Harry Kim lurking near the entrance.

Without looking back, Paris said, "Come on."

They were a few paces out into the corridor when Kim asked, "You okay?"

"Yep," Paris said.

"What about B'Elanna? Even through the bulkhead, she sounded really pissed."

"Do you blame her?"

"The captain told me about your mother. I'm so sorry. I mean, I was angry with you for a long time, but I've never on my worst day questioned your fitness as a parent."

"Thanks," Paris said.

"You know I always wanted to make first officer," Kim said, "but not like this."

"Well, don't get comfortable," Paris said. "It's not permanent."

"I know that," Kim said. "It's going to be okay. You'll fix this."

Paris nodded, wondering as each minute passed if this was going to be a more difficult task than he had been telling himself.

When they reached the turbolift, Paris directed it to deck six.

"Where are we going?" Kim asked.

Paris turned to him, his face hard. "I love three women. Right now, two of them are furious with me. Before we get started I need to spend a few minutes with the only one who still thinks I hang the moon."

Kim nodded, understanding. "Is Miral playing Captain Proton yet?"

"Nope, too scary," Paris said as they exited the lift and hurried toward the holodeck.

"Flotter?"

"*Way too scary,*" Paris replied. "She's at the park."

"Works for me." Kim smiled. "Let's build her a really big sand castle."

As they entered the holodeck, Paris couldn't stop thinking about how impermanent castles built of sand were.

VESTA

Seven considered all that Admiral Janeway had told her of Axum's recovery, his current status, and Starfleet Medical's request. It was a relief, but she was not deceived about the peril she was about to face.

"I will comply with Starfleet's request," she stated.

The admiral had made her case from behind the desk in her new quarters aboard the *Vesta.* She rose from her chair and moved to the other side, resting against its edge and crossing her arms. "Why?" she asked.

"To refuse would be to place you and the Full Circle fleet in an untenable position with Starfleet Command. I am permitted to serve here at their pleasure. I have never considered requesting a commission to formalize my relationship with

Starfleet. Had I done so, there would be no question of my obligation to follow their orders. If I refuse, they would surely insist that you deny me the opportunity to continue with the fleet."

"I'm a big girl, Seven. I can handle Starfleet Command. You don't have to go, if you don't want to."

"Billions are dead because of the Borg; hundreds of thousands more, perhaps, because of the Caeliar. Both are part of me. Assuming I am allowed to work with those currently trying to cure the disease, I believe I will be able to assist them."

"So this is expediency?" Janeway asked.

"I need to see Axum," Seven replied evenly. "If what you say is true, he sacrificed a great deal on my behalf. If what I have sensed from him is accurate, he is in danger and I cannot stand idly by hoping for the best. If I can help him, I must."

"I understand," Janeway said. "I just want to make sure you are going into this with your eyes open."

"I am."

"Chakotay told me you believe Axum is being tortured," Janeway said.

"That is his perception. Whether or not it is the intention of those now holding him is unclear. I intend to keep an open mind when evaluating their procedures, but I will not conscience behavior that violates our shared moral obligations."

"Nor would I," Janeway assured her. "Tom Paris and Doctor Sharak will accompany you, and Sharak will be near at hand should you find anything the least bit out of the ordinary. I will provide all of you with classified codes so you can reach me at any time. I have also seen to it that Icheb is assigned to Starfleet Medical Research for his current internship."

"He is too young to be a part of this," Seven insisted.

"Not anymore," Janeway said.

Seven paused, then asked, "Did you consider sending the Doctor in Sharak's place?"

"I did not."

"Why?"

Janeway stood upright at this, stepping past Seven and refusing to meet her eyes as she said, "The Doctor saved Axum's life but failed to establish a solid working relationship with the officers now entrusted with his continuing care and study. Starfleet Medical doesn't want him directly involved. I cannot change their minds. However, I will expect him to continue to study what we know of the disease, and should he make any promising breakthroughs, they will be forwarded to Starfleet Medical immediately."

"I see," Seven said, then added, "Is there something wrong with the Doctor's program?"

Turning back, Janeway said, "Why do you ask?"

"The last time I was with him there was a discrepancy in his vocal subroutines. I had only heard it once before, when his ethical subroutines had been compromised."

Janeway nodded. "I'll have Reg run a full diagnostic."

"I think that would be wise," Seven said. "If you will excuse me now, there are many pressing matters I must attend to before I depart in the morning."

"Of course," Janeway said. "And Seven?"

"Yes?"

Janeway looked at her with a mixture of fear and resignation. "If you find yourself in need of . . . anything, contact my mother. I know she'd love to see you again."

"Thank you," Seven said.

Once Seven had departed, Janeway returned to her desk and considered the padd before her. She had seriously contemplated showing it to Seven, but given all she was now facing, the admiral could not. Janeway felt certain that at some point, Seven might have to know of its contents; maybe when she returned.

When that time came, Janeway would likely share some, if not all, of the contents of Zimmerman's message with her.

For now, only the admiral and the Doctor's creator would remain aware of the alteration that had been made. Prior to encoding the file, Janeway reviewed it one more time.

Admiral Janeway,

I'm Lewis Zimmerman. I know my face is familiar to you, and right now I wish I'd taken the time when you were closer to home to meet with you, just to introduce myself. In all honesty, I prefer to remain behind the scenes. My work usually speaks for me. Tonight, I can't do that.

I've recorded this message for transmission in the event a complete diagnostic of the Doctor's program is run by a third party in the next six months. Should it be required, I'll assume that some of my work has not been integrated as well into the Doctor's program as I anticipated and that he is exhibiting behavior that is cause for concern.

I beg you not to share with him what I am about to tell you.

I was surprised to hear from him early this afternoon. We're not what you would call close. Part of the alterations I have made included wiping our last conversation from his memory.

You don't have children, do you, Admiral? Me either. But I'd venture to guess that many of the officers who have served with you over the years have taken the place of those non-existent offspring. To hear the Doctor tell it, you are a fierce protector of your people. He's even referred to it as a maternal instinct from time to time. I didn't plan on feeling anything similar for the Doctor or any of my creations. But we both know how different he is. I've studied his evolving matrix during many a long night, searching for the spark of sentience we now take for granted in him. To reproduce that would be something, indeed. But I've long suspected that his development has been as much a product of nurture as nature. He is what he is because we both made him that way. I provided the programming, and you provided the experiences that in combination have done the unimaginable.

I wish sometimes this hadn't come to pass. Were he any other program, I could alter his matrix or delete him without second thought. As it is, when he is troubled or has lost his way, I feel the same painful impatience I so often saw in my own father. He was as ill-equipped to raise a son as I am, and I never asked to be a father. But that doesn't change anything now.

The Doctor contacted me because he is experiencing intense emotional distress. Disruptions of this magnitude in the past have led to cascade failure; I was terrified to risk that while he's so far away. He advised me that the last time this happened you were critical in helping him work through the stages of grief that accompanied an impossible ethical choice. Were this matter so cut and dried, I would have suggested he do the same. But it isn't.

As you are no doubt aware, the Doctor comes as close as he can to loving a woman named Seven of Nine. I've seen her and applaud his ambition while loathing his naiveté. She broke his heart, but he somehow integrated that pain into his program in such a way that it did not damage him permanently. He tells himself her happiness is more important than his. If that's not love, I don't know what is. And until now, that pleasant fiction has sustained him.

Apparently fairly recently Seven chose to enter a more intimate relation with a man the Doctor is convinced will cause her terrible pain. He insisted that his concern was for her as a friend and that he did not know the best way to broach the topic with her. He believed he could convince her of the folly of this choice. You and I both know that's not how it works. If we could direct our hearts to love only those most likely to keep it safe, how much easier would our lives be? It's painful, to be sure, to lose the affection or lack the ability to claim the affection of someone we care for deeply. But it's often infinitely more painful to live and work in close quarters with someone who not only cannot return our feelings, but who gives them to another we find unworthy of them.

I told him to transfer out of the fleet. He wouldn't hear of it. And given the recent trauma Reg and I inflicted on him by creating Meegan, I knew better than to push too hard. Frankly, I'm surprised he sought my counsel at all.

But then, it hit me. The Doctor's problem is actually one I failed to anticipate because I never expected him to exceed his programming. It's my fault, and I had to try and fix it.

When organic beings suffer, we often seek short-term consolations, but the reality is that time is the only thing to offer eventual solace. We are blessed with memories that fade. The day someone dies the pain is excruciating. Months, sometimes years, later, it's hard to see their face clearly in our mind's eye anymore.

And the same is true of our hearts. The impact of emotional turmoil fades the further we travel from the initial shock, otherwise we would never dare risk love again.

The Doctor can't do that. His memories are permanent, fixed in his matrix, and when called on, live forever with the same emotional intensity as if they had just occurred. He's not programmed to forget. But I see now that like any other man, he should have been.

I didn't think it was fair to rob the Doctor of all his most potent memories of Seven. Most of them must be maintained in order for him to continue serving as a doctor, and many are integral to the development of his compassion. But I believed I could create a patch that would lessen the intensity of those memories . . . allow them to diminish in power the way ours do. I segregated the files in question quite easily and "muted" them, so to speak. I also inserted a subroutine that would provide a brief pleasant sensation, not unlike an analgesic for us, when he tried to access the affected memories. I don't want him to know his memories have been altered. I don't want to risk another mystery that leads to cascade failure. I just wanted to offer him a little relief.

I don't know how well it's going to work. I only had a few hours to write the patch and upload it before Pathfinder closed our comm window. It's probably not my best work. But I had to help him somehow. My instinct was that of any parent, to take away as much of their child's pain as they can.

His last diagnostic I saw indicated the patch was completely integrated, but there were unforeseen irregularities. Files that should have been unaffected were marked with minute corruptions. So if he suddenly, or more likely, slowly over time, loses some of his ability to access key memory centers, or confuses events that have occurred in the past, you'll know the reason why.

I can't imagine that we'll lose him altogether. You, as his commanding officer, will see the signs first, especially since you know what to look for. I tried to run this by Reg, but he was unwilling to discuss any of the Doctor's personal matters with me, and I understand why.

Should his matrix fully integrate the changes, I expect the only visible alteration will be in regards to Seven of Nine. He should now hold her in the same esteem he holds the rest of the crew, but no more. And her personal choices should not be of concern to him. Were he organic, he would have eventually reached this on his own. As it is, I just tried to make that possible for him.

If you have problems, you know where to reach me, Admiral.

Hoping fervently she would never have cause to discuss this with Zimmerman or anyone else, Janeway encoded the file and moved on to the next problem on her list: the opening of formal diplomatic relations with the Confederacy of the Worlds of the First Quadrant.

Tapping her combadge lightly, she said, "Decan to the admiral's office."

He had entered before her hand fell from her combadge.

"Have we received any new reports from our officers stationed aboard *Demeter*?"

"We have," Decan said, offering her a padd. "It is obvious that they are choosing their words carefully, aware that their transmissions are being monitored. They have been extended extreme hospitality during their stay and arrangements are moving forward in preparation of the formal assembly of greeting scheduled for the evening of our arrival at the Confederacy."

"Do we have the details of that assembly yet?" Janeway asked.

"They are subject to constant revision, as is usually the case with such ceremonies. We have been advised that the Presider of the Confederacy has chosen to greet our delegation personally at the opening of the assembly. We are assured that this is unusual and a great honor."

"Indeed," Janeway said.

Kathryn Janeway had spent the last several months preparing for whatever the future held. That command of the fleet was now hers was a positive development; more than she'd dared hope when she returned to Earth. But the time also had come for her to resume one of her duties as an admiral that she had struggled with: *diplomat*. Rank had its rewards, to be sure, but they were fleeting, and sometimes they were a prelude to conflicts that sorely tried her patience.

In a way, it was like preparing for any battle. But the weapons here were not energy based. They were words and gestures, and both could be just as deadly as a phaser.

One moment, one hour, one day at a time, she reminded herself, suddenly conscious of how badly she wanted to speak with Chakotay. She hated the way their reunion had ended. She knew she had disappointed him just as surely as he had disappointed her. But that didn't change the fact that for her to succeed, for *them* to succeed, they must move beyond it.

More than the future of *her* fleet was now at stake.

Epilogue

DEMETER

". . . In a little more than a week, Starfleet, and by extension the Federation, has attained celebrity status among these people. I don't know if they really want an alliance with us as much as confirmation that their achievements here dwarf those of the Federation. Time will tell. But they're going to have to swallow a large helping of humility once our diplomatic delegations begin their work in earnest. And I'm positively dying to see what our people make of some of their more quaint *customs.*" Leaning back and stretching his arms over his head, Counselor Cambridge considered ending his report, but added, "*They're not as much like us as we would like to believe. I don't think the apple has fallen quite as far from their ancestral tree as we hoped. The ancient wave forms who warned us off had a point. They like power; for them it is not a means to an end, it is the end. I fear . . .*"

His work was interrupted by a notice from the ship's computer.

INCOMING MESSAGE FOR COUNSELOR CAMBRIDGE.

"From whom?" Cambridge asked.

MISSION SPECIALIST SEVEN OF NINE.

"Computer, suspend log entry and play incoming message," Cambridge ordered, smiling.

The moment he saw her face, ice rushed through his veins.

"I did not wish to inform you of my decision in this manner, but there was no alternative."

"Computer, pause message."

The counselor took a moment to collect himself, and then resumed the playback.

"Voyager *has regrouped with the* Vesta *and the* Galen. *Admiral Janeway has returned and now officially commands the fleet. She advised me that Axum was recovered by a remote Starbase in the Beta Quadrant. Starfleet Medical has requested that I return to the Alpha Quadrant immediately, and I have chosen to honor that request."*

"Of course you have, my dear," Cambridge said.

"A new illness has arisen on three Federation worlds: a plague Starfleet Medical believes is caused by Caeliar catoms. I spoke briefly with the Doctor, who saved Axum's life by providing him with a small number of my catoms. This explains my connection to Axum, as well as the disturbing events I witnessed during those connections."

"Remind me to thank the Doctor the next time I see him," Cambridge said through gritted teeth.

"I believe I will be able to assist those studying the disease. I also believe it is essential that I see Axum. It should comfort you to know that Doctor Sharak and Commander Paris will accompany me to Earth."

"It goes from bad to worse."

"Had it been possible, I would have requested that you return with me as well. It was not. And that request would have been selfish. You are needed by Captain Chakotay. Nothing has, or will, change between us. I will rejoin the fleet as soon as possible. Until then . . ."

"Computer, end playback," Cambridge ordered abruptly.

He didn't need to hear the rest. Whatever Seven said, whatever she might honestly *believe,* was of no consequence.

He knew the truth.

STARFLEET MEDICAL,
CLASSIFIED OPERATIONS FACILITY

"Report, Ensign."

"Seven of Nine is en route, Commander."

"Excellent."

"She is bringing *Voyager's* CMO with her."

"That shouldn't be a problem. Will the modifications to the chambers be complete before she arrives?"

"Yes, sir."

"And the expedition?"

"They are set to launch at zero five hundred hours tomorrow."

"Thank you, Ensign. Dismissed."

The young science officer inclined his head before turning briskly on his heel.

The Commander returned his attention to his latest test results. They were frustrating, to say the least. Despite his ability to now visualize and extract catomic molecules from his patient, they remained impervious to his programming efforts.

He did not doubt that access to a wider range of samples would change those results.

It *had* to.

Billions of Federation citizens were counting on him, *depending* on him. Those tasked with protecting them had failed.

He would not.

The adventure will continue in

Star Trek: Voyager—Acts of Contrition

ACKNOWLEDGMENTS

This one comes with a great deal of gratitude to my readers. I've done what I can to forge a new path for the crew of the *Starship Voyager* and the fleet that accompanies her, but the enthusiasm with which this work has been received must be credited with its continuation. I appreciate each and every one of you.

Special thanks this time around are due to Mark Rademaker. I'm enchanted by his design for the *Demeter.* He keeps my footing sure when it comes to all manner of technical stuff, and any errors found here are my fault, not his. Also to my fellow writers who are always quick to answer my questions . . . Heather Jarman, David Mack, Chris Bennett, David R. George III, Mike Martin and Dayton Ward. David George's encouragement as I began to map out our new direction was particularly insightful.

And extra special thanks to Malcolm for the quote.

My editors, as always, are a blessing, and their continued faith in me is a great gift.

My agent, Maura, is simply the best.

My family and friends sustain me, and their patience knows no bounds. My mother, Patricia, my brothers, Matt and Paul, my other mothers, Vivian and Ollie, never seem as surprised as I am when I learn I get to write another book for Trek. Lynne's support is integral to every aspect of my life. Candy, Sam, Jen, Tina, Julie, Stephanie, and the amazing children they created that share my world inspire me daily.

Maggie is my second goddaughter and has grown into such an astonishingly caring, strong, and beautiful young woman. This book is hers and is dedicated with all my love.

Anorah, there simply aren't words for what you have given me. The constant light and passionate joy are overwhelming most of the time. To know you at all is an honor. To be loved so completely by you is richness beyond measure.

David, my heart, your sacrifices are never forgotten, and your support makes our lives possible. I just cannot imagine who I would be without you.

Thank you, one and all.

ABOUT THE AUTHOR

Kirsten Beyer is the author of *Star Trek: Voyager: Full Circle; Star Trek: Voyager: Unworthy; Star Trek: Voyager: Children of the Storm; Star Trek: Voyager: The Eternal Tide;* the last *Buffy* book ever, *One Thing or Your Mother; Star Trek: Voyager: String Theory: Book 2: Fusion;* the *Alias* APO novel *Once Lost;* and she contributed the short story "Isabo's Shirt" to the *Distant Shores* anthology as well as the short story "Widow's Weeds" to *Space Grunts.*

Kirsten appeared in the Los Angeles productions of *Johnson Over Jordan, This Old Planet,* and Harold Pinter's *The Hothouse,* which the *L.A. Times* called "unmissable." She also appeared in the Geffen Playhouse's world premiere of *Quills* and has been seen on *General Hospital* and *Passions,* among other TV shows.

Kirsten has undergraduate degrees in English literature and theater arts and a master of fine arts from UCLA. She is currently working on the next *Voyager* novel, and when time permits, her first original novel.

She lives in Los Angeles with her husband, David, and their daughter, Anorah.